Bracebridge Hall Or The Humorists

By

Washington Irving

Loki's Publishing

BRACEBRIDGE HALL; OR, THE HUMOURISTS
A MEDLEY.

Under this cloud I walk, Gentlemen; pardon my rude assault. I am a traveller who, having surveyed most of the terrestrial angles of this globe, am hither arrived, to peruse this little spot.

—CHRISTMAS ORDINARY.

Contents

The Author. Worthy Reader!

On again taking pen in hand, I would fain make a few observations at the outset, by way of bespeaking a right understanding. The volumes which I have already published have met with a reception far beyond my most sanguine expectations. I would willingly attribute this to their intrinsic merits; but, in spite of the vanity of authorship, I cannot but be sensible that their success has, in a great measure, been owing to a less flattering cause. It has been a matter of marvel, to my European readers, that a man from the wilds of America should express himself in tolerable English. I was looked upon as something new and strange in literature; a kind of demi-savage, with a feather in his hand, instead of on his head; and there was a curiosity to hear what such a being had to say about civilized society.

This novelty is now at an end, and of course the feeling of indulgence which it produced. I must now expect to bear the scrutiny of sterner criticism, and to be measured by the same standard with contemporary writers; and the very favor which has been shown to my previous writings, will cause these to be treated with the greater rigour; as there is nothing for which the world is apt to punish a man more severely, than for having been over-praised. On this head, therefore, I wish to forestall the censoriousness of the reader; and I entreat he will not think the worse of me for the many injudicious things that may have been said in my commendation.

I am aware that I often travel over beaten ground, and treat of subjects that have already been discussed by abler pens. Indeed, various authors have been mentioned as my models, to whom I should feel flattered if I thought I bore the slightest resemblance; but in truth I write after no model that I am conscious of, and I write with no idea of imitation or competition. In venturing occasionally on topics that have already been almost exhausted by English authors, I do it, not with the presumption of challenging a comparison, but with the hope that some new interest may be given to such topics, when discussed by the pen of a stranger.

If, therefore, I should sometimes be found dwelling with fondness on subjects that are trite and commonplace with the reader, I beg that the circumstances under which I write may be kept in recollection. Having been born and brought up in a new country, yet educated from infancy in the literature of an old one, my mind was early filled with historical and poetical associations, connected with places, and manners, and customs of Europe; but which could rarely be applied to those of my own country. To a mind thus peculiarly prepared, the most ordinary objects and scenes, on arriving in Europe, are full of strange matter and interesting novelty. England is as classic ground to an American as Italy is to an Englishman; and old London teems with as much historical association as mighty Rome.

Indeed, it is difficult to describe the whimsical medley of ideas that throng upon his mind, on landing among English scenes. He, for the first time, sees a world about which he has been reading and thinking in every stage of his existence. The recollected ideas of infancy, youth, and manhood; of the nursery, the school, and the study, come swarming at once upon him; and his attention is distracted between great and little objects; each of which, perhaps, awakens an equally delightful train of remembrances.

But what more especially attracts his notice, are those peculiarities which distinguish an old country and an old state of society from a new one. I have never yet grown familiar enough with the crumbling monuments of past ages, to blunt the intense interest with which I at first beheld them. Accustomed always to scenes where history was, in a manner, in anticipation; where every thing in art was new and progressive, and pointed to the future rather than to the past; where, in short, the works of man gave no ideas but those of young existence, and prospective improvement; there was something inexpressibly touching in the sight of enormous piles of architecture, gray with antiquity, and sinking into-decay. I cannot describe the mute but deep-felt enthusiasm with which I have contemplated a vast monastic ruin, like Tintern Abbey, buried in the bosom of a quiet valley, and shut up from the world, as though it had existed merely for itself; or a warrior pile, like Conway Castle, standing in stern loneliness on its rocky height, a mere hollow yet threatening phantom of departed power. They spread a grand, and melancholy, and, to me, an unusual charm over the landscape; I, for the first time, beheld signs of national old age, and empire's decay, and proofs of the transient and perishing glories of art, amidst the ever-springing and reviving fertility of nature.

But, in fact, to me every thing was full of matter; the footsteps of history were every where to be traced; and poetry had breathed over and sanctified the land. I experienced the delightful freshness of feeling of a child, to whom every thing is new. I pictured to myself a set of inhabitants and a mode of life for every habitation that I saw, from the aristocratical mansion, amidst the lordly repose of stately groves and solitary parts, to the straw-thatched cottage, with its scanty garden and its cherished woodbine. I thought I never could be sated with the sweetness and freshness of a country so completely carpeted with verdure; where every air breathed of the balmy pasture, and the honey-suckled hedge. I was continually coming upon some little document of poetry, in the blossomed hawthorn, the daisy, the cowslip, the primrose, or some other simple object that has received a supernatural value from the muse. The first time that I heard the song of the nightingale, I was intoxicated more by the delicious crowd of remembered associations than by the melody of its notes; and I shall never forget the thrill of ecstasy with which I first saw the lark rise, almost from beneath my feet, and wing its musical flight up into the morning sky.

In this way I traversed England, a grown-up child, delighted by every object, great and small; and betraying a wondering ignorance, and simple enjoyment, that provoked many a stare and a smile from my wiser and more experienced fellow-travellers. Such too was the odd confusion of associations that kept breaking upon me, as I first approached London. One of my earliest wishes had been to see this great metropolis. I had read so much about it in the earliest books that had been put into my infant hands; and I had heard so much about it from those around me who had come from the "old countries." I was familiar with the names of its streets, and squares, and public places, before I knew those of my native city. It was, to me, the great centre of the world, round which every thing seemed to revolve. I recollect contemplating so wistfully, when a boy, a paltry little print of the Thames, and London Bridge, and St. Paul's, that was in front of an old magazine; and a picture of Kensington Gardens, with gentlemen in three-cornered hats and broad skirts, and ladies in hoops and lappets, that hung up in my bed-room; even the venerable cut of St. John's Gate, that has stood, time out of mind, in front of the Gentleman's Magazine, was not without its charms to me; and I envied the odd-looking little men that appeared to be loitering about its arches.

How then did my heart warm when the towers of Westminster Abbey were pointed out to me, rising above the rich groves of St. James's Park, with a thin blue haze about their gray pinnacles! I could not behold this great mausoleum of what is most illustrious in our paternal history, without feeling my enthusiasm in a glow. With what eagerness did I explore every part of the metropolis! I was not content with those matters which occupy the dignified research of the learned traveller; I delighted to call up all the feelings of childhood, and to seek after those objects which had been the wonders of my infancy. London Bridge, so famous in nursery songs; the far-famed Monument; Gog and Magog, and the Lions in the Tower, all brought back many a recollection of infantile delight, and of good old beings, now no more, who had gossiped about them to my wondering ear. Nor was it without a recurrence of childish interest, that I first peeped into Mr. Newberry's shop, in St. Paul's Church-yard, that fountain-head of literature. Mr. Newberry was the first that ever filled my infant mind with the idea of a great and good man. He published all the picture-books of the day; and, out of his abundant love for children, he charged "nothing for either paper or print, and only a penny-halfpenny for the binding!"

I have mentioned these circumstances, worthy reader, to show you the whimsical crowd of associations that are apt to beset my mind on mingling among English scenes. I hope they may, in some measure, plead my apology, should I be found harping upon stale and trivial themes, or indulging an over-fondness for any thing antique and obsolete. I know it is the humour, not to say cant of the day, to run riot about old times, old books, old customs, and old buildings; with myself, however, as far as I have caught the contagion, the feeling is genuine. To a man from a young country, all old things are in a manner new; and he may surely be excused in being a little curious about antiquities, whose native land, unfortunately, cannot boast of a single ruin.

Having been brought up, also, in the comparative simplicity of a republic, I am apt to be struck with even the ordinary circumstances incident to an aristocratical state of society. If, however, I should at any time amuse myself by pointing out some of the eccentricities, and some of the poetical characteristics of the latter, I would not be understood as pretending to decide upon its political merits. My only aim is to paint characters and manners. I am no politician. The more I have considered the study of politics, the more I have found it full of perplexity; and I have contented myself, as I have in my religion, with the faith in which I was brought up, regulating my own conduct by its precepts; but leaving to abler heads the task of making converts.

I shall continue on, therefore, in the course I have hitherto pursued; looking at things poetically, rather than politically; describing them as they are, rather than pretending to point out how they should be; and endeavouring to see the world in as pleasant a light as circumstances will permit.

I have always had an opinion that much good might be done by keeping mankind in good-humour with one another. I may be wrong in my philosophy, but I shall continue to practise it until convinced of its fallacy. When I discover the world to be all that it has been represented by sneering cynics and whining poets, I will turn to and abuse it also; in the meanwhile, worthy reader, I hope you will not think lightly of me, because I cannot believe this to be so very bad a world as it is represented.

Thine truly,
Geoffrey Crayon.

The Hall.

The ancient house, and the best for housekeeping in this county or the next; and though the master of it write but squire, I know no lord like him.
—Merry Beggars.

The reader, if he has perused the volumes of the Sketch-Book, will probably recollect something of the Bracebridge family, with which I once passed a Christmas. I am now on another visit to the Hall, having been invited to a wedding which is shortly to take place. The Squire's second son, Guy, a fine, spirited young captain in the army, is about to be married to his father's ward, the fair Julia Templeton. A gathering of relations and friends has already commenced, to celebrate the joyful occasion; for the old gentleman is an enemy to quiet, private weddings. "There is nothing," he says, "like launching a young couple gayly, and cheering them from the shore; a good outset is half the voyage."

Before proceeding any farther, I would beg that the Squire might not be confounded with that class of hard-riding, foxhunting gentlemen so often described, and, in fact, so nearly extinct in England. I use this rural title partly because it is his universal appellation throughout the neighbourhood, and partly because it saves me the frequent repetition of his name, which is one of those rough old English names at which Frenchmen exclaim in despair.

The Squire is, in fact, a lingering specimen of the old English country gentleman; rusticated a little by living almost entirely on his estate, and something of a humourist, as Englishmen are apt to become when they have an opportunity of living in their own way. I like his hobby passing well, however, which is, a bigoted devotion to old English manners and customs; it jumps a little with my own humor, having as yet a lively and unsated curiosity about the ancient and genuine characteristics of my "father land."

There are some traits about the Squire's family, also, which appear to me to be national. It is one of those old aristocratical families, which, I believe, are peculiar to England, and scarcely understood in other countries; that is to say, families of the ancient gentry, who, though destitute of titled rank, maintain a high ancestral pride; who look down upon all nobility of recent creation, and would consider it a sacrifice of dignity to merge the venerable name of their house in a modern title.

This feeling is very much fostered by the importance which they enjoy on their hereditary domains. The family mansion is an old manor-house, standing in a retired and beautiful part of Yorkshire. Its inhabitants have been always regarded, through the surrounding country, as "the great ones of the earth;" and the little village near the Hall looks up to the Squire with almost feudal homage. An old manor-house, and an old family of this kind, are rarely to be met with at the present day; and it is probably the peculiar humour of the Squire that has retained this secluded specimen of English housekeeping in something like the genuine old style.

I am again quartered in the panelled chamber, in the antique wing of the house. The prospect from the window, however, has quite a different aspect from that which it wore on my winter visit. Though early in the month of April, yet a few warm, sunshiny days have drawn forth the beauties of the spring, which, I think, are always most captivating on their first opening. The parterres of the old-fashioned garden are gay with flowers; and the gardener has brought out his exotics, and placed them along the stone balustrades. The trees are clothed with green buds and tender leaves. When I throw open my jingling casement, I smell the odour of mignonette, and hear the hum of the bees from the flowers against the sunny wall, with the varied song of the throstle, and the cheerful notes of the tuneful little wren.

While sojourning in this strong-hold of old fashions, it is my intention to make occasional sketches of the scenes and characters before me. I would have it understood, however, that I am not writing a novel, and have nothing of intricate plot, or marvellous adventure, to promise the reader. The Hall of which I treat, has, for aught I know, neither trap-door, nor sliding-panel, nor donjon-keep; and indeed appears to have no mystery about it. The family is a worthy, well-meaning family, that, in all probability, will eat and drink, and go to bed, and get up regularly, from one end of my work to the other; and the Squire is so kind-hearted an old gentleman, that I see no likelihood of his throwing any kind of distress in the way of the approaching nuptials. In a word, I cannot foresee a single extraordinary event that is likely to occur in the whole term of my sojourn at the Hall.

I tell this honestly to the reader, lest, when he finds me dallying along, through every-day English scenes, he may hurry ahead, in hopes of meeting with some marvellous adventure further on. I invite him, on the contrary, to ramble gently on with me, as he would saunter out into the fields, stopping occasionally to gather a flower, or listen to a bird, or admire a prospect, without any anxiety to arrive at the end of his career. Should I, however, in the course of my loiterings about this old mansion, see or hear anything curious, that might serve to vary the monotony of this every-day life, I shall not fail to report it for the reader's entertainment:

> *For freshest wits I know will soon be wearie*
> *Of any book, how grave so e'er it be,*
> *Except it have odd matter, strange and merrie,*
> *Well sauc'd with lies and glared all with glee.*[1]

---

[1] Mirror for Magistrates.

The Busy Man.

*A decayed gentleman, who lives most upon his own mirth and my
master's means, and much good do him with it. He does hold my
master up with his stories, and songs, and catches, and such tricks
and jigs, you would admire—he is with him now.*
—Jovial Crew.

By no one has my return to the Hall been more heartily greeted than by
Mr. Simon Bracebridge, or Master Simon, as the Squire most commonly
calls him. I encountered him just as I entered the park, where he was
breaking a pointer, and he received me with all the hospitable cordiality
with which a man welcomes a friend to another one's house. I have
already introduced him to the reader as a brisk old bachelor-looking little
man; the wit and superannuated beau of a large family connection, and the
Squire's factotum. I found him, as usual, full of bustle; with a thousand
petty things to do, and persons to attend to, and in chirping good-humour;
for there are few happier beings than a busy idler; that is to say, a man who
is eternally busy about nothing.

I visited him, the morning after my arrival, in his chamber, which is in
a remote corner of the mansion, as he says he likes to be to himself, and
out of the way. He has fitted it up in his own taste, so that it is a perfect
epitome of an old bachelor's notions of convenience and arrangement. The
furniture is made up of odd pieces from all parts of the house, chosen on
account of their suiting his notions, or fitting some corner of his apartment;
and he is very eloquent in praise of an ancient elbow-chair, from which he
takes occasion to digress into a censure on modern chairs, as having
degenerated from the dignity and comfort of high-backed antiquity.

Adjoining to his room is a small cabinet, which he calls his study. Here
are some hanging shelves, of his own construction, on which are several
old works on hawking, hunting, and farriery, and a collection or two of
poems and songs of the reign of Elizabeth, which he studies out of
compliment to the Squire; together with the Novelist's Magazine, the

Sporting Magazine; the Racing Calendar, a volume or two of the Newgate Calendar, a book of peerage, and another of heraldry.

His sporting dresses hang on pegs in a small closet; and about the walls of his apartment are hooks to hold his fishing-tackle, whips, spurs, and a favourite fowling-piece, curiously wrought and inlaid, which he inherits from his grandfather. He has, also, a couple of old single-keyed flutes, and a fiddle which he has repeatedly patched and mended himself, affirming it to be a veritable Cremona, though I have never heard him extract a single note from it that was not enough to make one's blood run cold.

From this little nest his fiddle will often be heard, in the stillness of mid-day, drowsily sawing some long-forgotten tune; for he prides himself on having a choice collection of good old English music, and will scarcely have any thing to do with modern composers. The time, however, at which his musical powers are of most use, is now and then of an evening, when he plays for the children to dance in the hall, and he passes among them and the servants for a perfect Orpheus.

His chamber also bears evidence of his various avocations: there are half-copied sheets of music; designs for needle-work; sketches of landscapes, very indifferently executed; a camera lucida; a magic lantern, for which he is endeavoring to paint glasses; in a word, it is the cabinet of a man of many accomplishments, who knows a little of everything, and does nothing well.

After I had spent some time in his apartment, admiring the ingenuity of his small inventions, he took me about the establishment, to visit the stables, dog-kennel, and other dependencies, in which he appeared like a general visiting the different quarters of his camp; as the Squire leaves the control of all these matters to him, when he is at the Hall. He inquired into the state of the horses; examined their feet; prescribed a drench for one, and bleeding for another; and then took me to look at his own horse, on the merits of which he dwelt with great prolixity, and which, I noticed, had the best stall in the stable.

After this I was taken to a new toy of his and the Squire's, which he termed the falconry, where there were several unhappy birds in durance, completing their education. Among the number was a fine falcon, which Master Simon had in especial training, and he told me that he would show me, in a few days, some rare sport of the good old-fashioned kind. In the course of our round, I noticed that the grooms, game-keeper, whippers-in, and other retainers, seemed all to be on somewhat of a familiar footing with Master Simon, and fond of having a joke with him, though it was evident they had great deference for his opinion in matters relating to their functions.

There was one exception, however, in a testy old huntsman, as hot as a pepper-corn; a meagre, wiry old fellow, in a threadbare velvet jockey cap, and a pair of leather breeches, that, from much wear, shone, as though they had been japanned. He was very contradictory and pragmatical, and apt, as I thought, to differ from Master Simon now and then, out of mere captiousness. This was particularly the case with respect to the treatment of the hawk, which the old man seemed to have under his peculiar care, and, according to Master Simon, was in a fair way to ruin: the latter had a vast deal to say about *casting*, and *imping*, and *gleaming*, and *enseaming*, and giving the hawk the *rangle*, which I saw was all heathen Greek to old Christy; but he maintained his point notwithstanding, and seemed to hold all this technical lore in utter disrespect.

I was surprised with the good-humour with which Master Simon bore his contradictions, till he explained the matter tom e afterwards. Old Christy is the most ancient servant in the place, having lived among dogs and horses the greater part of a century, and been in the service of Mr. Bracebridge's father. He knows the pedigree of every horse on the place, and has bestrode the great-great-grandsires of most of them. He can give a circumstantial detail of every fox-hunt for the last sixty or seventy years, and has a history for every stag's head about the house, and every hunting trophy nailed to the door of the dog-kennel.

All the present race have grown up under his eye, and humour him in his old age. He once attended the Squire to Oxford, when he was a student there, and enlightened the whole university with his hunting lore. All this is enough to make the old man opinionated, since he finds, on all these matters of first-rate importance, he knows more than the rest of the world. Indeed, Master Simon had been his pupil, and acknowledges that he derived his first knowledge in hunting from the instructions of Christy: and I much question whether the old man does not still look upon him rather as a greenhorn.

On our return homewards, as we were crossing the lawn in front of the house, we heard the porter's bell ring at the lodge, and shortly afterwards, a kind of cavalcade advanced slowly up the avenue. At sight of it my companion paused, considered it for a moment, and then, making a sudden exclamation, hurried away to meet it. As it approached, I discovered a fair, fresh-looking elderly lady, dressed in an old-fashioned riding-habit, with a broad-brimmed white beaver hat, such as may be seen in Sir Joshua Reynolds' paintings. She rode a sleek white pony, and was followed by a footman in rich livery, mounted on an over-fed hunter. At a little distance in the rear came an ancient cumbrous chariot, drawn by two very corpulent horses, driven by as corpulent a coachman, beside whom sat a page dressed in a fanciful green livery. Inside of the chariot was a starched prim personage, with a look somewhat between a lady's companion and a lady's maid; and two pampered curs, that showed their ugly faces, and barked out of each window.

There was a general turning out of the garrison, to receive this new comer. The Squire assisted her to alight, and saluted her affectionately; the fair Julia flew into her arms, and they embraced with the romantic fervour of boarding-school friends: she was escorted into the house by Julia's lover, towards whom she showed distinguished favour; and a line of the old servants, who had collected in the Hall, bowed most profoundly as she passed.

I observed that Master Simon was most assiduous and devout in his attentions upon this old lady. He walked by the side of her pony, up the avenue; and, while she was receiving the salutations of the rest of the family, he took occasion to notice the fat coachman; to pat the sleek carriage horses, and, above all, to say a civil word to my lady's gentlewoman, the prim, sour-looking vestal in the chariot.

I had no more of his company for the rest of the morning. He was swept off in the vortex that followed in the wake of this lady. Once indeed he paused for a moment, as he was hurrying on some errand of the good lady's, to let me know that this was Lady Lillycraft, a sister of the Squire's, of large fortune, which the captain would inherit, and that her estate lay in one of the best sporting counties in all England.

Family Servants.

Verily old servants are the vouchers of worthy housekeeping. They are like rats in a mansion, or mites in a cheese, bespeaking the antiquity and fatness of their abode.

In my casual anecdotes of the Hall, I may often he tempted to dwell on circumstances of a trite and ordinary nature, from their appearing to me illustrative of genuine national character. It seems to be the study of the Squire to adhere, as much as possible, to what he considers the old landmarks of English manners. His servants all understand his ways, and for the most part have been accustomed to them from infancy; so that, upon the whole, his household presents one of the few tolerable specimens that can now be met with, of the establishment of an English country gentleman of the old school.

By the by, the servants are not the least characteristic part of the household: the housekeeper, for instance, has been born and brought up at the Hall, and has never been twenty miles from it; yet she has a stately air, that would not disgrace a lady that had figured at the court of Queen Elizabeth.

I am half inclined to think that she has caught it from living so much among the old family pictures. It may, however, be owing to a consciousness of her importance in the sphere in which she has always moved; for she is greatly respected in the neighbouring village, and among the farmers' wives, and has high authority in the household, ruling over the servants with quiet, but undisputed sway.

She is a thin old lady, with blue eyes and pointed nose and chin. Her dress is always the same as to fashion. She wears a small, well-starched ruff, a laced stomacher, full petticoats, and a gown festooned and open in front, which, on particular occasions, is of ancient silk, the legacy of some former dame of the family, or an inheritance from her mother, who was housekeeper before her. I have a reverence for these old garments, as I make no doubt they have figured about these apartments in days long past, when they have set off the charms of some peerless family beauty; and I have sometimes looked from the old housekeeper to the neighbouring portraits, to see whether I could not recognize her antiquated brocade in the dress of some one of those long-waisted dames that smile on me from the walls.

Her hair, which is quite white, is frizzed out in front, and she wears over it a small cap, nicely plaited, and brought down under the chin. Her manners are simple and primitive, heightened a little by a proper dignity of station.

The Hall is her world, and the history of the family the only history she knows, excepting that which she has read in the Bible. She can give a biography of every portrait in the picture gallery, and is a complete family chronicle.

She is treated with great consideration by the Squire. Indeed, Master Simon tells me that there is a traditional anecdote current among the servants, of the Squire's having been seen kissing her in the picture gallery, when they were both young. As, however, nothing further was ever noticed between them, the circumstance caused no great scandal; only she was observed to take to reading Pamela shortly afterwards, and refused the hand of the village inn-keeper, whom she had previously smiled on.

The old butler, who was formerly footman, and a rejected admirer of hers, used to tell the anecdote now and then, at those little cabals that will occasionally take place among the most orderly servants, arising from the common propensity of the governed to talk against administration; but he has left it off, of late years, since he has risen into place, and shakes his head rebukingly when it is mentioned.

It is certain that the old lady will, to this day, dwell on the looks of the Squire when he was a young man at college; and she maintains that none of his sons can compare with their father when he was of their age, and was dressed out in his full suit of scarlet, with his hair craped and powdered, and his three-cornered hat.

She has an orphan niece, a pretty, soft-hearted baggage, named Phoebe Wilkins, who has been transplanted to the Hall within a year or two, and been nearly spoiled for any condition of life. She is a kind of attendant and companion of the fair Julia's; and from loitering about the young lady's apartments, reading scraps of novels, and inheriting second-hand finery, has become something between a waiting-maid and a slipshod fine lady.

She is considered a kind of heiress among the servants, as she will inherit all her aunt's property; which, if report be true, must be a round sum of good golden guineas, the accumulated wealth of two housekeepers' savings; not to mention the hereditary wardrobe, and the many little valuables and knick-knacks, treasured up in the housekeepers' room. Indeed, the old housekeeper has the reputation, among the servants and the villagers, of being passing rich; and there is a japanned chest of drawers, and a large iron-bound coffer in her room, which are supposed, by the house-maids, to hold treasures of wealth.

The old lady is a great friend of Master Simon, who, indeed, pays a little court to her, as to a person high in authority; and they have many discussions on points of family history, in which, notwithstanding his extensive information, and pride of knowledge, he commonly admits her superior accuracy. He seldom returns to the Hall, after one of his visits to the other branches of the family, without bringing Mrs. Wilkins some remembrance from the ladies of the house where he has been staying.

Indeed, all the children of the house look up to the old lady with habitual respect and attachment, and she seems almost to consider them as her own, from their having grown up under her eye. The Oxonian, however, is her favourite, probably from, being the youngest, though he is the most mischievous, and has been apt to play tricks upon her from boyhood.

I cannot help mentioning one little ceremony, which, I believe, is peculiar to the Hall. After the cloth is removed at dinner, the old housekeeper sails into the room and stands behind the Squire's chair, when he fills her a glass of wine with his own hands, in which she drinks the health of the company in a truly respectful yet dignified manner, and then retires. The Squire received the custom from his father, and has always continued it.

There is a peculiar character about the servants of old English families that reside principally in the country. They have a quiet, orderly, respectful mode of doing their duties. They are always neat in their persons, and appropriately, and if I may use the phrase, technically dressed; they move about the house without hurry or noise; there is nothing of the bustle of employment, or the voice of command; nothing of that obtrusive housewifery that amounts to a torment. You are not persecuted by the process of making you comfortable; yet every thing is done, and is done well. The work of the house is performed as if by magic, but it is the magic of system. Nothing is done by fits and starts, nor at awkward seasons; the whole goes on like well-oiled clock-work, where there is no noise nor jarring in its operations.

English servants, in general, are not treated with great indulgence, nor rewarded by many commendations; for the English are laconic and reserved toward their domestics; but an approving nod and a kind word from master or mistress, goes as far here, as an excess of praise or indulgence elsewhere. Neither do servants often exhibit any animated marks of affection to their employers; yet, though quiet, they are strong in their attachments; and the reciprocal regard of masters and servants, though not ardently expressed, is powerful and lasting in old English families.

The title of "an old family servant" carries with it a thousand kind associations, in all parts of the world; and there is no claim upon the home-bred charities of the heart more irresistible than that of having been "born in the house." It is common to see gray-headed domestics of this kind attached to an English family of the "old school," who continue in it to the day of their death, in the enjoyment of steady, unaffected kindness, and the performance of faithful, unofficious duty. I think such instances of attachment speak well for both master and servant, and the frequency of them speaks well for national character.

These observations, however, hold good only with families of the description I have mentioned; and with such as are somewhat retired, and pass the greater part of their time in the country.

As to the powdered menials that throng the halls of fashionable town residences, they equally reflect the character of the establishments to which they belong; and I know no more complete epitomes of dissolute heartlessness and pampered inutility.

But, the good "old family servant!"—the one who has always been linked, in idea, with the home of our heart; who has led us to school in the days of prattling childhood; who has been the confidant of our boyish cares, and schemes, and enterprises; who has hailed us as we came home at vacations, and been the promoter of all our holiday sports; who, when we, in wandering manhood, have left the paternal roof, and only return thither at intervals—will welcome us with a, joy inferior only to that of our parents; who, now grown gray and infirm with age, still totters about the house of our fathers, in fond and faithful servitude; who claims us, in a manner, as his own; and hastens with querulous eagerness to anticipate his fellow-domestics in waiting upon us at table; and who, when we retire at night to the chamber that still goes by our name, will linger about the room to have one more kind look, and one more pleasant word about times that are past—who does not experience towards such a being a feeling of almost filial affection?

I have met with several instances of epitaphs on the gravestones of such valuable domestics, recorded with the simple truth of natural feeling. I have two before me at this moment; one copied from a tombstone of a church-yard in Warwickshire:

"Here lieth the body of Joseph Batte, confidential servant to George Birch, Esq., of Hamstead Hall. His grateful friend and master caused this inscription to be written in memory of his discretion, fidelity, diligence, and continence. He died (a bachelor) aged 84, having lived 44 years in the same family."

The other was taken from a tombstone in Eltham churchyard:

"Here lie the remains of Mr. James Tappy, who departed this life on the 8th of September, 1818, aged 84, after a faithful service of 60 years in one family; by each individual of which he lived respected, and died lamented by the sole survivor."

Few monuments, even of the illustrious, have given me the glow about the heart that I felt while copying this honest epitaph in the church-yard of Eltham. I sympathized with this "sole survivor" of a family mourning over the grave of the faithful follower of his race, who had been, no doubt, a living memento of times and friends that had passed away; and in considering this record of long and devoted service, I called to mind the touching speech of Old Adam, in "As You Like It," when tottering after the youthful son of his ancient master:

"Master, go on, and I will follow thee
To the last gasp, with love and loyalty!"

NOTE.—I cannot but mention a tablet which I have seen somewhere in the chapel of Windsor Castle, put up by the late king to the memory of a family servant, who had been a faithful attendant of his lamented daughter, the Princess Amelia. George III. possessed much of the strong domestic feeling of the old English country gentleman; and it is an incident curious in monumental history, and creditable to the human heart, a monarch erecting a monument in honour of the humble virtues of a menial.

The Widow.

She was so charitable and pitious
She would weep if that she saw a mous
Caught in a trap, if it were dead or Wed:
Of small hounds had she, that she fed
With rost flesh, milke, and wastel bread,
But sore wept she if any of them were dead,
Or if man smote them with a yard smart.
—CHAUCER.

Notwithstanding the whimsical parade made by Lady Lillycraft on her arrival, she has none of the petty stateliness that I had imagined; but, on the contrary, she has a degree of nature and simple-heartedness, if I may use the phrase, that mingles well with her old-fashioned manners and harmless ostentation. She dresses in rich silks, with long waist; she rouges considerably, and her hair, which is nearly white, is frizzed out, and put up with pins. Her face is pitted with the small-pox, but the delicacy of her features shows that she may once have been beautiful; and she has a very fair and well-shaped hand and arm, of which, if I mistake not, the good lady is still a little vain.

I have had the curiosity to gather a few particulars concerning her. She was a great belle in town, between thirty and forty years since, and reigned for two seasons with all the insolence of beauty, refusing several excellent offers; when, unfortunately, she was robbed of her charms and her lovers by an attack of the small-pox. She retired immediately into the country, where she some time after inherited an estate, and married a baronet, a former admirer, whose passion had suddenly revived; "having," as he said, "always loved her mind rather than her person."

The baronet did not enjoy her mind and fortune above six months, and had scarcely grown very tired of her, when he broke his neck in a fox-chase, and left her free, rich, and disconsolate. She has remained on her estate in the country ever since, and has never shown any desire to return to town, and revisit the scene of her early triumphs and fatal malady. All her favourite recollections, however, revert to that short period of her youthful beauty. She has no idea of town but as it was at that time; and continually forgets that the place and people must have changed materially in the course of nearly half a century. She will often speak of the toasts of those days as if still reigning; and, until very recently, used to talk with delight of the royal family, and the beauty of the young princes and princesses. She cannot be brought to think of the present king otherwise than as an elegant young man, rather wild, but who danced a minuet divinely; and before he came to the crown, would often mention him as the "sweet young prince."

She talks also of the walks in Kensington Garden, where the gentlemen appeared in gold-laced coats, and cocked hats, and the ladies in hoops, and swept so proudly along the grassy avenues; and she thinks the ladies let themselves sadly down in their dignity, when they gave up cushioned head-dresses, and high-heeled shoes. She has much to say too of the officers who were in the train of her admirers; and speaks familiarly of many wild young blades, that are now, perhaps, hobbling about watering-places with crutches and gouty shoes.

Whether the taste the good lady had of matrimony discouraged her or not, I cannot say; but though her merits and her riches have attracted many suitors, she has never been tempted to venture again into the happy state. This is singular, too, for she seems of a most soft and susceptible heart; is always talking of love and connubial felicity, and is a great stickler for old-fashioned gallantry, devoted attentions, and eternal constancy, on the part of the gentlemen. She lives, however, after her own taste. Her house, I am told, must have been built and furnished about the time of Sir Charles Grandison: every thing about it is somewhat formal and stately; but has been softened down into a degree of voluptuousness, characteristic of an old lady, very tender-hearted and romantic, and that loves her ease. The cushions of the great arm-chairs, and wide sofas, almost bury you when you sit down on them. Flowers of the most rare and delicate kind are placed about the rooms, and on little japanned stands; and sweet bags lie about the tables and mantel-pieces. The house is full of pet dogs, Angora cats, and singing birds, who are as carefully waited upon as she is herself.

She is dainty in her living, and a little of an epicure, living on white meats, and little lady-like dishes, though her servants have substantial old English fare, as their looks bear witness. Indeed, they are so indulged, that they are all spoiled; and when they lose their present place, they will be fit for no other. Her ladyship is one of those easy-tempered beings that are always doomed to be much liked, but ill served by their domestics, and cheated by all the world.

Much of her time is passed in reading novels, of which she has a most extensive library, and has a constant supply from the publishers in town. Her erudition in this line of literature is immense; she has kept pace with the press for half a century. Her mind is stuffed with love-tales of all kinds, from the stately amours of the old books of chivalry, down to the last blue-covered romance, reeking from the press; though she evidently gives the preference to those that came out in the days of her youth, and when she was first in love. She maintains that there are no novels written now-a-days equal to Pamela and Sir Charles Grandison; and she places the Castle of Otranto at the head of all romances.

She does a vast deal of good in her neighbourhood, and is imposed upon by every beggar in the county. She is the benefactress of a village adjoining to her estate, and takes an especial interest in all its love-affairs. She knows of every courtship that is going on; every lovelorn damsel is sure to find a patient listener and a sage adviser in her ladyship. She takes great pains to reconcile all love-quarrels, and should any faithless swain persist in his inconstancy, he is sure to draw on himself the good lady's violent indignation.

I have learned these particulars partly from Frank Bracebridge, and partly from Master Simon. I am now able to account for the assiduous attention of the latter to her ladyship. Her house is one of his favourite resorts, where he is a very important personage. He makes her a visit of business once a year, when he looks into all her affairs; which, as she is no manager, are apt to get into confusion. He examines the books of the overseer, and shoots about the estate, which, he says, is well stocked with game, notwithstanding that it is poached by all the vagabonds in the neighbourhood.

It is thought, as I before hinted, that the captain will inherit the greater part of her property, having always been her chief favourite; for, in fact, she is partial to a red coat. She has now come to the Hall to be present at his nuptials, having a great disposition to interest herself in all matters of love and matrimony.

The Lovers.

Rise up, my love, my fair one, and come away; for, lo, the winter is past, the rain is over and gone; the flowers appear on the earth; the time of the singing of birds is come, and the voice of the turtle is heard in the land.
—SONG OF SOLOMON.

To a man who is a little of a philosopher, and a bachelor to boot; and who, by dint of some experience in the follies of life, begins to look with a learned eye upon the ways of man, and eke of woman; to such a man, I say, there is something very entertaining in noticing the conduct of a pair of young lovers. It may not be as grave and scientific a study as the loves of the plants, but it is certainly as interesting.

I have, therefore, derived much pleasure, since my arrival at the Hall, from observing the fair Julia and her lover. She has all the delightful, blushing consciousness of an artless girl, inexperienced in coquetry, who has made her first conquest; while the captain regards her with that mixture of fondness and exultation with which a youthful lover is apt to contemplate so beauteous a prize.

I observed them yesterday in the garden, advancing along one of the retired walks. The sun was shining with delicious warmth, making great masses of bright verdure, and deep blue shade. The cuckoo, that "harbinger of spring," was faintly heard from a distance; the thrush piped from the hawthorn; and the yellow butterflies sported, and toyed, and coquetted in the air.

The fair Julia was leaning on her lover's arm, listening to his conversation, with her eyes cast down, a soft blush on her cheek, and a quiet smile on her lips, while in the hand that hung negligently by her side was a bunch of flowers. In this way they were sauntering slowly along; and when I considered them and the scene in which they were moving, I could not but think it a thousand pities that the season should ever change, or that young people should ever grow older, or that blossoms should give way to fruit, or that lovers should ever get married.

From what I have gathered of family anecdote, I understand that the fair Julia is the daughter of a favourite college friend of the Squire; who, after leaving Oxford, had entered the army, and served for many years in India, where he was mortally wounded in a skirmish with the natives. In his last moments he had, with a faltering pen, recommended his wife and daughter to the kindness of his early friend.

The widow and her child returned to England helpless and almost hopeless. When Mr. Bracebridge received accounts of their situation, he hastened to their relief. He reached them just in time to soothe the last moments of the mother, who was dying of a consumption, and to make her happy in the assurance that her child should never want a protector.

The good Squire returned with his prattling charge to his strong-hold; where he had brought her up with a tenderness truly paternal. As he has taken some pains to superintend her education, and form her taste, she has grown up with many of his notions, and considers him the wisest, as well as the best of men. Much of her time, too, has been passed with Lady Lillycraft, who has instructed her in the manners of the old school, and enriched her mind with all kinds of novels and romances. Indeed, her ladyship has had a great hand in promoting the match between Julia and the captain, having had them together at her country-seat, the moment she found there was an attachment growing up between them; the good lady being never so happy as when she has a pair of turtles cooing about her.

I have been pleased to see the fondness with which the fair Julia is regarded by the old servants at the Hall. She has been a pet with them from childhood, and every one seems to lay some claim to her education; so that it is no wonder that she should be extremely accomplished. The gardener taught her to rear flowers, of which she is extremely fond. Old Christy, the pragmatical huntsman, softens when she approaches; and as she sits lightly and gracefully in her saddle, claims the merit of having taught her to ride; while the housekeeper, who almost looks upon her as a daughter, intimates that she first gave her an insight into the mysteries of the toilet, having been dressing-maid, in her young days, to the late Mrs. Bracebridge. I am inclined to credit this last claim, as I have noticed that the dress of the young lady had an air of the old school, though managed with native taste, and that her hair was put up very much in the style of Sir Peter Lely's portraits in the picture gallery.

Her very musical attainments partake of this old-fashioned character, and most of her songs are such as are not at the present day to be found on the piano of a modern performer. I have, however, seen so much of modern fashions, modern accomplishments, and modern fine ladies, that I relish this tinge of antiquated style in so young and lovely a girl; and I have had as much pleasure in hearing her warble one of the old songs of Herrick, or Carew, or Suckling, adapted to some simple old melody, as I have had from listening to a lady amateur skylark it up and down through the finest bravura of Rossini or Mozart. We have very pretty music in the evenings, occasionally, between her and the captain, assisted sometimes by Master Simon, who scrapes, dubiously, on his violin; being very apt to get out, and to halt a note or two in the rear. Sometimes he even thrums a little on the piano, and takes a part in a trio, in which his voice can generally be distinguished by a certain quavering tone, and an occasional false note.

I was praising the fair Julia's performance to him, after one of her songs, when I found he took to himself the whole credit of having formed her musical taste, assuring me that she was very apt; and, indeed, summing up her whole character in his knowing way, by adding, that "she was a very nice girl, and had no nonsense about her."

Family Reliques.

My Infelice's face, her brow, her eye,
The dimple on her cheek: and such sweet skill
Hath from the cunning workman's pencil flown,
These lips look fresh and lively as her own.
False colours last after the true be dead.
Of all the roses grafted on her cheeks,
Of all the graces dancing in her eyes,
Of all the music set upon her tongue,
Of all that was past woman's excellence
In her white bosom; look, a painted board
Circumscribes all!
—DEKKER.

An old English family mansion is a fertile subject for study. It abounds with illustrations of former times, and traces of the tastes, and humours, and manners of successive generations. The alterations and additions, in different styles of architecture; the furniture, plate, pictures, hangings; the warlike and sporting implements of different ages and fancies; all furnish food for curious and amusing speculation. As the Squire is very careful in collecting and preserving all family reliques, the Hall is full of remembrances of the kind. In looking about the establishment, I can picture to myself the characters and habits that have prevailed at different eras of the family history. I have mentioned, on a former occasion, the armour of the crusader which hangs up in the Hall. There are also several jack-boots, with enormously thick soles and high heels, that belonged to a set of cavaliers, who filled the Hall with the din and stir of arms during the time of the Covenanters. A number of enormous drinking vessels of antique fashion, with huge Venice glasses, and green-hock-glasses, with the apostles in relief on them, remain as monuments of a generation or two of hard livers, that led a life of roaring revelry, and first introduced the gout into the family.

I shall pass over several more such indications of temporary tastes of the Squire's predecessors; but I cannot forbear to notice a pair of antlers in the great hall, which is one of the trophies of a hard-riding squire of former times, who was the Nimrod of these parts. There are many traditions of his wonderful feats in hunting still existing, which are related by old Christy, the huntsman, who gets exceedingly nettled if they are in the least doubted. Indeed, there is a frightful chasm, a few miles from the Hall, which goes by the name of the Squire's Leap, from his having cleared it in the ardour of the chase; there can be no doubt of the fact, for old Christy shows the very dints of the horse's hoofs on the rocks on each side of the chasm.

Master Simon holds the memory of this squire in great veneration, and has a number of extraordinary stories to tell concerning him, which he repeats at all hunting dinners; and I am told that they wax more and more marvellous the older they grow. He has also a pair of Rippon spurs which belonged to this mighty hunter of yore, and which he only wears on particular occasions.

The place, however, which abounds most with mementos of past times, is the picture gallery; and there is something strangely pleasing, though melancholy, in considering the long rows of portraits which compose the greater part of the collection. They furnish a kind of narrative of the lives of the family worthies, which I am enabled to read with the assistance of the venerable housekeeper, who is the family chronicler, prompted occasionally by Master Simon. There is the progress of a fine lady, for instance, through a variety of portraits. One represents her as a little girl, with a long waist and hoop, holding a kitten in her arms, and ogling the spectator out of the corners of her eyes, as if she could not turn her head. In another, we find her in the freshness of youthful beauty, when she was a celebrated belle, and so hard-hearted as to cause several unfortunate gentlemen to run desperate and write bad poetry. In another, she is depicted as a stately dame, in the maturity of her charms; next to the portrait of her husband, a gallant colonel in full-bottomed wig and gold-laced hat, who was killed abroad; and, finally, her monument is in the church, the spire of which may be seen from the window, where her effigy is carved in marble, and represents her as a venerable dame of seventy-six.

In like manner, I have followed some of the family great men through a series of pictures, from early boyhood to the robe of dignity, or truncheon of command; and so on by degrees, until they were garnered up in the common repository, the neighbouring church.

There is one group that particularly interested me. It consisted of four sisters, of nearly the same age, who flourished about a century since, and, if I may judge from their portraits, were extremely beautiful. I can imagine what a scene of gayety and romance this old mansion must have been, when they were in the heyday of their charms; when they passed like beautiful visions through its halls, or stepped daintily to music in the revels and dances of the cedar gallery; or printed, with delicate feet, the velvet verdure of these lawns. How must they have been looked up to with mingled love, and pride, and reverence by the old family servants; and followed with almost painful admiration by the aching eyes of rival admirers! How must melody, and song, and tender serenade, have breathed about these courts, and their echoes whispered to the loitering tread of lovers! How must these very turrets have made the hearts of the young galliards thrill, as they first discerned them from afar, rising from among the trees, and pictured to themselves the beauties casketed like gems within these walls! Indeed, I have discovered about the place several faint records of this reign of love and romance, when the Hall was a kind of Court of Beauty.

Several of the old romances in the library have marginal notes expressing sympathy and approbation, where there are long speeches extolling ladies' charms, or protesting eternal fidelity, or bewailing the cruelty of some tyrannical fair one. The interviews, and declarations, and parting scenes of tender lovers, also bear the marks of having been frequently read, and are scored and marked with notes of admiration, and have initials written on the margins; most of which annotations have the day of the month and year annexed to them. Several of the windows, too, have scraps of poetry engraved on them with diamonds, taken from the writings of the fair Mrs. Philips, the once celebrated Orinda. Some of these seem to have been inscribed by lovers; and others, in a delicate and unsteady hand, and a little inaccurate in the spelling, have evidently been written by the young ladies themselves, or by female friends, who have been on visits to the Hall. Mrs. Philips seems to have been their favourite author, and they have distributed the names of her heroes and heroines among their circle of intimacy. Sometimes, in a male hand, the verse bewails the cruelty of beauty, and the sufferings of constant love; while in a female hand it prudishly confines itself to lamenting the parting of female friends. The bow-window of my bed-room, which has, doubtless, been inhabited by one of these beauties, has several of these inscriptions. I have one at this moment before my eyes, called "Camilla parting with Leonora:"

"How perish'd is the joy that's past,
  The present how unsteady!
What comfort can be great and last,
  When this is gone already;"

And close by it is another, written, perhaps, by some adventurous lover, who had stolen into the lady's chamber during her absence:

"THEODOSIUS TO CAMILLA.

I'd rather in your favour live,
  Than in a lasting name;
And much a greater rate would give
  For happiness than fame.

THEODOSIUS. 1700."

When I look at these faint records of gallantry and tenderness; when I contemplate the fading portraits of these beautiful girls, and think, too, that they have long since bloomed, reigned, grown old, died, and passed away, and with them all their graces, their triumphs, their rivalries, their admirers; the whole empire of love and pleasure in which they ruled—"all dead, all buried, all forgotten," I find a cloud of melancholy stealing over the present gayeties around me. I was gazing, in a musing mood, this very morning, at the portrait of the lady whose husband was killed abroad, when the fair Julia entered the gallery, leaning on the arm of the captain. The sun shone through the row of windows on her as she passed along, and she seemed to beam out each time into brightness, and relapse into shade, until the door at the bottom of the gallery closed after her. I felt a sadness of heart at the idea, that this was an emblem of her lot: a few more years of sunshine and shade, and all this life and loveliness, and enjoyment, will have ceased, and nothing be left to commemorate this beautiful being but one more perishable portrait; to awaken, perhaps, the trite speculations of some future loiterer, like myself, when I and my scribblings shall have lived through our brief existence, and been forgotten.

An Old Soldier

I've worn some leather out abroad; let out a heathen soul or two; fed this good sword with the black blood of pagan Christians; converted a few infidels with it.—But let that pass.
—The Ordinary.

The Hall was thrown into some little agitation, a few days since, by the arrival of General Harbottle. He had been expected for several days, and had been looked for, rather impatiently, by several of the family. Master Simon assured me that I would like the general hugely, for he was a blade of the old school, and an excellent table companion. Lady Lillycraft, also, appeared to be somewhat fluttered, on the morning of the general's arrival, for he had been one of her early admirers; and she recollected him only as a dashing young ensign, just come upon the town. She actually spent an hour longer at her toilette, and made her appearance with her hair uncommonly frizzed and powdered, and an additional quantity of rouge. She was evidently a little surprised and shocked, therefore, at finding the lithe, dashing ensign transformed into a corpulent old general, with a double chin; though it was a perfect picture to witness their salutations; the graciousness of her profound curtsy, and the air of the old school with which the general took off his hat, swayed it gently in his hand, and bowed his powdered head.

All this bustle and anticipation has caused me to study the general with a little more attention than, perhaps, I should otherwise have done; and the few days that he has already passed at the Hall have enabled me, I think, to furnish a tolerable likeness of him to the reader.

He is, as Master Simon observed, a soldier of the old school, with powdered head, side locks, and pigtail. His face is shaped like the stern of a Dutch man-of-war, narrow at top and wide at bottom, with full rosy cheeks and a double chin; so that, to use the cant of the day, his organs of eating may be said to be powerfully developed.

The general, though a veteran, has seen very little active service, except the taking of Seringapatam, which forms an era in his history. He wears a large emerald in his bosom, and a diamond on his finger, which he got on that occasion, and whoever is unlucky enough to notice either, is sure to involve himself in the whole history of the siege. To judge from the general's conversation, the taking of Seringapatam is the most important affair that has occurred for the last century.

On the approach of warlike times on the continent, he was rapidly promoted to get him out of the way of younger officers of merit; until, having been hoisted to the rank of general, he was quietly laid on the shelf. Since that time, his campaigns have been principally confined to watering-places; where he drinks the waters for a slight touch of the liver which he got in India; and plays whist with old dowagers, with whom he has flirted in his younger days. Indeed, he talks of all the fine women of the last half century, and, according to hints which he now and then drops, has enjoyed the particular smiles of many of them.

He has seen considerable garrison duty, and can speak of almost every place famous for good quarters, and where the inhabitants give good dinners. He is a diner out of first-rate currency, when in town; being invited to one place, because he has been seen at another. In the same way he is invited about the country-seats, and can describe half the seats in the kingdom, from actual observation; nor is any one better versed in court gossip, and the pedigrees and intermarriages of the nobility.

As the general is an old bachelor, and an old beau, and there are several ladies at the Hall, especially his quondam flame Lady Jocelyne, he is put rather upon his gallantry. He commonly passes some time, therefore, at his toilette, and takes the field at a late hour every morning, with his hair dressed out and powdered, and a rose in his button-hole. After he has breakfasted, he walks up and down the terrace in the sunshine, humming an air, and hemming between every stave, carrying one hand behind his back, and with the other touching his cane to the ground, and then raising it up to his shoulder. Should he, in these morning promenades, meet any of the elder ladies of the family, as he frequently does Lady Lillycraft, his hat is immediately in his hand, and it is enough to remind one of those courtly groups of ladies and gentlemen, in old prints of Windsor terrace, or Kensington garden.

He talks frequently about "the service," and is fond of humming the old song,

Why, soldiers, why,
Should we be melancholy, boys?
Why, soldiers, why,
Whose business 't is to die!

I cannot discover, however, that the general has ever run any great risk of dying, excepting from an apoplexy or an indigestion. He criticises all the battles on the continent, and discusses the merits of the commanders, but never fails to bring the conversation, ultimately, to Tippoo Saib and Seringapatam. I am told that the general was a perfect champion at drawing-rooms, parades, and watering-places, during the late war, and was looked to with hope and confidence by many an old lady, when labouring under the terror of Buonaparte's invasion.

He is thoroughly loyal, and attends punctually on levees when in town. He has treasured up many remarkable sayings of the late king, particularly one which the king made to him on a field-day, complimenting him on the excellence of his horse. He extols the whole royal family, but especially the present king, whom he pronounces the most perfect gentleman and best whist-player in Europe. The general swears rather more than is the fashion of the present day; but it was the mode in the old school. He is, however, very strict in religious matters, and a staunch churchman. He repeats the responses very loudly in church, and is emphatical in praying for the king and royal family.

At table, his loyalty waxes very fervent with his second bottle, and the song of "God save the King" puts him into a perfect ecstasy. He is amazingly well contented with the present state of things, and apt to get a little impatient at any talk about national ruin and agricultural distress. He says he has travelled about the country as much as any man, and has met with nothing but prosperity; and to confess the truth, a great part of his time is spent in visiting from one country-seat to another, and riding about the parks of his friends. "They talk of public distress," said the general this day to me, at dinner, as he smacked a glass of rich burgundy, and cast his eyes about the ample board; "they talk of public distress, but where do we find it, sir? I see none. I see no reason why any one has to complain. Take my word for it, sir, this talk about public distress is all humbug!"

The Widow's Retinue.

Little dogs and all!
—Lear.

In giving an account of the arrival of Lady Lillycraft at the Hall, I ought to have mentioned the entertainment which I derived from witnessing the unpacking of her carriage, and the disposing of her retinue. There is something extremely amusing to me in the number of factitious wants, the loads of imaginary conveniences, but real encumbrances, with which the luxurious are apt to burthen themselves. I like to watch the whimsical stir and display about one of these petty progresses. The number of robustious footmen and retainers of all kinds bustling about, with looks of infinite gravity and importance, to do almost nothing. The number of heavy trunks, and parcels, and bandboxes belonging to my lady; and the solicitude, exhibited about some humble, odd-looking box, by my lady's maid; the cushions piled in the carriage to make a soft seat still softer, and to prevent the dreaded possibility of a jolt; the smelling-bottles, the cordials, the baskets of biscuit and fruit; the new publications; all provided to guard against hunger, fatigue, or ennui; the led horses, to vary the mode of travelling; and all this preparation and parade to move, perhaps, some very good-for-nothing personage about a little space of earth!

I do not mean to apply the latter part of these observations to Lady Lillycraft, for whose simple kind-heartedness I have a very great respect, and who is really a most amiable and worthy being. I cannot refrain, however, from mentioning some of the motley retinue she has brought with her; and which, indeed, bespeak the overflowing kindness of her nature, which requires her to be surrounded with objects on which to lavish it.

In the first place, her ladyship has a pampered coachman, with a red face, and cheeks that hang down like dew-laps. He evidently domineers over her a little with respect to the fat horses; and only drives out when he thinks proper, and when he thinks it will be "good for the cattle."

She has a favourite page, to attend upon her person; a handsome boy of about twelve years of age, but a mischievous varlet, very much spoiled, and in a fair way to be good for nothing. He is dressed in green, with a profusion of gold cord and gilt buttons about his clothes. She always has one or two attendants of the kind, who are replaced by others as soon as they grow to fourteen years of age. She has brought two dogs with her, also, out of a number of pets which she maintains at home. One is a fat spaniel, called Zephyr—though heaven defend me from such a zephyr! He is fed out of all shape and comfort; his eyes are nearly strained out of his head; he wheezes with corpulency, and cannot walk without great difficulty. The other is a little, old, gray-muzzled curmudgeon, with an unhappy eye, that kindles like a coal if you only look at him; his nose turns up; his mouth is drawn into wrinkles, so as to show his teeth; in short, he has altogether the look of a dog far gone in misanthropy, and totally sick of the world. When he walks, he has his tail curled up so tight that it seems to lift his feet from the ground; and he seldom makes use of more than three legs at a time, keeping the other drawn up as a reserve. This last wretch is called Beauty.

These dogs are full of elegant ailments, unknown to vulgar dogs; and are petted and nursed by Lady Lillycraft with the tenderest kindness. They are pampered and fed with delicacies by their fellow-minion, the page; but their stomachs are often weak and out of order, so that they cannot eat; though I have now and then seen the page give them a mischievous pinch, or thwack over the head, when his mistress was not by. They have cushions for their express use, on which they lie before the fire, and yet are apt to shiver and moan if there is the least draught of air. When any one enters the room, they make a most tyrannical barking that is absolutely deafening. They are insolent to all the other dogs of the establishment. There is a noble stag-hound, a great favourite of the Squire's, who is a privileged visitor to the parlour; but the moment he makes his appearance, these intruders fly at him with furious rage; and I have admired the sovereign indifference and contempt with which he seems to look down upon his puny assailants. When her ladyship drives out, these dogs are generally carried with her to take the air; when they look out of each window of the carriage, and bark at all vulgar pedestrian dogs. These dogs are a continual source of misery to the household as they are always in the way, they every now and then get their toes trod on, and then there is a yelping on their part, and a loud lamentation on the part of their mistress, that fills the room with clamour and confusion.

Lastly, there is her ladyship's waiting-gentlewoman, Mrs. Hannah, a prim, pragmatical old maid; one of the most intolerable and intolerant virgins that ever lived. She has kept her virtue by her until it has turned sour, and now every word and look smacks of verjuice. She is the very opposite to her mistress, for one hates, and the other loves, all mankind. How they first came together I cannot imagine; but they have lived together for many years; and the abigail's temper being tart and encroaching, and her ladyship's easy and yielding, the former has got the complete upper hand, and tyrannizes over the good lady in secret.

Lady Lillycraft now and then complains of it, in great confidence, to her friends, but hushes up the subject immediately, if Mrs. Hannah makes her appearance. Indeed, she has been so accustomed to be attended by her, that she thinks she could not do without her; though one great study of her life, is to keep Mrs. Hannah in good-humour, by little presents and kindnesses.

Master Simon has a most devout abhorrence, mingled with awe, for this ancient spinster. He told me the other day, in a whisper, that she was a cursed brimstone—in fact, he added another epithet, which I would not repeat for the world. I have remarked, however, that he is always extremely civil to her when they meet.

Ready-Money Jack.

My purse, it is my privy wyfe,
This song I dare both syng and say,
It keepeth men from grievous stryfe
When every man for himself shall pay.
As I ryde in ryche array
For gold and silver men wyll me floryshe;
But thys matter I dare well saye,
Every gramercy myne own purse.
—Book of Hunting.

On the skirts of the neighbouring village, there lives a kind of small potentate, who, for aught I know, is a representative of one of the most ancient legitimate lines of the present day; for the empire over which he reigns has belonged to his family time out of mind. His territories comprise a considerable number of good fat acres; and his seat of power is in an old farm-house, where he enjoys, unmolested, the stout oaken chair of his ancestors. The personage to whom I allude is a sturdy old yeoman of the name of John Tibbets, or rather, Ready-Money Jack Tibbets, as he is called throughout the neighbourhood.

The first place where he attracted my attention was in the church-yard on Sunday; where he sat on a tombstone after the service, with his hat a little on one side, holding forth to a small circle of auditors; and, as I presumed, expounding the law and the prophets; until, on drawing a little nearer, I found he was only expatiating on the merits of a brown horse. He presented so faithful a picture of a substantial English yeoman, such as he is often described in books, heightened, indeed, by some little finery, peculiar to himself, that I could not but take note of his whole appearance.

He was between fifty and sixty, of a strong, muscular frame, and at least six feet high, with a physiognomy as grave as a lion's, and set off with short, curling, iron-gray locks. His shirt-collar was turned down, and displayed a neck covered with the same short, curling, gray hair; and he wore a coloured silk neckcloth, tied very loosely, and tucked in at the bosom, with a green paste brooch on the knot. His coat was of dark green cloth, with silver buttons, on each of which was engraved a stag, with his own name, John Tibbets, underneath. He had an inner waistcoat of figured chintz, between which and his coat was another of scarlet cloth, unbuttoned. His breeches were also left unbuttoned at the knees, not from any slovenliness, but to show a broad pair of scarlet garters. His stockings were blue, with white clocks; he wore large silver shoe-buckles; a broad paste buckle in his hatband; his sleeve-buttons were gold seven-shilling pieces; and he had two or three guineas hanging as ornaments to his watch-chain.

On making some inquiries about him, I gathered that he was descended from a line of farmers, that had always lived on the same spot, and owned the same property; and that half of the church-yard was taken up with the tombstones of his race. He has all his life been an important character in the place. When a youngster, he was one of the most roaring blades of the neighbourhood. No one could match him at wrestling, pitching the bar, cudgel play, and other athletic exercises. Like the renowned Pinner of Wakefield, he was the village champion; carried off the prize at all the fairs, and threw his gauntlet at the country round. Even to this day, the old people talk of his prowess, and undervalue, in comparison, all heroes of the green that have succeeded him; nay, they say, that if Ready-Money Jack were to take the field even now, there is no one could stand before him.

When Jack's father died, the neighbours shook their heads, and predicted that young hopeful would soon make way with the old homestead; but Jack falsified all their predictions. The moment he succeeded to the paternal farm, he assumed a new character; took a wife; attended resolutely to his affairs, and became an industrious, thrifty farmer. With the family property, he inherited a set of old family maxims, to which he steadily adhered. He saw to everything himself; put his own hand to the plough; worked hard; ate heartily; slept soundly; paid for every thing in cash down; and never danced, except he could do it to the music of his own money in both pockets. He has never been without a hundred or two pounds in gold by him, and never allows a debt to stand unpaid. This has gained him his current name, of which, by the by, he is a little proud; and has caused him to be looked upon as a very wealthy man by all the village.

Notwithstanding his thrift, however, he has never denied himself the amusements of life, but has taken a share in every passing pleasure. It is his maxim that "he that works hard can afford to play." He is, therefore, an attendant at all the country fairs and wakes, and has signalized himself by feats of strength and prowess on every village green in the shire. He often makes his appearance at horse-races, and sports his half guinea, and even his guinea at a time; keeps a good horse for his own riding, and to this day is fond of following the hounds, and is generally in at the death. He keeps up the rustic revels, and hospitalities too, for which his paternal farm-house has always been noted; has plenty of good cheer and dancing at harvest-home, and, above all, keeps the "merry night,"[2] as it is termed, at Christmas. With all his love of amusement, however, Jack is by no means a boisterous, jovial companion. He is seldom known to laugh even in the midst of his gayety; but maintains the same grave, lion-like demeanour. He is very slow at comprehending a joke; and is apt to sit puzzling at it with a perplexed look, while the rest of the company is in a roar. This gravity has, perhaps, grown on him with the growing weight of his character; for he is gradually rising into patriarchal dignity in his native place. Though he no longer takes an active part in athletic sports, yet he always presides at them, and is appealed to on all occasions as umpire. He maintains the peace on the village green at holiday games, and quells all brawls and quarrels by collaring the parties and shaking them heartily, if refractory. No one ever pretends to raise a hand against him, or to contend against his decisions; the young men having grown up in habitual awe of his prowess, and in implicit deference to him as the champion and lord of the green.

He is a regular frequenter of the village inn, the landlady having been a sweetheart of his in early life, and he having always continued on kind terms with her. He seldom, however, drinks any thing but a draught of ale; smokes his pipe, and pays his reckoning before leaving the tap-room. Here

---

[2] MERRY NIGHT—a rustic merry-making in a farm-house about Christmas, common in some parts of Yorkshire. There is abundance of homely fare, tea, cakes, fruit, and ale; various feats of agility, amusing games, romping, dancing, and kissing withal. They commonly break up at midnight.

he "gives his little senate laws;" decides bets, which are very generally referred to him; determines upon the characters and qualities of horses; and, indeed, plays now and then the part of a judge in settling petty disputes between neighbours, which otherwise might have been nursed by country attorneys into tolerable law-suits. Jack is very candid and impartial in his decisions, but he has not a head to carry a long argument, and is very apt to get perplexed and out of patience if there is much pleading. He generally breaks through the argument with a strong voice, and brings matters to a summary conclusion, by pronouncing what he calls the "upshot of the business," or, in other words, "the long and the short of the matter."

Jack once made a journey to London, a great many years since, which has furnished him with topics of conversation ever since. He saw the old king on the terrace at Windsor, who stopped, and pointed him out to one of the princesses, being probably struck with Jack's truly yeoman-like appearance. This is a favourite anecdote with him, and has no doubt had a great effect in making him a most loyal subject ever since, in spite of taxes and poors' rates. He was also at Bartholomew fair, where he had half the buttons cut off his coat; and a gang of pick-pockets, attracted by his external show of gold and silver, made a regular attempt to hustle him as he was gazing at a show; but for once they found that they had caught a tartar; for Jack enacted as great wonders among the gang as Samson did among the Philistines. One of his neighbours, who had accompanied him to town, and was with him at the fair, brought back an account of his exploits, which raised the pride of the whole village; who considered their champion as having subdued all London, and eclipsed the achievements of Friar Tuck, or even the renowned Robin Hood himself.

Of late years, the old fellow has begun to take the world easily; he works less, and indulges in greater leisure, his son having grown up, and succeeded to him both in the labours of the farm, and the exploits of the green. Like all sons of distinguished men, however, his father's renown is a disadvantage to him, for he can never come up to public expectation. Though a fine active fellow of three-and-twenty, and quite the "cock of the walk," yet the old people declare he is nothing like what Ready-Money Jack was at his time of life. The youngster himself acknowledges his inferiority, and has a wonderful opinion of the old man, who indeed taught him all his athletic accomplishments, and holds such a sway over him, that I am told, even to this day, he would have no hesitation to take him in hands, if he rebelled against paternal government.

The Squire holds Jack in very high esteem, and shows him to all his visitors, as a specimen of old English "heart of oak." He frequently calls at his house, and tastes some of his homebrewed, which is excellent. He made Jack a present of old Tusser's "Hundred Points of good Husbandrie," which has furnished him with reading ever since, and is his text-book, and manual in all agricultural and domestic concerns. He has made dog's ears at the most favourite passages, and knows many of the poetical maxims by heart.

Tibbets, though not a man to be daunted or flattered by high acquaintances; and though he cherishes a sturdy independence of mind and manner, yet is evidently gratified by the attentions of the Squire, whom he has known from boyhood, and pronounces "a true gentleman every inch of him." He is also on excellent terms with Master Simon, who is a kind of privy counsellor to the family; but his great favourite is the Oxonian, whom he taught to wrestle and play at quarter-staff when a boy, and considers the most promising young gentleman in the whole country.

Bachelors.

The Bachelor most joyfully
In pleasant plight doth pass his dales,
Good fellowship and companie
He doth maintain and keep alwaies.
—*EVEN'S Old Ballads.*

There is no character in the comedy of human life that is more difficult to play well, than that of an old Bachelor. When a single gentleman, therefore, arrives at that critical period when he begins to consider it an impertinent question to be asked his age, I would advise him, to look well to his ways. This period, it is true, is much later with some men than with others; I have witnessed more than once the meeting of two wrinkled old lads of this kind, who had not seen each other for several years, and have been amused by the amicable exchange of compliments on each other's appearance, that takes place on such occasions. There is always one invariable observation: "Why, bless my soul! you look younger than when I last saw you!" Whenever a man's friends begin to compliment him about looking young, he may be sure that they think he is growing old.

I am led to make these remarks by the conduct of Master Simon and the general, who have become great cronies. As the former is the younger by many years, he is regarded as quite a youthful blade by the general, who moreover looks upon him as a man of great wit and prodigious acquirements. I have already hinted that Master Simon is a family beau, and considered rather a young fellow by all the elderly ladies of the connexion; for an old bachelor, in an old family connexion, is something like an actor in a regular dramatic corps, who seems to "flourish in immortal youth," and will continue to play the Romeos and Rangers for half a century together.

Master Simon, too, is a little of the chameleon, and takes a different hue with every different companion: he is very attentive and officious, and somewhat sentimental, with Lady Lillycraft; copies out little namby-pamby ditties and love-songs for her, and draws quivers, and doves, and darts, and Cupids, to be worked on the corners of her pocket-handkerchiefs. He indulges, however, in very considerable latitude with the other married ladies of the family; and has many sly pleasantries to whisper to them, that provoke an equivocal laugh and a tap of the fan. But when he gets among young company, such as Frank Bracebridge, the Oxonian, and the general, he is apt to put on the mad wag, and to talk in a very bachelor-like strain about the sex.

In this he has been encouraged by the example of the general, whom he looks up to as a man who has seen the world. The general, in fact, tells shocking stories after dinner, when the ladies have retired, which he gives as some of the choice things that are served up at the Mulligatawney club; a knot of boon companions in London. He also repeats the fat jokes of old Major Pendergast, the wit of the club, and which, though the general can hardly repeat them for laughing, always make Mr. Bracebridge look grave, he having a great antipathy to an indecent jest. In a word, the general is a complete instance of the declension in gay life, by which a young man of pleasure is apt to cool down into an obscene old gentleman.

I saw him and Master Simon, an evening or two since, conversing with a buxom milkmaid in a meadow; and from their elbowing each other now and then, and the general's shaking his shoulders, blowing up his cheeks, and breaking out into a short fit of irrepressible laughter, I had no doubt they were playing the mischief with the girl.

As I looked at them through a hedge, I could not but think they would have made a tolerable group for a modern picture of Susannah and the two elders. It is true, the girl seemed in nowise alarmed at the force of the enemy; and I question, had either of them been alone, whether she would not have been more than they would have ventured to encounter. Such veteran roysters are daring wags when together, and will put any female to the blush with their jokes; but they are as quiet as lambs when they fall singly into the clutches of a fine woman.

In spite of the general's years, he evidently is a little vain of his person, and ambitious of conquests. I have observed him on Sunday in church, eyeing the country girls most suspiciously; and have seen him leer upon them with a downright amorous look, even when he has been gallanting Lady Lillycraft, with great ceremony, through the church-yard. The general, in fact, is a veteran in the service of Cupid, rather than of Mars, having signalized himself in all the garrison towns and country quarters, and seen service in every ball-room of England. Not a celebrated beauty but he has laid siege to; and if his word may be taken in a matter wherein no man is apt to be over-veracious, it is incredible the success he has had with the fair. At present he is like a worn-out warrior, retired from service; but who still cocks his beaver with a military air, and talks stoutly of fighting whenever he comes within the smell of gunpowder.

I have heard him speak his mind very freely over his bottle, about the folly of the captain in taking a wife; as he thinks a young soldier should care for nothing but his "bottle and kind landlady." But, in fact, he says the service on the continent has had a sad effect upon the young men; they have been ruined by light wines and French quadrilles. "They've nothing," he says, "of the spirit of the old service. There are none of your six-bottle men left, that were the souls of a mess dinner, and used to play the very deuce among the women."

As to a bachelor, the general affirms that he is a free and easy man, with no baggage to take care of but his portmanteau; but a married man, with his wife hanging on his arm, always puts him in mind of a chamber candlestick, with its extinguisher hitched to it. I should hot mind all this, if it were merely confined to the general; but I fear he will be the ruin of my friend, Master Simon, who already begins to echo his heresies, and to talk in the style of a gentleman that has seen life, and lived upon the town. Indeed, the general seems to have taken Master Simon in hand, and talks of showing him the lions when he comes to town, and of introducing him to a knot of choice spirits at the Mulligatawney club; which, I understand, is composed of old nabobs, officers in the Company's employ, and other "men of Ind," that have seen service in the East, and returned home burnt out with curry, and touched with the liver complaint. They have their regular club, where they eat Mulligatawney soup, smoke the hookah, talk about Tippoo Saib, Seringapatam, and tiger-hunting; and are tediously agreeable in each other's company.

Wives.

Believe me, man, there is no greater blisse
Than is the quiet joy of loving wife;
Which whoso wants, half of himselfe doth misse.
Friend without change, playfellow without strife,
Food without fulnesse, counsaile without pride,
Is this sweet doubling of our single life.
—SIR P. SIDNEY.

There is so much talk about matrimony going on around me, in consequence of the approaching event for which we are assembled at the Hall, that I confess I find my thoughts singularly exercised on the subject. Indeed, all the bachelors of the establishment seem to be passing through a kind of fiery ordeal; for Lady Lillycraft is one of those tender, romance-read dames of the old school, whose mind is filled with flames and darts, and who breathe nothing but constancy and wedlock. She is for ever immersed in the concerns of the heart; and, to use a poetical phrase, is perfectly surrounded by "the purple light of love." The very general seems to feel the influence of this sentimental atmosphere; to melt as he approaches her ladyship, and, for the time, to forget all his heresies about matrimony and the sex.

The good lady is generally surrounded by little documents of her prevalent taste; novels of a tender nature; richly bound little books of poetry, that are filled with sonnets and love tales, and perfumed with rose-leaves; and she has always an album at hand, for which she claims the contributions of all her friends. On looking over this last repository, the other day, I found a series of poetical extracts, in the Squire's handwriting, which might have been intended as matrimonial hints to his ward. I was so much struck with several of them, that I took the liberty of copying them out. They are from the old play of Thomas Davenport, published in 1661, entitled "The City Night-Cap;" in which is drawn out and exemplified, in the part of Abstemia, the character of a patient and faithful wife, which, I think, might vie with that of the renowned Griselda.

I have often thought it a pity that plays and novels should always end at the wedding, and should not give us another act, and another volume, to let us know how the hero and heroine conducted themselves when married. Their main object seems to be merely to instruct young ladies how to get husbands, but not how to keep them: now this last, I speak it with all due diffidence, appears to me to be a desideratum in modern married life. It is appalling to those who have not yet adventured into the holy state, to see how soon the flame of romantic love burns out, or rather is quenched in matrimony; and how deplorably the passionate, poetic lover declines into the phlegmatic, prosaic husband. I am inclined to attribute this very much to the defect just mentioned in the plays and novels, which form so important a branch of study of our young ladies; and which teach them how to be heroines, but leave them totally at a loss when they come to be wives. The play from which the quotations before me were made, however, is an exception to this remark; and I cannot refuse myself the pleasure of adducing some of them for the benefit of the reader, and for the honour of an old writer, who has bravely attempted to awaken dramatic interest in favour of a woman, even after she was married!

The following is a commendation of Abstemia to her husband Lorenzo:

> *She's modest, but not sullen, and loves silence;*
> *Not that she wants apt words, (for when she speaks,*
> *She inflames love with wonder,) but because*
> *She calls wise silence the soul's harmony.*
> *She's truly chaste; yet such a foe to coyness,*
> *The poorest call her courteous; and which is excellent,*
> *(Though fair and young) she shuns to expose herself*
> *To the opinion of strange eyes. She either seldom*
> *Or never walks abroad but in your company.*
> *And then with such sweet bashfulness, as if*
> *She were venturing on crack'd ice, and takes delight*
> *To step into the print your foot hath made,*
> *And will follow you whole fields; so she will drive*
> *Tediousness out of time, with her sweet character.*

Notwithstanding all this excellence, Abstemia has the misfortune to incur the unmerited jealousy of her husband. Instead, however, of resenting his harsh treatment with clamorous upbraidings, and with the stormy violence of high, windy virtue, by which the sparks of anger are so often blown into a flame, she endures it with the meekness of conscious, but patient, virtue; and makes the following beautiful appeal to a friend who has witnessed her long suffering:

> ———*Hast thou not seen me*
> *Bear all his injuries, as the ocean suffers*
> *The angry bark to plough through her bosom,*
> *And yet is presently so smooth, the eye*
> *Cannot perceive where the wide wound was made?*

Lorenzo, being wrought on by false representations, at length repudiates her. To the last, however, she maintains her patient sweetness, and her love for him, in spite of his cruelty. She deplores his error, even more than his unkindness; and laments the delusion which has turned his very affection into a source of bitterness. There is a moving pathos in her parting address to Lorenzo, after their divorce:

> ———*Farewell, Lorenzo,*
> *Whom my soul doth love: if you e'er marry,*
> *May you meet a good wife; so good, that you*
> *May not suspect her, nor may she be worthy*
> *Of your suspicion; and if you hear hereafter*
> *That I am dead, inquire but my last words,*
> *And you shall know that to the last I lov'd you.*
> *And when you walk forth with your second choice*
> *Into the pleasant fields, and by chance talk of me,*
> *Imagine that you see me, lean and pale,*
> *Strewing your path with flowers.—*
> *But may she never live to pay my debts: (weeps)*
> *If but in thought she wrong you, may she die*
> *In the conception of the injury.*

Pray make me wealthy with one kiss: farewell, sir:
Let it not grieve you when you shall remember
That I was innocent: nor this forget,
Though innocence here suffer, sigh, and groan,
She walks but thorow thorns to find a throne.

In a short time Lorenzo discovers his error, and the innocence of his injured wife. In the transports of his repentance, he calls to mind all her feminine excellence; her gentle, uncomplaining, womanly fortitude under wrongs and sorrows:

————Oh, Abstemia!
How lovely thou lookest now! now thou appearest
Chaster than is the morning's modesty
That rises with a blush, over whose bosom
The western wind creeps softly; now I remember
How, when she sat at table, her obedient eye
Would dwell on mine, as if it were not well,
Unless it look'd where I look'd: oh how proud
She was, when she could cross herself to please me!
But where now is this fair soul? Like a silver cloud
She hath wept herself, I fear, into the dead sea.
And will be found no more.

It is but doing right by the reader, if interested in the fate of Abstemia by the preceding extracts, to say, that she was restored to the arms and affections of her husband, rendered fonder than ever, by that disposition in every good heart, to atone for past injustice, by an overflowing measure of returning kindness:

Thou wealth, worth more than kingdoms; I am now
Confirmed past all suspicion; thou art far
Sweeter in thy sincere truth than a sacrifice
Deck'd up for death with garlands. The Indian winds
That blow from off the coast and cheer the sailor
With the sweet savour of their spices, want

The delight flows in thee.

I have been more affected and interested by this little dramatic picture, than by many a popular love tale; though, as I said before, I do not think it likely either Abstemia or patient Grizzle stand much chance of being taken for a model. Still I like to see poetry now and then extending its views beyond the wedding-day, and teaching a lady how to make herself attractive even after marriage. There is no great need of enforcing on an unmarried lady the necessity of being agreeable; nor is there any great art requisite in a youthful beauty to enable her to please. Nature has multiplied attractions around her. Youth is in itself attractive. The freshness of budding beauty needs no foreign aid to set it off; it pleases merely because it is fresh, and budding, and beautiful. But it is for the married state that a woman needs the most instruction, and in which she should be most on her guard to maintain her powers of pleasing. No woman can expect to be to her husband all that he fancied her when he was a lover. Men are always doomed to be duped, not so much by the arts of the sex, as by their own imaginations. They are always wooing goddesses, and marrying mere mortals. A woman should, therefore, ascertain what was the charm that rendered her so fascinating when a girl, and endeavour to keep it up when she has become a wife. One great thing undoubtedly was, the chariness of herself and her conduct, which an unmarried female always observes. She should maintain the same niceness and reserve in her person and habits, and endeavour still to preserve a freshness and virgin delicacy in the eye of her husband. She should remember that the province of woman is to be wooed, not to woo; to be caressed, not to caress. Man is an ungrateful being in love; bounty loses instead of winning him. The secret of a woman's power does not consist so much in giving, as in withholding.

A woman may give up too much even to her husband. It is to a thousand little delicacies of conduct that she must trust to keep alive passion, and to protect herself from that dangerous familiarity, that thorough acquaintance with every weakness and imperfection incident to matrimony. By these means she may still maintain her power, though she has surrendered her person, and may continue the romance of love even beyond the honeymoon.

"She that hath a wise husband," says Jeremy Taylor, "must entice him to an eternal dearnesse by the veil of modesty, and the grave robes of chastity, the ornament of meekness, and the jewels of faith and charity. She must have no painting but blushings; her brightness must be purity, and she must shine round about with sweetness and friendship; and she shall be pleasant while she lives, and desired when she dies."

I have wandered into a rambling series of remarks on a trite subject, and a dangerous one for a bachelor to meddle with. That I may not, however, appear to confine my observations entirely to the wife, I will conclude with another quotation from Jeremy Taylor, in which the duties of both parties are mentioned; while I would recommend his sermon on the marriage-ring to all those who, wiser than myself, are about entering the happy state of wedlock.

"There is scarce any matter of duty but it concerns them both alike, and is only distinguished by names, and hath its variety by circumstances and little accidents: and what in one is called love, in the other is called reverence; and what in the wife is obedience, the same in the man is duty. He provides, and she dispenses; he gives commandments, and she rules by them; he rules her by authority, and she rules him by love; she ought by all means to please him, and he must by no means displease her."

Story Telling.

A favorite evening pastime at the Hall, and one which the worthy Squire is fond of promoting, is story telling, "a good, old-fashioned fire-side amusement," as he terms it. Indeed, I believe he promotes it, chiefly, because it was one of the choice recreations in those days of yore, when ladies and gentlemen were not much in the habit of reading. Be this as it may, he will often, at supper-table, when conversation flags, call on some one or other of the company for a story, as it was formerly the custom to call for a song; and it is edifying to see the exemplary patience, and even satisfaction, with which the good old gentleman will sit and listen to some hackneyed tale that he has heard for at least a hundred times.

In this way, one evening, the current of anecdotes and stories ran upon mysterious personages that have figured at different times, and filled the world with doubt and conjecture; such as the Wandering Jew, the Man with the Iron Mask, who tormented the curiosity of all Europe; the Invisible Girl, and last, though not least, the Pig-faced Lady.

At length, one of the company was called upon that had the most unpromising physiognomy for a story teller, that ever I had seen. He was a thin, pale, weazen-faced man, extremely nervous, that had sat at one corner of the table, shrunk up, as it were, into himself, and almost swallowed up in the cape of his coat, as a turtle in its shell.

The very demand seemed to throw him into a nervous agitation; yet he did not refuse. He emerged his head out of his shell, made a few odd grimaces and gesticulations, before he could get his muscles into order, or his voice under command, and then offered to give some account of a mysterious personage that he had recently encountered in the course of his travels, and one whom he thought fully entitled to being classed with the Man with the Iron Mask.

I was so much struck with his extraordinary narrative, that I have written it out to the best of my recollection, for the amusement of the reader. I think it has in it all the elements of that mysterious and romantic narrative, so greedily sought after at the present day.

The Stout Gentleman.
A STAGE-COACH ROMANCE.

"I'll cross it, though it blast me!"
—Hamlet.

It was a rainy Sunday, in the gloomy month of November. I had been detained, in the course of a journey, by a slight indisposition, from which I was recovering; but I was still feverish, and was obliged to keep within doors all day, in an inn of the small town of Derby. A wet Sunday in a country inn!—whoever has had the luck to experience one can alone judge of my situation.

The rain pattered against the casements; the bells tolled for church with a melancholy sound. I went to the windows, in quest of something to amuse the eye; but it seemed as if I had been placed completely out of the reach of all amusement. The windows of my bed-room looked out among tiled roofs and stacks of chimneys, while those of my sitting-room commanded a full view of the stable-yard. I know of nothing more calculated to make a man sick of this world, than a stable-yard on a rainy day. The place was littered with wet straw, that had been kicked about by travellers and stable-boys. In one corner was a stagnant pool of water, surrounding an island of muck; there were several half-drowned fowls crowded together under a cart, among which was a miserable, crest-fallen cock, drenched out of all life and spirit; his drooping tail matted, as it were, into a single feather, along which the water trickled from his back; near the cart was a half-dozing cow chewing the cud, and standing patiently to be rained on, with wreaths of vapor rising from her reeking hide; a wall-eyed horse, tired of the loneliness of the stable, was poking his spectral head out of the window, with the rain dripping on it from the eaves; an unhappy cur, chained to a dog-house hard by, uttered something every now and then, between a bark and a yelp; a drab of a kitchen-wench tramped backwards and forwards through the yard in pattens, looking as sulky as the weather itself; every thing, in short, was comfortless and forlorn, excepting a crew of hard-drinking ducks, assembled like boon companions round a puddle, and making a riotous noise over their liquor.

I was lonely and listless, and wanted amusement. My room soon became insupportable. I abandoned it, and sought what is technically called the travellers'-room. This is a public room set apart at most inns for the accommodation of a class of wayfarers called travellers, or riders; a kind of commercial knights-errant, who are incessantly scouring the kingdom in gigs, on horseback, or by coach. They are the only successors that I know of, at the present day, to the knights-errant of yore. They lead the same kind of roving adventurous life, only changing the lance for a driving-whip, the buckler for a pattern-card, and the coat of mail for an upper Benjamin. Instead of vindicating the charms of peerless beauty, they rove about spreading the fame and standing of some substantial tradesman or manufacturer, and are ready at any time to bargain in his name; it being the fashion now-a-days to trade, instead of fight, with one another. As the room of the hotel, in the good old fighting times, would be hung round at night with the armour of wayworn warriors, such as coats of mail, falchions, and yawning helmets; so the travellers room is garnished with the harnessing of their successors, with box-coats, whips of all kinds, spurs, gaiters, and oil-cloth covered hats.

I was in hopes of finding some of these worthies to talk with, but was disappointed. There were, indeed, two or three in the room; but I could make nothing of them. One was just finishing his breakfast, quarrelling with his bread and butter, and huffing the waiter; another buttoned on a pair of gaiters, with many execrations at Boots for not having cleaned his shoes well; a third sat drumming on the table with his fingers, and looking at the rain as it streamed down the window-glass; they all appeared infected by the weather, and disappeared, one after the other, without exchanging a word.

I sauntered to the window, and stood gazing at the people picking their way to church, with petticoats hoisted mid-leg high, and dripping umbrellas. The bell ceased to toll, and the streets became silent. I then amused myself with watching the daughters of a tradesman opposite; who, being confined to the house for fear of wetting their Sunday finery, played off their charms at the front windows, to fascinate the chance tenants of the inn. They at length were summoned away by a vigilant vinegar-faced mother, and I had nothing further from without to amuse me.

What was I to do to pass away the long-lived day? I was sadly nervous and lonely; and every thing about an inn seems calculated to make a dull day ten times duller. Old newspapers, smelling of beer and tobacco-smoke, and which I had already read half-a-dozen times—good-for-nothing books, that were worse than rainy weather. I bored myself to death with an old volume of the Lady's Magazine. I read all the commonplaced names of ambitious travellers scrawled on the panes of glass; the eternal families of the Smiths, and the Browns, and the Jacksons, and the Johnsons, and all the other sons; and I deciphered several scraps of fatiguing inn-window poetry which I have met with in all parts of the world.

The day continued lowering and gloomy; the slovenly, ragged, spongy clouds drifted heavily along; there was no variety even in the rain: it was one dull, continued, monotonous patter—patter—patter, excepting that now and then I was enlivened by the idea of a brisk shower, from the rattling of the drops upon a passing umbrella.

It was quite *refreshing* (if I may be allowed a hackneyed phrase of the day) when, in the course of the morning, a horn blew, and a stage-coach whirled through the street, with outside passengers stuck all over it, cowering under cotton umbrellas, and seethed together, and reeking with the steams of wet box-coats and upper Benjamins.

The sound brought out from their lurking-places a crew of vagabond boys, and vagabond dogs, and the carroty-headed hostler, and that nondescript animal ycleped Boots, and all the other vagabond race that infest the purlieus of an inn; but the bustle was transient; the coach again whirled on its way; and boy and dog, and hostler and Boots, all slunk back again to their holes; the street again became silent, and the rain continued to rain on. In fact, there was no hope of its clearing up; the barometer pointed to rainy weather; mine hostess' tortoise-shell cat sat by the fire washing her face, and rubbing her paws over her ears; and, on referring to the almanac, I found a direful prediction stretching from the top of the page to the bottom through the whole month, "expect—much—rain—about—this—time."

I was dreadfully hipped. The hours seemed as if they would never creep by. The very ticking of the clock became irksome. At length the stillness of the house was interrupted by the ringing of a bell. Shortly after, I heard the voice of a waiter at the bar: "The stout gentleman in No. 13 wants his breakfast. Tea and bread and butter with ham and eggs; the eggs not to be too much done."

In such a situation as mine, every incident is of importance.

Here was a subject of speculation presented to my mind, and ample exercise for my imagination. I am prone to paint pictures to myself, and on this occasion I had some materials to work upon. Had the guest up-stairs been mentioned as Mr. Smith, or Mr. Brown, or Mr. Jackson, or Mr. Johnson, or merely as "the gentleman in No. 13," it would have been a perfect blank to me. I should have thought nothing of it; but "The stout gentleman!"—the very name had something in it of the picturesque. It at once gave the size; it embodied the personage to my mind's eye, and my fancy did the rest.

He was stout, or, as some term it, lusty; in all probability, therefore, he was advanced in life, some people expanding as they grow old. By his breakfasting rather late, and in his own room, he must be a man accustomed to live at his ease, and above the necessity of early rising; no doubt a round, rosy, lusty old gentleman.

There was another violent ringing. The stout gentleman was impatient for his breakfast. He was evidently a man of importance; "well-to-do in the world;" accustomed to be promptly waited upon; of a keen appetite, and a little cross when hungry; "perhaps," thought I, "he maybe be some London Alderman; or who knows but he may be a Member of Parliament?"

The breakfast was sent up and there was a short interval of silence; he was, doubtless, making the tea. Presently there was a violent ringing, and before it could be answered, another ringing still more violent. "Bless me! what a choleric old gentleman!" The waiter came down in a huff. The butter was rancid, the eggs were overdone, the ham was too salt:—the stout gentleman was evidently nice in his eating; one of those who eat and growl, and keep the waiter on the trot, and live in a state militant with the household.

The hostess got into a fume. I should observe that she was a brisk, coquettish woman; a little of a shrew, and something of a slammerkin, but very pretty withal; with a nincompoop for a husband, as shrews are apt to have. She rated the servants roundly for their negligence in sending up so bad a breakfast, but said not a word against the stout gentleman; by which I clearly perceived that he must be a man of consequence, entitled to make a noise and to give trouble at a country inn. Other eggs, and ham, and bread and butter, were sent up. They appeared to be more graciously received; at least there was no further complaint.

I had not made many turns about the travellers'-room, when there was another ringing. Shortly afterwards there was a stir and an inquest about the house. The stout gentleman wanted the Times or the Chronicle newspaper. I set him down, therefore, for a whig; or rather, from his being so absolute and lordly where he had a chance, I suspected him of being a radical. Hunt, I had heard, was a large man; "who knows," thought I, "but it is Hunt himself!"

My curiosity began to be awakened. I inquired of the waiter who was this stout gentleman that was making all this stir; but I could get no information; nobody seemed to know his name. The landlords of bustling inns seldom trouble their heads about the names or occupations of their transient guests. The colour of a coat, the shape or size of the person, is enough to suggest a travelling name. It is either the tall gentleman, or the short gentleman, or the gentleman in black, or the gentleman in snuff-colour; or, as in the present instance, the stout gentleman. A designation of the kind once hit on answers every purpose, and saves all further inquiry.

Rain—rain—rain! pitiless, ceaseless rain! No such thing as putting a foot out of doors, and no occupation nor amusement within. By and by I heard some one walking overhead. It was in the stout gentleman's room. He evidently was a large man, by the heaviness of his tread; and an old man, from his wearing such creaking soles. "He is doubtless," thought I, "some rich old square-toes, of regular habits, and is now taking exercise after breakfast."

I now read all the advertisements of coaches and hotels that were stuck about the mantel-piece. The Lady's Magazine had become an abomination to me; it was as tedious as the day itself. I wandered out, not knowing what to do, and ascended again to my room. I had not been there long, when there was a squall from a neighbouring bed-room. A door opened and slammed violently; a chamber-maid, that I had remarked for having a ruddy, good-humoured face, went down-stairs in a violent flurry. The stout gentleman had been rude to her.

This sent a whole host of my deductions to the deuce in a moment. This unknown personage could not be an old gentleman; for old gentlemen are not apt to be so obstreperous to chamber-maids. He could not be a young gentleman; for young gentlemen are not apt to inspire such indignation. He must be a middle-aged man, and confounded ugly into the bargain, or the girl would not have taken the matter in such terrible dudgeon. I confess I was sorely puzzled.

In a few minutes I heard the voice of my landlady. I caught a glance of her as she came tramping up-stairs; her face glowing, her cap flaring, her tongue wagging the whole way. "She'd have no such doings in her house, she'd warrant! If gentlemen did spend money freely, it was no rule. She'd have no servant maids of hers treated in that way, when they were about their work, that's what she wouldn't!"

As I hate squabbles, particularly with women, and above all with pretty women, I slunk back into my room, and partly closed the door; but my curiosity was too much excited not to listen. The landlady marched intrepidly to the enemy's citadel, and entered it with a storm: the door closed after her. I heard her voice in high windy clamour for a moment or two. Then it gradually subsided, like a gust of wind in a garret; then there was a laugh; then I heard nothing more.

After a little while, my landlady came out with an odd smile on her face, adjusting her cap, which was a little on one side. As she wont down-stairs, I heard the landlord ask her what was the matter; she said, "Nothing at all, only the girl's a fool." I was more than ever perplexed what to make of this unaccountable personage, who could put a good-natured chamber-maid in a passion, and send away a termagant landlady in smiles. He could not be so old, nor cross, nor ugly either.

I had to go to work at his picture again, and to paint him entirely different. I now set him down for one of those stout gentlemen that are frequently met with, swaggering about the doors of country inns. Moist, merry fellows, in Belcher handkerchiefs, whose bulk is a little assisted by malt liquors. Men who have seen the world, and been sworn at Highgate; who are used to tavern life; up to all the tricks of tapsters, and knowing in the ways of sinful publicans. Free-livers on a small scale; who are prodigal within the compass of a guinea; who call all the waiters by name, touzle the maids, gossip with the landlady at the bar, and prose over a pint of port, or a glass of negus, after dinner.

The morning wore away in forming of these and similar surmises. As fast as I wove one system of belief, some movement of the unknown would completely overturn it, and throw all my thoughts again into confusion. Such are the solitary operations of a feverish mind. I was, as I have said, extremely nervous; and the continual meditation on the concerns of this invisible personage began to have its effect:—I was getting a fit of the fidgets.

Dinner-time came. I hoped, the stout gentleman might dine in the travellers'-room, and that I might at length get a view of his person; but no—he had dinner served in his own room. What could be the meaning of this solitude and mystery? He could not be a radical; there was something too aristocratical in thus keeping himself apart from the rest of the world, and condemning himself to his own dull company throughout a rainy day. And then, too, he lived too well for a discontented politician. He seemed to expatiate on a variety of dishes, and to sit over his wine like a jolly friend of good living. Indeed, my doubts on this head were soon at an end; for he could not have finished his first bottle before I could faintly hear him humming a tune; and on listening, I found it to be "God save the King." 'Twas plain, then, he was no radical, but a faithful subject; one that grew loyal over his bottle, and was ready to stand by king and constitution, when he could stand by nothing else. But who could he be? My conjectures began to run wild. Was he not some personage of distinction, traveling incog.? "God knows!" said I, at my wit's end; "it may be one of the royal family for aught I know, for they are all stout gentlemen!"

The weather continued rainy. The mysterious unknown kept his room, and, as far as I could judge, his chair, for I did not hear him move. In the meantime, as the day advanced, the travellers'-room began to be frequented. Some, who had just arrived, came in buttoned up in box-coats; others came home, who had been dispersed about the town. Some took their dinners, and some their tea. Had I been in a different mood, I should have found entertainment in studying this peculiar class of men. There were two especially, who were regular wags of the road, and up to all the standing jokes of travellers. They had a thousand sly things to say to the waiting-maid, whom they called Louisa, and Ethelinda, and a dozen other fine names, changing the name every time, and chuckling amazingly at their own waggery. My mind, however, had become completely engrossed by the stout gentleman. He had kept my fancy in chase during a long day, and it was not now to be diverted from the scent.

The evening gradually wore away. The travellers read the papers two or three times over. Some drew round the fire, and told long stories about their horses, about their adventures, their overturns, and breakings down. They discussed the credits of different merchants and different inns; and the two wags told several choice anecdotes of pretty chamber-maids, and kind landladies. All this passed as they were quietly taking what they called their night-caps, that is to say, strong glasses of brandy and water and sugar, or some other mixture of the kind; after which they one after another rang for "Boots" and the chamber-maid, and walked off to bed in old shoes cut down into marvellously uncomfortable slippers.

There was only one man left; a short-legged, long-bodied, plethoric fellow, with a very large, sandy head. He sat by himself, with a glass of port wine negus, and a spoon; sipping and stirring, and meditating and sipping, until nothing was left but the spoon. He gradually fell asleep bolt upright in his chair, with the empty glass standing before him; and the candle seemed to fall asleep too, for the wick grew long, and black, and cabbaged at the end, and dimmed the little light that remained in the chamber. The gloom that now prevailed was contagious. Around hung the shapeless, and almost spectral, box-coats of departed travellers, long since buried in deep sleep. I only heard the ticking of the clock, with the deep-drawn breathings of the sleeping topers, and the drippings of the rain, drop—drop—drop, from the eaves of the house. The church-bells chimed midnight. All at once the stout gentleman began to walk overhead, pacing slowly backwards and forwards. There was something extremely awful in all this, especially to one in my state of nerves. These ghastly greatcoats, these guttural breathings, and the creaking footsteps of this mysterious being. His steps grew fainter and fainter, and at length died away. I could bear it no longer. I was wound up to the desperation of a hero of romance. "Be he who or what he may," said I to myself, "I'll have a sight of him!" I seized a chamber candle, and hurried up to number 13. The door stood ajar. I hesitated—I entered: the room was deserted. There stood a large, broad-bottomed elbow chair at a table, on which was an empty tumbler, and a "Times" newspaper, and the room smelt powerfully of Stilton cheese.

The mysterious stranger had evidently but just retired. I turned off, sorely disappointed, to my room, which had been changed to the front of the house. As I went along the corridor, I saw a large pair of boots, with dirty, waxed tops, standing at the door of a bed-chamber. They doubtless belonged to the unknown; but it would not do to disturb so redoubtable a personage in his den; he might discharge a pistol, or something worse, at my head. I went to bed, therefore, and lay awake half the night in a terrible nervous state; and even when I fell asleep, I was still haunted in my dreams by the idea of the stout gentleman and his wax-topped boots.

I slept rather late the next morning, and was awakened by some stir and bustle in the house, which I could not at first comprehend; until getting more awake, I found there was a mail-coach starting from the door. Suddenly there was a cry from below, "The gentleman has forgot his umbrella! look for the gentleman's umbrella in No. 13!" I heard an immediate scampering of a chamber-maid along the passage, and a shrill reply as she ran, "Here it is! here's the gentleman's umbrella!"

The mysterious stranger then was on the point of setting off. This was the only chance I should ever have of knowing him. I sprang out of bed, scrambled to the window, snatched aside the curtains, and just caught a glimpse of the rear of a person getting in at the coach-door. The skirts of a brown coat parted behind, and gave me a full view of the broad disk of a pair of drab breeches. The door closed—"all right!" was the word—the coach whirled off:—and that was all I ever saw of the stout gentleman!

Forest Trees.

"A living gallery of aged trees."

One of the favourite themes of boasting with the Squire, is the noble trees on his estate, which, in truth, has some of the finest that I have seen in England. There is something august and solemn in the great avenues of stately oaks that gather their branches together high in air, and seem to reduce the pedestrians beneath them to mere pigmies. "An avenue of oaks or elms," the Squire observes, "is the true colonnade that should lead to a gentleman's house. As to stone and marble, any one can rear them at once—they are the work of the day; but commend me to the colonnades that have grown old and great with the family, and tell by their grandeur how long the family has endured."

The Squire has great reverence for certain venerable trees, gray with moss, which he considers as the ancient nobility of his domain. There is the ruin of an enormous oak, which has been so much battered by time and tempest, that scarce any thing is left; though he says Christy recollects when, in his boyhood, it was healthy and nourishing, until it was struck by lightning. It is now a mere trunk, with one twisted bough stretching up into the air, leaving a green branch at the end of it. This sturdy wreck is much valued by the Squire; he calls it his standard-bearer, and compares it to a veteran warrior beaten down in battle, but bearing up his banner to the last. He has actually had a fence built round it, to protect it as much as possible from further injury.

It is with great difficulty that the Squire can ever be brought to have any tree cut down on his estate. To some he looks with reverence, as having been planted by his ancestors; to others with a kind of paternal affection, as having been planted by himself; and he feels a degree of awe in bringing down, with a few strokes of the axe, what it has cost centuries to build up. I confess I cannot but sympathize, in some degree, with the good Squire on the subject. Though brought up in a country overrun with forests, where trees are apt to be considered mere encumbrances, and to be laid low without hesitation or remorse, yet I could never see a fine tree hewn down without concern. The poets, who are naturally lovers of trees, as they are of every thing that is beautiful, have artfully awakened great interest in their favour, by representing them as the habitations of sylvan deities; insomuch that every great tree had its tutelar genius, or a nymph, whose existence was limited to its duration. Evelyn, in his Sylva, makes several pleasing and fanciful allusions to this superstition. "As the fall," says he, "of a very aged oak, giving a crack like thunder, has often been heard at many miles' distance; constrained though I often am to fell them with reluctancy, I do not at any time remember to have heard the groans of those nymphs (grieving to be dispossessed of their ancient habitations) without some emotion and pity." And again, in alluding to a violent storm that had devastated the woodlands, he says, "Methinks I still hear, sure I am that I still feel, the dismal groans of our forests; the late dreadful hurricane having subverted so many thousands of goodly oaks, prostrating the trees, laying them in ghastly postures, like whole regiments fallen in battle by the sword of the conqueror, and crushing all that grew beneath them. The public accounts," he adds, "reckon no less than three thousand brave oaks in one part only of the forest of Dean blown down."

I have paused more than once in the wilderness of America, to contemplate the traces of some blast of wind, which seemed to have rushed down from the clouds, and ripped its way through the bosom of the woodlands; rooting up, shivering, and splintering the stoutest trees, and leaving a long track of desolation. There was something awful in the vast havoc made among these gigantic plants; and in considering their magnificent remains, so rudely torn and mangled, and hurled down to perish prematurely on their native soil, I was conscious of a strong movement of the sympathy so feelingly expressed by Evelyn. I recollect, also, hearing a traveller of poetical Temperament expressing the kind of horror which he felt on Beholding on the banks of the Missouri, an oak of prodigious size, which had been, in a manner, overpowered by an enormous wild grape-vine. The vine had clasped its huge folds round the trunk, and from thence had wound about every branch and twig, until the mighty tree had withered in its embrace. It seemed like Laocoon struggling ineffectually in the hideous coils of the monster Python. It was the lion of trees perishing in the embraces of a vegetable boa.

I am fond of listening to the conversation of English gentlemen on rural concerns, and of noticing with what taste and discrimination, and what strong, unaffected interest they will discuss topics, which, in other countries, are abandoned to mere woodmen, or rustic cultivators. I have heard a noble earl descant on park and forest scenery with the science and feeling of a painter. He dwelt on the shape and beauty of particular trees on his estate, with as much pride and technical precision as though he had been discussing the merits of statues in his collection I found that he had even gone considerable distances to examine trees which were celebrated among rural amateurs; for it seems that trees, like horses, have their established points of excellence; and that there are some in England which enjoy very extensive celebrity among tree-fanciers, from being perfect in their kind.

There is something nobly simple and pure in such a taste: it argues, I think, a sweet and generous nature, to have this strong relish for the beauties of vegetation, and this friendship for the hardy and glorious sons of the forest. There is a grandeur of thought connected with this part of rural economy. It is, if I may be allowed the figure, the heroic line of husbandry. It is worthy of liberal, and free-born, and aspiring men. He who plants an oak, looks forward to future ages, and plants for posterity. Nothing can be less selfish than this. He cannot expect to sit in its shade, nor enjoy its shelter; but he exults in the idea that the acorn which he has buried in the earth shall grow up into a lofty pile, and shall keep on flourishing, and increasing, and benefiting mankind, long after he shall have ceased to tread his paternal fields. Indeed, it is the nature of such occupations to lift the thoughts above mere worldliness. As the leaves of trees are said to absorb all noxious qualities of the air, and to breathe forth a purer atmosphere, so it seems to me as if they drew from us all sordid and angry passions, and breathed forth peace and philanthropy. There is a serene and settled majesty in woodland scenery, that enters into the soul, and dilates and elevates it, and fills it with noble inclinations. The ancient and hereditary groves, too, that embower this island, are most of them full of story. They are haunted by the recollections of great spirits of past ages, who have sought for relaxation among them from the tumult of arms, or the toils of state, or have wooed the muse beneath their shade. Who can walk, with soul unmoved, among the stately groves of Penshurst, where the gallant, the amiable, the elegant Sir Philip Sidney passed his boyhood; or can look without fondness upon the tree that is said to have been planted on his birthday; or can ramble among the classic bowers of Hagley; or can pause among the solitudes of Windsor Forest, and look at the oaks around, huge, gray, and time-worn, like the old castle towers, and not feel as if he were surrounded by so many monuments of long-enduring glory? It is, when viewed in this light, that planted groves, and stately avenues, and cultivated parks, have an advantage over the more luxuriant beauties of unassisted nature. It is that they teem with moral associations, and keep up the ever-interesting story of human existence.

It is incumbent, then, on the high and generous spirits of an ancient nation, to cherish these sacred groves that surround their ancestral mansions, and to perpetuate them to their descendants. Republican as I am by birth, and brought up as I have been in republican principles and habits, I can feel nothing of the servile reverence for titled rank, merely because it is titled; but I trust that I am neither churl nor bigot in my creed. I can both see and feel how hereditary distinction, when it falls to the lot of a generous mind, may elevate that mind into true nobility. It is one of the effects of hereditary rank, when it falls thus happily, that it multiplies the duties, and, as it were, extends the existence of the possessor. He does not feel himself a mere individual link in creation, responsible only for his own brief term of being. He carries back his existence in proud recollection, and he extends it forward in honourable anticipation. He lives with his ancestry, and he lives with his posterity. To both does he consider himself involved in deep responsibilities. As he has received much from those that have gone before, so he feels bound to transmit much to those who are to come after him. His domestic undertakings seem to imply a longer existence than those of ordinary men; none are so apt to build and plant for future centuries, as noble-spirited men, who have received their heritages from foregone ages.

I cannot but applaud, therefore, the fondness and pride with which I have noticed English gentlemen, of generous temperaments, and high aristocratic feelings, contemplating those magnificent trees, which rise like towers and pyramids, from the midst of their paternal lands. There is an affinity between all nature, animate and inanimate: the oak, in the pride and lustihood of its growth, seems to me to take its range with the lion and the eagle, and to assimilate, in the grandeur of its attributes, to heroic and intellectual man. With its mighty pillar rising straight and direct towards heaven, bearing up its leafy honours from the impurities of earth, and supporting them aloft in free air and glorious sunshine, it is an emblem of what a true nobleman *should be*; a refuge for the weak, a shelter for the oppressed, a defence for the defenceless; warding off from them the peltings of the storm, or the scorching rays of arbitrary power. He who is *this*, is an ornament and a blessing to his native land. He who is *otherwise*, abuses his eminent advantages; abuses the grandeur and prosperity which he has drawn from the bosom of his country. Should tempests arise, and he be laid prostrate by the storm, who would mourn over his fall? Should he be borne down by the oppressive hand of power, who would murmur at his fate?—"Why cumbereth he the ground?"

A Literary Antiquary.

Printed bookes he contemnes, as a novelty of this latter age; but a manuscript he pores on everlastingly; especially if the cover be all moth-eaten, and the dust make a parenthesis betweene every syllable.
—Mico-Cosmographie, 1638.

The Squire receives great sympathy and support, in his antiquated humours, from the parson, of whom I made some mention on my former visit to the Hall, and who acts as a kind of family chaplain. He has been cherished by the Squire almost constantly, since the time that they were fellow-students at Oxford; for it is one of the peculiar advantages of these great universities, that they often link the poor scholar to the rich patron, by early and heart-felt ties, that last through life, without the usual humiliations of dependence and patronage. Under the fostering protection of the Squire, therefore, the little parson has pursued his studies in peace. Having lived almost entirely among books, and those, too, old books, he is quite ignorant of the world, and his mind is as antiquated as the garden at the Hall, where the flowers are all arranged in formal beds, and the yew-trees clipped into urns and peacocks.

His taste for literary antiquities was first imbibed in the Bodleian Library at Oxford; where, when a student, he passed many an hour foraging among the old manuscripts. He has since, at different times, visited most of the curious libraries in England, and has ransacked many of the cathedrals. With all his quaint and curious learning, he has nothing of arrogance or pedantry; but that unaffected earnestness and guileless simplicity which seem to belong to the literary antiquary.

He is a dark, mouldy little man, and rather dry in his manner; yet, on his favourite theme, he kindles up, and at times is even eloquent. No fox-hunter, recounting his last day's sport, could be more animated than I have seen the worthy parson, when relating his search after a curious document, which he had traced from library to library, until he fairly unearthed it in the dusty chapter-house of a cathedral. When, too, he describes some venerable manuscript, with its rich illuminations, its thick creamy vellum, its glossy ink, and the odour of the cloisters that seemed to exhale from it, he rivals the enthusiasm of a Parisian epicure, expatiating on the merits of a Perigord pie, or a *Patté de Strasbourg*.

His brain seems absolutely haunted with love-sick dreams about gorgeous old works in "silk linings, triple gold bands, and tinted leather, locked up in wire cases, and secured from the vulgar hands of the mere reader;" and, to continue the happy expressions of an ingenious writer, "dazzling one's eyes like eastern beauties, peering through their jealousies."[3]

He has a great desire, however, to read such works in the old libraries and chapter-houses to which they belong; for he thinks a black-letter volume reads best in one of those venerable chambers where the light struggles through dusty lancet windows and painted glass; and that it loses half its zest, if taken away from the neighbourhood of the quaintly-carved oaken book-case and Gothic reading-desk. At his suggestion, the Squire has had the library furnished in this antique taste, and several of the windows glazed with painted glass, that they may throw a properly tempered light upon the pages of their favourite old authors.

The parson, I am told, has been for some time meditating a commentary on Strutt, Brand, and Douce, in which he means to detect them in sundry dangerous errors in respect to popular games and superstitions; a work to which the Squire looks forward with great interest. He is, also, a casual contributor to that long-established repository of national customs and antiquities, the Gentleman's Magazine, and is one of those that every now and then make an inquiry concerning some obsolete custom or rare legend; nay, it is said that several of his communications have been at least six inches in length. He frequently receives parcels by coach from different parts of the kingdom, containing mouldy volumes and almost illegible manuscripts; for it is singular what an active correspondence is kept up among literary antiquaries, and how soon the fame of any rare volume, or unique copy, just discovered among the rubbish of a library, is circulated among them. The parson is more busy than common just now, being a little flurried by an advertisement of a work, said to be preparing for the press, on the mythology of the middle

---

[3] D'Israeli—Curiosities of Literature.

ages. The little man has long been gathering together all the hobgoblin tales he could collect, illustrative of the superstitions of former times; and he is in a complete fever lest this formidable rival should take the field before him.

Shortly after my arrival at the Hall, I called at the parsonage, in company with Mr. Bracebridge and the general. The parson had not been seen for several days, which was a matter of some surprise, as he was an almost daily visitor at the Hall. We found him in his study; a small dusky chamber, lighted by a lattice window that looked into the church-yard, and was overshadowed by a yew-tree. His chair was surrounded by folios and quartos, piled upon the floor, and his table was covered with books and manuscripts. The cause of his seclusion was a work which he had recently received, and with which he had retired in rapture from the world, and shut himself up to enjoy a literary honeymoon undisturbed. Never did boarding-school girl devour the pages of a sentimental novel, or Don Quixote a chivalrous romance, with more intense delight than did the little man banquet on the pages of this delicious work. It was Dibdin's Bibliographical Tour; a work calculated to have as intoxicating an effect on the imaginations of literary antiquaries, as the adventures of the heroes of the round table, on all true knights; or the tales of the early American voyagers on the ardent spirits of the age, filling them with dreams of Mexican and Peruvian mines, and of the golden realm of El Dorado.

The good parson had looked forward to this bibliographical expedition as of far greater importance than those to Africa or the North Pole. With what eagerness had he seized upon the history of the enterprise! with what interest had he followed the redoubtable bibliographer and his graphical squire in their adventurous roamings among Norman castles, and cathedrals, and French libraries, and German convents and universities; penetrating into the prison-houses of vellum manuscripts, and exquisitely illuminated missals, and revealing their beauties to the world!

When the parson had finished a rapturous eulogy on this most curious and entertaining work, he drew forth from a little drawer a manuscript, lately received from a correspondent, which had perplexed him sadly. It was written in Norman French, in very ancient characters, and so faded and mouldered away as to be almost illegible. It was apparently an old Norman drinking song, that might have been brought over by one of

William the Conqueror's carousing followers. The writing was just legible enough to keep a keen antiquity-hunter on a doubtful chase; here and there he would be completely thrown out, and then there would be a few words so plainly written as to put him on the scent again. In this way he had been led on for a whole day, until he had found himself completely at fault.

The Squire endeavoured to assist him, but was equally baffled. The old general listened for some time to the discussion, and then asked the parson if he had read Captain Morris's, or George Stevens's, or Anacreon Moore's bacchanalian songs? On the other replying in the negative, "Oh, then," said the general, with a sagacious nod, "if you want a drinking song, I can furnish you with the latest collection—I did not know you had a turn for those kind of things; and I can lend you the Encyclopedia of Wit into the bargain. I never travel without them; they're excellent reading at an inn."

It would not be easy to describe the odd look of surprise and perplexity of the parson, at this proposal; or the difficulty the Squire had in making the general comprehend, that though a jovial song of the present day was but a foolish sound in the ears of wisdom, and beneath the notice of a learned man, yet a trowl, written by a tosspot several hundred years since, was a matter worthy of the gravest research, and enough to set whole colleges by the ears.

I have since pondered much on this matter, and have figured to myself what may be the fate of our current literature, when retrieved, piecemeal, by future antiquaries, from among the rubbish of ages. What a Magnus Apollo, for instance, will Moore become, among sober divines and dusty schoolmen! Even his festive and amatory songs, which are now the mere quickeners of our social moments, or the delights of our drawing-rooms, will then become matters of laborious research and painful collation. How many a grave professor will then waste his midnight oil, or worry his brain through a long morning, endeavouring to restore the pure text, or illustrate the biographical hints of "Come, tell me, says Rosa, as kissing and kissed;" and how many an arid old bookworm, like the worthy little parson, will give up in despair, after vainly striving to fill up some fatal hiatus in "Fanny of Timmol"!

Nor is it merely such exquisite authors as Moore that are doomed to consume the oil of future antiquaries. Many a poor scribbler, who is now, apparently, sent to oblivion by pastrycooks and cheese-mongers, will then rise again in fragments, and flourish in learned immortality.

After all, thought I, time is not such an invariable destroyer as he is represented. If he pulls down, he likewise builds up; if he impoverishes one, he enriches another; his very dilapidations furnish matter for new works of controversy, and his rust is more precious than the most costly gilding. Under his plastic hand, trifles rise into importance; the nonsense of one age becomes the wisdom of another; the levity of the wit gravitates into the learning of the pedant, and an ancient farthing moulders into infinitely more value than a modern guinea.

The Farm-House.

————"Love and hay
Are thick sown, but come up full of thistles."
—BEAUMONT AND FLETCHER.

I was so much pleased with the anecdotes which were told me of Ready-Money Jack Tibbets, that I got Master Simon, a day or two since, to take me to his house. It was an old-fashioned farm-house built with brick, with curiously twisted chimneys. It stood at a little distance from the road, with a southern exposure, looking upon a soft green slope of meadow. There was a small garden in front, with a row of bee-hives humming among beds of sweet herbs and flowers. Well-scoured milking tubs, with bright copper hoops, hung on the garden paling. Fruit trees were trained up against the cottage, and pots of flowers stood in the windows. A fat, superannuated mastiff lay in the sunshine at the door; with a sleek cat sleeping peacefully across him.

Mr. Tibbets was from home at the time of our calling, but we were received with hearty and homely welcome by his wife; a notable, motherly woman, and a complete pattern for wives; since, according to Master Simon's account, she never contradicts honest Jack, and yet manages to have her own way, and to control him in every thing.

She received us in the main room of the house, a kind of parlour and hall, with great brown beams of timber across it, which Mr. Tibbets is apt to point out with some exultation, observing, that they don't put such timber in houses now-a-days. The furniture was old-fashioned, strong, and highly polished; the walls were hung with coloured prints of the story of the Prodigal Son, who was represented in a red coat and leather breeches. Over the fire-place was a blunderbuss, and a hard-favoured likeness of Ready-Money Jack, taken when he was a young man, by the same artist that painted the tavern sign; his mother having taken a notion that the Tibbets had as much right to have a gallery of family portraits as the folks at the Hall.

The good dame pressed us very much to take some refreshment, and tempted us with a variety of household dainties, so that we were glad to compound by tasting some of her homemade wines. While we were there, the son and heir-apparent came home; a good-looking young fellow, and something of a rustic beau. He took us over the premises, and showed us the whole establishment. An air of homely but substantial plenty prevailed throughout; every thing was of the best materials, and in the best condition. Nothing was out of place, or ill made; and you saw every where the signs of a man that took care to have the worth of his money, and that paid as he went.

The farm-yard was well stocked; under a shed was a taxed cart, in trim order, in which Ready-Money Jack took his wife about the country. His well-fed horse neighed from the stable, and when led out into the yard, to use the words of young Jack, "he shone like a bottle;" for he said the old man made it a rule that every thing about him should fare as well as he did himself.

I was pleased to see the pride which the young fellow seemed to have of his father. He gave us several particulars concerning his habits, which were pretty much to the effect of those I have already mentioned. He had never suffered an account to stand in his life, always providing the money before he purchased any thing; and, if possible, paying in gold and silver. He had a great dislike to paper money, and seldom went without a considerable sum in gold about him. On my observing that it was a wonder he had never been waylaid and robbed, the young fellow smiled at the idea of any one venturing upon such an exploit, for I believe he thinks the old man would be a match for Robin Hood and all his gang.

I have noticed that Master Simon seldom goes into any house without having a world of private talk with some one or other of the family, being a kind of universal counsellor and confidant. We had not been long at the farm, before the old dame got him into a corner of her parlour, where they had a long, whispering conference together; in which I saw, by his shrugs, that there were some dubious matters discussed, and by his nods that he agreed with every thing she said.

After we had come out, the young man accompanied us a little distance, and then, drawing Master Simon aside into a green lane, they walked and talked together for nearly half an hour. Master Simon, who has the usual propensity of confidants to blab every thing to the next friend they meet with, let me know that there was a love affair in question; the young fellow having been smitten with the charms of Phoebe Wilkins, the pretty niece of the housekeeper at the Hall. Like most other love concerns, it had brought its troubles and perplexities. Dame Tibbets had long been on intimate, gossiping terms with the housekeeper, who often visited the farm-house; but when the neighbours spoke to her of the likelihood of a match between her son and Phoebe Wilkins, "Marry come up!" she scouted the very idea. The girl had acted as lady's maid; and it was beneath the blood of the Tibbets', who had lived on their own lands time out of mind, and owed reverence and thanks to nobody, to have the heir-apparent marry a servant!

These vapourings had faithfully been carried to the housekeeper's ear, by one of their mutual go-between friends. The old housekeeper's blood, if not as ancient, was as quick as that of Dame Tibbets. She had been accustomed to carry a high head at the Hall, and among the villagers; and her faded brocade rustled with indignation at the slight cast upon her alliance by the wife of a petty farmer. She maintained that her niece had been a companion rather than a waiting-maid to the young ladies. "Thank heavens, she was not obliged to work for her living, and was as idle as any young lady in the land; and when somebody died, would receive something that would be worth the notice of some folks, with all their ready money."

A bitter feud had thus taken place between the two worthy dames, and the young people were forbidden to think of one another. As to young Jack, he was too much in love to reason upon the matter; and being a little heady, and not standing in much awe of his mother, was ready to sacrifice the whole dignity of the Tibbets' to his passion. He had lately, however, had a violent quarrel with his mistress, in consequence of some coquetry on her part, and at present stood aloof. The politic mother was exerting all her ingenuity to widen the accidental breach; but, as is most commonly the case, the more she meddled with this perverse inclination of the son, the stronger it grew. In the meantime, old Ready-Money was kept completely in the dark; both parties were in awe and uncertainty as to what might be his way of taking the matter, and dreaded to awaken the sleeping lion. Between father and son, therefore, the worthy Mrs. Tibbets was full of business, and at her wit's end. It is true there was no great danger of honest Ready-Money's finding the thing out, if left to himself; for he was of a most unsuspicious temper, and by no means quick of apprehension; but there was daily risk of his attention being aroused, by the cobwebs which his indefatigable wife was continually spinning about his nose.

Such is the distracted state of politics, in the domestic empire of Ready-Money Jack; which only shows the intrigues and internal dangers to which the best-regulated governments are liable. In this perplexed situation of their affairs, both mother and son have applied to Master Simon for counsel; and, with all his experience in meddling with other people's concerns, he finds it an exceedingly difficult part to play, to agree with both parties, seeing that their opinions and wishes are so diametrically opposite.

Horsemanship.

A coach was a strange monster in those days, and the sight put both horse and man into amazement. Some said it was a great crabshell brought out of China, and some imagined it to be one of the pagan temples, in which the canibals adored the divell.
—TAYLOR, THE WATER POET.

I have made casual mention, more than once, of one of the Squire's antiquated retainers, old Christy, the huntsman. I find that his crabbed humour is a source of much entertainment among the young men of the family; the Oxonian, particularly, takes a mischievous pleasure, now and then, in slyly rubbing the old man against the grain, and then smoothing him down again; for the old fellow is as ready to bristle up his back as a porcupine. He rides a venerable hunter called Pepper, which is a counterpart of himself, a heady cross-grained animal, that frets the flesh off its bones; bites, kicks, and plays all manner of villainous tricks. He is as tough, and nearly as old as his rider, who has ridden him time out of mind, and is, indeed, the only one that can do any thing with him. Sometimes, however, they have a complete quarrel, and a dispute for mastery, and then, I am told, it is as good as a farce to see the heat they both get into, and the wrong-headed contest that ensues; for they are quite knowing in each other's ways, and in the art of teasing and fretting each other. Notwithstanding these doughty brawls, however, there is nothing that nettles old Christy sooner than to question the merits of the horse; which he upholds as tenaciously as a faithful husband will vindicate the virtues of the termagant spouse, that gives him a curtain lecture every night of his life.

The young men call old Christy their "professor of equitation;" and in accounting for the appellation, they let me into some particulars of the Squire's mode of bringing up his children. There is an odd mixture of eccentricity and good sense in all the opinions of my worthy host. His mind is like modern Gothic, where plain brick-work is set off with pointed arches and quaint tracery. Though the main ground-work of his opinions is correct, yet he has a thousand little notions, picked up from old books, which stand out whimsically on the surface of his mind.

Thus, in educating his boys, he chose Peachem, Markam, and such like old English writers, for his manuals. At an early age he took the lads out of their mother's hands, who was disposed, as mothers are apt to be, to make fine, orderly children of them, that should keep out of sun and rain and never soil their hands, nor tear their clothes.

In place of this, the Squire turned them loose to run free and wild about the park, without heeding wind or weather. He was, also, particularly attentive in making them bold and expert horsemen; and these were the days when old Christy, the huntsman, enjoyed great importance, as the lads were put under his care to practise them at the leaping-bars, and to keep an eye upon them in the chase.

The Squire always objected to their riding in carriages of any kind, and is still a little tenacious on this point. He often rails against the universal use of carriages, and quotes the words of honest Nashe to that effect. "It was thought," says Nashe, in his Quaternio, "a kind of solecism, and to savour of effeminacy, for a young gentleman in the flourishing time of his age to creep into a coach, and to shroud himself from wind and weather: our great delight was to outbrave the blustering Boreas upon a great horse; to arm and prepare ourselves to go with Mars and Bellona into the field, was our sport and pastime; coaches and caroches we left unto them for whom they were first invented, for ladies and gentlemen, and decrepit age and impotent people."

The Squire insists that the English gentlemen have lost much of their hardiness and manhood, since the introduction of carriages. "Compare," he will say, "the fine gentleman of former times, ever on horseback, booted and spurred, and travel-stained, but open, frank, manly, and chivalrous, with the fine gentleman of the present day, full of affectation and effeminacy, rolling along a turnpike in his voluptuous vehicle. The young men of those days were rendered brave, and lofty, and generous in their notions, by almost living in their saddles, and having their foaming steeds 'like proud seas under them.' There is something," he adds, "in bestriding a fine horse that makes a man feel more than mortal. He seems to have doubled his nature, and to have added to his own courage and sagacity the power, the speed, and stateliness of the superb animal on which he is mounted."

"It is a great delight," says old Nashe, "to see a young gentleman with his skill and cunning, by his voice, rod, and spur, better to manage and to command the great Bucephalus, than the strongest Milo, with all his strength; one while to see him make him tread, trot, and gallop the ring; and one after to see him make him gather up roundly; to bear his head steadily; to run a full career swiftly; to stop a sudden lightly; anon after to see him make him advance, to yerke, to go back, and sidelong, to turn on either hand; to gallop the gallop galliard; to do the capriole, the chambetta, and dance the curvetty."

In conformity to these ideas, the Squire had them all on horseback at an early age, and made them ride, slapdash, about the country, without flinching at hedge, or ditch, or stone wall, to the imminent danger of their necks.

Even the fair Julia was partially included in this system; and, under the instructions of old Christy, has become one of the best horsewomen in the country. The Squire says it is better than all the cosmetics and sweeteners of the breath that ever were invented. He extols the horsemanship of the ladies in former times, when Queen Elizabeth would scarcely suffer the rain to stop her accustomed ride. "And then think," he will say, "what nobler and sweeter beings it made them. What a difference must there be, both in mind and body, between a joyous, high-spirited dame of those days, glowing with health and exercise, freshened by every breeze that blows, seated loftily and gracefully on her saddle, with plume on head, and hawk on hand, and her descendant of the present day, the pale victim of routs and ball-rooms, sunk languidly in one corner of an enervating carriage."

The Squire's equestrian system has been attended with great success; for his sons, having passed through the whole course of instruction without breaking neck or limb, are now healthful, spirited, and active, and have the true Englishman's love for a horse. If their manliness and frankness are praised in their father's hearing, he quotes the old Persian maxim, and says, they have been taught "to ride, to shoot, and to speak the truth."

It is true, the Oxonian has now and then practised the old gentleman's doctrines a little in the extreme. He is a gay youngster, rather fonder of his horse than his book, with a little dash of the dandy; though the ladies all declare that he is "the flower of the flock." The first year that he was sent to Oxford, he had a tutor appointed to overlook him, a dry chip of the university. When he returned home in the vacation, the Squire made many inquiries about how he liked his college, his studies, and his tutor.

"Oh, as to my tutor, sir, I've parted with him some time since."

"You have! and, pray, why so?"

"Oh, sir, hunting was all the go at our college, and I was a little short of funds; so I discharged my tutor, and took a horse, you know."

"Ah, I was not aware of that, Tom," said the Squire, mildly.

When Tom returned to college, his allowance was doubled, that he might be enabled to keep both horse and tutor.

Love Symptoms.

I will now begin to sigh, read poets, look pale, go neatly, and be most
apparently in love.
—MARSTON.

I should not be surprised, if we should have another pair of turtles at the Hall; for Master Simon has informed me, in great confidence, that he suspects the general of some design upon the susceptible heart of Lady Lillycraft. I have, indeed, noticed a growing attention and courtesy in the veteran towards her ladyship; he softens very much in her company, sits by her at table, and entertains her with long stories about Seringapatam, and pleasant anecdotes of the Mulligatawney club. I have even seen him present her with a full-blown rose from the hot-house, in a style of the most captivating gallantry, and it was accepted with great suavity and graciousness; for her ladyship delights in receiving the homage and attention of the sex.

Indeed, the general was one of the earliest admirers that dangled in her train, during her short reign of beauty; and they flirted together for half a season in London, some thirty or forty years since. She reminded him lately, in the course of a conversation about former days, of the time when he used to ride a white horse, and to canter so gallantly by the side of her carriage in Hyde Park; whereupon I have remarked that the veteran has regularly escorted her since, when she rides out on horseback; and, I suspect, he almost persuades himself that he makes as captivating an appearance as in his youthful days.

It would be an interesting and memorable circumstance in the chronicles of Cupid, if this spark of the tender passion, after lying dormant for such a length of time, should again be fanned into a flame, from amidst the ashes of two burnt-out hearts. It would be an instance of perdurable fidelity, worthy of being placed beside those recorded in one of the Squire's favourite tomes, commemorating the constancy of the olden times; in which times, we are told, "Men and wymmen coulde love togyders seven yeres, and no licours lustes were betwene them, and thenne was love, trouthe, and feythfulnes; and lo in lyke wyse was used love in King Arthur's dayes."[4]

Still, however, this may be nothing but a little venerable flirtation, the general being a veteran dangler, and the good lady habituated to these kind of attentions. Master Simon, on the other hand, thinks the general is looking about him with the wary eye of an old campaigner; and, now that he is on the wane, is desirous of getting into warm winter-quarters. Much allowance, however, must be made for Master Simon's uneasiness on the subject, for he looks on Lady Lillycraft's house as one of his strongholds, where he is lord of the ascendant; and, with all his admiration of the general, I much doubt whether he would like to see him lord of the lady and the establishment.

There are certain other symptoms, notwithstanding, that give an air of probability to Master Simon's intimations. Thus, for instance, I have observed that the general has been very assiduous in his attentions to her ladyship's dogs, and has several times exposed his fingers to imminent jeopardy, in attemptingto pat Beauty on the head. It is to be hoped his advances to the mistress will be more favourably received, as all his overtures towards a caress are greeted by the pestilent little cur with a wary kindling of the eye, and a most venomous growl.

He has, moreover, been very complaisant towards my lady's gentlewoman, the immaculate Mrs. Hannah, whom he used to speak of in a way that I do not choose to mention. Whether she has the same suspicions with Master Simon or not, I cannot say; but she receives his civilities with no better grace than the implacable Beauty; unscrewing her mouth into a most acid smile, and looking as though she could bite a piece out of him. In short, the poor general seems to have as formidable foes to contend with, as a hero of ancient fairy tale; who had to fight his way to his enchanted princess through ferocious monsters of every kind, and to encounter the brimstone terrors of some fiery dragon.

There is still another circumstance, which inclines me to give very considerable credit to Master Simon's suspicions. Lady Lillycraft is very fond of quoting poetry, and the conversation often turns upon it, on which occasions the general is thrown completely out. It happened the other day

---

[4] Morte d' Arthur.

that Spenser's Fairy Queen was the theme for the greater part of the morning, and the poor general sat perfectly silent. I found him not long after in the library, with spectacles on nose, a book in his hand, and fast asleep. On my approach, he awoke, slipt the spectacles into his pocket, and began to read very attentively. After a little while he put a paper in the place, and laid the volume aside, which I perceived was the Fairy Queen. I have had the curiosity to watch how he got on in his poetical studies; but though I have repeatedly seen him with the book in his hand, yet I find the paper has not advanced above three or four pages; the general being extremely apt to fall asleep when he reads.

Falconry.

Ne is there hawk which mantleth on her perch,
Whether high tow'ring or accousting low,
But I the measure of her flight doe search,
And all her prey and all her diet know.
—SPENSER.

There are several grand sources of lamentation furnished to the worthy Squire, by the improvement of society and the grievous advancement of knowledge; among which there is none, I believe, that causes him more frequent regret than the unfortunate invention of gunpowder. To this he continually traces the decay of some favourite custom, and, indeed, the general downfall of all chivalrous and romantic usages. "English soldiers," he says, "have never been the men they were in the days of the cross-bow and the long-bow; when they depended upon the strength of the arm, and the English archer could draw a cloth-yard shaft to the head. These were the times when, at the battles of Cressy, Poietiers, and Agincourt, the French chivalry was completely destroyed by the bowmen of England. The yeomanry, too, have never been what they were, when, in times of peace, they were constantly exercised with the bow, and archery was a favourite holiday pastime."

Among the other evils which have followed in the train of this fatal invention of gunpowder, the Squire classes the total decline of the noble art of falconry. "Shooting," he says, "is a skulking, treacherous, solitary sport, in comparison; but hawking was a gallant, open, sunshiny recreation; it was the generous sport of hunting carried into the skies."

"It was, moreover," he says, "according to Braithwate, the stately amusement of 'high and mounting spirits;' for as the old Welsh proverb affirms in those tunes, 'you might know a gentleman by his hawk, horse, and grayhound.' Indeed, a cavalier was seldom seen abroad without his hawk on his fist; and even a lady of rank did not think herself completely equipped, in riding forth, unless she had a tassel-gentel held by jesses on her delicate hand. It was thought in those excellent days, according to an old writer, 'quite sufficient for noblemen to winde their horn, and to carry their hawke fair; and leave study and learning to the children of mean people.'"

Knowing the good Squire's hobby, therefore, I have not been surprised at finding that, among the various recreations of former times which he has endeavoured to revive in the little world in which he rules, he has bestowed great attention on the noble art of falconry. In this he, of course, has been seconded by his indefatigable coadjutor, Master Simon; and even the parson has thrown considerable light on their labours, by various hints on the subject, which he has met with in old English works. As to the precious work of that famous dame, Juliana Barnes; the Gentleman's Academie, by Markham; and the other well-known treatises that were the manuals of ancient sportsmen, they have them at their fingers' ends; but they have more especially studied some old tapestry in the house, whereon is represented a party of cavaliers and stately dames, with doublets, caps, and flaunting feathers, mounted on horse, with attendants on foot, all in animated pursuit of the game.

The Squire has discountenanced the killing of any hawks in his neighbourhood, but gives a liberal bounty for all that are brought him alive; so that the Hall is well stocked with all kinds of birds of prey. On these he and Master Simon have exhausted their patience and ingenuity, endeavouring to "reclaim" them, as it is termed, and to train them up for the sport; but they have met with continual checks and disappointments. Their feathered school has turned out the most untractable and graceless scholars: nor is it the least of their trouble to drill the retainers who were to act as ushers under them, and to take immediate charge of these refractory birds. Old Christy and the gamekeeper both, for a time, set their faces against the whole plan of education; Christy having been nettled at hearing what he terms a wild-goose chase put on a par with a fox-hunt; and the gamekeeper having always been accustomed to look upon hawks as arrant poachers, which it was his duty to shoot down, and nail, in terrorem, against the out-houses.

Christy has at length taken the matter in hand, but has done still more mischief by his intermeddling. He is as positive and wrong-headed about this, as he is about hunting. Master Simon has continual disputes with him, as to feeding and training the hawks. He reads to him long passages from the old authors I have mentioned; but Christy, who cannot read, has a sovereign contempt for all book-knowledge, and persists in treating the hawks according to his own notions, which are drawn from his experience, in younger days, in the rearing of game-cocks.

The consequence is, that, between these jarring systems, the poor, birds have had a most trying and unhappy time of it. Many have fallen victims to Christy's feeding and Master Simon's physicking; for the latter has gone to work *secundum artem*, and has given them all the vomitings and scourings laid down in the books; never were poor hawks so fed and physicked before. Others have been lost by being but half "reclaimed," or tamed; for on being taken into the field, they have "raked" after the game quite out of hearing of the call, and never returned to school.

All these disappointments had been petty, yet sore grievances to the Squire, and had made him to despond about success. He has lately, however, been made happy by the receipt of a fine Welsh falcon, which Master Simon terms a stately high-flyer. It is a present from the Squire's friend, Sir Watkyn Williams Wynne; and is, no doubt, a descendant of some ancient line of Welsh princes of the air, that have long lorded it over their kingdom of clouds, from Wynnstay to the very summit of Snowden, or the brow of Penmanmawr.

Ever since the Squire received this invaluable present, he has been as impatient to sally forth and make proof of it, as was Don Quixote to assay his suit of armour. There have been some demurs as to whether the bird was in proper health and training; but these have been overruled by the vehement desire to play with a new toy; and it has been determined, right or wrong, in season or out of season, to have a day's sport in hawking to-morrow.

The Hall, as usual, whenever the Squire is about to make some new sally on his hobby, is all agog with the thing. Miss Templeton, who is brought up in reverence for all her guardian's humours, has proposed to be of the party; and Lady Lillycraft has talked also of riding out to the scene of action and looking on. This has gratified the old gentleman extremely; he hails it as an auspicious omen of the revival of falconry, and does not despair but the time will come when it will be again the pride of a fine lady to carry about a noble falcon, in preference to a parrot or a lap-dog.

I have amused myself with the bustling preparations of that busy spirit, Master Simon, and the continual thwartings he receives from that genuine son of a pepper-box, old Christy. They have had half-a-dozen consultations about how the hawk is to be prepared for the morning's sport. Old Nimrod, as usual, has always got in a pet, upon which Master Simon has invariably given up the point, observing, in a good-humoured tone, "Well, well, have it your own way, Christy; only don't put yourself in a passion;" a reply which always nettles the old man ten times more than ever.

Hawking.

The soaring hawk, from fist that flies,
Her falconer doth constrain
Some times to range the ground about
To find her out again;
And if by sight or sound of bell,
His falcon he may see,
Wo ho! he cries, with cheerful voice—
The gladdest man is he.
—Handful of Pleasant Delites.

At an early hour this morning, the Hall was in a bustle preparing for the sport of the day. I heard Master Simon whistling and singing under my window at sunrise, as he was preparing the jesses for the hawk's legs, and could distinguish now and then a stanza of one of his favourite old ditties:

"In peascod time, when hound to horn
Gives note that buck be kill'd;
And little boy, with pipe of corn,
Is tending sheep a-field," &c.

A hearty breakfast, well flanked by cold meats, was served up in the great hall. The whole garrison of retainers and hangers-on were in motion, re-enforced by volunteer idlers from the village. The horses were led up and down before the door; every body had something to say, and something to do, and hurried hither and thither; there was a direful yelping of dogs; some that were to accompany us being eager to set off, and others that were to stay at home being whipped back to their kennels. In short, for once, the good Squire's mansion might have been taken as a good specimen of one of the rantipole establishments of the good old feudal times.

Breakfast being finished, the chivalry of the Hall prepared to take the field. The fair Julia was of the party, in a hunting-dress, with a light plume of feathers in her riding-hat. As she mounted her favourite galloway, I remarked, with pleasure, that old Christy forgot his usual crustiness, and hastened to adjust her saddle and bridle. He touched his cap, as she smiled on him, and thanked him; and then, looking round at the other attendants, gave a knowing nod of his head, in which I read pride and exultation at the charming appearance of his pupil.

Lady Lillycraft had likewise determined to witness the sport. She was dressed in her broad white beaver, tied under the chin, and a riding-habit of the last century. She rode her sleek, ambling pony, whose motion was as easy as a rocking-chair; and was gallantly escorted by the general, who looked not unlike one of the doughty heroes in the old prints of the battle of Blenheim. The parson, likewise, accompanied her on the other side; for this was a learned amusement, in which he took great interest; and, indeed, had given much counsel, from his knowledge of old customs.

At length every thing was arranged, and off we set from the Hall. The exercise on horseback puts one in fine spirits; and the scene was gay and animating. The young men of the family accompanied Miss Templeton. She sat lightly and gracefully in her saddle, her plumes dancing and waving in the air; and the group had a charming effect, as they appeared and disappeared among the trees, cantering along, with the bounding animation of youth. The Squire and Master Simon rode together, accompanied by old Christy, mounted on Pepper. The latter bore the hawk on his fist, as he insisted the bird was most accustomed to him. There was a rabble rout on foot, composed of retainers from the Hall, and some idlers from the village, with two or three spaniels, for the purpose of starting the game.

A kind of corps de reserve came on quietly in the rear, composed of Lady Lillycraft, General Harbottle, the parson, and a fat footman. Her ladyship ambled gently along on her pony, while the general, mounted on a tall hunter, looked down upon her with an air of the most protecting gallantry.

For my part, being no sportsman, I kept with this last party, or rather lagged behind, that I might take in the whole picture; and the parson occasionally slackened his pace, and jogged on in company with me.

The sport led us at some distance from the Hall, in a soft meadow, reeking with the moist verdure of spring. A little river ran through it, bordered by willows, which had put forth their tender early foliage. The sportsmen were in quest of herons, which were said to keep about this stream.

There was some disputing, already, among the leaders of the sport. The Squire, Master Simon, and old Christy, came every now and then to a pause, to consult together, like the field officers in an army; and I saw, by certain motions of the head, that Christy was as positive as any old wrong-headed German commander.

As we were prancing up this quiet meadow, every sound we made was answered by a distinct echo, from the sunny wall of an old building, that lay on the opposite margin of the stream; and I paused to listen to this "spirit of a sound," which seems to love such quiet and beautiful places. The parson informed me that this was the ruin of an ancient grange, and was supposed, by the country people, to be haunted by a dobbie, a kind of rural sprite, something like Robin-good-fellow. They often fancied the echo to be the voice of the dobbie answering them, and were rather shy of disturbing it after dark. He added, that the Squire was very careful of this ruin, on account of the superstition connected with it. As I considered this local habitation of an "airy nothing," I called to mind the fine description of an echo in Webster's Duchess of Malfry:

—*"Yond side o' th' river lies a wall,*
Piece of a cloister, which, in my opinion,
Gives the best echo that you ever heard:
So plain in the distinction of our words,
That many have supposed it a spirit
That answers."

The parson went on to comment on a pleasing and fanciful appellation which the Jews of old gave to the echo, which they called Bath-kool, that is to say, "the daughter of the voice;" they considered it an oracle, supplying in the second temple the want of the urim and thummim, with which the first was honoured.[5] The little man was just entering very largely

---

[5] Bekker's Monde enchanté.

and learnedly upon the subject, when we were startled by a prodigious bawling, shouting, and yelping. A flight of crows, alarmed by the approach of our forces, had suddenly risen from a meadow; a cry was put up by the rabble rout on foot—"Now, Christy! now is your time, Christy!" The Squire and Master Simon, who were beating up the river banks In quest of a heron, called out eagerly to Christy to keep quiet; the old man, vexed and bewildered by the confusion of voices, completely lost his head; in his flurry he slipped off the hood, cast off the falcon, and away flew the crows, and away soared the hawk.

I had paused on a rising ground, close to Lady Lillycraft and her escort, from whence I had a good view of the sport. I was pleased with the appearance of the party in the meadow, riding along in the direction that the bird flew; their bright beaming faces turned up to the bright skies as they watched the game; the attendants on foot scampering along, looking up, and calling out; and the dogs bounding and yelping with clamorous sympathy.

The hawk had singled out a quarry from among the carrion crew. It was curious to see the efforts of the two birds to get above each other; one to make the fatal swoop, the other to avoid it. Now they crossed athwart a bright feathery cloud, and now they were against the clear blue sky. I confess, being no sportsman, I was more interested for the poor bird that was striving for its life, than for the hawk that was playing the part of a mercenary soldier. At length the hawk got the upper hand, and made a rushing stoop at her quarry, but the latter made as sudden a surge downwards, and slanting up again, evaded the blow, screaming and making the best of his way for a dry tree on the brow of a neighbouring hill; while the hawk, disappointed of her blow, soared up again into the air, and appeared to be "raking" off. It was in vain old Christy called, and whistled, and endeavoured to lure her down: she paid no regard to him; and, indeed, his calls were drowned in the shouts and yelps of the army of militia that had followed him into the field.

Just then an exclamation from Lady Lillycraft made me turn my head. I beheld a complete confusion among the sportsmen in the little vale below us. They were galloping and running towards the edge of a bank; and I was shocked to see Miss Templeton's horse galloping at large without his rider. I rode to the place to which the others were hurrying, and when I reached the bank, which almost overhung the stream, I saw at the foot of it, the fair Julia, pale, bleeding, and apparently lifeless, supported in the arms of her frantic lover.

In galloping heedlessly along, with her eyes turned upward, she had unwarily approached too near the bank; it had given way with her, and she and her horse had been precipitated to the pebbled margin of the river.

I never saw greater consternation. The captain was distracted; Lady Lillycraft fainting; the Squire in dismay, and Master Simon at his wit's end. The beautiful creature at length showed signs of returning life; she opened her eyes; looked around her upon the anxious group, and comprehending in a moment the nature of the scene, gave a sweet smile, and putting her hand in her lover's, exclaimed, feebly, "I am not much hurt, Guy!" I could have taken her to my heart for that single exclamation.

It was found, indeed, that she had escaped almost miraculously, with a contusion on the head, a sprained ankle, and some slight bruises. After her wound was stanched, she was taken to a neighbouring cottage, until a carriage could be summoned to convey her home; and when this had arrived, the cavalcade which had issued forth so gayly on this enterprise, returned slowly and pensively to the Hall.

I had been charmed by the generous spirit shown by this young creature, who, amidst pain and danger, had been anxious only to relieve the distress of those around her. I was gratified, therefore, by the universal concern displayed by the domestics on our return. They came crowding down the avenue, each eager to render assistance. The butler stood ready with some curiously delicate cordial; the old housekeeper was provided with half-a-dozen nostrums, prepared by her own hands, according to the family receipt-book; while her niece, the melting Phoebe, having no other way of assisting, stood wringing her hands, and weeping aloud.

The most material effect that is likely to follow this accident, is a postponement of the nuptials, which were close at hand. Though I commiserate the impatience of the captain on that account, yet I shall not otherwise be sorry at the delay, as it will give me a better opportunity of studying the characters here assembled, with which I grow more and more entertained.

I cannot but perceive that the worthy Squire is quite disconcerted at the unlucky result of his hawking experiment, and this unfortunate illustration of his eulogy on female equitation. Old Christy, too, is very waspish, having been sorely twitted by Master Simon for having let his hawk fly at carrion. As to the falcon, in the confusion occasioned by the fair Julia's disaster, the bird was totally forgotten. I make no doubt she has made the best of her way back to the hospitable Hall of Sir Watkyn Williams Wynne; and may very possibly, at this present writing, be pluming her wings among the breezy bowers of Wynnstay.

St. Mark's Eve.

O 't is a fearful thing to be no more.
Or if to be, to wander after death!
To walk as spirits do, in brakes all day,
And, when the darkness comes, to glide in paths
That lead to graves; and in the silent vault,
Where lies your own pale shroud, to hover o'er it,
Striving to enter your forbidden corpse.
—DRYDEN.

The conversation this evening at the supper-table took a curious turn, on the subject of a superstition, formerly very prevalent in this part of the country, relative to the present night of the year, which is the Eve of St. Mark's. It was believed, the parson informed us, that if any one would watch in the church porch on this eve, for three successive years, from eleven to one o'clock at night, he would see, on the third year, the shades of those of the parish who were to die in the course of the year, pass by him into church, clad in their usual apparel.

Dismal as such a sight would be, he assured us that it was formerly a frequent thing for persons to make the necessary vigils. He had known more than one instance in his time. One old woman, who pretended to have seen this phantom procession, was an object of great awe for the whole year afterwards, and caused much uneasiness and mischief. If she shook her head mysteriously at a person, it was like a death-warrant; and she had nearly caused the death of a sick person, by looking ruefully in at the window.

There was also an old man, not many years since, of a sullen, melancholy temperament, who had kept two vigils, and began to excite some talk in the village, when, fortunately for the public comfort, he died shortly after his third watching; very probably from a cold that he had taken, as the night was tempestuous. It was reported about the village, however, that he had seen his own phantom pass by him into the church.

This led to the mention of another superstition of an equally strange and melancholy kind, which, however, is chiefly confined to Wales. It is respecting what are called corpse-candles, little wandering fires, of a pale bluish light, that move about like tapers in the open air, and are supposed to designate the way some corpse is to go. One was seen at Lanyler, late at night, hovering up and down, along the bank of the Istwith, and was watched by the neighbours until they were tired, and went to bed. Not long afterwards there came a comely country lass, from Montgomeryshire, to see her friends, who dwelt on the opposite side of the river. She thought to ford the stream at the very place where the light had been first seen, but was dissuaded on account of the height of the flood. She walked to and fro along the bank, just where the candle had moved, waiting for the subsiding of the water. She at length endeavored to cross, but the poor girl was drowned in the attempt.[6]

There was something mournful in this little anecdote of rural superstition, that seemed to affect all the listeners. Indeed, it is curious to remark how completely a conversation of the kind will absorb the attention of a circle, and sober down its gayety, however boisterous. By degrees I noticed that every one was leaning forward over the table, with eyes earnestly fixed upon the parson; and at the mention of corpse-candles which had been seen about the chamber of a young lady who died on the eve of her wedding-day, Lady Lillycraft turned pale.

I have witnessed the introduction of stories of the kind into various evening circles; they were often commenced in jest, and listened to with smiles; but I never knew the most gay or the most enlightened of audiences, that were not, if the conversation continued for any length of time, completely and solemnly interested in it. There is, I believe, a degree of superstition lurking in every mind; and I doubt if any one can thoroughly examine all his secret notions and impulses, without detecting it, hidden, perhaps, even from himself. It seems, in fact, to be a part of our nature, like instinct in animals, acting independently of our reason. It is often found existing in lofty natures, especially those that are poetical and aspiring. A great and extraordinary poet of our day, whose life and writings evince a mind subject to powerful exaltations, is said to believe in omens and secret intimations. Caesar, it is well known, was greatly under

---

[6] Aubrey's Miscel.

the influence of such belief; and Napoleon had his good and evil days, and his presiding star.

As to the worthy parson, I have no doubt that he is strongly inclined to superstition. He is naturally credulous, and passes so much of his time searching out popular traditions and supernatural tales, that his mind has probably become infected by them. He has lately been immersed in the Demonolatria of Nicholas Remigus, concerning supernatural occurrences in Lorraine, and the writings of Joachimus Camerius, called by Vossius the Phoenix of Germany; and he entertains the ladies with stories from them, that make them almost afraid to go to bed at night. I have been charmed myself with some of the wild little superstitions which he has adduced from Blefkénius, Scheffer, and others, such as those of the Laplanders about the domestic spirits which wake them at night, and summon them to go and fish; of Thor, the deity of thunder, who has power of life and death, health and sickness, and who, armed with the rainbow, shoots his arrows at those evil demons that live on the tops of rocks and mountains, and infest the lakes; of the Jubles or Juhlafolket, vagrant troops of spirits, which roam the air, and wander up and down by forests and mountains, and the moonlight sides of hills.

The parson never openly professes his belief in ghosts, but I have remarked that he has a suspicious way of pressing great names into the defence of supernatural doctrines, and making philosophers and saints fight for him. He expatiates at large on the opinions of the ancient philosophers about larves, or nocturnal phantoms, the spirits of the wicked, which wandered like exiles about the earth; and about those spiritual beings which abode in the air, but descended occasionally to earth, and mingled among mortals, acting as agents between them and the gods. He quotes also from Philo the rabbi, the contemporary of the apostles, and, according to some, the friend of St. Paul, who says that the air is full of spirits of different ranks; some destined to exist for a time in mortal bodies, from which being emancipated, they pass and repass between heaven and earth, as agents or messengers in the service of the deity.

But the worthy little man assumes a bolder tone, when he quotes from the fathers of the church; such as St. Jerome, who gives it as the opinion of all the doctors, that the air is filled with powers opposed to each other; and Lactantius, who says that corrupt and dangerous spirits wander over the earth, and seek to console themselves for their own fall by effecting the ruin of the human race; and Clemens Alexandrinus, who is of opinion that the souls of the blessed have knowledge of what passes among men, the same as angels have.

I am now alone in my chamber, but these themes have taken such hold of my imagination, that I cannot sleep. The room in which I sit is just fitted to foster such a state of mind. The walls are hung with tapestry, the figures of which are faded, and look like unsubstantial shapes melting away from sight. Over the fire-place is the portrait of a lady, who, according to the housekeeper's tradition, pined to death for the loss of her lover in the battle of Blenheim. She has a most pale and plaintive countenance, and seems to fix her eyes mournfully upon me. The family have long since retired. I have heard their steps die away, and the distant doors clap to after them. The murmur of voices, and the peal of remote laughter, no longer reach the ear. The clock from the church, in which so many of the former inhabitants of this house lie buried, has chimed the awful hour of midnight.

I have sat by the window and mused upon the dusky landscape, watching the lights disappearing, one by one, from the distant village; and the moon rising in her silent majesty, and leading up all the silver pomp of heaven. As I have gazed upon these quiet groves and shadowy lawns, silvered over, and imperfectly lighted by streaks of dewy moonshine, my mind has been crowded by "thick-coming fancies" concerning those spiritual beings which

> ————*"walk the earth*
> *Unseen, both when we wake and when we sleep."*

Are there, indeed, such beings? Is this space between us and the deity filled up by innumerable orders of spiritual beings, forming the same gradations between the human soul and divine perfection, that we see prevailing from humanity downwards to the meanest insect? It is a sublime and beautiful doctrine, inculcated by the early fathers, that there are guardian angels appointed to watch over cities and nations; to take care of the welfare of good men, and to guard and guide the steps of helpless infancy. "Nothing," says St. Jerome, "gives up a greater idea of the dignity of our soul, than that God has given each of us, at the moment of our birth, an angel to have care of it."

Even the doctrine of departed spirits returning to visit the scenes and beings which were dear to them during the body's existence, though it has been debased by the absurd superstitions of the vulgar, in itself is awfully solemn and sublime.

However lightly it may be ridiculed, yet the attention involuntarily yielded to it whenever it is made the subject of serious discussion; its prevalence in all ages and countries, and even among newly-discovered nations, that have had no previous interchange of thought with other parts of the world, prove it to be one of those mysteries, and almost instinctive beliefs, to which, if left to ourselves, we should naturally incline.

In spite of all the pride of reason and philosophy, a vague doubt will still lurk in the mind, and perhaps will never be perfectly eradicated; as it is concerning a matter that does not admit of positive demonstration. Every thing connected with our spiritual nature is full of doubt and difficulty. "We are fearfully and wonderfully made;" we are surrounded by mysteries, and we are mysteries even to ourselves. Who yet has been able to comprehend and describe the nature of the soul, its connection with the body, or in what part of the frame it is situated? We know merely that it does exist; but whence it came, and when it entered into us, and how it is retained, and where it is seated, and how it operates, are all matters of mere speculation, and contradictory theories. If, then, we are thus ignorant of this spiritual essence, even while it forms a part of ourselves, and is continually present to our consciousness, how can we pretend to ascertain or to deny its powers and operations when released from its fleshy prison-house? It is more the manner, therefore, in which this superstition has been degraded, than its intrinsic absurdity, that has brought it into contempt. Raise it above the frivolous purposes to which it has been applied, strip it of the gloom and horror with which it has been surrounded, and there is none of the whole circle of visionary creeds that could more delightfully elevate the imagination, or more tenderly affect the heart. It would become a sovereign comfort at the bed of death, soothing the bitter tear wrung from us by the agony of our mortal separation. What could be more consoling than the idea, that the souls of those whom we once loved were permitted to return and watch over our welfare?—that affectionate and guardian spirits sat by our pillows when we slept, keeping a vigil over our most helpless hours?—that beauty and innocence which had languished into the tomb, yet smiled unseen around us, revealing themselves in those blest dreams wherein we live over again the hours of past endearment? A belief of this kind would, I should think, be a new incentive to virtue; rendering us circumspect even in our most secret moments, from the idea that those we once loved and honoured were invisible witnesses of all our actions.

It would take away, too, from that loneliness and destitution which we are apt to feel more and more as we get on in our pilgrimage through the wilderness of this world, and find that those who set forward with us, lovingly and cheerily, on the journey, have, one by one, dropped away from our side. Place the superstition in this light, and I confess I should like to be a believer in it. I see nothing in it that is incompatible with the tender and merciful nature of our religion, nor revolting to the wishes and affections of the heart.

There are departed beings that I have loved as I never again shall love in this world;—that have loved me as I never again shall be loved! If such beings do ever retain in their blessed spheres the attachments which they felt on earth—if they take an interest in the poor concerns of transient mortality, and are permitted to hold communion with those whom they have loved on earth, I feel as if now, at this deep hour of night, in this silence and solitude, I could receive their visitation with the most solemn, but unalloyed delight.

In truth, such visitations would be too happy for this world; they would be incompatible with the nature of this imperfect state of being. We are here placed in a mere scene of spiritual thraldom and restraint. Our souls are shut in and limited by bounds and barriers; shackled by mortal infirmities, and subject to all the gross impediments of matter. In vain would they seek to act independently of the body, and to mingle together in spiritual intercourse. They can only act here through their fleshy organs. Their earthly loves are made up of transient embraces and long separations. The most intimate friendship, of what brief and scattered portions of time does it consist! We take each other by the hand, and we exchange a few words and looks of kindness, and we rejoice together for a few short moments-and then days, months, years intervene, and we see and know nothing of each other. Or, granting that we dwell together for the full season of this our mortal life, the grave soon closes its gates between us, and then our spirits are doomed to remain in separation and widowhood; until they meet again in that more perfect state of being, where soul will dwell with soul in blissful communion, and there will be neither death, nor absence, nor any thing else to interrupt our felicity.

In the foregoing paper, I have alluded to the writings of some of the old Jewish rabbis. They abound with wild theories; but among them are many truly poetical flights; and their ideas are often very beautifully expressed. Their speculations on the nature of angels are curious and fanciful, though much resembling the doctrines of the ancient philosophers. In the writings of the Rabbi Eleazer is an account of the temptation of our first parents, and the fall of the angels, which the parson pointed out to me as having probably furnished some of the groundwork for "Paradise Lost."

According to Eleazer, the ministering angels said to the Deity, "What is there in man, that thou makest him of such importance? Is he any thing else than vanity? for he can scarcely reason a little on terrestrial things." To which God replied, "Do you imagine that I will be exalted and glorified only by you here above? I am the same below that I am here. Who is there among you that can call all the creatures by their names?" There was none found among them that could do so. At that moment Adam arose, and called all the creatures by their names. Seeing which, the ministering angels said among themselves, "Let us consult together how we may cause Adam to sin against the Creator, otherwise he will not fail to become our master."

Sammaël, who was a great prince in the heavens, was present at this council, with the saints of the first order, and the seraphim of six bands. Sammaël chose several out of the twelve orders to accompany him, and descended below, for the purpose of visiting all the creatures which God had created. He found none more cunning and more fit to do evil than the serpent.

The Rabbi then treats of the seduction and the fall of man; of the consequent fall of the demon, and the punishment which God inflicted on Adam, Eve, and the serpent. "He made them all come before him; pronounced nine maledictions on Adam and Eve, and condemned them to suffer death; and he precipitated Sammaël and all his band from heaven. He cut off the feet of the serpent, which had before the figure of a camel (Sammaël having been mounted on him), and he cursed him among all beasts and animals."

Gentility.

————True Gentrie standeth in the trade
Of virtuous life, not in the fleshy line;
For bloud is knit, but Gentrie is divine.
—Mirror for Magistrates.

I have mentioned some peculiarities of the Squire in the education of his sons; but I would not have it thought that his instructions were directed chiefly to their personal accomplishments. He took great pains also to form their minds, and to inculcate what he calls good old English principles, such as are laid down in the writings of Peachem and his contemporaries. There is one author of whom he cannot speak without indignation, which is Chesterfield. He avers that he did much, for a time, to injure the true national character, and to introduce, instead of open, manly sincerity, a hollow, perfidious courtliness. "His maxims," he affirms, "were calculated to chill the delightful enthusiasm of youth; to make them ashamed of that romance which is the dawn of generous manhood, and to impart to them a cold polish and a premature worldliness.

"Many of Lord Chesterfield's maxims would make a young man a mere man of pleasure; but an English gentleman should not be a mere man of pleasure. He has no right to such selfish indulgence. His ease, his leisure, his opulence, are debts due to his country, which he must ever stand ready to discharge. He should be a man at all points; simple, frank, courteous, intelligent, accomplished, and informed; upright, intrepid, and disinterested; one that can mingle among freemen; that can cope with statesmen; that can champion his country and its rights, either at home or abroad. In a country like England, where there is such free and unbounded scope for the exertion of intellect, and where opinion and example have such weight with the people, every gentleman of fortune and leisure should feel himself bound to employ himself in some way towards promoting the prosperity or glory of the nation. In a country where intellect and action are trammelled and restrained, men of rank and fortune may become idlers and triflers with impunity; but an English coxcomb is inexcusable; and this, perhaps, is the reason why he is the most offensive and insupportable coxcomb in the world."

The Squire, as Frank Bracebridge informs me, would often hold forth in this manner to his sons, when they were about leaving the paternal roof; one to travel abroad, one to go to the army, and one to the university. He used to have them with him in the library, which is hung with the portraits of Sidney, Surrey, Raleigh, Wyat, and others. "Look at those models of true English gentlemen, my sons," he would say with enthusiasm; "those were men that wreathed the graces of the most delicate and refined taste around the stern virtues of the soldier; that mingled what was gentle and gracious, with what was hardy and manly; that possessed the true chivalry of spirit, which is the exalted essence of manhood. They are the lights by which the youth of the country should array themselves. They were the patterns and idols of their country at home; they were the illustrators of its dignity abroad. 'Surrey,' says Camden, 'was the first nobleman that illustrated his high birth with the beauty of learning. He was acknowledged to be the gallantest man, the politest lover, and the completest gentleman of his time.' And as to Wyat, his friend Surrey most amiably testifies of him, that his person was majestic and beautiful, his visage 'stern and mild;' that he sung, and played the lute with remarkable sweetness; spoke foreign languages with grace and fluency, and possessed an inexhaustible fund of wit. And see what a high commendation is passed upon these illustrious friends: 'They were the two chieftains, who, having travelled into Italy, and there tasted the sweet and stately measures and style of the Italian poetry, greatly polished our rude and homely manner of vulgar poetry from what it had been before, and therefore may be justly called the reformers of our English poetry and style.' And Sir Philip Sidney, who has left us such monuments of elegant thought, and generous sentiment, and who illustrated his chivalrous spirit so gloriously in the field. And Sir Walter Raleigh, the elegant courtier, the intrepid soldier, the enterprising discoverer, the enlightened philosopher, the magnanimous martyr. These are the men for English gentlemen to study. Chesterfield, with his cold and courtly maxims, would have chilled and impoverished such spirits. He would have blighted all the budding romance of their temperaments. Sidney would never have written his Arcadia, nor Surrey have challenged the world in vindication of the beauties of his Geraldine. "These are the men, my sons," the Squire will continue, "that show to what our national character may be exalted, when its strong and powerful qualities are duly wrought up and refined. The solidest bodies are capable of the highest polish; and there is no character that may be wrought to a more exquisite and unsullied brightness, than that of the true English gentleman."

When Guy was about to depart for the army, the Squire again took him aside, and gave him a long exhortation. He warned him against that affectation of cool-blooded indifference, which he was told was cultivated by the young British officers, among whom it was a study to "sink the soldier" in the mere man of fashion. "A soldier," said he, "without pride and enthusiasm in his profession, is a mere sanguinary hireling. Nothing distinguishes him from the mercenary bravo, but a spirit of patriotism, or a thirst for glory. It is the fashion now-a-days, my son," said he, "to laugh at the spirit of chivalry; when that spirit is really extinct, the profession of the soldier becomes a mere trade of blood." He then set before him the conduct of Edward the Black Prince, who is his mirror of chivalry; valiant, generous, affable, humane; gallant in the field. But when he came to dwell on his courtesy toward his prisoner, the king of France; how he received him in his tent, rather as a conqueror than as a captive; attended on him at table like one of his retinue; rode uncovered beside him on his entry into London, mounted on a common palfrey, while his prisoner was mounted in state on a white steed of stately beauty; the tears of enthusiasm stood in the old gentleman's eyes.

Finally, on taking leave, the good Squire put in his son's hands, as a manual, one of his favourite old volumes, the life of the Chevalier Bayard, by Godefroy; on a blank page of which he had written an extract from the Morte d'Arthur, containing the eulogy of Sir Ector over the body of Sir Launcelot of the Lake, which the Squire considers as comprising the excellencies of a true soldier. "Ah, Sir Launcelot! thou wert head of all Christian knights; now there thou liest: thou wert never matched of none earthly knights-hands. And thou wert the curtiest knight that ever bare shield. And thou wert the truest friend to thy lover that ever bestrood horse; and thou wert the truest lover of a sinfull man that ever loved woman. And thou wert the kindest man that ever strook with sword; and thou wert the goodliest person that ever came among the presse of knights.

And thou wert the meekest man and the gentlest that ever eate in hall among ladies. And thou wert the sternest knight to thy mortal foe that ever put speare in the rest."

Fortune-Telling.

Each city, each town, and every village,
Affords us either an alms or pillage.
And if the weather be cold and raw.
Then in a barn we tumble on straw.
If warm and fair, by yea-cock and nay-cock,
The fields will afford us a hedge or a hay-cock.
—Merry Beggars.

As I was walking one evening with the Oxonian, Master Simon, and the general, in a meadow not far from the village, we heard the sound of a fiddle, rudely played, and looking in the direction from whence it came, we saw a thread of smoke curling up from among the trees. The sound of music is always attractive; for, wherever there is music, there is good-humour, or good-will. We passed along a footpath, and had a peep through a break in the hedge, at the musician and his party, when the Oxonian gave us a wink, and told us that if we would follow him we should have some sport.

It proved to be a gipsy encampment, consisting of three or four little cabins, or tents, made of blankets and sail-cloth, spread over hoops that were stuck in the ground. It was on one side of a green lane, close under a hawthorn hedge, with a broad beech-tree spreading above it. A small rill tinkled along close by, through the fresh sward, that looked like a carpet.

A tea-kettle was hanging by a crooked piece of iron, over a fire made from dry sticks and leaves, and two old gipsies, in red cloaks, sat crouched on the grass, gossiping over their evening cup of tea; for these creatures, though they live in the open air, have their ideas of fireside comforts. There were two or three children sleeping on the straw with which the tents were littered; a couple of donkeys were grazing in the lane, and a thievish-looking dog was lying before the fire. Some of the younger gipsies were dancing to the music of a fiddle, played by a tall, slender stripling, in an old frock-coat, with a peacock's feather stuck in his hat-band.

As we approached, a gipsy girl, with a pair of fine, roguish eyes, came up, and, as usual, offered to tell our fortunes. I could not but admire a certain degree of slattern elegance about the baggage. Her long black silken hair was curiously plaited in numerous small braids, and negligently put up in a picturesque style that a painter might have been proud to have devised.

Her dress was of figured chintz, rather ragged, and not over-clean but of a variety of most harmonious and agreeable colours; for these beings have a singularly fine eye for colours. Her straw hat was in her hand, and a red cloak thrown over one arm.

The Oxonian offered at once to have his fortune told, and the girl began with the usual volubility of her race; but he drew her on one side, near the hedge, as he said he had no idea of having his secrets overheard. I saw he was talking to her instead of she to him, and by his glancing towards us now and then, that he was giving the baggage some private hints. When they returned to us, he assumed a very serious air. "Zounds!" said he, "it's very astonishing how these creatures come by their knowledge; this girl has told me some things that I thought no one knew but myself!" The girl now assailed the general: "Come, your honour," said she, "I see by your face you're a lucky man; but you're not happy in your mind; you're not, indeed, sir; but have a good heart, and give me a good piece of silver, and I'll tell you a nice fortune."

The general had received all her approaches with a banter, and had suffered her to get hold of his hand; but at the mention of the piece of silver, he hemmed, looked grave, and, turning to us, asked if we had not better continue our walk. "Come, my master," said the girl, archly, "you'd not be in such a hurry, if you knew all that I could tell you about a fair lady that has a notion for you. Come, sir; old love burns strong; there's many a one comes to see weddings, that go away brides themselves."—Here the girl whispered something in a low voice, at which the general coloured up, was a little fluttered, and suffered himself to be drawn aside under the hedge, where he appeared to listen to her with great earnestness, and at the end paid her half-a-crown with the air of a man that has got the worth of his money. The girl next made her attack upon Master Simon, who, however, was too old a bird to be caught, knowing that it would end in an attack upon his purse, about which he is a little sensitive. As he has a great notion, however, of being considered a royster, he chucked her under the chin, played her off with rather broad jokes, and put on something of the rake-helly air, that we see now and then assumed on the stage, by the sad-boy gentleman of the old school. "Ah, your honour," said the girl, with a malicious leer, "you were not in such a tantrum last year, when I told you about the widow, you know who; but if you had taken a friend's advice, you'd never have come away from Doncaster races with a flea in your ear!" There was a secret sting in this speech, that seemed quite to disconcert Master Simon. He jerked away his hand in a pet, smacked his whip, whistled to his dogs, and intimated that it was high time to go home. The girl, however, was determined not to lose her harvest. She now turned upon me, and, as I have a weakness of spirit where there is a pretty face concerned, she soon wheedled me out of my money, and, in return, read me a fortune; which, if it prove true, and I am determined to believe it, will make me one of the luckiest men in the chronicles of Cupid.

I saw that the Oxonian was at the bottom of all this oracular mystery, and was disposed to amuse himself with the general, whose tender approaches to the widow have attracted the notice of the wag. I was a little curious, however, to know the meaning of the dark hints which had so suddenly disconcerted Master Simon; and took occasion to fall in the rear with the Oxonian on our way home, when he laughed heartily at my questions, and gave me ample information on the subject.

The truth of the matter is, that Master Simon has met with a sad rebuff since my Christmas visit to the Hall. He used at that time to be joked about a widow, a fine dashing woman, as he privately informed me. I had supposed the pleasure he betrayed on these occasions resulted from the usual fondness of old bachelors for being teased about getting married, and about flirting, and being fickle and false-hearted. I am assured, however, that Master Simon had really persuaded himself the widow had a kindness for him; in consequence of which he had been at some extraordinary expense in new clothes, and had actually got Frank Bracebridge to order him a coat from Stultz. He began to throw out hints about the importance of a man's settling himself in life before he grew old; he would look grave, whenever the widow and matrimony were mentioned in the same sentence;

and privately asked the opinion of the Squire and parson about the prudence of marrying a widow with a rich jointure, but who had several children.

An important member of a great family connexion cannot harp much upon the theme of matrimony, without its taking wind; and it soon got buzzed about that Mr. Simon Bracebridge was actually gone to Doncaster races, with a new horse; but that he meant to return in a curricle with a lady by his side. Master Simon did, indeed, go to the races, and that with a new horse; and the dashing widow did make her appearance in a curricle; but it was unfortunately driven by a strapping young Irish dragoon, with whom even Master Simon's self-complacency would not allow him to venture into competition, and to whom she was married shortly after.

It was a matter of sore chagrin to Master Simon for several months, having never before been fully committed. The dullest head in the family had a joke upon him; and there is no one that likes less to be bantered than an absolute joker. He took refuge for a time at Lady Lillycraft's, until the matter should blow over; and occupied himself by looking over her accounts, regulating the village choir, and inculcating loyalty into a pet bulfinch, by teaching him to whistle "God save the King."

He has now pretty nearly recovered from the mortification; holds up his head, and laughs as much as any one; again affects to pity married men, and is particularly facetious about widows, when Lady Lillycraft is not by. His only time of trial is when the general gets hold of him, who is infinitely heavy and persevering in his waggery, and will interweave a dull joke through the various topics of a whole dinner-time. Master Simon often parries these attacks by a stanza from his old work of "Cupid's Solicitor for Love:"

> "'Tis in vain to wooe a widow over long,
> In once or twice her mind you may perceive;
> Widows are subtle, be they old or young,
> And by their wiles young men they will deceive."

Love-Charms.

———Come, do not weep, my girl,
Forget him, pretty Pensiveness; there will
Come others, every day, as good as he.
—SIR J. SUCKLING.

The approach of a wedding in a family is always an event of great importance, but particularly so in a household like this, in a retired part of the country. Master Simon, who is a pervading spirit, and, through means of the butler and housekeeper, knows every thing that goes forward, tells me that the maid-servants are continually trying their fortunes, and that the servants'-hall has of late been quite a scene of incantation.

It is amusing to notice how the oddities of the head of a family flow down through all the branches. The Squire, in the indulgence of his love of every thing that smacks of old times, has held so many grave conversations with the parson at table, about popular superstitions and traditional rites, that they have been carried from the parlour to the kitchen by the listening domestics, and, being apparently sanctioned by such high authority, the whole house has become infected by them.

The servants are all versed in the common modes of trying luck, and the charms to insure constancy. They read their fortunes by drawing strokes in the ashes, or by repeating a form of words, and looking in a pail of water. St. Mark's Eve, I am told, was a busy time with them; being an appointed night for certain mystic ceremonies. Several of them sowed hemp-seed to be reaped by their true lovers; and they even ventured upon the solemn and fearful preparation of the dumb-cake. This must be done fasting, and in silence. The ingredients are handed down in traditional form: "An eggshell full of salt, an eggshell full of malt, and an eggshell full of barley-meal." When the cake is ready, it is put upon a pan over the fire, and the future husband will appear, turn the cake, and retire; but if a word is spoken or a fast is broken during this awful ceremony, there is no knowing what horrible consequences would ensue!

The experiments, in the present instance, came to no result; they that sowed the hemp-seed forgot the magic rhyme that they were to pronounce—so the true lover never appeared; and as to the dumb-cake, what between the awful stillness they had to keep, and the awfulness of the midnight hour, their hearts failed them when they had put the cake in the pan; so that, on the striking of the great house-clock in the servants'-hall, they were seized with a sudden panic, and ran out of the room, to which they did not return until morning, when they found the mystic cake burnt to a cinder.

The most persevering at these spells, however, is Phoebe Wilkins, the housekeeper's niece. As she is a kind of privileged personage, and rather idle, she has more time to occupy herself with these matters. She has always had her head full of love and matrimony. She knows the dream-book by heart, and is quite an oracle among the little girls of the family, who always come to her to interpret their dreams in the mornings.

During the present gayety of the house, however, the poor girl has worn a face full of trouble; and, to use the housekeeper's words, "has fallen into a sad hystericky way lately." It seems that she was born and brought up in the village, where her father was parish-clerk, and she was an early playmate and sweetheart of young Jack Tibbets. Since she has come to live at the Hall, however, her head has been a little turned. Being very pretty, and naturally genteel, she has been much noticed and indulged; and being the housekeeper's niece, she has held an equivocal station between a servant and a companion. She has learnt something of fashions and notions among the young ladies, which have effected quite a metamorphosis; insomuch that her finery at church on Sundays has given mortal offence to her former intimates in the village. This has occasioned the misrepresentations which have awakened the implacable family pride of Dame Tibbets. But what is worse, Phoebe, having a spice of coquetry in her disposition, showed it on one or two occasions to her lover, which produced a downright quarrel; and Jack, being very proud and fiery, has absolutely turned his back upon her for several successive Sundays.

The poor girl is full of sorrow and repentance, and would fain make up with her lover; but he feels his security, and stands aloof. In this he is doubtless encouraged by his mother, who is continually reminding him what he owes to his family; for this same family pride seems doomed to be the eternal bane of lovers.

As I hate to see a pretty face in trouble, I have felt quite concerned for the luckless Phoebe, ever since I heard her story. It is a sad thing to be thwarted in love at any time, but particularly so at this tender season of the year, when every living thing, even to the very butterfly, is sporting with its mate; and the green fields, and the budding groves, and the singing of the birds, and the sweet smell of the flowers, are enough to turn the head of a love-sick girl. I am told that the coolness of young Ready-Money lies very heavy at poor Phoebe's heart. Instead of singing about the house as formerly, she goes about pale and sighing, and is apt to break into tears when her companions are full of merriment.

Mrs. Hannah, the vestal gentlewoman of my Lady Lillycraft, has had long talks and walks with Phoebe, up and down the avenue of an evening; and has endeavoured to squeeze some of her own verjuice into the other's milky nature. She speaks with contempt and abhorrence of the whole sex, and advises Phoebe to despise all the men as heartily as she does. But Phoebe's loving temper is not to be curdled; she has no such thing as hatred or contempt for mankind in her whole composition. She has all the simple fondness of heart of poor, weak, loving woman; and her only thoughts at present are how to conciliate and reclaim her wayward swain.

The spells and love-charms, which are matters of sport to the other domestics, are serious concerns with this love-stricken damsel. She is continually trying her fortune in a variety of ways. I am told that she has absolutely fasted for six Wednesdays and three Fridays successively, having understood that it was a sovereign charm to insure being married to one's liking within the year. She carries about, also, a lock of her sweetheart's hair, and a riband he once gave her, being a mode of producing constancy in a lover. She even went so far as to try her fortune by the moon, which has always had much to do with lovers' dreams and fancies. For this purpose, she went out in the night of the full moon, knelt on a stone in the meadow, and repeated the old traditional rhyme:

"All hail to thee, moon, all hail to thee;
I pray thee, good moon, now show to me
The youth who my future husband shall be."

When she came back to the house, she was faint and pale, and went immediately to bed. The next morning she told the porter's wife that she had seen some one close by the hedge in the meadow, which she was sure was young Tibbets; at any rate, she had dreamt of him all night; both of which, the old dame assured her, were most happy signs. It has since turned out that the person in the meadow was old Christy, the huntsman, who was walking his nightly rounds with the great stag-hound; so that Phoebe's faith in the charm is completely shaken.

The Library.

Yesterday the fair Julia made her first appearance downstairs since her accident; and the sight of her spread an universal cheerfulness through the household. She was extremely pale, however, and could not walk without pain and difficulty. She was assisted, therefore, to a sofa in the library, which is pleasant and retired, looking out among trees; and so quiet, that the little birds come hopping upon the windows, and peering curiously into the apartment. Here several of the family gathered round, and devised means to amuse her, and make the day pass pleasantly. Lady Lillycraft lamented the want of some new novel to while away the time; and was almost in a pet, because the "Author of Waverley" had not produced a work for the last three months.

There was a motion made to call on the parson for some of his old legends or ghost stories; but to this Lady Lillycraft objected, as they were apt to give her the vapours. General Harbottle gave a minute account, for the sixth time, of the Disaster of a friend in India, who had his leg bitten off by a tiger, whilst he was hunting; and was proceeding to menace the company with a chapter or two about Tippoo Saib.

At length the captain bethought himself and said, he believed he had a manuscript tale lying in one corner of his campaigning trunk, which, if he could find, and the company were desirous, he would read to them. The offer was eagerly accepted. He retired, and soon returned with a roll of blotted manuscript, in a very gentlemanlike, but nearly illegible, hand, and a great part written on cartridge-paper.

"It is one of the scribblings," said he, "of my poor friend, Charles Lightly, of the dragoons. He was a curious, romantic, studious, fanciful fellow; the favourite, and often the unconscious butt of his fellow-officers, who entertained themselves with his eccentricities. He was in some of the hardest service in the peninsula, and distinguished himself by his gallantry. When the intervals of duty permitted, he was fond of roving about the country, visiting noted places, and was extremely fond of Moorish ruins.

When at his quarters, he was a great scribbler, and passed much of his leisure with his pen in his hand.

"As I was a much younger officer, and a very young man, he took me, in a manner, under his care, and we became close friends. He used often to read his writings to me, having a great confidence in my taste, for I always praised them. Poor fellow! he was shot down close by me, at Waterloo. We lay wounded together for some time, during a hard contest that took place near at hand. As I was least hurt, I tried to relieve him, and to stanch the blood which flowed from a wound in his breast. He lay with his head in my lap, and looked up thankfully in my face, but shook his head faintly, and made a sign that it was all over with him; and, indeed, he died a few minutes afterwards, just as our men had repulsed the enemy, and came to our relief. I have his favourite dog and his pistols to this day, and several of his manuscripts, which he gave to me at different times. The one I am now going to read, is a tale which he said he wrote in Spain, during the time that he lay ill of a wound received at Salamanca."

We now arranged ourselves to hear the story. The captain seated himself on the sofa, beside the fair Julia, who I had noticed to be somewhat affected by the picture he had carelessly drawn of wounds and dangers in a field of battle. She now leaned her arm fondly on his shoulder, and her eye glistened as it rested on the manuscript of the poor literary dragoon. Lady Lillycraft buried herself in a deep, well-cushioned elbow-chair. Her dogs were nestled on soft mats at her feet; and the gallant general took his station in an armchair, at her side, and toyed with her elegantly ornamented work-bag. The rest of the circle being all equally well accommodated, the captain began his story; a copy of which I have procured for the benefit of the reader.

The Student Of Salamanca.

What a life do I lead with my master; nothing but blowing of bellowes, beating of spirits, and scraping of croslets! It is a very secret science, for none almost can understand the language of it. Sublimation, almigation, calcination, rubification, albification, and fermentation; with as many termes unpossible to be uttered as the arte to be compassed.
—LILLY'S Gallathea.

Once upon a time, in the ancient city of Granada, there sojourned a young man of the name of Antonio de Castros. He wore the garb of a student of Salamanca, and was pursuing a course of reading in the library of the university; and, at intervals of leisure, indulging his curiosity by examining those remains of Moorish magnificence for which Granada is renowned.

Whilst occupied in his studies, he frequently noticed an old man of a singular appearance, who was likewise a visitor to the library. He was lean and withered, though apparently more from study than from age. His eyes, though bright and visionary, were sunk in his head, and thrown into shade by overhanging eyebrows. His dress was always the same: a black doublet; a short black cloak, very rusty and threadbare; a small ruff and a large overshadowing hat.

His appetite for knowledge seemed insatiable. He would pass whole days in the library, absorbed in study, consulting a multiplicity of authors, as though he were pursuing some interesting subject through all its ramifications; so that, in general, when evening came, he was almost buried among books and manuscripts.

The curiosity of Antonio was excited, and he inquired of the attendants concerning the stranger. No one could give him any information, excepting that he had been for some time past a casual frequenter of the library; that his reading lay chiefly among works treating of the occult sciences, and that he was particularly curious in his inquiries after Arabian manuscripts. They added, that he never held communication with any one, excepting to ask for particular works; that, after a fit of studious application, he would disappear for several days, and even weeks, and when he revisited the library, he would look more withered and haggard than ever. The student felt interested by this account; he was leading rather a desultory life, and had all that capricious curiosity which springs up in idleness. He determined to make himself acquainted with this book-worm, and find out who and what he was.

The next time that he saw the old man at the library, he commenced his approaches by requesting permission to look into one of the volumes with which the unknown appeared to have done. The latter merely bowed his head, in token of assent. After pretending to look through the volume with great attention, he returned it with many acknowledgments.

The stranger made no reply.

"May I ask, senor," said Antonio, with some hesitation, "may I ask what you are searching after in all these books?"

The old man raised his head, with an expression of surprise, at having his studies interrupted for the first time, and by so intrusive a question. He surveyed the student with a side glance from head to foot: "Wisdom, my son," said he, calmly; "and the search requires every moment of my attention." He then cast his eyes upon his book, and resumed his studies.

"But, father," said Antonio, "cannot you spare a moment to point out the road to others? It is to experienced travellers like you, that we strangers in the paths of knowledge must look for directions on our journey."

The stranger looked disturbed: "I have not time enough, my son, to learn," said he, "much less to teach. I am ignorant myself of the path of true knowledge; how then can I show it to others?"

"Well, but, father—"

"Senor," said the old man, mildly, but earnestly, "you must see that I have but few steps more to the grave. In that short space have I to accomplish the whole business of my existence. I have no time for words; every word is as one grain of sand of my glass wasted. Suffer me to be alone."

There was no replying to so complete a closing of the door of intimacy. The student found himself calmly but totally repulsed. Though curious and inquisitive, yet he was naturally modest, and on after-thoughts he blushed at his own intrusion. His mind soon became occupied by other objects. He passed several days wandering among the mouldering piles of Moorish architecture, those melancholy monuments of an elegant and voluptuous people. He paced the deserted halls of the Alhambra, the paradise of the Moorish kings. He visited the great court of the lions, famous for the perfidious massacre of the gallant Abencerrages. He gazed with admiration at its mosaic cupolas, gorgeously painted in gold and azure; its basins of marble, its alabaster vase, supported by lions, and storied with inscriptions.

His imagination kindled as he wandered among these scenes. They were calculated to awaken all the enthusiasm of a youthful mind. Most of the halls have anciently been beautified by fountains. The fine taste of the Arabs delighted in the sparkling purity and reviving freshness of water; and they erected, as it were, altars on every side, to that delicate element. Poetry mingles with architecture in the Alhambra. It breathes along the very walls. Wherever Antonio turned his eye, he beheld inscriptions in Arabic, wherein the perpetuity of Moorish power and splendour within these walls was confidently predicted.

Alas! how has the prophecy been falsified! Many of the basins, where the fountains had once thrown up their sparkling showers, were dry and dusty. Some of the palaces were turned into gloomy convents, and the barefoot monk paced through these courts, which had once glittered with the array, and echoed to the music, of Moorish chivalry.

In the course of his rambles, the student more than once encountered the old man of the library. He was always alone, and so full of thought as not to notice any one about him. He appeared to be intent upon studying those half-buried inscriptions, which, are found, here and there, among the Moorish ruins, and seem to murmur from the earth the tale of former greatness. The greater part of these have since been translated; but they were supposed by many at the time, to contain symbolical revelations, and golden maxims of the Arabian sages and astrologers. As Antonio saw the stranger apparently deciphering these inscriptions, he felt an eager longing to make his acquaintance, and to participate in his curious researches; but the repulse he had met with at the library deterred him from making any further advances.

He had directed his steps one evening to the sacred mount, which overlooks the beautiful valley watered by the Darro, the fertile plain of the Vega, and all that rich diversity of vale and mountain that surrounds

Granada with an earthly paradise. It was twilight when he found himself at the place, where, at the present day, are situated the chapels, known by the name of the Sacred Furnaces. They are so called from grottoes, in which some of the primitive saints are said to have been burnt. At the time of Antonio's visit, the place was an object of much curiosity. In an excavation of these grottoes, several manuscripts had recently been discovered, engraved on plates of lead. They were written in the Arabian language, excepting one, which was in unknown characters. The Pope had issued a bull, forbidding any one, under pain of excommunication, to speak of these manuscripts. The prohibition had only excited the greater curiosity; and many reports were whispered about, that these manuscripts contained treasures of dark and forbidden knowledge.

As Antonio was examining the place from whence these mysterious manuscripts had been drawn, he again observed the old man of the library wandering among the ruins. His curiosity was now fully awakened; the time and place served to stimulate it. He resolved to watch this groper after secret and forgotten lore, and to trace him to his habitation. There was something like adventure in the thing, that charmed his romantic disposition. He followed the stranger, therefore, at a little distance; at first cautiously, but he soon observed him to be so wrapped in his own thoughts, as to take little heed of external objects.

They passed along the skirts of the mountain, and then by the shady banks of the Darro. They pursued their way, for some distance from Granada, along a lonely road that led among the hills. The gloom of evening was gathering, and it was quite dark when the stranger stopped at the portal of a solitary mansion.

It appeared to be a mere wing, or ruined fragment, of what had once been a pile of some consequence. The walls were of great thickness; the windows narrow, and generally secured by iron bars. The door was of planks, studded with iron spikes, and had been of great strength, though at present it was much decayed. At one end of the mansion was a ruinous tower, in the Moorish style of architecture. The edifice had probably been a country retreat, or castle of pleasure, during the occupation of Granada by the Moors, and rendered sufficiently strong to withstand any casual assault in those warlike times.

The old man knocked at the portal. A light appeared at a small window just above it, and a female head looked out: it might have served as a model for one of Raphael's saints. The hair was beautifully braided, and gathered in a silken net; and the complexion, as well as could be judged from the light, was that soft, rich brunette, so becoming in southern beauty.

"It is I, my child," said the old man. The face instantly disappeared, and soon after a wicket-door in the large portal opened. Antonio, who had ventured near to the building, caught a transient sight of a delicate female form. A pair of fine black eyes darted a look of surprise at seeing a stranger hovering near, and the door was precipitately closed.

There was something in this sudden gleam of beauty that wonderfully struck the imagination of the student. It was like a brilliant, flashing from its dark casket. He sauntered about, regarding the gloomy pile with increasing interest. A few simple, wild notes, from among some rocks and trees at a little distance, attracted his attention. He found there a group of Gitanas, a vagabond gipsy race, which at that time abounded in Spain, and lived in hovels and caves of the hills about the neighbourhood of Granada. Some were busy about a fire, and others were listening to the uncouth music which one of their companions, seated on a ledge of the rock, was making with a split reed.

Antonio endeavoured to obtain some information of them, concerning the old building and its inhabitants. The one who appeared to be their spokesman was a gaunt fellow, with a subtle gait, a whispering voice, and a sinister roll of the eye. He shrugged his shoulders on the student's inquiries, and said that all was not right in that building. An old man inhabited it, whom nobody knew, and whose family appeared to be only a daughter and a female servant. He and his companions, he added, lived up among the neighbouring hills; and as they had been about at night, they had often seen strange lights, and heard strange sounds from the tower. Some of the country people, who worked in the vineyards among the hills, believed the old man to be one that dealt in the black art, and were not over-fond of passing near the tower at night; "but for our parts," said the Gitano, "we are not a people that trouble ourselves much with fears of that kind."

The student endeavoured to gain more precise information, but they had none to furnish him. They began to be solicitous for a compensation for what they had already imparted; and, recollecting the loneliness of the place, and the vagabond character of his companions, he was glad to give them a gratuity, and to hasten homewards.

He sat down to his studies, but his brain was too full of what he had seen and heard; his eye was upon the page, but his fancy still returned to the tower; and he was continually picturing the little window, with the beautiful head peeping out; or the door half open, and the nymph-like form within. He retired to bed, but the same object haunted his dreams. He was young and susceptible; and the excited state of his feelings, from wandering among the abodes of departed grace and gallantry, had predisposed him for a sudden impression from female beauty.

The next morning, he strolled again in the direction of the tower. It was still more forlorn, by the broad glare of day, than in the gloom of evening. The walls were crumbling, and weeds and moss were growing in every crevice. It had the look of a prison, rather than a dwelling-house. In one angle, however, he remarked a window which seemed an exception to the surrounding squalidness. There was a curtain drawn within it, and flowers standing on the window-stone. Whilst he was looking at it, the curtain was partially withdrawn, and a delicate white arm, of the most beautiful roundness, was put forth to water the flowers.

The student made a noise, to attract the attention of the fair florist. He succeeded. The curtain was further drawn, and he had a glance of the same lovely face he had seen the evening before; it was but a mere glance—the curtain again fell, and the casement closed. All this was calculated to excite the feelings of a romantic youth. Had he seen the unknown under other circumstances, it is probable that he would not have been struck with her beauty; but this appearance of being shut up and kept apart, gave her the value of a treasured gem. He passed and repassed before the house several times in the course of the day, but saw nothing more. He was there again in the evening. The whole aspect of the house was dreary. The narrow windows emitted no rays of cheerful light, to indicate that there was social life within. Antonio listened at the portal, but no sound of voices reached his ear. Just then he heard the clapping to of a distant door, and fearing to be detected in the unworthy act of eavesdropping, he precipitately drew off to the opposite side of the road, and stood in the shadow of a ruined archway.

He now remarked a light from a window in the tower. It was fitful and changeable; commonly feeble and yellowish, as if from a lamp; with an occasional glare of some vivid metallic colour, followed by a dusky glow. A column of dense smoke would now and then rise in the air, and hang like a canopy over the tower. There was altogether such a loneliness and seeming mystery about the building and its inhabitants, that Antonio was half inclined to indulge the country people's notions, and to fancy it the den of some powerful sorcerer, and the fair damsel he had seen to be some spell-bound beauty.

After some time had elapsed, a light appeared in the window where he had seen the beautiful arm. The curtain was down, but it was so thin that he could perceive the shadow of some one passing and repassing between it and the light. He fancied that he could distinguish that the form was delicate; and, from the alacrity of its movements, it was evidently youthful. He had not a doubt but this was the bed-chamber of his beautiful unknown.

Presently he heard the sound of a guitar, and a female voice singing. He drew near cautiously, and listened. It was a plaintive Moorish ballad, and he recognized in it the lamentations of one of the Abencerrages on leaving the walls of lovely Granada. It was full of passion and tenderness. It spoke of the delights of early life; the hours of love it had enjoyed on the banks of the Darro, and among the blissful abodes of the Alhambra. It bewailed the fallen honours of the Abencerrages, and imprecated vengeance on their oppressors. Antonio was affected by the music. It singularly coincided with the place. It was like the voice of past times echoed in the present, and breathing among the monuments of its departed glory.

The voice ceased; after a time the light disappeared, and all was still. "She sleeps!" said Antonio, fondly. He lingered about the building, with the devotion with which a lover lingers about the bower of sleeping beauty. The rising moon threw its silver beams on the gray walls, and glittered on the casement. The late gloomy landscape gradually became flooded with its radiance. Finding, therefore, that he could no longer move about in obscurity, and fearful that his loiterings might be observed, he reluctantly retired.

The curiosity which had at first drawn the young man to the tower, was now seconded by feelings of a more romantic kind. His studies were almost entirely abandoned. He maintained a kind of blockade of the old mansion; he would take a book with him, and pass a great part of the day under the trees in its vicinity; keeping a vigilant eye upon it, and endeavouring to ascertain what were the walks of his mysterious charmer. He found, however, that she never went out except to mass, when she was accompanied by her father. He waited at the door of the church, and offered her the holy water, in the hope of touching her hand; a little office of gallantry common in Catholic countries. She, however, modestly declined without raising her eyes to see who made the offer, and always took it herself from the font. She was attentive in her devotion; her eyes were never taken from the altar or the priest; and, on returning home, her countenance was almost entirely concealed by her mantilla.

Antonio had now carried on the pursuit for several days, and was hourly getting more and more interested in the chase, but never a step nearer to the game. His lurkings about the house had probably been noticed, for he no longer saw the fair face at the window, nor the white arm put forth to water the flowers. His only consolation was to repair nightly to his post of observation, and listen to her warbling; and if by chance he could catch a sight of her shadow, passing and repassing before the window, he thought himself most fortunate.

As he was indulging in one of these evening vigils, which were complete revels of the imagination, the sound of approaching footsteps made him withdraw into the deep shadow of the ruined archway opposite to the tower. A cavalier approached, wrapped in a large Spanish cloak. He paused under the window of the tower, and after a little while began a serenade, accompanied by his guitar, in the usual style of Spanish gallantry. His voice was rich and manly; he touched the instrument with skill, and sang with amorous and impassioned eloquence. The plume of his hat was buckled by jewels that sparkled in the moon-beams; and as he played on the guitar, his cloak falling off from one shoulder, showed him to be richly dressed. It was evident that he was a person of rank.

The idea now flashed across Antonio's mind, that the affections of his unknown beauty might be engaged. She was young, and doubtless susceptible; and it was not in the nature of Spanish females to be deaf and insensible to music and admiration. The surmise brought with it a feeling of dreariness. There was a pleasant dream of several days suddenly dispelled. He had never before experienced any thing of the tender passion; and, as its morning dreams are always delightful, he would fain have continued in the delusion.

"But what have I to do with her attachments?" thought he; "I have no claim on her heart, nor even on her acquaintance. How do I know that she is worthy of affection? Or if she is, must not so gallant a lover as this, with his jewels, his rank, and his detestable music, have completely captivated her? What idle humour is this that I have fallen into? I must again to my books. Study, study, will soon chase away all these idle fancies!"

The more he thought, however, the more he became entangled in the spell which his lively imagination had woven round him; and now that a rival had appeared, in addition to the other obstacles that environed this enchanted beauty, she appeared ten times more lovely and desirable. It was some slight consolation to him to perceive that the gallantry of the unknown met with no apparent return from the tower. The light at the window was extinguished. The curtain remained undrawn, and none of the customary signals were given to intimate that the serenade was accepted.

The cavalier lingered for some time about the place, and sang several other tender airs with a taste and feeling that made Antonio's heart ache; at length he slowly retired. The student remained with folded arms, leaning against the ruined arch, endeavouring to summon up resolution enough to depart; but there was a romantic fascination that still enchained him to the place. "It is the last time," said he, willing to compromise between his feelings and his judgment, "it is the last time; then let me enjoy the dream a few moments longer."

As his eye ranged about the old building to take a farewell look, he observed the strange light in the tower, which he had noticed on a former occasion. It kept beaming up, and declining, as before. A pillar of smoke rose in the air, and hung in sable volumes. It was evident the old man was busied in some of those operations that had gained him the reputation of a sorcerer throughout the neighbourhood.

Suddenly an intense and brilliant glare shone through the casement, followed by a loud report, and then a fierce and ruddy glow. A figure appeared at the window, uttering cries of agony or alarm, but immediately disappeared, and a body of smoke and flame whirled out of the narrow aperture. Antonio rushed to the portal, and knocked at it with vehemence. He was only answered by loud shrieks, and found that the females were already in helpless consternation. With an exertion of desperate strength he forced the wicket from its hinges, and rushed into the house.

He found himself in a small vaulted hall, and, by the light of the moon which entered at the door, he saw a staircase to the left. He hurried up it to a narrow corridor, through which was rolling a volume of smoke. He found here the two females in a frantic state of alarm; one of them clasped her hands, and implored him to save her father.

The corridor terminated in a spiral flight of steps, leading up to the tower. He sprang up it to a small door, through the chinks of which came a glow of light, and smoke was spuming out. He burst it open, and found himself in an antique vaulted chamber, furnished with a furnace and various chemical apparatus. A shattered retort lay on the stone floor; a quantity of combustibles, nearly consumed, with various half-burnt books and papers, were sending up an expiring flame, and filling the chamber with stifling smoke. Just within the threshold lay the reputed conjurer. He was bleeding, his clothes were scorched, and he appeared lifeless. Antonio caught him up, and bore him down the stairs to a chamber, in which there was a light, and laid him on a bed. The female domestic was despatched for such appliances as the house afforded; but the daughter threw herself frantically beside her parent, and could not be reasoned out of her alarm. Her dress was all in disorder; her dishevelled hair hung in rich confusion about her neck and bosom, and never was there beheld a lovelier picture of terror and affliction.

The skilful assiduities of the scholar soon produced signs of returning animation in his patient. The old man's wounds, though severe, were not dangerous. They had evidently been produced by the bursting of the retort; in his bewilderment he had been enveloped in the stifling metallic vapours, which had overpowered his feeble frame, and had not Antonio arrived to his assistance, it is possible he might never have recovered.

By slow degrees' he came to his senses. He looked about with a bewildered air at the chamber, the agitated group around, and the student who was leaning over him.

"Where am I?" said he wildly.

At the sound of his voice, his daughter uttered a faint exclamation of delight. "My poor Inez!" said he, embracing her; then, putting his hand to his head, and taking it away stained with blood, he seemed suddenly to recollect himself, and to be overcome with emotion.

"Ah!" cried he, "all is over with me! all gone! all vanished! gone in a moment! the labour of a lifetime lost!"

His daughter attempted to soothe him, but he became slightly delirious, and raved incoherently about malignant demons, and about the habitation of the green lion being destroyed. His wounds being dressed, and such other remedies administered as his situation required, he sunk into a state of quiet. Antonio now turned his attention to the daughter, whose sufferings had been little inferior to those of her father. Having with great difficulty succeeded in tranquillizing her fears, he endeavoured to prevail upon her to retire, and seek the repose so necessary to her frame, proffering to remain by her father until morning. "I am a stranger," said he, "it is true, and my offer may appear intrusive; but I see you are lonely and helpless, and I cannot help venturing over the limits of mere ceremony. Should you feel any scruple or doubt, however, say but a word, and I will instantly retire."

There was a frankness, a kindness, and a modesty, mingled in Antonio's deportment, that inspired instant confidence; and his simple scholar's garb was a recommendation in the house of poverty. The females consented to resign the sufferer to his care, as they would be the better able to attend to him on the morrow. On retiring, the old domestic was profuse in her benedictions; the daughter only looked her thanks; but as they shone through the tears that filled her fine black eyes, the student thought them a thousand times the most eloquent.

Here, then, he was, by a singular turn of chance, completely housed within this mysterious mansion. When left to himself, and the bustle of the scene was over, his heart throbbed as he looked round the chamber in which he was sitting. It was the daughter's room, the promised land toward which he had cast so many a longing gaze. The furniture was old, and had probably belonged to the building in its prosperous days; but every thing was arranged with propriety. The flowers that he had seen her attend stood in the window; a guitar leaned against a table, on which stood a crucifix, and before it lay a missal and a rosary. There reigned an air of purity and serenity about this little nestling-place of innocence; it was the emblem of a chaste and quiet mind. Some few articles of female dress lay on the chairs; and there was the very bed on which she had slept—the pillow on which her soft cheek had reclined! The poor scholar was treading enchanted ground; for what fairy land has more of magic in it, than the bedchamber of innocence and beauty?

From various expressions of the old man in his ravings, and from what he had noticed on a subsequent visit to the tower, to see that the fire was extinguished, Antonio had gathered that his patient was an alchymist. The philosopher's stone was an object eagerly sought after by visionaries in those days; but in consequence of the superstitious prejudices of the times, and the frequent persecutions of its votaries, they were apt to pursue their experiments in secret; in lonely houses, in caverns and ruins, or in the privacy of cloistered cells.

In the course of the night, the old man had several fits of restlessness and delirium; he would call out upon Theophrastus, and Geber, and Albertus Magnus, and other sages of his art; and anon would murmur about fermentation and projection, until, toward daylight, he once more sunk into a salutary sleep. When the morning sun darted his rays into the casement, the fair Inez, attended by the female domestic, came blushing into the chamber. The student now took his leave, having himself need of repose, but obtaining ready permission to return and inquire after the sufferer.

When he called again, he found the alchymist languid and in pain, but apparently suffering more in mind than in body. His delirium had left him, and he had been informed of the particulars of his deliverance, and of the subsequent attentions of the scholar. He could do little more than look his thanks, but Antonio did not require them; his own heart repaid him for all that he had done, and he almost rejoiced in the disaster that had gained him an entrance into this mysterious habitation. The alchymist was so helpless as to need much assistance; Antonio remained with him, therefore, the greater part of the day. He repeated his visit the next day, and the next. Every day his company seemed more pleasing to the invalid; and every day he felt his interest in the latter increasing. Perhaps the presence of the daughter might have been at the bottom of this solicitude.

He had frequent and long conversations with the alchymist. He found him, as men of his pursuits were apt to be, a mixture of enthusiasm and simplicity; of curious and extensive reading on points of little utility, with great inattention to the everyday occurrences of life, and profound ignorance of the world. He was deeply versed in singular and obscure branches of knowledge, and much given to visionary speculations. Antonio, whose mind was of a romantic cast, had himself given some attention to the occult sciences, and he entered upon these themes with an ardour that delighted the philosopher. Their conversations frequently turned upon astrology, divination, and the great secret. The old man would forget his aches and wounds, rise up like a spectre in his bed, and kindle into eloquence on his favourite topics. When gently admonished of his situation, it would but prompt him to another sally of thought.

"Alas, my son!" he would say, "is not this very decrepitude and suffering another proof of the importance of those secrets with which we are surrounded? Why are we trammelled by disease, withered by old age, and our spirits quenched, as it were, within, us, but because we have lost those secrets of life and youth which were known to our parents before their fall? To regain these, have philosophers been ever since aspiring; but just as they are on the point of securing the precious secrets for ever, the brief period of life is at an end; they die, and with them all their wisdom and experience. 'Nothing,' as De Nuysment observes, 'nothing is wanting for man's perfection but a longer life, less crossed with sorrows and maladies, to the attaining of the full and perfect knowledge of things.'"

At length Antonio so far gained on the heart of his patient, as to draw from him the outlines of his story.

Felix de Vasques, the alchymist, was a native of Castile, and of an ancient and honourable line. Early in life he had married a beautiful female, a descendant from one of the Moorish families. The marriage displeased his father, who considered the pure Spanish blood contaminated by this foreign mixture. It is true, the lady traced her descent from one of the Abencerrages, the most gallant of Moorish cavaliers, who had embraced the Christian faith on being exiled from the walls of Granada.

The injured pride of the father, however, was not to be appeased. He never saw his son afterwards, and on dying left him but a scanty portion of his estate; bequeathing the residue, in the piety and bitterness of his heart, to the erection of convents, and the performance of masses for souls in purgatory. Don Felix resided for a long time in the neighbourhood of Valladolid, in a state of embarrassment and obscurity. He devoted himself to intense study, having, while at the university of Salamanca, imbibed a taste for the secret sciences. He was enthusiastic and speculative; he went on from one branch of knowledge to another, until he became zealous in the search after the grand Arcanum.

He had at first engaged in the pursuit with the hopes of raising himself from his present obscurity, and resuming the rank and dignity to which his birth entitled him; but, as usual, it ended in absorbing every thought, and becoming the business of his existence. He was at length aroused from this mental abstraction, by the calamities of his household. A malignant fever swept off his wife and all his children, excepting an infant daughter. These losses for a time overwhelmed and stupefied him. His home had in a manner died away from around him, and he felt lonely and forlorn. When his spirit revived within him, he determined to abandon the scene of his humiliation and disaster; to bear away the child that was still left him beyond the scene of contagion, and never to return to Castile until he should be enabled to reclaim the honours of his line.

He had ever since been wandering and unsettled in his abode;— sometimes the resident of populous cities, at other times of absolute solitudes. He had searched libraries, meditated on inscriptions, visited adepts of different countries, and sought to gather and concentrate the rays which had been thrown by various minds upon the secrets of alchymy. He had at one time travelled quite to Padua to search for the manuscripts of Pietro d'Abano, and to inspect an urn which had been dug up near Este, supposed to have been buried by Maximus Olybius, and to have contained the grand elixir.[7]

---

[7] This urn was found in 1533. It contained a lesser one, in which was a burning lamp betwixt two small vials, the one of gold, the other of silver, both of them full of a very clear liquor. On the largest was an inscription, stating that Maximus Olybius shut up in this small vessel elements which he had prepared with great toil. There were many disquisitions among the learned on the subject. It was the most received opinion, that this Maximus Olybius was an inhabitant of Padua, that he had discovered the great secret, and that these vessels contained liquor, one to transmute metals to gold, and other to silver. The peasants who found the urns, imagining this precious liquor to be common water, spilt every drop, so that the art of transmuting metals remains as much a secret as ever.

While at Padua, he had met with an adept versed in Arabian lore, who talked of the invaluable manuscripts that must remain in the Spanish libraries, preserved from the spoils of the Moorish academies and universities; of the probability of meeting with precious unpublished writings of Geber, and Alfarabius, and Avicenna, the great physicians of the Arabian schools, who, it was well known, had treated much of alchymy; but, above all, he spoke of the Arabian tablets of lead, which had recently been dug up in the neighbourhood of Granada, and which, it was confidently believed among adepts, contained the lost secrets of the art.

The indefatigable alchymist once more bent his steps for Spain, full of renovated hope. He had made his way to Granada: he had wearied himself in the study of Arabic, in deciphering inscriptions, in rummaging libraries, and exploring every possible trace left by the Arabian sages.

In all his wanderings, he had been accompanied by Inez through the rough and the smooth, the pleasant and the adverse; never complaining, but rather seeking to soothe his cares by her innocent and playful caresses. Her instruction had been the employment and the delight of his hours of relaxation. She had grown up while they were wandering, and had scarcely ever known any home but by his side. He was family, friends, home, everything to her. He had carried her in his arms, when they first began their wayfaring; had nestled her, as an eagle does its young, among the rocky heights of the Sierra Morena; she had sported about him in childhood, in the solitudes of the Bateucas; had followed him, as a lamb does the shepherd, over the rugged Pyrenees, and into the fair plains of Languedoc; and now she was grown up to support his feeble steps among the ruined abodes of her maternal ancestors.

His property had gradually wasted away, in the course of his travels and his experiments. Still hope, the constant attendant of the alchymist, had led him on; ever on the point of reaping the reward of his labours, and ever disappointed. With the credulity that often attended his art, he attributed many of his disappointments to the machination of the malignant spirits that beset the paths of the alchymist and torment him in his solitary labours. "It is their constant endeavour," he observed, "to close up every avenue to those sublime truths, which would enable man to rise above the abject state into which he has fallen, and to return to his original perfection." To the evil offices of these demons, he attributed his late disaster. He had been on the very verge of the glorious discovery; never were the indications more completely auspicious; all was going on prosperously, when, at the critical moment which should have crowned his labours with success, and have placed him at the very summit of human power and felicity, the bursting of a retort had reduced his laboratory and himself to ruins.

"I must now," said he, "give up at the very threshold of success. My books and papers are burnt; my apparatus is broken. I am too old to bear up against these evils. The ardour that once inspired me is gone; my poor frame is exhausted by study and watchfulness, and this last misfortune has hurried me towards the grave." He concluded in a tone of deep dejection. Antonio endeavoured to comfort and reassure him; but the poor alchymist had for once awakened to a consciousness of the worldly ills that were gathering around him, and had sunk into despondency. After a pause, and some thoughtfulness and perplexity of brow, Antonio ventured to make a proposal.

"I have long," said he, "been filled with a love for the secret sciences, but have felt too ignorant and diffident to give myself up to them. You have acquired experience; you have amassed the knowledge of a lifetime; it were a pity it should be thrown away. You say you are too old to renew the toils of the laboratory; suffer me to undertake them. Add your knowledge to my youth and activity, and what shall we not accomplish? As a probationary fee, and a fund on which to proceed, I will bring into the common stock a sum of gold, the residue of a legacy, which has enabled me to complete my education. A poor scholar cannot boast much; but I trust we shall soon put ourselves beyond the reach of want; and if we should fail, why, I must depend, like other scholars, upon my brains to carry me through the world."

The philosopher's spirits, however, were more depressed than the student had imagined. This last shock, following in the rear of so many disappointments, had almost destroyed the reaction of his mind. The fire of an enthusiast, however, is never so low but that it may be blown again into a flame. By degrees, the old man was cheered and reanimated by the buoyancy and ardour of his sanguine companion. He at length agreed to accept of the services of the student, and once more to renew his experiments. He objected, however, to using the student's gold, notwithstanding that his own was nearly exhausted; but this objection was soon overcome; the student insisted on making it a common stock and common cause;—and then how absurd was any delicacy about such a trifle, with men who looked forward to discovering the philosopher's stone!

While, therefore, the alchymist was slowly recovering, the student busied himself in getting the laboratory once more in order. It was strewed with the wrecks of retorts and alembics, with old crucibles, boxes and phials of powders and tinctures, and half-burnt books and manuscripts.

As soon as the old man was sufficiently recovered, the studies and experiments were renewed. The student became a privileged and frequent visitor, and was indefatigable in his toils in the laboratory. The philosopher daily derived new zeal and spirits from the animation of his disciple. He was now enabled to prosecute the enterprise with continued exertion, having so active a coadjutor to divide the toil. While he was poring over the writings of Sandivogius, and Philalethes, and Dominus de Nuysment, and endeavouring to comprehend the symbolical language in which they have locked up their mysteries, Antonio would occupy himself among the retorts and crucibles, and keep the furnace in a perpetual glow.

With all his zeal, however, for the discovery of the golden art, the feelings of the student had not cooled as to the object that first drew him to this ruinous mansion. During the old man's illness, he had frequent opportunities of being near the daughter; and every day made him more sensible to her charms. There was a pure simplicity, and an almost passive gentleness, in her manners; yet with all this was mingled something, whether mere maiden shyness, or a consciousness of high descent, or a dash of Castilian pride, or perhaps all united, that prevented undue familiarity, and made her difficult of approach. The danger of her father, and the measures to be taken for his relief, had at first overcome this coyness and reserve, but as he recovered and her alarm subsided, she seemed to shrink from the familiarity she had indulged with the youthful stranger, and to become every day more shy and silent.

Antonio had read many books, but this was the first volume of womankind that he had ever studied. He had been captivated with the very title-page; but the further he read, the more he was delighted. She seemed formed to love; her soft black eye rolled languidly under its long silken lashes, and wherever it turned, it would linger and repose; there was tenderness in every beam. To him alone she was reserved and distant. Now that the common cares of the sick-room were at an end, he saw little more of her than before his admission to the house. Sometimes he met her on his way to and from the laboratory, and at such times there was ever a smile and a blush; but, after a simple salutation, she glided on and disappeared.

"'Tis plain," thought Antonio, "my presence is indifferent, if not irksome to her. She has noticed my admiration, and is determined to discourage it; nothing but a feeling of gratitude prevents her treating me with marked distaste—and then has she not another lover, rich, gallant, splendid, musical? how can I suppose she would turn her eyes from so brilliant a cavalier, to a poor obscure student, raking among the cinders of her father's laboratory?"

Indeed, the idea of the amorous serenader continually haunted his mind. He felt convinced that he was a favoured lover; yet, if so, why did he not frequent the tower?—why did he not make his approaches by noon-day? There was mystery in this eavesdropping and musical courtship. Surely Inez could not be encouraging a secret intrigue! Oh! no! she was too artless, too pure, too ingenuous! But then the Spanish females were so prone to love and intrigue; and music and moonlight were so seductive, and Inez had such a tender soul languishing in every look.—"Oh!" would the poor scholar exclaim, clasping his hands, "oh, that I could but once behold those loving eyes beaming on me with affection!"

It is incredible to those who have not experienced it, on what scanty aliment human life and human love may be supported. A dry crust, thrown now and then to a starving man, will give him a new lease of existence; and a faint smile, or a kind look, bestowed at casual intervals, will keep a lover loving on, when a man in his sober senses would despair.

When Antonio found himself alone in the laboratory, his mind would be haunted by one of these looks, or smiles, which he had received in passing. He would set it in every possible light, and argue on it with all the self-pleasing, self-teasing logic of a lover.

The country around him was enough to awaken that voluptuousness of feeling so favourable to the growth of passion. The window of the tower rose above the trees of the romantic valley of the Darro, and looked down upon some of the loveliest scenery of the Vega, where groves of citron and orange were refreshed by cool springs and brooks of the purest water.

The Xenel and the Darro wound their shining streams along the plain, and gleamed from among its bowers. The surrounding hills were covered with vineyards, and the mountains, crowned with snow, seemed to melt into the blue sky. The delicate airs that played about the tower were perfumed by the fragrance of myrtle and orange-blossoms, and the ear was charmed with the fond warbling of the nightingale, which, in these happy regions, sings the whole day long. Sometimes, too, there was the idle song of the muleteer, sauntering along the solitary road; or the notes of the guitar, from some group of peasants dancing in the shade. All these were enough to fill the head of the young lover with poetic fancies; and Antonio would picture to himself how he could loiter among those happy groves, and wander by those gentle rivers, and love away his life with Inez.

He felt at times impatient at his own weakness, and would endeavour to brush away these cobwebs of the mind. He would turn his thoughts, with sudden effort, to his occult studies, or occupy himself in some perplexing process; but often, when he had partially succeeded in fixing his attention, the sound of Inez's lute, or the soft notes of her voice, would come stealing upon the stillness of the chamber, and, as it were, floating round the tower. There was no great art in her performance; but Antonio thought he had never heard music comparable to this. It was perfect witchcraft to hear her warble forth some of her national melodies; those little Spanish romances and Moorish ballads, that transport the hearer, in idea, to the banks of the Guadalquivir, or the walls of the Alhambra, and make him dream of beauties, and balconies, and moonlight serenades.

Never was poor student more sadly beset than Antonio. Love is a troublesome companion in a study, at the best of tunes; but in the laboratory of an alchymist, his intrusion is terribly disastrous. Instead of attending to the retorts and crucibles, and watching the process of some experiment intrusted to his charge, the student would get entranced in one of these love-dreams, from which he would often be aroused by some fatal catastrophe. The philosopher, on returning from his researches in the libraries, would find every thing gone wrong, and Antonio in despair over the ruins of the whole day's work. The old man, however, took all quietly, for his had been a life of experiment and failure.

"We must have patience, my son," would he say, "as all the great masters that have gone before us have had. Errors, and accidents, and delays are what we have to contend with. Did not Pontanus err two hundred times, before he could obtain even the matter on which to found his experiments? The great Flamel, too, did he not labour four-and-twenty years, before he ascertained the first agent? What difficulties and hardships did not Cartilaceus encounter, at the very threshold of his discoveries? And Bernard de Treves, even after he had attained a knowledge of all the requisites, was he not delayed full three years? What you consider accidents, my son, are the machinations of our invisible enemies. The treasures and golden secrets of nature are surrounded by spirits hostile to man. The air about us teems with them. They lurk in the fire of the furnace, in the bottom of the crucible, and the alembic, and are ever on the alert to take advantage of those moments when our minds are wandering from intense meditation on the great truth that we are seeking. We must only strive the more to purify ourselves from, those gross and earthly feelings which becloud the soul, and prevent her from piercing into nature's arcana."

"Alas!" thought Antonio, "if to be purified from all earthly feeling requires that I should cease to love Inez, I fear I shall never discover the philosopher's stone!"

In this way, matters went on for some time, at the alchymist's. Day after day was sending the student's gold in vapour up the chimney; every blast of the furnace made him a ducat the poorer, without apparently helping him a jot nearer to the golden secret. Still the young man stood by, and saw piece after piece disappearing without a murmur: he had daily an opportunity of seeing Inez, and felt as if her favour would be better than silver or gold, and that every smile was worth a ducat.

Sometimes, in the cool of the evening, when the toils of the laboratory happened to be suspended, he would walk with the alchymist in what had once been a garden belonging to the mansion. There were still the remains of terraces and balustrades, and here and there a marble urn, or mutilated statue overturned, and buried among weeds and flowers run wild. It was the favourite resort of the alchymist in his hours of relaxation, where he would give full scope to his visionary flights. His mind was tinctured with the Rosicrucian doctrines. He believed in elementary beings; some favourable, others adverse to his pursuits; and, in the exaltation of his fancy, had often imagined that he held communion with them in his solitary walks, about the whispering groves and echoing walls of this old garden.

When accompanied by Antonio, he would prolong these evening recreations. Indeed, he sometimes did it out of consideration for his disciple, for he feared lest his too close application, and his incessant seclusion in the tower, should be injurious to his health. He was delighted and surprised by this extraordinary zeal and perseverance in so young a tyro, and looked upon him as destined to be one of the great luminaries of the art. Lest the student should repine at the time lost in these relaxations, the good alchymist would fill them up with wholesome knowledge, in matters connected with their pursuits; and would walk up and down the alleys with his disciple, imparting oral instruction, like an ancient philosopher. In all his visionary schemes, these breathed a spirit of lofty, though chimerical philanthropy, that won the admiration of the scholar. Nothing sordid nor sensual, nothing petty nor selfish, seemed to enter into his views, in respect to the grand discoveries he was anticipating. On the contrary, his imagination kindled with conceptions of widely dispensated happiness. He looked forward to the time when he should be able to go about the earth, relieving the indigent, comforting the distressed; and, by his unlimited means, devising and executing plans for the complete extirpation of poverty, and all its attendant sufferings and crimes. Never were grander schemes for general good, for the distribution of boundless wealth and universal competence, devised than by this poor, indigent alchymist in his ruined tower.

Antonio would attend these peripatetic lectures with all the ardour of a devotee; but there was another circumstance which may have given a secret charm to them. The garden was the resort also of Inez, where she took her walks of recreation; the only exercise that her secluded life permitted. As Antonio was duteously pacing by the side of his instructor, he would often catch a glimpse of the daughter, walking pensively about the alleys in the soft twilight. Sometimes they would meet her unexpectedly, and the heart of the student would throb with agitation. A blush, too, would crimson the cheek of Inez, but still she passed on and never joined them.

He had remained one evening until rather a late hour with the alchymist in this favourite resort. It was a delightful night after a sultry day, and the balmy air of the garden was peculiarly reviving. The old man was seated on a fragment of a pedestal, looking like a part of the ruin on which he sat. He was edifying his pupil by long lessons of wisdom from the stars, as they shone out with brilliant lustre in the dark-blue vault of a southern sky; for he was deeply versed in Behmen, and other of the Rosicrucians, and talked much of the signature of earthly things and passing events, which may be discerned in the heavens; of the power of the stars over corporeal beings, and their influence on the fortunes of the sons of men.

By degrees the moon rose and shed her gleaming light among the groves. Antonio apparently listened with fixed attention to the sage, but his ear was drinking in the melody of Inez's voice, who was singing to her lute in one of the moonlight glades of the garden. The old man, having exhausted his theme, sat gazing in silent reverie at the heavens. Antonio could not resist an inclination to steal a look at this coy beauty, who was thus playing the part of the nightingale, so sequestered and musical. Leaving the alchymist in his celestial reverie, he stole gently along one of the alleys. The music had ceased, and he thought he heard the sound of voices. He came to an angle of a copse that had screened a kind of green recess, ornamented by a marble fountain. The moon shone full upon the place, and by its light he beheld his unknown, serenading rival at the feet of Inez. He was detaining her by the hand, which he covered with kisses; but at sight of Antonio he started up and half drew his sword, while Inez, disengaged, fled back to the house.

All the jealous doubts and fears of Antonio were now confirmed. He did not remain to encounter the resentment of his happy rival at being thus interrupted, but turned from the place in sudden wretchedness of heart. That Inez should love another, would have been misery enough; but that she should be capable of a dishonourable amour, shocked him to the soul. The idea of deception in so young and apparently artless a being, brought with it that sudden distrust in human nature, so sickening to a youthful and ingenuous mind; but when he thought of the kind, simple parent she was deceiving, whose affections all centred in her, he felt for a moment a sentiment of indignation, and almost of aversion.

He found the alchymist still seated in his visionary contemplation of the moon. "Come hither, my son," said he, with his usual enthusiasm, "come, read with me in this vast volume of wisdom, thus nightly unfolded for our perusal. Wisely did the Chaldean sages affirm, that the heaven is as a mystic page, uttering speech to those who can rightly understand; warning them of good and evil, and instructing them in the secret decrees of fate."

The student's heart ached for his venerable master; and, for a moment, he felt the futility of his occult wisdom. "Alas! poor old man!" thought he, "of what avails all thy study? Little dost thou dream, while busied in airy speculations among the stars, what a treason against thy happiness is going on under thine eyes; as it were, in thy very bosom!—Oh Inez! Inez! where shall we look for truth and innocence, where shall we repose confidence in woman, if even you can deceive?"

It was a trite apostrophe, such as every lover makes when he finds his mistress not quite such a goddess as he had painted her. With the student, however, it sprung from honest anguish of heart. He returned to his lodgings, in pitiable confusion of mind. He now deplored the infatuation that had led him on until his feelings were so thoroughly engaged. He resolved to abandon his pursuits at the tower, and trust to absence to dispel the fascination by which he had been spellbound. He no longer thirsted after the discovery of the grand elixir: the dream of alchymy was over; for, without Inez, what was the value of the philosopher's stone?

He rose, after a sleepless night, with the determination of taking his leave of the alchymist, and tearing himself from Granada. For several days did he rise with the same resolution, and every night saw him come back to his pillow, to repine at his want of resolution, and to make fresh determinations for the morrow. In the meanwhile, he saw less of Inez than ever. She no longer walked in the garden, but remained almost entirely in her apartment. When she met him, she blushed more than usual; and once hesitated, as if she would have spoken; but, after a temporary embarrassment, and still deeper blushes, she made some casual observation, and retired. Antonio read, in this confusion, a consciousness of fault, and of that fault's being discovered. "What could she have wished to communicate? Perhaps to account for the scene in the garden;—but how can she account for it, or why should she account for it to me? What am I to her?—or rather, what is she to me?" exclaimed he, impatiently, with a new resolution to break through these entanglements of the heart, and fly from this enchanted spot for ever.

He was returning that very night to his lodgings, full of this excellent determination, when, in a shadowy part of the road, he passed a person whom he recognized, by his height and form, for his rival: he was going in the direction of the tower. If any lingering doubts remained, here was an opportunity of settling them completely. He determined to follow this unknown cavalier, and, under favour of the darkness, observe his movements. If he obtained access to the tower, or in any way a favourable reception, Antonio felt as if it would be a relief to his mind, and would enable him to fix his wavering resolution.

The unknown, as he came near the tower, was more cautious and stealthy in his approaches. He was joined under a clump of trees by another person, and they had much whispering together. A light was burning in the chamber of Inez; the curtain was down, but the casement was left open, as the night was warm. After some time, the light was extinguished. A considerable interval elapsed. The cavalier and his companion remained under covert of the trees, as if keeping watch. At length they approached the tower, with silent and cautious steps. The cavalier received a dark-lantern from his companion, and threw off his cloak. The other then softly brought something from the clump of trees, which Antonio perceived to be a light ladder: he placed it against the wall, and the serenader gently ascended. A sickening sensation came over Antonio. Here was indeed a confirmation of every fear. He was about to leave the place, never to return, when he heard a stifled shriek from Inez's chamber.

In an instant, the fellow that stood at the foot of the ladder lay prostrate on the ground. Antonio wrested a stiletto from his nerveless hand, and hurried up the ladder. He sprang in at the window, and found Inez struggling in the grasp of his fancied rival; the latter, disturbed from his prey, caught up his lantern, turned its light full upon Antonio, and, drawing his sword, made a furious assault; luckily the student saw the light gleam along the blade, and parried the thrust with the stiletto. A fierce, but unequal combat ensued. Antonio fought exposed to the full glare of the light, while his antagonist was in shadow: his stiletto, too, was but a poor defence against a rapier. He saw that nothing would save him but closing with his adversary, and getting within his weapon: he rushed furiously upon him, and gave him a severe blow with the stiletto; but received a wound in return from the shortened sword. At the same moment, a blow was inflicted from behind, by the confederate, who had ascended the ladder; it felled him to the floor, and his antagonists made their escape.

By this time, the cries of Inez had brought her father and the domestic into the room. Antonio was found weltering in his blood, and senseless. He was conveyed to the chamber of the alchymist, who now repaid in kind the attentions which the student had once bestowed upon him. Among his varied knowledge he possessed some skill in surgery, which at this moment was of more value than even his chymical lore. He stanched and dressed the wounds of his disciple, which on examination proved less desperate than he had at first apprehended. For a few days, however, his case was anxious, and attended with danger. The old man watched over him with the affection of a parent. He felt a double debt of gratitude towards him, on account of his daughter and himself; he loved him too as a faithful and zealous disciple; and he dreaded lest the world, should be deprived of the promising talents of so aspiring an alchymist.

An excellent constitution soon medicined his wounds; and there was a balsam in the looks and words of Inez, that had a healing effect on the still severer wounds which he carried in his heart. She displayed the strongest interest in his safety; she called him her deliverer, her preserver. It seemed as if her grateful disposition sought, in the warmth of its acknowledgments, to repay him for past coldness. But what most contributed to Antonio's recovery, was her explanation concerning his supposed rival. It was some time since he had first beheld her at church, and he had ever since persecuted her with his attentions. He had beset her in her walks, until she had been obliged to confine herself to the house, except when accompanied by her father. He had besieged her with letters, serenades, and every art by which he could urge a vehement, but clandestine and dishonourable suit. The scene in the garden was as much of a surprise to her as to Antonio. Her persecutor had been attracted by her voice, and had found his way over a ruined part of the wall. He had come upon her unawares; was detaining her by force, and pleading his insulting passion, when the appearance of the student interrupted him, and enabled her to make her escape. She had forborne to mention to her father the persecution which she suffered; she wished to spare him unavailing anxiety and distress, and had determined to confine herself more rigorously to the house; though it appeared that even here she had not been safe from his daring enterprise.

Antonio inquired whether she knew the name of this impetuous admirer? She replied that he had made his advances under a fictitious name; but that she had heard him once called by the name of Don Ambrosio de Loxa.

Antonio knew him, by report, for one of the most determined and dangerous libertines in all Granada. Artful, accomplished, and, if he chose to be so, insinuating; but daring and headlong in the pursuit of his pleasures; violent and implacable in his resentments. He rejoiced to find that Inez had been proof against his seductions, and had been inspired with aversion by his splendid profligacy; but he trembled to think of the dangers she had run, and he felt solicitude about the dangers that must yet environ her.

At present, however, it was probable the enemy had a temporary quietus. The traces of blood had been found for some distance from the ladder, until they were lost among thickets; and as nothing had been heard or seen of him since, it was concluded that he had been seriously wounded.

As the student recovered from his wounds, he was enabled to join Inez and her father in their domestic intercourse. The chamber in which they usually met had probably been a saloon of state in former times. The floor was of marble; the walls partially covered with remains of tapestry; the chairs, richly carved and gilt, were crazed with age, and covered with tarnished and tattered brocade. Against the wall hung a long rusty rapier, the only relic that the old man retained of the chivalry of his ancestors. There might have been something to provoke a smile, in the contrast between the mansion and its inhabitants; between present poverty and the graces of departed grandeur; but the fancy of the student had thrown so much romance about the edifice and its inmates, that every thing was clothed with charms. The philosopher, with his broken-down pride, and his strange pursuits, seemed to comport with the melancholy ruin he inhabited; and there was a native elegance of spirit about the daughter, that showed she would have graced the mansion in its happier days.

What delicious moments were these to the student! Inez was no longer coy and reserved. She was naturally artless and confiding; though the kind of persecution she had experienced from one admirer had rendered her, for a time, suspicious and circumspect toward the other. She now felt an entire confidence in the sincerity and worth of Antonio, mingled with an overflowing gratitude. When her eyes met his, they beamed with sympathy and kindness; and Antonio, no longer haunted by the idea of a favoured rival, once more aspired to success.

At these domestic meetings, however, he had little opportunity of paying his court, except by looks. The alchymist, supposing him, like himself, absorbed in the study of alchymy, endeavoured to cheer the tediousness of his recovery by long conversations on the art. He even brought several of his half-burnt volumes, which the student had once rescued from the flames, and rewarded him for their preservation, by reading copious passages. He would entertain him with the great and good acts of Flamel, which he effected through means of the philosopher's stone, relieving widows and orphans, founding hospitals, building churches, and what not; or with the interrogatories of King Kalid, and the answers of Morienus, the Roman hermit of Jerusalem; or the profound questions which Elardus, a necromancer of the province of Catalonia, put to the devil, touching the secrets of alchymy, and the devil's replies.

All these were couched, in occult language, almost unintelligible to the unpractised ear of the disciple. Indeed, the old man delighted in the mystic phrases and symbolical jargon in which the writers that have treated of alchymy have wrapped their communications; rendering them incomprehensible except to the initiated. With what rapture would he elevate his voice at a triumphant passage, announcing the grand discovery! "Thou shalt see," would he exclaim, in the words of Henry Kuhnrade,[8] "th e stone of the philosophers (our king) go forth of the bed-chamber of his glassy sepulchre into the theatre of this world; that is to say, regenerated and made perfect, a shining carbuncle, a most temperate splendour, whose most subtle and depurated parts are inseparable, united into one with a concordial mixture, exceeding equal, transparent as chrystal, shining red like a ruby, permanently colouring or ringing, fixt in all temptations or tryals; yea, in the examination of the burning sulphur itself, and the

---

[8] Amphitheatre of the Eternal Wisdom.

devouring waters, and in the most vehement persecution of the fire, always incombustible and permanent as a salamander!"

The student had a high veneration for the fathers of alchymy, and a profound respect for his instructor; but what was Henry Kuhnrade, Geber, Lully, or even Albertus Magnus himself, compared to the countenance of Inez, which presented such a page of beauty to his perusal? While, therefore, the good alchymist was doling out knowledge by the hour, his disciple would forget books, alchymy, every thing but the lovely object before him. Inez, too, unpractised in the science of the heart, was gradually becoming fascinated by the silent attentions of her lover. Day by day, she seemed more and more perplexed by the kindling and strangely pleasing emotions of her bosom. Her eye was often cast down in thought. Blushes stole to her cheek without any apparent cause, and light, half-suppressed sighs would follow these short fits of musing. Her little ballads, though the same that she had always sung, yet breathed a more tender spirit. Either the tones of her voice were more soft and touching, or some passages were delivered with a feeling she had never before given them. Antonio, beside his love for the abstruse sciences, had a pretty turn for music; and never did philosopher touch the guitar more tastefully. As, by degrees, he conquered the mutual embarrassment that kept them asunder, he ventured to accompany Inez in some of her songs. He had a voice full of fire and tenderness: as he sang, one would have thought, from the kindling blushes of his companion, that he had been pleading his own passion in her ear. Let those who would keep two youthful hearts asunder, beware of music. Oh! this leaning over chairs, and conning the same music-book, and entwining of voices, and melting away in harmonies!—the German waltz is nothing to it.

The worthy alchymist saw nothing of all this. His mind could admit of no idea that was not connected with the discovery of the grand arcanum, and he supposed his youthful coadjutor equally devoted. He was a mere child as to human nature; and, as to the passion of love, whatever he might once have felt of it, he had long since forgotten that there was such an idle passion in existence. But, while he dreamed, the silent amour went on. The very quiet and seclusion of the place were favourable to the growth of romantic passion. The opening bud of love was able to put forth leaf by leaf, without an adverse wind to check its growth. There was neither officious friendship to chill by its advice, nor insidious envy to wither by its sneers, nor an observing world to look on and stare it out of countenance. There was neither declaration, nor vow, nor any other form of Cupid's canting school. Their hearts mingled together, and understood each other without the aid of language. They lapsed into the full current of affection, unconscious of its depth, and thoughtless of the rocks that might lurk beneath its surface. Happy lovers! who wanted nothing to make their felicity complete, but the discovery of the philosopher's stone!

At length, Antonio's health was sufficiently restored to enable him to return to his lodgings in Granada. He felt uneasy, however, at leaving the tower, while lurking danger might surround its almost defenceless inmates. He dreaded lest Don Ambrosio, recovered from his wounds, might plot some new attempt, by secret art, or open violence. From all that he had heard, he knew him to be too implacable to suffer his defeat to pass unavenged, and too rash and fearless, when his arts were unavailing, to stop at any daring deed in the accomplishment of his purposes. He urged his apprehensions to the alchymist and his daughter, and proposed that they should abandon the dangerous vicinity of Granada.

"I have relations," said he, "in Valentia, poor indeed, but worthy and affectionate. Among them you will find friendship and quiet, and we may there pursue our labours unmolested." He went on to paint the beauties and delights of Valentia, with all the fondness of a native, and all the eloquence with which a lover paints the fields and groves which he is picturing as the future scenes of his happiness. His eloquence, backed by the apprehensions of Inez, was successful with the alchymist, who, indeed, had led too unsettled a life to be particular about the place of his residence; and it was determined, that, as soon as Antonio's health was perfectly restored, they should abandon the tower, and seek the delicious neighbourhood of Valentia.[9]

---

[9] Here are the strongest silks, the sweetest wines, the excellent'st almonds, the best oyls, and beautifull'st females of all Spain. The very bruit animals make themselves beds of rosemary, and other fragrant flowers hereabouts; and when one is at sea, if the winde blow from the shore, he may smell this soyl before he comes in sight of it, many leagues off, by the strong odoriferous scent it casts. As it is the most pleasant, so it is also the temperat'st clime of all Spain, and they commonly call it the second Italy;

To recruit his strength, the student suspended his toils in the laboratory, and spent the few remaining days, before departure, in taking a farewell look at the enchanting environs of Granada. He felt returning health and vigour, as he inhaled the pure temperate breezes that play about its hills; and the happy state of his mind contributed to his rapid recovery. Inez was often the companion of his walks. Her descent, by the mother's side, from one of the ancient Moorish families, gave her an interest in this once favourite seat of Arabian power. She gazed with enthusiasm upon its magnificent monuments, and her memory was filled with the traditional tales and ballads of Moorish chivalry. Indeed, the solitary life she had led, and the visionary turn of her father's mind, had produced an effect upon her character, and given it a tinge of what, in modern days, would be termed romance. All this was called into full force by this new passage; for, when a woman first begins to love, life is all romance to her.

In one of their evening strolls, they had ascended to the mountain of the Sun, where is situated the Generaliffe, the palace of pleasure, in the days of Moorish dominion, but now a gloomy convent of Capuchins. They had wandered about its garden, among groves of orange, citron, and cypress, where the waters, leaping in torrents, or gushing in fountains, or tossed aloft in sparkling jets, fill the air with music and freshness.

There is a melancholy mingled with all the beauties of this garden, that gradually stole over the feelings of the lovers. The place is full of the sad story of past times. It was the favourite abode of the lovely queen of Granada, where she was surrounded by the delights of a gay and voluptuous court. It was here, too, amidst her own bowers of roses, that her slanderers laid the base story of her dishonour, and struck a fatal blow to the line of the gallant Abencerrages.

The whole garden has a look of ruin and neglect. Many of the fountains are dry and broken; the streams have wandered from their marble channels, and are choked by weeds and yellow leaves. The reed whistles to the wind, where it had once sported among roses, and shaken perfume from the orange-blossom. The convent-bell flings its sullen sound, or the drowsy vesper-hymn floats along these solitudes, which once resounded

---

which made the Moors, whereof many thousands were disterr'd, and banish'd hence to Barbary, to think that Paradise was in that part of the heavens which hung over this citie.—HOWELL'S Letters.

with the song, and the dance, and the lover's serenade. Well may the Moors lament over the loss of this earthly paradise; well may they remember it in their prayers, and beseech Heaven to restore it to the faithful; well may their ambassadors smite their breasts when they behold these monuments of their race, and sit down and weep among the fading glories of Granada!

It is impossible to wander about these scenes of departed love and gayety, and not feel the tenderness of the heart awakened. It was then that Antonio first ventured to breathe his passion, and to express by words what his eyes had long since so eloquently revealed. He made his avowal with fervour, but with frankness. He had no gay prospects to hold out: he was a poor scholar, dependent on his "good spirits to feed and clothe him." But a woman in love is no interested calculator. Inez listened to him with downcast eyes, but in them was a humid gleam that showed her heart was with him. She had no prudery in her nature; and she had not been sufficiently in society to acquire it. She loved him with all the absence of worldliness of a genuine woman; and, amidst timid smiles and blushes, he drew from her a modest acknowledgment of her affection.

They wandered about the garden, with that sweet intoxication of the soul which none but happy lovers know. The world about them was all fairy land; and, indeed, it spread forth one of its fairest scenes before their eyes, as if to fulfil their dream of earthly happiness. They looked out from between groves of orange, upon the towers of Granada below them; the magnificent plain of the Vega beyond, streaked with evening sunshine, and the distant hills tinted with rosy and purple hues: it seemed an emblem of the happy future, that love and hope were decking out for them.

As if to make the scene complete, a group of Andalusians struck up a dance, in one of the vistas of the garden, to the guitars of two wandering musicians. The Spanish music is wild and plaintive, yet the people dance to it with spirit and enthusiasm. The picturesque figures of the dancers; the girls with their hair in silken nets that hung in knots and tassels down their backs, their mantillas floating round their graceful forms, their slender feet peeping from under their basquinas, their arms tossed up in the air to play the castanets, had a beautiful effect on this airy height, with the rich evening landscape spreading out below them.

When the dance was ended, two of the parties approached Antonio and Inez; one of them began a soft and tender Moorish ballad, accompanied by the other on the lute. It alluded to the story of the garden, the wrongs of the fair queen of Granada, and the misfortunes of the Abencerrages. It was one of those old ballads that abound in this part of Spain, and live, like echoes, about the ruins of Moorish greatness. The heart of Inez was at that moment open to every tender impression; the tears rose into her eyes, as she listened to the tale. The singer approached nearer to her; she was striking in her appearance;—young, beautiful, with a mixture of wildness and melancholy in her fine black eyes. She fixed them mournfully and expressively on Inez, and, suddenly varying her manner, sang another ballad, which treated of impending danger and treachery. All this might have passed for a mere accidental caprice of the singer, had there not been something in her look, manner, and gesticulation that made it pointed and startling.

Inez was about to ask the meaning of this evidently personal application of the song, when she was interrupted by Antonio, who gently drew her from the place. Whilst she had been lost in attention to the music, he had remarked a group of men, in the shadows of the trees, whispering together. They were enveloped in the broad hats and great cloaks so much worn by the Spanish, and, while they were regarding himself and Inez attentively, seemed anxious to avoid observation. Not knowing what might be their character or intention, he hastened to quit a place where the gathering shadows of evening might expose them to intrusion and insult. On their way down the hill, as they passed through the wood of elms, mingled with poplars and oleanders, that skirts the road leading from the Alhambra, he again saw these men apparently following at a distance; and he afterwards caught sight of them among the trees on the banks of the Darro. He said nothing on the subject to Inez, nor her father, for he would not awaken unnecessary alarm; but he felt at a loss how to ascertain or to avert any machinations that might be devising against the helpless inhabitants of the tower.

He took his leave of them late at night, full of this perplexity. As he left the dreary old pile, he saw some one lurking in the shadow of the wall, apparently watching his movements. He hastened after the figure, but it glided away, and disappeared among some ruins. Shortly after he heard a low whistle, which was answered from a little distance. He had no longer a doubt but that some mischief was on foot, and turned to hasten back to the tower, and put its inmates on their guard. He had scarcely turned, however, before he found himself suddenly seized from behind by some one of Herculean strength. His struggles were in vain; he was surrounded by armed men. One threw a mantle over him that stifled his cries, and enveloped him in its folds; and he was hurried off with irresistible rapidity.

The next day passed without the appearance of Antonio at the alchymist's. Another, and another day succeeded, and yet he did not come; nor had any thing been heard of him at his lodgings. His absence caused, at first, surprise and conjecture, and at length alarm. Inez recollected the singular intimations of the ballad-singer upon the mountain, which seemed to warn her of impending danger, and her mind was full of vague forebodings. She sat listening to every sound at the gate, or footstep on the stairs. She would take up her guitar and strike a few notes, but it would not do; her heart was sickening with suspense and anxiety. She had never before felt what it was to be really lonely. She now was conscious of the force of that attachment which had taken possession of her breast; for never do we know how much we love, never do we know how necessary the object of our love is to our happiness, until we experience the weary void of separation.

The philosopher, too, felt the absence of his disciple almost as sensibly as did his daughter. The animating buoyancy of the youth had inspired him with new ardour, and had given to his labours the charm of full companionship. However, he had resources and consolations of which his daughter was destitute. His pursuits were of a nature to occupy every thought, and keep the spirits in a state of continual excitement. Certain indications, too, had lately manifested themselves, of the most favourable nature. Forty days and forty nights had the process gone on successfully; the old man's hopes were constantly rising, and he now considered the glorious moment once more at hand, when he should obtain not merely the major lunaria, but likewise the tinctura solaris, the means of multiplying gold, and of prolonging existence. He remained, therefore, continually shut up in his laboratory, watching his furnace; for a moment's inadvertency might once more defeat all his expectations.

He was sitting one evening at one of his solitary vigils, wrapped up in meditation; the hour was late, and his neighbour, the owl, was hooting from the battlement of the tower, when he heard the door open behind him. Supposing it to be his daughter coming to take her leave of him for the night, as was her frequent practice, he called her by name, but a harsh voice me this ear in reply. He was grasped by the arms, and, looking up, perceived three strange men in the chamber. He attempted to shake them off, but in vain. He called for help, but they scoffed at his cries. "Peace, dotard!" cried one: "think'st thou the servants of the most holy inquisition are to be daunted by thy clamours? Comrades, away with him!"

Without heeding his remonstrances and entreaties, they seized upon his books and papers, took some note of the apartment, and the utensils, and then bore him off a prisoner.

Inez, left to herself, had passed a sad and lonely evening; seated by a casement which looked into the garden, she had pensively watched star after star sparkle out of the blue depths of the sky, and was indulging a crowd of anxious thoughts about her lover, until the rising tears began to flow. She was suddenly alarmed by the sound of voices, that seemed to come from a distant part of the mansion. There was, not long after, a noise of several persons descending the stairs. Surprised at these unusual sounds in their lonely habitation, she remained for a few moments in a state of trembling, yet indistinct apprehension, when the servant rushed into the room, with terror in her countenance, and informed her that her father was carried off by armed men.

Inez did not stop to hear further, but flew down-stairs to overtake them. She had scarcely passed the threshold, when she found herself in the grasp of strangers.—"Away!—away!" cried she, wildly, "do not stop me—let me follow my father."

"We come to conduct you to him, senora," said one of the men, respectfully.

"Where is he, then?"

"He is gone to Granada," replied the man: "an unexpected circumstance requires his presence there immediately; but he is among friends."

"We have no friends in Granada," said Inez, drawing back; but then the idea of Antonio rushed into her mind; something relating to him might have call her father thither. "Is senor Antonio de Castros with him?" demanded she, with agitation.

"I know not, senora," replied the man. "It is very possible. I only know that your father is among friends, and is anxious for you to follow him."

"Let us go, then," cried she, eagerly. The men led her a little distance to where a mule was waiting, and, assisting her to mount, they conducted her slowly towards the city.

Granada was on that evening a scene of fanciful revel. It was one of the festivals of the Maestranza, an association of the nobility to keep up some of the gallant customs of ancient chivalry. There had been a representation of a tournament in one of the squares; the streets would still occasionally resound with the beat of a solitary drum, or the bray of a trumpet from some straggling party of revellers. Sometimes they were met by cavaliers, richly dressed in ancient costumes, attended by their squires; and at one time they passed in sight of a palace brilliantly illuminated, from whence came the mingled sounds of music and the dance. Shortly after, they came to the square where the mock tournament had been held. It was thronged by the populace, recreating themselves among booths and stalls where refreshments were sold, and the glare of torches showed the temporary galleries, and gay-coloured awnings, and armorial trophies, and other paraphernalia of the show. The conductors of Inez endeavoured to keep out of observation, and to traverse a gloomy part of the square; but they were detained at one place by the pressure of a crowd surrounding a party of wandering musicians, singing one of those ballads of which the Spanish populace are so passionately fond. The torches which were held by some of the crowd, threw a strong mass of light upon Inez, and the sight of so beautiful a being, without mantilla or veil, looking so bewildered, and conducted by men who seemed to take no gratification in the surrounding gayety, occasioned expressions of curiosity. One of the ballad-singers approached, and striking her guitar with peculiar earnestness, began to sing a doleful air, full of sinister forebodings. Inez started with surprise. It was the same ballad-singer that had addressed her in the garden of the Generaliffe.

It was the same air that she had then sung. It spoke of impending dangers; they seemed, indeed, to be thickening around her. She was anxious to speak with the girl, and to ascertain whether she really had a knowledge of any definite evil that was threatening her; but, as she attempted to address her, the mule, on which she rode, was suddenly seized, and led forcibly through the throng by one of her conductors, while she saw another addressing menacing words to the ballad-singer. The latter raised her hand with a warning gesture, as Inez lost sight of her.

While she was yet lost in perplexity, caused by this singular occurrence, they stopped at the gate of a large mansion. One of her attendants knocked, the door was opened, and they entered a paved court. "Where are we?" demanded Inez, with anxiety. "At the house of a friend, senora," replied the man. "Ascend this staircase with me, and in a moment you will meet your father."

They ascended a staircase, that led to a suite of splendid apartments. They passed through several, until they came to an inner chamber. The door opened—some one approached; but what was her terror at perceiving, not her father, but Don Ambrosio!

The men who had seized upon the alchymist had, at least, been more honest in their professions. They were, indeed, familiars of the inquisition. He was conducted in silence to the gloomy prison of that horrible tribunal. It was a mansion whose very aspect withered joy, and almost shut out hope. It was one of those hideous abodes which the bad passions of men conjure up in this fair world, to rival the fancied dens of demons and the accursed.

Day after day went heavily by, without anything to mark the lapse of time, but the decline and reappearance of the light that feebly glimmered through the narrow window of the dungeon in which the unfortunate alchymist was buried rather than confined. His mind was harassed with uncertainties and fears about his daughter, so helpless and inexperienced. He endeavoured to gather tidings of her from the man who brought his daily portion of food. The fellow stared, as if astonished at being asked a question in that mansion of silence and mystery, but departed without saying a word. Every succeeding attempt was equally fruitless.

The poor alchymist was oppressed by many griefs; and it was not the least, that he had been again interrupted in his labours on the very point of success. Never was alchymist so near attaining the golden secret—a little longer, and all his hopes would have been realized. The thoughts of these disappointments afflicted him more even than the fear of all that he might suffer from the merciless inquisition. His waking thoughts would follow him into his dreams. He would be transported in fancy to his laboratory, busied again among retorts and alembics, and surrounded by Lully, by D'Abano, by Olybius, and the other masters of the sublime art. The moment of projection would arrive; a seraphic form would rise out of the furnace, holding forth a vessel containing the precious elixir; but, before he could grasp the prize, he would awake, and find himself in a dungeon.

All the devices of inquisitorial ingenuity were employed to ensnare the old man, and to draw from him evidence that might be brought against himself, and might corroborate certain secret information that had been given against him. He had been accused of practising necromancy and judicial astrology, and a cloud of evidence had been secretly brought forward to substantiate the charge. It would be tedious to enumerate all the circumstances, apparently corroborative, which had been industriously cited by the secret accuser. The silence which prevailed about the tower, its desolateness, the very quiet of its inhabitants, had been adduced as proofs that something sinister was perpetrated within. The alchymist's conversations and soliloquies in the garden had been overheard and misrepresented. The lights and strange appearances at night, in the tower, were given with violent exaggerations. Shrieks and yells were said to have been heard from thence at midnight, when, it was confidently asserted, the old man raised familiar spirits by his incantations, and even compelled the dead to rise from their graves, and answer to his questions.

The alchymist, according to the custom of the inquisition, was kept in complete ignorance of his accuser; of the witnesses produced against him; even of the crimes of which he was accused. He was examined generally, whether he knew why he was arrested, and was conscious of any guilt that might deserve the notice of the holy office? He was examined as to his country, his life, his habits, his pursuits, his actions, and opinions. The old man was frank and simple in his replies; he was conscious of no guilt, capable of no art, practised in no dissimulation. After receiving a general admonition to bethink himself whether he had not committed any act deserving of punishment and to prepare, by confession, to secure the well known mercy of the tribunal, he was remanded to his cell.

He was now visited in his dungeon by crafty familiars of the inquisition, who, under pretence of sympathy and kindness, came to beguile the tediousness of his imprisonment with friendly conversation. They casually introduced the subject of alchymy, on which they touched with great caution and pretended indifference. There was no need of such craftiness. The honest enthusiast had no suspicion in his nature: the moment they touched upon his favourite theme, he forgot his misfortunes and imprisonment, and broke forth into rhapsodies about the divine science.

The conversation was artfully turned to the discussion of elementary beings. The alchymist readily avowed his belief in them; and that there had been instances of their attending upon philosophers, and administering to their wishes. He related many miracles said to have been performed by Apollonius Thyaneus, through the aid of spirits or demons; insomuch that he was set up by the heathens in opposition to the Messiah; and was even regarded with reverence by many Christians. The familiars eagerly demanded whether he believed Apollonius to be a true and worthy philosopher. The unaffected piety of the alchymist protected him even in the midst of his simplicity; for he condemned Apollonius as a sorcerer and an impostor. No art could draw from him an admission that he had ever employed or invoked spiritual agencies in the prosecution of his pursuits, though he believed himself to have been frequently impeded by their invisible interference.

The inquisitors were sorely vexed at not being able to inveigle him into a confession of a criminal nature; they attributed their failure to craft, to obstinacy, to every cause but the right one, namely, that the harmless visionary had nothing guilty to confess. They had abundant proof of a secret nature against him; but it was the practice of the inquisition to endeavour to procure confession from the prisoners. An auto da fé was at hand; the worthy fathers were eager for his conviction, for they were always anxious to have a good number of culprits condemned to the stake, to grace these solemn triumphs. He was at length brought to a final examination.

The chamber of trial was spacious and gloomy. At one end was a huge crucifix, the standard of the inquisition. A long table extended through the centre of the room, at which sat the inquisitors and their secretary; at the other end, a stool was placed for the prisoner.

He was brought in, according to custom, bare-headed and bare-legged. He was enfeebled by confinement and affliction; by constantly brooding over the unknown fate of his child, and the disastrous interruption of his experiments. He sat bowed down and listless; his head sunk upon his breast; his whole appearance that of one "past hope, abandoned, and by himself given over."

The accusation alleged against him was now brought forward in a specific form; he was called upon by name, Felix de Vasquez, formerly of Castile, to answer to the charges of necromancy and demonology. He was told that the charges were amply substantiated; and was asked whether he was ready, by full confession, to throw himself upon the well-known mercy of the holy inquisition.

The philosopher testified some slight surprise at the nature of the accusation, but simply replied, "I am innocent."

"What proof have you to give of your innocence?"

"It rather remains for you to prove your charges," said the old man. "I am a stranger and a sojourner in the land, and know no one out of the doors of my dwelling. I can give nothing in my vindication but the word of a nobleman and a Castilian."

The inquisitor shook his head, and went on to repeat the various inquiries that had before been made as to his mode of life and pursuits. The poor alchymist was too feeble and too weary at heart to make any but brief replies. He requested that some man of science might examine his laboratory, and all his books and papers, by which it would be made abundantly evident that he was merely engaged in the study of alchymy.

To this the inquisitor observed, that alchymy had become a mere covert for secret and deadly sins. That the practisers of it were apt to scruple at no means to satisfy their inordinate greediness of gold. Some had been known to use spells and impious ceremonies; to conjure the aid of evil spirits; nay, even to sell their souls to the enemy of mankind, so that they might riot in boundless wealth while living.

The poor alchymist had heard all patiently, or, at least, passively. He had disdained to vindicate his name otherwise than by his word; he had smiled at the accusations of sorcery, when applied merely to himself; but when the sublime art, which had been the study and passion of his life, was assailed, he could no longer listen in silence. His head gradually rose from his bosom; a hectic colour came in faint streaks to his cheek; played about there, disappeared, returned, and at length kindled into a burning glow. The clammy dampness dried from his forehead; his eyes, which had nearly been extinguished, lighted up again, and burned with their wonted and visionary fires. He entered into a vindication of his favourite art. His voice at first was feeble and broken; but it gathered strength as he proceeded, until it rolled in a deep and sonorous volume. He gradually rose from his seat, as he rose with his subject; he threw back the scanty black mantle which had hitherto wrapped his limbs; the very uncouthness of his form and looks gave an impressive effect to what he uttered; it was as though a corpse had become suddenly animated.

He repelled with scorn the aspersions cast upon alchymy by the ignorant and vulgar. He affirmed it to be the mother of all art and science, citing the opinions of Paracelsus, Sandivogius, Raymond Lully, and others, in support of his assertions. He maintained that it was pure and innocent and honourable both in its purposes and means. What were its objects? The perpetuation of life and youth, and the production of gold. "The elixir vitae," said he, "is no charmed potion, but merely a concentration of those elements of vitality which nature has scattered through her works. The philosopher's stone, or tincture, or powder, as it is variously called, is no necromantic talisman, but consists simply of those particles which gold contains within itself for its reproduction; for gold, like other things, has its seed within itself, though bound up with inconceivable firmness, from the vigour of innate fixed salts and sulphurs. In seeking to discover the elixir of life, then," continued he, "we seek only to apply some of nature's own specifics against the disease and decay to which our bodies are subjected; and what else does the physician, when he tasks his art, and uses subtle compounds and cunning distillations, to revive our languishing powers, and avert the stroke of death for a season?

"In seeking to multiply the precious metals, also, we seek but to germinate and multiply, by natural means, a particular species of nature's productions; and what else does the husbandman, who consults times and seasons, and, by what might be deemed a natural magic, from the mere scattering of his hand, covers a whole plain with golden vegetation? The mysteries of our art, it is true, are deeply and darkly hidden; but it requires so much the more innocence and purity of thought, to penetrate unto them.

No, father! the true alchymist must be pure in mind and body; he must be temperate, patient, chaste, watchful, meek, humble, devout. 'My son,' says Hermes Trismegestes, the great master of our art, 'my son, I recommend you above all things to fear God.' And indeed it is only by devout castigation of the senses, and purification of the soul that the alchymist is enabled to enter into the sacred chambers of truth. 'Labour, pray, and read,' is the motto of our science. As De Nuysment well observes, 'These high and singular favours are granted unto none, save only unto the sons of God, (that is to say, the virtuous and devout,) who, under his paternal benediction, have obtained the opening of the same, by the helping hand of the queen of arts, divine Philosophy.' Indeed, so sacred has the nature of this knowledge been considered, that we are told it has four times been expressly communicated by God to man, having made a part of that cabalistical wisdom which was revealed to Adam to console him for the loss of Paradise; and to Moses in the bush, and to Solomon in a dream, and to Esdras by the angel.

"So far from demons and malign spirits being the friends and abettors of the alchymist, they are the continual foes with which he has to contend. It is their constant endeavour to shut up the avenues to those truths which would enable him to rise above the abject state into which he has fallen, and return to that excellence which was his original birthright. For what would be the effect of this length of days, and this abundant wealth, but to enable the possessor to go on from art to art, from science to science, with energies unimpaired by sickness, uninterrupted by death? For this have sages and philosophers shut themselves up in cells and solitudes; buried themselves in caves and dens of the earth; turning from the joys of life, and the pleasance of the world; enduring scorn, poverty, persecution. For this was Raymond Lully stoned to death in Mauritania. For this did the immortal Pietro D'Abano suffer persecution at Padua, and, when he escaped from his oppressors by death, was despitefully burnt in effigy. For this have illustrious men of all nations intrepidly suffered martyrdom. For this, if unmolested, have they assiduously employed the latest hour of life, the expiring throb of existence; hoping to the last that they might yet seize upon the prize for which they had struggled, and pluck themselves back even from the very jaws of the grave!

"For, when once the alchymist shall have attained the object of his toils; when the sublime secret shall be revealed to his gaze, how glorious will be the change in his condition! How will he emerge from his solitary retreat, like the sun breaking forth from the darksome chamber of the night, and darting his beams throughout the earth! Gifted with perpetual youth and boundless riches, to what heights of wisdom may he attain! How may he carry on, uninterrupted, the thread of knowledge, which has hitherto been snapped at the death of each philosopher! And, as the increase of wisdom is the increase of virtue, how may he become the benefactor of his fellow-men; dispensing, with liberal but cautious and discriminating hand, that inexhaustible wealth which is at his disposal; banishing poverty, which is the cause of so much sorrow and wickedness; encouraging the arts; promoting discoveries, and enlarging all the means of virtuous enjoyment! His life will be the connecting band of generations. History will live in his recollection; distant ages will speak with his tongue. The nations of the earth will look to him as their preceptor, and kings will sit at his feet and learn wisdom. Oh glorious! oh celestial alchymy!"—

Here he was interrupted by the inquisitor, who had suffered him to go on thus far, in hopes of gathering something from his unguarded enthusiasm. "Senor," said he, "this is all rambling, visionary talk. You are charged with sorcery, and in defence you give us a rhapsody about alchymy. Have you nothing better than this to offer in your defence?"

The old man slowly resumed his seat, but did not deign a reply. The fire that had beamed in his eye gradually expired. His cheek resumed its wonted paleness; but he did not relapse into inanity. He sat with a steady, serene, patient look. Like one prepared not to contend, but to suffer.

His trial continued for a long time, with cruel mockery of justice, for no witnesses were ever in this court confronted with the accused, and the latter had continually to defend himself in the dark. Some unknown and powerful enemy had alleged charges against the unfortunate alchymist, but who he could not imagine. Stranger and sojourner as he was in the land, solitary and harmless in his pursuits, how could he have provoked such hostility? The tide of secret testimony, however, was too strong against him; he was convicted of the crime of magic, and condemned to expiate his sins at the stake, at the approaching auto da fé.

While the unhappy alchymist was undergoing his trial at the inquisition, his daughter was exposed to trials no less severe. Don Ambrosio, into whose hands she had fallen, was, as has before been intimated, one of the most daring and lawless profligates in all Granada. He was a man of hot blood and fiery passions, who stopped at nothing in the gratification of his desires; yet with all this he possessed manners, address, and accomplishments, that had made him eminently successful among the sex. From the palace to the cottage he had extended his amorous enterprises; his serenades harassed the slumbers of half the husbands in Granada; no balcony was too high for his adventurous attempts, nor any cottage too lowly for his perfidious seductions. Yet he was as fickle as he was ardent; success had made him vain and capricious; he had no sentiment to attach him to the victim of his arts; and many a pale cheek and fading eye, languishing amidst the sparkling of jewels, and many a breaking heart, throbbing under the rustic bodice, bore testimony to his triumphs and his faithlessness.

He was sated, however, by easy conquests, and wearied of a life of continual and prompt gratification. There had been a degree of difficulty and enterprise in the pursuit of Inez that he had never before experienced. It had aroused him from the monotony of mere sensual life, and stimulated him with the charm of adventure. He had become an epicure in pleasure; and now that he had this coy beauty in his power, he was determined to protract his enjoyment, by the gradual conquest of her scruples and downfall of her virtue. He was vain of his person and address, which he thought no woman could long withstand; and it was a kind of trial of skill to endeavour to gain, by art and fascination, what he was secure of obtaining at any time by violence.

When Inez, therefore, was brought into his presence by his emissaries, he affected not to notice her terror and surprise, but received her with formal and stately courtesy. He was too wary a fowler to flutter the bird when just entangled in the net. To her eager and wild inquiries about her father, he begged her not to be alarmed; that he was safe, and had been there, but was engaged elsewhere in an affair of moment, from which he would soon return; in the meantime, he had left word that she should await his return in patience. After some stately expressions of general civility, Don Ambrosio made a ceremonious bow and retired.

The mind of Inez was full of trouble and perplexity. The stately formality of Don Ambrosio was so unexpected as to check the accusations and reproaches that were springing to her lips. Had he had evil designs, would he have treated her with such frigid ceremony when he had her in his power? But why, then, was she brought to his house? Was not the mysterious disappearance of Antonio connected with this? A thought suddenly darted into her mind. Antonio had again met with Don Ambrosio—they had fought—Antonio was wounded—perhaps dying! It was him to whom her father had gone—it was at his request that Don Ambrosio had sent for them, to soothe his dying moments! These, and a thousand such horrible suggestions, harassed her mind; but she tried in vain to get information from the domestics; they knew nothing but that her father had been there, had gone, and would soon return.

Thus passed a night of tumultuous thought, and vague yet cruel apprehensions. She knew not what to do or what to believe—whether she ought to fly, or to remain; but if to fly, how was she to extricate herself?—and where was she to seek her father? As the day dawned without any intelligence of him, her alarm increased; at length a message was brought from him, saying that circumstances prevented his return to her, but begging her to hasten to him without delay.

With an eager and throbbing heart did she set forth with the men that were to conduct her. She little thought, however, that she was merely changing her prison-house. Don Ambrosio had feared lest she should be traced to his residence in Granada; or that he might be interrupted there before he could accomplish his plan of seduction. He had her now conveyed, therefore, to a mansion which he possessed in one of the mountain solitudes in the neighbourhood of Granada; a lonely, but beautiful retreat. In vain, on her arrival, did she look around for her father or Antonio; none but strange faces met her eye: menials, profoundly respectful, but who knew nor saw anything but what their master pleased.

She had scarcely arrived before Don Ambrosio made his appearance, less stately in his manner, but still treating her with the utmost delicacy and deference. Inez was too much agitated and alarmed to be baffled by his courtesy, and became vehement in her demand to be conducted to her father.

Don Ambrosio now put on an appearance of the greatest embarrassment and emotion. After some delay, and much pretended confusion, he at length confessed that the seizure of her father was all a stratagem; a mere false alarm, to procure him the present opportunity of having access to her, and endeavouring to mitigate that obduracy, and conquer that repugnance, which he declared had almost driven him to distraction.

He assured her that her father was again at home in safety, and occupied in his usual pursuits; having been fully satisfied that his daughter was in honourable hands, and would soon be restored to him. It was in vain that she threw herself at his feet, and implored to be set at liberty; he only replied by gentle entreaties, that she would pardon the seeming violence he had to use; and that she would trust a little while to his honour. "You are here," said he, "absolute mistress of every thing: nothing shall be said or done to offend you; I will not even intrude upon your ear the unhappy passion that is devouring my heart. Should you require it, I will even absent myself from your presence; but, to part with you entirely at present, with your mind full of doubts and resentments, would be worse than death to me. No, beautiful Inez, you must first know me a little better, and know by my conduct that my passion for you is as delicate and respectful as it is vehement."

The assurance of her father's safety had relieved Inez from one cause of torturing anxiety, only to render her fears the more violent on her own account. Don Ambrosio, however, continued to treat her with artful deference, that insensibly lulled her apprehensions. It is true she found herself a captive, but no advantage appeared to be taken of her helplessness. She soothed herself with the idea that a little while would suffice to convince Don Ambrosio of the fallacy of his hopes, and that he would be induced to restore her to her home. Her transports of terror and affliction, therefore, subsided, in a few days, into a passive, yet anxious melancholy, with which she awaited the hoped-for event.

In the meanwhile, all those artifices were employed that are calculated to charm the senses, ensnare the feelings, and dissolve the heart into tenderness. Don Ambrosio was a master of the subtle arts of seduction. His very mansion breathed an enervating atmosphere of languor and delight. It was here, amidst twilight saloons and dreamy chambers, buried among groves of orange and myrtle, that he shut himself up at times from the prying world, and gave free scope to the gratification of his pleasures.

The apartments were furnished in the most sumptuous and voluptuous manner; the silken couches swelled to the touch, and sunk in downy softness beneath the slightest pressure. The paintings and statues, all told some classic tale of love, managed, however, with an insidious delicacy; which, while it banished the grossness that might disgust, was the more calculated to excite the imagination. There the blooming Adonis was seen, not breaking away to pursue the boisterous chase, but crowned with flowers, and languishing in the embraces of celestial beauty. There Acis wooed his Galatea in the shade, with the Sicilian sea spreading in halcyon serenity before them. There were depicted groups of fauns and dryads, fondly reclining in summer bowers, and listening to the liquid piping of the reed; or the wanton satyrs, surprising some wood-nymph during her noontide slumber. There, too, on the storied tapestry, might be seen the chaste Diana, stealing, in the mystery of moonlight, to kiss the sleeping Endymion; while Cupid and Psyche, entwined in immortal marble, breathed on each other's lips the early kiss of love.

The ardent rays of the sun were excluded from these balmy halls; soft and tender music from unseen musicians floated around, seeming to mingle with the perfumes that were exhaled from a thousand flowers. At night, when the moon shed a fairy light over the scene, the tender serenade would rise from among the bowers of the garden, in which the fine voice of Don Ambrosio might often be distinguished; or the amorous flute would be heard along the mountain, breathing in its pensive cadences the very soul of a lover's melancholy.

Various entertainments were also devised to dispel her loneliness, and to charm away the idea of confinement. Groups of Andalusian dancers performed, in the splendid saloons, the various picturesque dances of their country; or represented little amorous ballets, which turned upon some pleasing scene of pastoral coquetry and courtship. Sometimes there were bands of singers, who, to the romantic guitar, warbled forth ditties full of passion and tenderness.

Thus all about her enticed to pleasure and voluptuousnesss; but the heart of Inez turned with distaste from this idle mockery. The tears would rush into her eyes, as her thoughts reverted from this scene of profligate splendour, to the humble but virtuous home from whence she had been betrayed; or if the witching power of music ever soothed her into a tender reverie, it was to dwell with fondness on the image of Antonio. But if Don Ambrosio, deceived by this transient calm, should attempt at such time to whisper his passion, she would start as from a dream, and recoil from him with involuntary shuddering.

She had passed one long day of more than ordinary sadness, and in the evening a band of these hired performers were exerting all the animating powers of song and dance to amuse her. But while the lofty saloon resounded with their warblings, and the light sound of feet upon its marble pavement kept time to the cadence of the song, poor Inez, with her face buried in the silken couch on which she reclined, was only rendered more wretched by the sound of gayety.

At length her attention was caught by the voice of one of the singers, that brought with it some indefinite recollections. She raised her head, and cast an anxious look at the performers, who, as usual, were at the lower end of the saloon.

One of them advanced a little before the others. It was a female, dressed in a fanciful, pastoral garb, suited to the character she was sustaining; but her countenance was not to be mistaken. It was the same ballad-singer that had twice crossed her path, and given her mysterious intimations of the lurking mischief that surrounded her. When the rest of the performances were concluded, she seized a tambourine, and, tossing it aloft, danced alone to the melody of her own voice. In the course of her dancing, she approached to where Inez reclined: and as she struck the tambourine, contrived dexterously to throw a folded paper on the couch. Inez seized it with avidity, and concealed it in her bosom. The singing and dancing were at an end; the motley crew retired; and Inez, left alone, hastened with anxiety to unfold the paper thus mysteriously conveyed. It was written in an agitated, and almost illegible handwriting: "Be on your guard! you are surrounded by treachery. Trust not to the forbearance of Don Ambrosio; you are marked out for his prey. An humble victim to his perfidy gives you this warning; she is encompassed by too many dangers to be more explicit.—Your father is in the dungeons of the inquisition!"

The brain of Inez reeled, as she read this dreadful scroll. She was less filled with alarm at her own danger, than horror at her father's situation.

The moment Don Ambrosio appeared, she rushed and threw herself at his feet, imploring him to save her father. Don Ambrosio stared with astonishment; but immediately regaining his self-possession, endeavoured to soothe her by his blandishments, and by assurances that her father was in safety. She was not to be pacified; her fears were too much aroused to be trifled with. She declared her knowledge of her father's being a prisoner of the inquisition, and reiterated her frantic supplications that he would save him.

Don Ambrosio paused for a moment in perplexity, but was too adroit to be easily confounded. "That your father is a prisoner," replied he, "I have long known. I have concealed it from you, to save you from fruitless anxiety. You now know the real reason of the restraint I have put upon your liberty: I have been protecting instead of detaining you. Every exertion has been made in your father's favour; but I regret to say, the proofs of the offences of which he stands charged have been too strong to be controverted. Still," added he, "I have it in my power to save him; I have influence, I have means at my beck; it may involve me, it is true, in difficulties, perhaps in disgrace; but what would I not do, in the hope of being rewarded by your favour? Speak, beautiful Inez," said he, his eyes kindling with sudden eagerness; "it is with you to say the word that seals your father's fate. One kind word—say but you will be mine, and you will behold me at your feet, your father at liberty and in affluence, and we shall all be happy!"

Inez drew back from him with scorn and disbelief. "My father," exclaimed she, "is too innocent and blameless to be convicted of crime; this is some base, some cruel artifice!" Don Ambrosio repeated his asseverations, and with them also his dishonourable proposals; but his eagerness overshot its mark: her indignation and her incredulity were alike awakened by his base suggestions; and he retired from her presence, checked and awed by the sudden pride and dignity of her demeanour.

The unfortunate Inez now became a prey to the most harrowing anxieties. Don Ambrosio saw that the mask had fallen from his face, and that the nature of his machinations was revealed. He had gone too far to retrace his steps, and assume the affectation of tenderness and respect; indeed, he was mortified and incensed at her insensibility to his attractions, and now only sought to subdue her through her fears. He daily represented to her the dangers that threatened her father, and that it was in his power alone to avert them. Inez was still incredulous. She was too ignorant of the nature of the inquisition, to know that even innocence was not always a protection from its cruelties; and she confided too surely in the virtue of her father, to believe that any accusation could prevail against him.

At length Don Ambrosio, to give an effectual blow to her confidence, brought her the proclamation of the approaching auto da fé, in which the prisoners were enumerated. She glanced her eye over it, and beheld her father's name, condemned to the stake for sorcery!

For a moment she stood transfixed with horror. Don Ambrosio seized upon the transient calm. "Think, now, beautiful Inez," said he, with a tone of affected tenderness, "his life is still in your hands; one word from you, one kind word, and I can yet save him."

"Monster! wretch!" cried she, coming to herself, and recoiling from him with insuperable abhorrence: "'Tis you that are the cause of this—'tis you that are his murderer!" Then, wringing her hands, she broke forth into exclamations of the most frantic agony.

The perfidious Ambrosio saw the torture of her soul, and anticipated from it a triumph. He saw that she was in no mood, during her present paroxysm, to listen to his words; but he trusted that the horrors of lonely rumination would break down her spirit, and subdue her to his will. In this, however, he was disappointed. Many were the vicissitudes of mind of the wretched Inez; at one time, she would embrace his knees, with piercing supplications; at another, she would shrink with nervous horror at his very approach; but any intimation of his passion only excited the same emotion of loathing and detestation.

At length the fatal day drew nigh. "To-morrow," said Don Ambrosio, as he left her one evening, "to-morrow is the auto da fé. To-morrow you will hear the sound of the bell that tolls your father to his death. You will almost see the smoke that rises from the funeral pile. I leave you to yourself. It is yet in my power to save him. Think whether you can stand to-morrow's horrors without shrinking! Think whether you can endure the after-reflection, that you were the cause of his death, and that merely through a perversity in refusing proffered happiness."

What a night was it to Inez!—her heart already harassed and almost broken, by repeated and protracted anxieties; her strength wasted and enfeebled. On every side, horrors awaited her; her father's death, her own dishonour—there seemed no escape from misery or perdition. "Is there no relief from man—no pity in heaven?" exclaimed she. "What —what have we done, that we should be thus wretched?"

As the dawn approached, the fever of her mind arose to agony; a thousand times did she try the doors and windows of her apartment, in the desperate hope of escaping. Alas! with all the splendour of her prison, it was too faithfully secured for her weak hands to work deliverance. Like a poor bird, that beats its wings against its gilded cage, until it sinks panting in despair, so she threw herself on the floor in hopeless anguish. Her blood grew hot in her veins, her tongue was parched, her temples throbbed with violence, she gasped rather than breathed; it seemed as if her brain was on fire. "Blessed Virgin!" exclaimed she, clasping her hands and turning up her strained eyes, "look down with pity, and support me in this dreadful hour!"

Just as the day began to dawn, she heard a key turn softly in the door of her apartment. She dreaded lest it should be Don Ambrosio; and the very thought of him gave her a sickening pang. It was a female clad in a rustic dress, with her face concealed by her mantilla. She stepped silently into the room, looked cautiously round, and then, uncovering her face, revealed the well-known features of the ballad-singer. Inez uttered an exclamation of surprise, almost of joy. The unknown started back, pressed her finger on her lips enjoining silence, and beckoned her to follow. She hastily wrapped herself in her veil, and obeyed. They passed with quick, but noiseless steps through an antechamber, across a spacious hall, and along a corridor; all was silent; the household was yet locked in sleep. They came to a door, to which the unknown applied a key. Inez's heart misgave her; she knew not but some new treachery was menacing her; she laid her cold hand on the stranger's arm: "Whither are you leading me?" said she. "To liberty," replied the other, in a whisper.

"Do you know the passages about this mansion?"

"But too well!" replied the girl, with a melancholy shake of the head. There was an expression of sad veracity in her countenance, that was not to be distrusted. The door opened on a small terrace, which was overlooked by several windows of the mansion.

"We must move across this quickly," said the girl, "or we may be observed."

They glided over it, as if scarce touching the ground. A flight of steps led down into the garden; a wicket at the bottom was readily unbolted: they passed with breathless velocity along one of the alleys, still in sight of the mansion, in which, however, no person appeared to be stirring. At length they came to a low private door in the wall, partly hidden by a fig-tree. It was secured by rusty bolts, that refused to yield to their feeble efforts.

"Holy Virgin!" exclaimed the stranger, "what is to be done? one moment more, and we may be discovered."

She seized a stone that lay near by: a few blows, and the bolt flew back; the door grated harshly as they opened it, and the next moment they found themselves in a narrow road.

"Now," said the stranger, "for Granada as quickly as possible! The nearer we approach it, the safer we shall be; for the road will be more frequented."

The imminent risk they ran of being pursued and taken, gave supernatural strength to their limbs; they flew, rather than ran. The day had dawned; the crimson streaks on the edge of the horizon gave tokens of the approaching sunrise; already the light clouds that floated in the western sky were tinged with gold and purple; though the broad plain of the Vega, which now began to open upon their view, was covered with the dark haze of morning. As yet they only passed a few straggling peasants on the road, who could have yielded them no assistance in case of their being overtaken. They continued to hurry forward, and had gained a considerable distance, when the strength of Inez, which had only been sustained by the fever of her mind, began to yield to fatigue: she slackened her pace, and faltered.

"Alas!" said she, "my limbs fail me! I can go no farther!"

"Bear up, bear up," replied her companion, cheeringly; "a little farther, and we shall be safe: look! yonder is Granada, just showing itself in the valley below us. A little farther, and we shall come to the main road, and then we shall find plenty of passengers to protect us."

Inez, encouraged, made fresh efforts to get forward, but her weary limbs were unequal to the eagerness of her mind; her mouth and throat were parched by agony and terror: she gasped for breath, and leaned for support against a rock. "It is all in vain!" exclaimed she; "I feel as though I should faint."

"Lean on me," said the other; "let us get into the shelter of yon thicket, that will conceal us from the view; I hear the sound of water, which will refresh you."

With much difficulty they reached the thicket, which overhung a small mountain-stream, just where its sparkling waters leaped over the rock and fell into a natural basin. Here Inez sank upon the ground, exhausted. Her companion brought water in the palms of her hands, and bathed her pallid temples. The cooling drops revived her; she was enabled to get to the margin of the stream, and drink of its crystal current; then, reclining her head on the bosom of her deliverer, she was first enabled to murmur forth her heartfelt gratitude.

"Alas!" said the other, "I deserve no thanks; I deserve not the good opinion you express. In me you behold a victim of Don Ambrosio's arts. In early years he seduced me from the cottage of my parents: look! at the foot of yonder blue mountain, in the distance, lies my native village: but it is no longer a home for me. From thence he lured me, when I was too young for reflection; he educated me, taught me various accomplishments, made me sensible to love, to splendour, to refinement; then, having grown weary of me, he neglected me, and cast me upon the world. Happily the accomplishments he taught me have kept me from utter want; and the love with which he inspired me has kept me from farther degradation. Yes! I confess my weakness; all his perfidy and wrongs cannot efface him from my heart. I have been brought up to love him; I have no other idol: I know him to be base, yet I cannot help adoring him. I am content to mingle among the hireling throng that administer to his amusements, that I may still hover about him, and linger in those halls where I once reigned mistress. What merit, then, have I in assisting your escape? I scarce know whether I am acting from sympathy and a desire to rescue another victim from his power; or jealousy, and an eagerness to remove too powerful a rival!"

While she was yet speaking, the sun rose in all its splendour; first lighting up the mountain summits, then stealing down height by height, until its rays gilded the domes and towers of Granada, which they could partially see from between the trees, below them. Just then the heavy tones of a bell came sounding from a distance, echoing, in sullen clang, along the mountain. Inez turned pale at the sound. She knew it to be the great bell of the cathedral, rung at sunrise on the day of the auto da fé, to give note of funeral preparation. Every stroke beat upon her heart, and inflicted an absolute, corporeal pang. She started up wildly. "Let us begone!" cried she; "there is not a moment for delay!"

"Stop!" exclaimed the other; "yonder are horsemen coming over the brow of that distant height; if I mistake not, Don Ambrosio is at their head.—Alas! 'tis he! we are lost. Hold!" continued she; "give me your scarf and veil; wrap yourself in this mantilla. I will fly up yon footpath that leads to the heights. I will let the veil flutter as I ascend; perhaps they may mistake me for you, and they must dismount to follow me. Do you hasten forward: you will soon reach the main road. You have jewels on your fingers: bribe the first muleteer you meet, to assist you on your way."

All this was said with hurried and breathless rapidity. The exchange of garments was made in an instant. The girl darted up the mountain-path, her white veil fluttering among the dark shrubbery, while Inez, inspired with new strength, or rather new terror, flew to the road, and trusted to Providence to guide her tottering steps to Granada.

All Granada was in agitation on the morning of this dismal day. The heavy bell of the cathedral continued to utter its clanging tones, that pervaded every part of the city, summoning all persons to the tremendous spectacle that was about to be exhibited. The streets through which the procession was to pass were crowded with the populace. The windows, the roofs, every place that could admit a face or a foothold, were alive with spectators. In the great square, a spacious scaffolding, like an amphitheatre, was erected, where the sentences of the prisoners were to be read, and the sermon of faith to be preached; and close by were the stakes prepared, where the condemned were to be burnt to death. Seats were arranged for the great, the gay, the beautiful; for such is the horrible curiosity of human nature, that this cruel sacrifice was attended with more eagerness than a theatre, or even a bull-feast.

As the day advanced, the scaffolds and balconies were filled with expecting multitudes; the sun shone brightly upon fair faces and gallant dresses; one would have thought it some scene of elegant festivity, instead of an exhibition of human agony and death. But what a different spectacle and ceremony was this, from those which Granada exhibited in the days of her Moorish splendour! "Her galas, her tournaments, her sports of the ring, her fêtes of St. John, her music, her Zambras, and admirable tilts of canes! Her serenades, her concerts, her songs in Generaliffe! The costly liveries of the Abencerrages, their exquisite inventions, the skill and valour of the Alabaces, the superb dresses of the Zegries, Mazas, and Gomeles!"[10]—All these were at an end. The days of chivalry were over. Instead of the prancing cavalcade, with neighing steed and lively trumpet; with burnished lance, and helm, and buckler; with rich confusion of plume, and scarf, and banner, where purple, and scarlet, and green, and orange, and every gay colour, were mingled with cloth of gold and fair embroidery; instead of this, crept on the gloomy pageant of superstition, in cowl and sackcloth; with cross and coffin, and frightful symbols of human suffering. In place of the frank, hardy knight, open and brave, with his lady's favour in his casque, and amorous motto on his shield, looking, by gallant deeds, to win the smile of beauty, came the shaven, unmanly monk, with downcast eyes, and head and heart bleached in the cold cloister, secretly exulting in this bigot triumph.

The sound of the bells gave notice that the dismal procession was advancing. It passed slowly through the principal streets of the city, bearing in advance the awful banner of the Holy Office. The prisoners walked singly, attended by confessors, and guarded by familiars of the inquisition. They were clad in different garments, according to the nature of their punishments; those who were to suffer death wore the hideous Samarra, painted with flames and demons. The procession was swelled by choirs of boys, different religious orders and public dignitaries, and above all, by the fathers of the faith, moving "with slow pace, and profound gravity, truly triumphing as becomes the principal generals of that great victory."[11]

As the sacred banner of the inquisition advanced, the countless throng sunk on their knees before it; they bowed their faces to the very earth as it passed, and then slowly rose again, like a great undulating billow. A murmur of tongues prevailed as the prisoners approached, and eager eyes

---

[10] Rodd's Civil Wars of Granada.

[11] Gonsalvius, p. 135.

were strained, and fingers pointed, to distinguish the different orders of penitents, whose habits denoted the degree of punishment they were to undergo. But as those drew near whose frightful garb marked them as destined to the flames, the noise of the rabble subsided; they seemed almost to hold in their breath; filled with that strange and dismal interest with which we contemplate a human being on the verge of suffering and death.

It is an awful thing—a voiceless, noiseless multitude! The hushed and gazing stillness of the surrounding thousands, heaped on walls, and gates, and roofs, and hanging, as it were, in clusters, heightened the effect of the pageant that moved drearily on. The low murmuring of the priests could now be heard in prayer and exhortation, with the faint responses of the prisoners, and now and then the voices of the choir at a distance, chanting the litanies of the saints.

The faces of the prisoners were ghastly and disconsolate. Even those who had been pardoned, and wore the Sanbenito, or penitential garment, bore traces of the horrors they had undergone. Some were feeble and tottering, from long confinement; some crippled and distorted by various tortures; every countenance was a dismal page, on which might be read the secrets of their prison-house. But in the looks of those condemned to death, there was something fierce and eager. They seemed men harrowed up by the past, and desperate as to the future. They were anticipating, with spirits fevered by despair, and fixed and clenched determination, the vehement struggle with agony and death which they were shortly to undergo. Some cast now and then a wild and anguished look about them, upon the shining day; the "sun-bright palaces," the gay, the beautiful world, which they were soon to quit for ever; or a glance of sudden indignation at the thronging thousands, happy in liberty and life, who seemed, in contemplating their frightful situation, to exult in their own comparative security.

One among the condemned, however, was an exception to these remarks. It was an aged man, somewhat bowed down, with a serene, though dejected countenance, and a beaming, melancholy eye. It was the alchymist. The populace looked upon him with a degree of compassion, which they were not prone to feel towards criminals condemned by the inquisition; but when they were told that he was convicted of the crime of magic, they drew back with awe and abhorrence.

The procession had reached the grand square. The first part had already mounted the scaffolding, and the condemned were approaching. The press of the populace became excessive, and was repelled, as it were, in billows by the guards. Just as the condemned were entering the square, a shrieking was heard among the crowd. A female, pale, frantic, dishevelled, was seen struggling through the multitude. "My father! my father!" was all the cry she uttered, but it thrilled through every heart. The crowd instinctively drew back, and made way for her as she advanced.

The poor alchymist had made his peace with Heaven, and, by a hard struggle, had closed his heart upon the world, when the voice of his child called him once more back to worldly thought and agony. He turned towards the well-known voice; his knees smote together; he endeavoured to stretch forth his pinioned arms, and felt himself clasped in the embraces of his child. The emotions of both were too agonizing for utterance. Convulsive sobs and broken exclamations, and embraces more of anguish than tenderness, were all that passed between them. The procession was interrupted for a moment. The astonished monks and familiars were filled with involuntary respect, at the agony of natural affection. Ejaculations of pity broke from the crowd, touched by the filial piety, the extraordinary and hopeless anguish, of so young and beautiful a being.

Every attempt to soothe her, and prevail on her to retire, was unheeded; at length they endeavoured to separate her from her father by force. The movement roused her from her temporary abandonment. With a sudden paroxysm of fury, she snatched a sword from one of the familiars. Her late pale countenance was flushed with rage, and fire flashed from her once soft and languishing eyes. The guards shrunk back with awe. There was something in this filial frenzy, this feminine tenderness wrought up to desperation, that touched even their hardened hearts. They endeavoured to pacify her, but in vain. Her eye was eager and quick, as the she-wolf's guarding her young. With one arm she pressed her father to her bosom, with the other she menaced every one that approached.

The patience of the guards was soon exhausted. They had held back in awe, but not in fear. With all her desperation the weapon was soon wrested from her feeble hand, and she was borne shrieking and struggling among the crowd. The rabble murmured compassion; but such was the dread inspired by the inquisition, that no one attempted to interfere.

The procession again resumed its march. Inez was ineffectually struggling to release herself from the hands of the familiars that detained her, when suddenly she saw Don Ambrosio before her. "Wretched girl!" exclaimed he with fury, "why have you fled from your friends? Deliver her," said he to the familiars, "to my domestics; she is under my protection."

His creatures advanced to seize her. "Oh, no! oh, no!" cried she, with new terrors, and clinging to the familiars, "I have fled from no friends. He is not my protector! He is the murderer of my father!"

The familiars were perplexed; the crowd pressed on, with eager curiosity. "Stand off!" cried the fiery Ambrosio, dashing the throng from around him. Then turning to the familiars, with sudden moderation, "My friends," said he, "deliver this poor girl to me. Her distress has turned her brain; she has escaped from her friends and protectors this morning; but a little quiet and kind treatment will restore her to tranquillity."

"I am not mad! I am not mad!" cried she, vehemently. "Oh, save me!—save me from these men! I have no protector on earth but my father, and him they are murdering!"

The familiars shook their heads; her wildness corroborated the assertions of Don Ambrosio, and his apparent rank commanded respect and belief. They relinquished their charge to him, and he was consigning the struggling Inez to his creatures.

"Let go your hold, villain!" cried a voice from among the crowd—and Antonio was seen eagerly tearing his way through the press of people.

"Seize him! seize him!" cried Don Ambrosio to the familiars, "'tis an accomplice of the sorcerer's."

"Liar!" retorted Antonio, as he thrust the mob to the right and left, and forced himself to the spot.

The sword of Don Ambrosio flashed in an instant from the scabbard; the student was armed, and equally alert. There was a fierce clash of weapons: the crowd made way for them as they fought, and closed again, so as to hide them from the view of Inez. All was tumult and confusion for a moment; when there was a kind of shout from the spectators, and the mob again opening, she beheld, as she thought, Antonio weltering in his blood.

This new shock was too great for her already overstrained intellect. A giddiness seized upon her; every thing seemed to whirl before her eyes; she gasped some incoherent words, and sunk senseless upon the ground.

Days—weeks elapsed, before Inez returned to consciousness. At length she opened her eyes, as if out of a troubled sleep. She was lying upon a magnificent bed, in a chamber richly furnished with pier-glasses, and massive tables inlaid with silver, of exquisite workmanship. The walls were covered with tapestry; the cornices richly gilded; through the door, which stood open, she perceived a superb saloon, with statues and crystal lustres, and a magnificent suite of apartments beyond. The casements of the room were open to admit the soft breath of summer, which stole in, laden with perfumes from a neighbouring garden; from whence, also, the refreshing sound of fountains and the sweet notes of birds came in mingled music to her ear.

Female attendants were moving, with noiseless step, about the chamber; but she feared to address them. She doubted whether this was not all delusion, or whether she was not still in the palace of Don Ambrosio, and that her escape, and all its circumstances, had not been but a feverish dream. She closed her eyes again, endeavouring to recall the past, and to separate the real from the imaginary. The last scenes of consciousness, however, rushed too forcibly, with all their horrors, to her mind to be doubted, and she turned shuddering from the recollection, to gaze once more on the quiet and serene magnificence around her. As she again opened her eyes, they rested on an object that at once dispelled every alarm. At the head of her bed sat a venerable form, watching over her with a look of fond anxiety—it was her father!

I will not attempt to describe the scene that ensued; nor the moments of rapture which more than repaid all the sufferings that her affectionate heart had undergone. As soon as their feelings had become more calm, the alchymist stepped out of the room to introduce a stranger, to whom he was indebted for his life and liberty. He returned, leading in Antonio, no longer in his poor scholar's garb, but in the rich dress of a nobleman.

The feelings of Inez were almost overpowered by these sudden reverses, and it was some time before she was sufficiently composed to comprehend the explanation of this seeming romance.

It appeared that the lover, who had sought her affections in the lowly guise of a student, was only son and heir of a powerful grandee of Valentia. He had been placed at the university of Salamanca; but a lively curiosity, and an eagerness for adventure, had induced him to abandon the university, without his father's consent, and to visit various parts of Spain. His rambling inclination satisfied, he had remained incognito for a time at Granada, until, by farther study and self-regulation, he could prepare himself to return home with credit, and atone for his transgressions against paternal authority.

How hard he had studied, does not remain on record. All that we know is his romantic adventure of the tower. It was at first a mere youthful caprice, excited by a glimpse of a beautiful face. In becoming a disciple of the alchymist, he probably thought of nothing more than pursuing a light love affair. Farther acquaintance, however, had completely fixed his affections; and he had determined to conduct Inez and her father to Valentia, and to trust to her merits to secure his father's consent to their union.

In the meantime, he had been traced to his concealment. His father had received intelligence of his being entangled in the snares of a mysterious adventurer and his daughter, and likely to become the dupe of the fascinations of the latter. Trusty emissaries had been despatched to seize upon him by main force, and convey him without delay to the paternal home.

What eloquence he had used with his father, to convince him of the innocence, the honour, and the high descent of the alchymist, and of the exalted worth of his daughter, does not appear. All that we know is, that the father, though a very passionate, was a very reasonable man, as appears by his consenting that his son should return to Granada, and conduct Inez as his affianced bride to Valentia.

Away, then, Don Antonio hurried back, full of joyous anticipations. He still forbore to throw off his disguise, fondly picturing to himself what would be the surprise of Inez, when, having won her heart and hand as a poor wandering scholar, he should raise her and her father at once to opulence and splendour.

On his arrival he had been shocked at finding the tower deserted by its inhabitants. In vain he sought for intelligence concerning them; a mystery hung over their disappearance which he could not penetrate, until he was thunderstruck, on accidentally reading a list of the prisoners at the impending auto da fé, to find the name of his venerable master among the condemned.

It was the very morning of the execution. The procession was already on its way to the grand square. Not a moment was to be lost. The grand inquisitor was a relation of Don Antonio, though they had never met. His first impulse was to make himself known; to exert all his family influence, the weight of his name, and the power of his eloquence, in vindication of the alchymist. But the grand inquisitor was already proceeding, in all his pomp, to the place where the fatal ceremony was to be performed. How was he to be approached? Antonio threw himself into the crowd, in a fever of anxiety, and was forcing his way to the scene of horror, where he arrived just in time to rescue Inez, as has been mentioned.

It was Don Ambrosio that fell in their contest. Being desperately wounded, and thinking his end approaching, he had confessed to an attending father of the inquisition, that he was the sole cause of the alchymist's condemnation, and that the evidence on which it was grounded was altogether false. The testimony of Don Antonio came in corroboration of this avowal; and his relationship to the grand inquisitor had, in all probability, its proper weight. Thus was the poor alchymist snatched, in a manner, from the very flames; and so great had been the sympathy awakened in his case, that for once a populace rejoiced at being disappointed of an execution.

The residue of the story may readily be imagined, by every one versed in this valuable kind of history. Don Antonio espoused the lovely Inez, and took her and her father with him to Valentia. As she had been a loving and dutiful daughter, so she proved a true and tender wife. It was not long before Don Antonio succeeded to his father's titles and estates, and he and his fair spouse were renowned for being the handsomest and happiest couple in all Valentia.

As to Don Ambrosio, he partially recovered to the enjoyment of a broken constitution and a blasted name, and hid his remorse and disgrace in a convent; while the poor victim of his arts, who had assisted Inez in her escape, unable to conquer the early passion that he had awakened in her bosom, though convinced of the baseness of the object, retired from the world, and became an humble sister in a nunnery.

The worthy alchymist took up his abode with his children. A pavilion, in the garden of their palace, was assigned to him as a laboratory, where he resumed his researches with renovated ardour, after the grand secret. He was now and then assisted by his son-in-law; but the latter slackened grievously in his zeal and diligence, after marriage. Still he would listen with profound gravity and attention to the old man's rhapsodies, and his quotations from Paracelsus, Sandivogius, and Pietro D'Abano, which daily grew longer and longer. In this way the good alchymist lived on quietly and comfortably, to what is called a good old age, that is to say, an age that is good for nothing; and unfortunately for mankind, was hurried out of life in his ninetieth year, just as he was on the point of discovering the Philosopher's Stone.

Such was the story of the captain's friend, with which we whiled away the morning. The captain was, every now and then, interrupted by questions and remarks, which I have not mentioned, lest I should break the continuity of the tale. He was a little disturbed, also, once or twice, by the general, who fell asleep, and breathed rather hard, to the great horror and annoyance of Lady Lillycraft. In a long and tender love scene, also, which was particularly to her ladyship's taste, the unlucky general, having his head a little sunk upon his breast, kept making a sound at regular intervals, very much like the word *pish*, long drawn out. At length he made an odd abrupt guttural sound, that suddenly awoke him; he hemmed, looked about with a slight degree of consternation, and then began to play with her ladyship's work-bag, which, however, she rather pettishly withdrew. The steady sound of the captain's voice was still too potent a soporific for the poor general; he kept gleaming up and sinking in the socket, until the cessation of the tale again roused him, when he started awake, put his foot down upon Lady Lillycraft's cur, the sleeping Beauty, which yelped and seized him by the leg, and, in a moment, the whole library resounded with yelpings and exclamations. Never did man more completely mar his fortunes while he was asleep. Silence being at length restored, the company expressed their thanks to the captain, and gave various opinions of the story. The parson's mind, I found, had been continually running upon the leaden manuscripts, mentioned in the beginning, as dug up at Granada, and he put several eager questions to the captain on the subject. The general could not well make out the drift of the story, but thought it a little confused. "I am glad, however," said he, "that they burnt the old chap of the tower; I have no doubt he was a notorious impostor."

Volume Second.

Under this cloud I walk, Gentlemen; pardon my rude assault. I am a traveller, who, having surveyed most of the terrestrial angles of this globe, am hither arrived, to peruse this little spot.
—Christmas Ordinary.

English Country Gentlemen.

His certain life, that never can deceive him,
Is full of thousand sweets, and rich content;
The smooth-leaved beeches in the field receive him
With coolest shade, till noontide's heat be spent.
His life is neither tost in boisterous seas
Or the vexatious world; or lost in slothful ease.
Pleased and full blest he lives, when he his God can please.
—Phineas Fletcher.

I take great pleasure in accompanying the Squire in his Perambulations about his estate, in which he is often attended by a kind of cabinet council. His prime minister, the steward, is a very worthy and honest old man, that assumes a right of way; that is to say, a right to have his own way, from having lived time out of mind on the place. He loves the estate even better than he does the Squire; and thwarts the latter sadly in many of his projects of improvement, being a little prone to disapprove of every plan that does not originate with himself.

In the course of one of these perambulations, I have known the Squire to point out some important alteration which he was contemplating, in the disposition or cultivation of the grounds; this, of course, would be opposed by the steward, and a long argument would ensue, over a stile, or on a rising piece of ground, until the Squire, who has a high opinion of the other's ability and integrity, would be fain to give up the point. This concession, I observed, would immediately mollify the old man; and, after walking over a field or two in silence, with his hands behind his back, chewing the cud of reflection, he would suddenly turn to the Squire, and observe, that "he had been turning the matter over in his mind, and, upon the whole, he believed he would take his honour's advice."

Christy, the huntsman, is another of the Squire's occasional attendants, to whom he continually refers in all matters of local history, as to a chronicle of the estate, having, in a manner, been acquainted with many of the trees, from the very time that they were acorns. Old Nimrod, as has been shown, is rather pragmatical in those points of knowledge on which he values himself; but the Squire rarely contradicts him, and is, in fact, one of the most indulgent potentates that ever was henpecked by his ministry.

He often laughs about it himself, and evidently yields to these old men more from the bent of his own humour than from any want of proper authority. He likes this honest independence of old age, and is well aware that these trusty followers love and honour him in their hearts. He is perfectly at ease about his own dignity, and the respect of those around him; nothing disgusts him sooner than any appearance of fawning or sycophancy.

I really have seen no display of royal state, that could compare with one of the Squire's progresses about his paternal fields and through his hereditary woodlands, with several of these faithful adherents about him, and followed by a body-guard of dogs. He encourages a frankness and manliness of deportment among his dependants, and is the personal friend of his tenants; inquiring into their concerns, and assisting them in times of difficulty and hardship. This has rendered him one of the most popular, and of course one of the happiest, of landlords.

Indeed, I do not know a more enviable condition of life, than that of an English gentleman, of sound judgment and good feelings, who passes the greater part of his time on an hereditary estate in the country. From the excellence of the roads, and the rapidity and exactness of the public conveyances, he is enabled to command all the comforts and conveniences, all the intelligence and novelties of the capital, while he is removed from its hurry and distraction. He has ample means of occupation and amusement, within his own domains; he may diversify his time, by rural occupations, by rural sports, by study, and by the delights of friendly society collected within his own hospitable halls.

Or, if his views and feelings are of a more extensive and liberal nature, he has it greatly in his power to do good, and to have that good immediately reflected back upon himself. He can render essential services to his country, by assisting in the disinterested administration of the laws; by watching over the opinions and principles of the lower orders around him; by diffusing among them those lights which may be important to their welfare; by mingling frankly among them, gaining their confidence, becoming the immediate auditor of their complaints, informing himself of their wants, making himself a channel through which their grievances may be quietly communicated to the proper sources of mitigation and relief; or by becoming, if need be, the intrepid and incorruptible guardian of their liberties—the enlightened champion of their rights.

All this, it appears to me, can be done without any sacrifice of personal dignity, without any degrading arts of popularity, without any truckling to vulgar prejudices or concurrence in vulgar clamour; but by the steady influence of sincere and friendly counsel, of fair, upright, and generous deportment. Whatever may be said of English mobs and English demagogues, I have never met with a people more open to reason, more considerate in their tempers, more tractable by argument in the roughest times, than the English. They are remarkably quick at discerning and appreciating whatever is manly and honourable. They are, by nature and habit, methodical and orderly; and they feel the value of all that is regular and respectable. They may occasionally be deceived by sophistry, and excited into turbulence by public distresses and the misrepresentations of designing men; but open their eyes, and they will eventually rally round the landmarks of steady truth and deliberate good sense. They are fond of established customs; they are fond of long-established names; and that love of order and quiet which characterizes the nation, gives a vast influence to the descendants of the old families, whose forefathers have been lords of the soil from time immemorial.

It is when the rich and well-educated and highly-privileged classes neglect their duties, when they neglect to study the interests, and conciliate the affections, and instruct the opinions, and champion the rights of the people, that the latter become discontented and turbulent, and fall into the hands of demagogues: the demagogue always steps in, where the patriot is wanting. There is a common high-handed cant among the high-feeding, and, as they fancy themselves, high-minded men, about putting down the mob; but all true physicians know that it is better to sweeten the blood than attack the tumour, to apply the emollient rather than the cautery. It is absurd, in a country like England, where there is so much freedom, and such a jealousy of right, for any man to assume an aristocratical tone, and to talk superciliously of the common people. There is no rank that makes him independent of the opinions and affections of his fellow-men; there is no rank nor distinction that severs him from his fellow-subjects; and if, by any gradual neglect or assumption on the one side, and discontent and jealousy on the other, the orders of society should really separate, let those who stand on the eminence beware that the chasm is not mining at their feet. The orders of society, in all well-constituted governments, are mutually bound together, and important to each other; there can be no such thing in a free government as a vacuum; and whenever one is likely to take place, by the drawing off of the rich and intelligent from the poor, the bad passions of society will rush in to fill up the space, and rend the whole asunder.

Though born and brought up in a republic, and more and more confirmed in republican principles by every year's observation and experience, yet I am not insensible to the excellence that may exist in other forms of government, nor to the fact that they may be more suitable to the situation and circumstances of the countries in which they exist: I have endeavoured rather to look at them as they are, and to observe how they are calculated to effect the end which they propose. Considering, therefore, the mixed nature of the government of this country, and its representative form, I have looked with admiration at the manner in which the wealth and influence and intelligence were spread over its whole surface; not as in some monarchies, drained from the country, and collected in towns and cities. I have considered the great rural establishments of the nobility, and the lesser establishments of the gentry, as so many reservoirs of wealth and intelligence distributed about the kingdom, apart from the towns, to irrigate, freshen, and fertilize the surrounding country. I have looked upon them, too, as the august retreat of patriots and statesmen, where, in the enjoyment of honourable independence and elegant leisure, they might train up their minds to appear in those legislative assemblies, whose debates and decisions form the study and precedents of other nations, and involve the interests of the world.

I have been both surprised and disappointed, therefore, at finding that on this subject I was often indulging in an Utopian dream, rather than a well-founded opinion. I have been concerned at finding that these fine estates were too often involved, and mortgaged, or placed in the hands of creditors, and the owners exiled from their paternal lands. There is an extravagance, I am told, that runs parallel with wealth; a lavish expenditure among the great; a senseless competition among the aspiring; a heedless, joyless dissipation among all the upper ranks, that often beggars even these splendid establishments, breaks down the pride and principles of their possessors, and makes too many of them mere place-hunters, or shifting absentees. It is thus that so many are thrown into the hands of government; and a court, which ought to be the most pure and honourable in Europe, is so often degraded by noble, but importunate time-servers. It is thus, too, that so many become exiles from their native land, crowding the hotels of foreign countries, and expending upon thankless strangers the wealth so hardly drained from their laborious peasantry. I have looked upon these latter with a mixture of censure and concern. Knowing the almost bigoted fondness of an Englishman for his native home, I can conceive what must be their compunction and regret, when, amidst the sunburnt plains of France, they call to mind the green fields of England; the hereditary groves which they have abandoned; and the hospitable roof of their fathers, which they have left desolate, or to be inhabited by strangers. But retrenchment is no plea for abandonment of country. They nave risen with the prosperity of the land; let them abide its fluctuations, and conform to its fortunes. It is not for the rich to fly, because the country is suffering: let them share, in their relative proportion, the common lot; they owe it to the land that has elevated them to honour and affluence. When the poor have to diminish their scanty morsels of bread; when they have to compound with the cravings of nature, and study with how little they can do, and not be starved; it is not then for the rich to fly, and diminish still farther the resources of the poor, that they themselves may live in splendour in a cheaper country. Let them rather retire to their estates, and there practise retrenchment. Let them return to that noble simplicity, that practical good sense, that honest pride, which form the foundation of true English character, and from them they may again rear the edifice of fair and honourable prosperity.

On the rural habits of the English nobility and gentry, on the manner in which they discharge their duties of their patrimonial possessions, depend greatly the virtue and welfare of the nation. So long as they pass the greater part of their time in the quiet and purity of the country; surrounded by the monuments of their illustrious ancestors; surrounded by every thing that can inspire generous pride, noble emulation, and amiable and magnanimous sentiment; so long they are safe, and in them the nation may repose its interests and its honour. But the moment that they become the servile throngers of court avenues, and give themselves up to the political intrigues and heartless dissipations of the metropolis, that moment they lose the real nobility Of their natures, and become the mere leeches of the country.

That the great majority of nobility and gentry in England are endowed with high notions of honour and independence, I thoroughly believe. They have evidenced it lately on very important questions, and have given an example of adherence to principle, in preference to party and power, that must have astonished many of the venal and obsequious courts of Europe. Such are the glorious effects of freedom, when infused into a constitution. But it seems to me, that they are apt to forget the positive nature of their duties, and to fancy that their eminent privileges are only so many means of self-indulgence. They should recollect, that in a constitution like that of England, the titled orders are intended to be as useful as they are ornamental, and it is their virtues alone that can render them both. Their duties are divided between the sovereign and the subjects; surrounding and giving lustre and dignity to the throne, and at the same time tempering and mitigating its rays, until they are transmitted in mild and genial radiance to the people. Born to leisure and opulence, they owe the exercise of their talents, and the expenditure of their wealth, to their native country. They may be compared to the clouds; which, being drawn up by the sun, and elevated in the heavens, reflect and magnify his splendour; while they repay the earth, from which they derive their sustenance, by returning their treasures to its bosom in fertilizing showers.

A Bachelor's Confessions.

"I'll live a private, pensive single life."
—The Collier of Croydon.

I was sitting in my room, a morning or two since, reading, when some one tapped at the door, and Master Simon entered. He had an unusually fresh appearance; he had put on a bright green riding-coat, with a bunch of violets in the button-hole, and had the air of an old bachelor trying to rejuvenate himself. He had not, however, his usual briskness and vivacity; but loitered about the room with somewhat of absence of manner, humming the old song—"Go, lovely rose, tell her that wastes her time and me;" and then, leaning against the window, and looking upon the landscape, he uttered a very audible sigh. As I had not been accustomed to see Master Simon in a pensive mood, I thought there might be some vexation preying on his mind, and I endeavoured to introduce a cheerful strain of conversation; but he was not in the vein to follow it up, and proposed that we should take a walk.

It was a beautiful morning, of that soft vernal temperature, that seems to thaw all the frost out of one's blood, and to set all nature in a ferment. The very fishes felt its influence; the cautious trout ventured out of his dark hole to seek his mate; the roach and the dace rose up to the surface of the brook to bask in the sunshine, and the amorous frog piped from among the rushes. If ever an oyster can really fall in love, as has been said or sung, it must be on such a morning.

The weather certainly had its effect even upon Master Simon, for he seemed obstinately bent upon the pensive mood. Instead of stepping briskly along, smacking his dog-whip, whistling quaint ditties, or telling sporting anecdotes, he leaned on my arm, and talked about the approaching nuptials; from whence he made several digressions upon the character of womankind, touched a little upon the tender passion, and made sundry very excellent, though rather trite, observations upon disappointments in love. It was evident that he had something on his mind which he wished to impart, but felt awkward in approaching it. I was curious to see to what this strain would lead; but was determined not to assist him. Indeed, I mischievously pretended to turn the conversation, and talked of his usual topics, dogs, horses, and hunting; but he was very brief in his replies, and invariably got back, by hook or by crook, into the sentimental vein.

At length we came to a clump of trees that overhung a whispering brook, with a rustic bench at their feet. The trees were grievously scored with letters and devices, which had grown out of all shape and size by the growth of the bark; and it appeared that this grove had served as a kind of register of the family loves from time immemorial. Here Master Simon made a pause, pulled up a tuft of flowers, threw them one by one into the water, and at length, turning somewhat abruptly upon me, asked me if I had ever been in love. I confess the question startled me a little, as I am not over-fond of making confessions of my amorous follies; and above all, should never dream of choosing my friend Master Simon for a confidant. He did not wait, however, for a reply; the inquiry was merely a prelude to a confession on his own part, and after several circumlocutions and whimsical preambles, he fairly disburthened himself of a very tolerable story of his having been crossed in love.

The reader will, very probably, suppose that it related to the gay widow who jilted him not long since at Doncaster races;—no such thing. It was about a sentimental passion that he once had for a most beautiful young lady, who wrote poetry and played on the harp. He used to serenade her; and, indeed, he described several tender and gallant scenes, in which he was evidently picturing himself in his mind's eye as some elegant hero of romance, though, unfortunately for the tale, I only saw him as he stood before me, a dapper little old bachelor, with a face like an apple that has dried with the bloom on it.

What were the particulars of this tender tale, I have already forgotten; indeed, I listened to it with a heart like a very pebble-stone, having hard work to repress a smile while Master Simon was putting on the amorous swain, uttering every now and then a sigh, and endeavouring to look sentimental and melancholy.

All that I recollect is that the lady, according to his account, was certainly a little touched; for she used to accept all the music that he copied for her harp, and all the patterns that he drew for her dresses; and he began to flatter himself, after a long course of delicate attentions, that he was gradually fanning up a gentle flame in her heart, when she suddenly accepted the hand of a rich, boisterous, fox-hunting baronet, without either music or sentiment, who carried her by storm after a fortnight's courtship.

Master Simon could not help concluding by some observation about "modest merit," and the power of gold over the sex. As a remembrance of his passion, he pointed out a heart carved on the bark of one of the trees; but which, in the process of time, had grown out into a large excrescence; and he showed me a lock of her hair, which he wore in a true-lover's knot, in a large gold brooch.

I have seldom met with an old bachelor that had not, at some time or other, his nonsensical moment, when he would become tender and sentimental, talk about the concerns of the heart, and have some confession of a delicate nature to make. Almost every man has some little trait of romance in his life, which he looks back to with fondness, and about which he is apt to grow garrulous occasionally. He recollects himself as he was at the time, young and gamesome; and forgets that his hearers have no other idea of the hero of the tale, but such as he may appear at the time of telling it; peradventure, a withered, whimsical, spindle-shanked old gentleman. With married men, it is true, this is not so frequently the case: their amorous romance is apt to decline after marriage; why, I cannot for the life of me imagine; but with a bachelor, though it may slumber, it never dies. It is always liable to break out again in transient flashes, and never so much as on a spring morning in the country; or on a winter evening when seated in his solitary chamber stirring up the fire and talking of matrimony.

The moment that Master Simon had gone through his confession, and, to use the common phrase, "had made a clean breast of it," he became quite himself again. He had settled the point which had been worrying his mind, and doubtless considered himself established as a man of sentiment in my opinion. Before we had finished our morning's stroll, he was singing as blithe as a grasshopper, whistling to his dogs, and telling droll stories: and I recollect that he was particularly facetious that day at dinner on the subject of matrimony, and uttered several excellent jokes, not to be found in Joe Miller, that made the bride elect blush and look down; but set all the old gentlemen at the table in a roar, and absolutely brought tears into the general's eyes.

English Gravity.

"Merrie England!"
—Ancient Phrase.

There is nothing so rare as for a man to ride his hobby without molestation. I find the Squire has not so undisturbed an indulgence in his humours as I had imagined; but has been repeatedly thwarted of late, and has suffered a kind of well-meaning persecution from a Mr. Faddy, an old gentleman of some weight, at least of purse, who has recently moved into the neighbourhood. He is a worthy and substantial manufacturer, who, having accumulated a large fortune by dint of steam-engines and spinning-jennies, has retired from business, and set up for a country gentleman. He has taken an old country-seat, and refitted it; and painted and plastered it, until it looks not unlike his own manufactory. He has been particularly careful in mending the walls and hedges, and putting up notices of spring-guns and man-traps in every part of his premises. Indeed, he shows great jealousy about his territorial rights, having stopped up a footpath that led across his fields, and given warning, in staring letters, that whoever was found trespassing on those grounds would be prosecuted with the utmost rigour of the law. He has brought into the country with him all the practical maxims of town, and the bustling habits of business; and is one of those sensible, useful, prosing, troublesome, intolerable old gentlemen, that go about wearying and worrying society with excellent plans for public utility.

He is very much disposed to be on intimate terms with the Squire, and calls on him every now and then, with some project for the good of the neighbourhood, which happens to run diametrically opposite to some one or other of the Squire's peculiar notions; but which is "too sensible a measure" to be openly opposed. He has annoyed him excessively, by enforcing the vagrant laws; persecuting the gipsies, and endeavouring to suppress country wakes and holiday games; which he considers great nuisances, and reprobates as causes of the deadly sin of idleness.

There is evidently in all this a little of the ostentation of newly-acquired consequence; the tradesman is gradually swelling into the aristocrat; and he begins to grow excessively intolerant of every thing that is not genteel. He has a great deal to say about "the common people;" talks much of his park, his preserves, and the necessity of enforcing the game-laws more strictly; and makes frequent use of the phrase, "the gentry of the neighbourhood."

He came to the Hall lately, with a face full of business, that he and the Squire, to use his own words, "might lay their heads together," to hit upon some mode of putting a stop to the frolicking at the village on the approaching May-day. It drew, he said, idle people together from all parts of the neighbourhood, who spent the day fiddling, dancing, and carousing, instead of staying at home to work for their families.

Now, as the Squire, unluckily, is at the bottom of these May-day revels, it may be supposed that the suggestions of the sagacious Mr. Faddy were not received with the best grace in the world. It is true, the old gentleman is too courteous to show any temper to a guest in his own house; but no sooner was he gone, than the indignation of the Squire found vent, at having his poetical cobwebs invaded by this buzzing, bluebottle fly of traffic. In his warmth, he inveighed against the whole race of manufacturers, who, I found, were sore disturbers of his comfort. "Sir," said he, with emotion, "it makes my heart bleed, to see all our fine streams dammed up, and bestrode by cotton-mills; our valleys smoking with steam-engines, and the din of the hammer and the loom scaring away all our rural delight. What's to become of merry old England, when its manor-houses are all turned into manufactories, and its sturdy peasantry into pin-makers and stocking-weavers? I have looked in vain for merry Sherwood, and all the greenwood haunts of Robin Hood; the whole country is covered with manufacturing towns. I have stood on the ruins of Dudley Castle, and looked round, with an aching heart, on what were once its feudal domains of verdant and beautiful country. Sir, I beheld a mere *campus phlegrae*; a region of fire; reeking with coal-pits, and furnaces, and smelting-houses, vomiting forth flames and smoke. The pale and ghastly people, toiling among vile exhalations, looked more like demons than human beings; the clanking wheels and engines, seen through the murky atmosphere, looked like instruments of torture in this pandemonium. What is to become of the country, with these evils rankling in its very core? Sir, these manufacturers will be the ruin of our rural manners; they will destroy the national character; they will not leave materials for a single line of poetry!"

The Squire is apt to wax eloquent on such themes; and I could hardly help smiling at this whimsical lamentation over national industry and public improvement. I am told, however, that he really grieves at the growing spirit of trade, as destroying the charm of life. He considers every new shorthand mode of doing things, as an inroad of snug sordid method; and thinks that this will soon become a mere matter-of-fact world, where life will be reduced to a mathematical calculation of conveniences, and every thing will be done by steam.

He maintains, also, that the nation has declined in its free and joyous spirit, in proportion as it has turned its attention to commerce and manufactures; and that, in old times, when England was an idler, it was also a merrier little island. In support of this opinion, he adduces the frequency and splendour of ancient festivals and merry-makings, and the hearty spirit with which they were kept up by all classes of people. His memory is stored with the accounts given by Stow, in his Survey of London, of the holiday revels at the inns of court, the Christmas mummeries, and the masquings and bonfires about the streets. London, he says, in those days, resembled the continental cities in its picturesque manners and amusements. The court used to dance after dinner, on public occasions. After the coronation dinner of Richard II, for example, the king, the prelates, the nobles, the knights, and the rest of the company, danced in Westminster Hall to the music of the minstrels. The example of the court was followed by the middling classes, and so down to the lowest, and the whole nation was a dancing, jovial nation. He quotes a lively city picture of the times, given by Stow, which resembles the lively scenes one may often see in the gay city of Paris; for he tells us that on holidays, after evening prayers, the maidens in London used to assemble before the door, in sight of their masters and dames, and while one played on a timbrel, the others danced for garlands, hanged athwart the street.

"Where will we meet with such merry groups now-a-days?" the Squire will exclaim, shaking his head mournfully;—"and then as to the gayety that prevailed in dress throughout all ranks of society, and made the very streets so fine and picturesque: 'I have myself,' says Gervaise Markham, 'met an ordinary tapster in his silk stockings, garters deep fringed with gold lace, the rest of his apparel suitable, with cloak lined with velvet!' Nashe, too, who wrote in 1593, exclaims at the finery of the nation: 'England, the player's stage of gorgeous attire, the ape of all nations' superfluities, the continual masquer in outlandish habiliments.'"

Such are a few of the authorities quoted by the Squire, by way of contrasting what he supposes to have been the former vivacity of the nation with its present monotonous character. "John Bull," he will say, "was then a gay cavalier, with his sword by his side and a feather in his cap; but he is now a plodding citizen, in snuff-coloured coat and gaiters."

By the by, there really appears to have been some change in the national character, since the days of which the Squire is so fond of talking; those days when this little island acquired its favourite old title of "merry England." This may be attributed in part to the growing hardships of the times, and the necessity of turning the whole attention to the means of subsistence; but England's gayest customs prevailed at times when her common people enjoyed comparatively few of the comforts and conveniences that they do at present. It may be still more attributed to the universal spirit of gain, and the calculating habits that commerce has introduced; but I am inclined to attribute it chiefly to the gradual increase of the liberty of the subject, and the growing freedom and activity of opinion.

A free people are apt to be grave and thoughtful. They have high and important matters to occupy their minds. They feel that it is their right, their interest, and their duty, to mingle in public concerns, and to watch over the general welfare. The continual exercise of the mind on political topics gives intenser habits of thinking, and a more serious and earnest demeanour. A nation becomes less gay, but more intellectually active and vigorous. It evinces less play of the fancy, but more power of the imagination; less taste and elegance, but more grandeur of mind; less animated vivacity, but deeper enthusiasm.

It is when men are shut out of the regions of manly thought, by a despotic government; when every grave and lofty theme is rendered perilous to discussion and almost to reflection; it is then that they turn to the safer occupations of taste and amusement; trifles rise to importance, and occupy the craving activity of intellect. No being is more void of care and reflection than the slave; none dances more gayly, in his intervals of labour; but make him free, give him rights and interests to guard, and he becomes thoughtful and laborious.

The French are a gayer people than the English. Why? Partly from temperament, perhaps; but greatly because they have been accustomed to governments which surrounded the free exercise of thought with danger, and where he only was safe who shut his eyes and ears to public events, and enjoyed the passing pleasure of the day. Within late years, they have had more opportunity of exercising their minds; and within late years, the national character has essentially changed. Never did the French enjoy such a degree of freedom as they do at this moment; and at this moment the French are comparatively a grave people.

Gipsies.

What's that to absolute freedom; such as the very beggars have; to feast and revel here to-day, and yonder to-morrow; next day where they please; and so on still, the whole country or kingdom over? There's liberty! the birds of the air can take no more.
—Jovial Crew.

Since the meeting with the gipsies, which I have related in a former paper, I have observed several of them haunting the purlieus of the Hall, in spite of a positive interdiction of the Squire. They are part of a gang that has long kept about this neighbourhood, to the great annoyance of the farmers, whose poultry-yards often suffer from their nocturnal invasions. They are, however, in some measure patronized by the Squire, who considers the race as belonging to the good old times; which, to confess the private truth, seem to have abounded with good-for-nothing characters.

This roving crew is called "Starlight Tom's Gang," from the name of its chieftain, a notorious poacher. I have heard repeatedly of the misdeeds of this "minion of the moon;" for every midnight depredation that takes place in park, or fold or farm-yard, is laid to his charge. Starlight Tom, in fact, answers to his name; he seems to walk in darkness, and, like a fox, to be traced in the morning by the mischief he has done. He reminds me of that fearful personage in the nursery rhyme:

> *Who goes round the house at night?*
> *None but bloody Tom!*
> *Who steals all the sheep at night?*
> *None but one by one!*

In short, Starlight Tom is the scapegoat of the neighbourhood, but so cunning and adroit, that there is no detecting him. Old Christy and the game-keeper have watched many a night, in hopes of entrapping him; and Christy often patrols the park with his dogs, for the purpose, but all in vain.

It is said that the Squire winks hard at his misdeeds, having an indulgent feeling towards the vagabond, because of his being very expert at all kinds of games, a great shot with the cross-bow, and the best morris-dancer in the country.

The Squire also suffers the gang to lurk unmolested about the skirts of his estate, on condition that they do not come about the house. The approaching wedding, however, has made a kind of Saturnalia at the Hall, and has caused a suspension of all sober rule. It has produced a great sensation throughout the female part of the household; not a housemaid but dreams of wedding favours, and has a husband running in her head. Such a time is a harvest for the gipsies: there is a public footpath leading across one part of the park, by which they have free ingress, and they are continually hovering about the grounds, telling the servant-girls' fortunes, or getting smuggled in to the young ladies.

I believe the Oxonian amuses himself very much by furnishing them with hints in private, and bewildering all the weak brains in the house with their wonderful revelations. The general certainly was very much astonished by the communications made to him the other evening by the gipsy girl: he kept a wary silence towards us on the subject, and affected to treat it lightly; but I have noticed that he has since redoubled his attentions to Lady Lillycraft and her dogs.

I have seen also Phoebe Wilkins, the housekeeper's pretty and love-sick niece, holding a long conference with one of these old sibyls behind a large tree in the avenue, and often looking round to see that she was not observed. I make no doubt that she was endeavouring to get some favourable augury about the result of her love-quarrel with young Ready-Money, as oracles have always been more consulted on love affairs than upon any thing else. I fear, however, that in this instance the response was not so favourable as usual; for I perceived poor Phoebe returning pensively towards the house, her head hanging down, her hat in her hand, and the riband trailing along the ground.

At another time, as I turned a corner of a terrace, at the bottom of the garden, just by a clump of trees, and a large stone urn, I came upon a bevy of the young girls of the family, attended by this same Phoebe Wilkins. I was at a loss to comprehend the meaning of their blushing and giggling, and their apparent agitation, until I saw the red cloak of a gipsy vanishing among the shrubbery. A few moments after, I caught sight of Master Simon and the Oxonion stealing along one of the walks of the garden, chuckling and laughing at their successful waggery; having evidently put the gipsy up to the thing, and instructed her what to say.

After all, there is something strangely pleasing in these tamperings with the future, even where we are convinced of the fallacy of the prediction. It is singular how willingly the mind will half deceive itself, and with what a degree of awe we will listen to these babblers about futurity. For my part, I cannot feel angry with these poor vagabonds, that seek to deceive us into bright hopes and expectations. I have always been something of a castle-builder, and have found my liveliest pleasures to arise from the illusions which fancy has cast over commonplace realities. As I get on in life, I find it more difficult to deceive myself in this delightful manner; and I should be thankful to any prophet, however false, that would conjure the clouds which hang over futurity into palaces, and all its doubtful regions into fairy-land.

The Squire, who, as I have observed, has a private good-will towards gipsies, has suffered considerable annoyance on their account. Not that they requite his indulgence with ingratitude, for they do not depredate very flagrantly on his estate; but because their pilferings and misdeeds occasion loud murmurs in the village. I can readily understand the old gentleman's humour on this point; I have a great toleration for all kinds of vagrant sunshiny existence, and must confess I take a pleasure in observing the ways of gipsies. The English, who are accustomed to them from childhood, and often suffer from their petty depredations, consider them as mere nuisances; but I have been very much struck with their peculiarities. I like to behold their clear olive complexions, their romantic black eyes, their raven locks, their lithe, slender figures; and hear them in low silver tones dealing forth magnificent promises of honours and estates, of world's wealth, and ladies' love.

Their mode of life, too, has something in it very fanciful and picturesque. They are the free denizens of nature, and maintain a primitive independence, in spite of law and gospel; of county gaols and country magistrates. It is curious to see this obstinate adherence to the wild, unsettled habits of savage life transmitted from generation to generation, and preserved in the midst of one of the most cultivated, populous, and systematic countries in the world. They are totally distinct from the busy, thrifty people about them. They seem to be, like the Indians of America, either above or below the ordinary cares and anxieties of mankind. Heedless of power, of honours, of wealth; and indifferent to the fluctuations of times; the rise or fall of grain, or stock, or empires, they seem to laugh at the tolling, fretting world around them, and to live according to the philosophy of the old song:

"Who would ambition shun,
And loves to lie i' the sun,
Seeking the food he eats,
And pleased with what he gets,
Come hither, come hither, come hither;
  Here shall he see
  No enemy,
But winter and rough weather."

In this way, they wander from county to county; keeping about the purlieus of villages, or in plenteous neighbourhoods, where there are fat farms and rich country-seats. Their encampments are generally made in some beautiful spot—either a green shady nook of a road; or on the border of a common, under a sheltering hedge; or on the skirts of a fine spreading wood. They are always to be found lurking about fairs, and races, and rustic gatherings, wherever there is pleasure, and throng, and idleness. They are the oracles of milk-maids and simple serving-girls; and sometimes have even the honour of perusing the white hands of gentlemen's daughters, when rambling about their fathers' grounds. They are the bane of good housewives and thrifty farmers, and odious in the eyes of country justices; but, like all other vagabond beings, they have something to commend them to the fancy. They are among the last traces, in these matter-of-fact days, of the motley population of former times; and are whimsically associated in my mind with fairies and witches, Robin Goodfellow, Robin Hood, and the other fantastical personages of poetry.

May-Day Customs.

Happy the age, and harmless were the dayes,
(For then true love and amity was found,)
When every village did a May-pole raise,
And Whitsun ales and May-games did abound:
And all the lusty yonkers in a rout,
With merry lasses daunc'd the rod about,
Then friendship to their banquets bid the guests,
And poore men far'd the better for their feasts.
—PASQUIL'S Palinodia.

The month of April has nearly passed away, and we are fast approaching that poetical day, which was considered, in old times, as the boundary that parted the frontiers of winter and summer. With all its caprices, however, I like the month of April. I like these laughing and crying days, when sun and shade seem to run in billows over the landscape. I like to see the sudden shower coursing over the meadow, and giving all nature a greener smile; and the bright sunbeams chasing the flying cloud, and turning all its drops into diamonds.

I was enjoying a morning of the kind, in company with the Squire, in one of the finest parts of the park. We were skirting a beautiful grove, and he was giving me a kind of biographical account of several of his favourite forest trees, when he heard the strokes of an axe from the midst of a thick copse. The Squire paused and listened, with manifest signs of uneasiness. He turned his steps in the direction of the sound. The strokes grew louder and louder as we advanced; there was evidently a vigorous arm wielding the axe. The Squire quickened his pace, but in vain; a loud crack, and a succeeding crash, told that the mischief had been done, and some child of the forest laid low. When we came to the place, we found Master Simon and several others standing about a tall and beautifully straight young tree, which had just been felled.

The Squire, though a man of most harmonious dispositions, was completely put out of tune by this circumstance. He felt like a monarch witnessing the murder of one of his liege subjects, and demanded, with some asperity, the meaning of the outrage. It turned out to be an affair of Master Simon's, who had selected the tree, from its height and straightness, for a May-pole, the old one which stood on the village green being unfit for farther service. If any thing could have soothed the ire of my worthy host, it would have been the reflection that his tree had fallen for so good a cause; and I saw that there was a great struggle between his fondness for his groves, and his devotion to May-day. He could not contemplate the prostrate tree, however, without indulging in lamentation, and making a kind of funeral eulogy, like Mark Antony over the body of Caesar; and he forbade that any tree should thenceforward be cut down on his estate, without a warrant from himself; being determined, he said, to hold the sovereign power of life and death in his own hands.

This mention of the May-pole struck my attention, and I inquired whether the old customs connected with it were really kept up in this part of the country. The Squire shook his head mournfully; and I found I had touched on one of his tender points, for he grew quite melancholy in bewailing the total decline of old May-day. Though it is regularly celebrated in the neighbouring village, yet it has been merely resuscitated by the worthy Squire, and is kept up in a forced state of existence at his expense. He meets with continual discouragements; and finds great difficulty in getting the country bumpkins to play their parts tolerably. He manages to have every year a "Queen of the May;" but as to Robin Hood, Friar Tuck, the Dragon, the Hobby-Horse, and all the other motley crew that used to enliven the day with their mummery, he has not ventured to introduce them.

Still I looked forward with some interest to the promised shadow of old May-day, even though it be but a shadow; and I feel more and more pleased with the whimsical yet harmless hobby of my host, which is surrounding him with agreeable associations, and making a little world of poetry about him. Brought up, as I have been, in a new country, I may appreciate too highly the faint vestiges of ancient customs which I now and then meet with, and the interest I express in them may provoke a smile from those who are negligently suffering them to pass away. But with whatever indifference they may be regarded by those "to the manner born," yet in my mind the lingering flavour of them imparts a charm to rustic life, which nothing else could readily supply.

I shall never forget the delight I felt on first seeing a May-pole. It was on the banks of the Dee, close by the picturesque old bridge that stretches across the river from the quaint little city of Chester. I had already been carried back into former days, by the antiquities of that venerable place; the examination of which is equal to turning over the pages of a black-letter volume, or gazing on the pictures in Froissart. The May-pole on the margin of that poetic stream completed the illusion. My fancy adorned it with wreaths of flowers, and peopled the green bank with all the dancing revelry of May-day. The mere sight of this May-pole gave a glow to my feelings, and spread a charm over the country for the rest of the day; and as I traversed a part of the fair plain of Cheshire, and the beautiful borders of Wales, and looked from among swelling hills down a long green valley, through which "the Deva wound its wizard stream," my imagination turned all into a perfect Arcadia.

Whether it be owing to such poetical associations early instilled into my mind, or whether there is, as it were, a sympathetic revival and budding forth of the feelings at this season, certain it is, that I always experience, wherever I may be placed, a delightful expansion of the heart at the return of May. It is said that birds about this time will become restless in their cages, as if instinct with the season, conscious of the revelry that is going on in the groves, and impatient to break from their bondage, and join in the jubilee of the year. In like manner I have felt myself excited, even in the midst of the metropolis, when the windows, which had been churlishly closed all winter, were again thrown open to receive the balmy breath of May; when the sweets of the country were breathed into the town, and flowers were cried about the streets. I have considered the treasures of flowers thus poured in, as so many missives from nature, inviting us forth to enjoy the virgin beauty of the year, before its freshness is exhaled by the heats of sunny summer.

One can readily imagine what a gay scene it must have been in jolly old London, when the doors were decorated with flowering branches, when every hat was decked with hawthorn, and Robin Hood, Friar Tuck, Maid Marian, the morris-dancers, and all the other fantastic masks and revellers, were performing their antics about the May-pole in every part of the city.

I am not a bigoted admirer of old times and old customs, merely because of their antiquity: but while I rejoice in the decline of many of the rude usages and coarse amusements of former days, I cannot but regret that this innocent and fanciful festival has fallen into disuse. It seemed appropriate to this verdant and pastoral country, and calculated to light up the too pervading gravity of the nation. I value every custom that tends to infuse poetical feeling into the common people, and to sweeten and soften the rudeness of rustic manners, without destroying their simplicity. Indeed, it is to the decline of this happy simplicity, that the decline of this custom may be traced; and the rural dance on the green, and the homely May-day pageant, have gradually disappeared, in proportion as the peasantry have become expensive and artificial in their pleasures, and too knowing for simple enjoyment.

Some attempts, the Squire informs me, have been made of late years, by men of both taste and learning, to rally back the popular feeling to these standards of primitive simplicity; but the time has gone by, the feeling has become chilled by habits of gain and traffic, the country apes the manners and amusements of the town, and little is heard of May-day at present, except from the lamentations of authors, who sigh after it from among the brick walls of the city:

"For O, for O, the Hobby-Horse is forgot."

Village Worthies.

Nay, I tell you, I am so well beloved in our town, that not the worst dog in the street will hurt my little finger.
—Collier of Croydon.

As the neighbouring village is one of those out-of-the-way, but gossiping, little places where a small matter makes a great stir, it is not to be supposed that the approach of a festival like that of May-day can be regarded with indifference, especially since it is made a matter of such moment by the great folks at the Hall. Master Simon, who is the faithful factotum of the worthy Squire, and jumps with his humour in every thing, is frequent just now in his visits to the village, to give directions for the impending fête; and as I have taken the liberty occasionally of accompanying him, I have been enabled to get some insight into the characters and internal politics of this very sagacious little community.

Master Simon is in fact the Caesar of the village. It is true the Squire is the protecting power, but his factotum is the active and busy agent. He intermeddles in all its concerns, is acquainted with all the inhabitants and their domestic history, gives counsel to the old folks in their business matters, and the young folks in their love affairs, and enjoys the proud satisfaction of being a great man in a little world.

He is the dispenser, too, of the Squire's charity, which is bounteous; and, to do Master Simon justice, he performs this part of his functions with great alacrity. Indeed, I have been entertained with the mixture of bustle, importance, and kind-heartedness which he displays. He is of too vivacious a temperament to comfort the afflicted by sitting down, moping and whining, and blowing noses in concert: but goes whisking about like a sparrow, chirping consolation into every hole and corner of the village. I have seen an old woman, in a red cloak, hold him for half an hour together with some long phthisical tale of distress, which Master Simon listened to with many a bob of the head, smack of his dog-whip, and other symptoms of impatience, though he afterwards made a most faithful and circumstantial report of the case to the Squire. I have watched him, too, during one of his pop visits into the cottage of a superannuated villager, who is a pensioner of the Squire, where he fidgeted about the room without sitting down, made many excellent off-hand reflections with the old invalid, who was propped up in his chair, about the shortness of life, the certainty of death, and the necessity of preparing for "that awful change;" quoted several texts of scripture very incorrectly, but much to the edification of the cottager's wife; and on coming out, pinched the daughter's rosy cheek, and wondered what was in the young men that such a pretty face did not get a husband.

He has also his cabinet counsellors in the village, with whom he is very busy just now, preparing for the May-day ceremonies. Among these is the village tailor, a pale-faced fellow, that plays the clarionet in the church choir; and; being a great musical genius, has frequent meetings of the band at his house, where they "make night hideous" by their concerts. He is, in consequence, high in favour with Master Simon; and, through his influence, has the making, or rather marring, of all the liveries of the Hall; which generally look as though they had been cut out by one of those scientific tailors of the Flying Island of Laputa, who took measure of their customers with a quadrant. The tailor, in fact, might rise to be one of the moneyed men of the village, were he not rather too prone to gossip, and keep holidays, and give concerts, and blow all his substance, real and personal, through his clarionet; which literally keeps him poor, both in body and estate. He has for the present thrown by all his regular work, and suffered the breeches of the village to go unmade and unmended, while he is occupied in making garlands of party-coloured rags, in imitation of flowers, for the decoration of the May-pole.

Another of Master Simon's counsellors is the apothecary, a short and rather fat man, with a pair of prominent eyes, that diverge like those of a lobster. He is the village wise man; very sententious, and full of profound remarks on shallow subjects. Master Simon often quotes his sayings, and mentions him as rather an extraordinary man; and even consults him occasionally, in desperate cases of the dogs and horses. Indeed, he seems to have been overwhelmed by the apothecary's philosophy, which is exactly one observation deep, consisting of indisputable maxims, such as may be gathered from the mottoes of tobacco-boxes. I had a specimen of his philosophy, in my very first conversation with him; in the course of which he observed, with great solemnity and emphasis, that "man is a compound of wisdom and folly;" upon which Master Simon, who had hold of my arm, pressed very hard upon it, and whispered in my ear "That's a devilish shrewd remark!"

The Schoolmaster.

There will be no mosse stick to the stone of Sisiphus, no grasse hang on the heeles of Mercury, no butter cleave on the bread of a traveller. For as the eagle at every flight loseth a feather, which maketh her bauld in her age, so the traveller in every country loseth some fleece, which maketh him a beggar in his youth, by buying that for a pound which he cannot sell again for a penny—repentance.
—LILLY'S Euphues.

Among the worthies of the village that enjoy the peculiar confidence of Master Simon, is one who has struck my fancy so much that I have thought him worthy of a separate notice. It is Slingsby, the schoolmaster, a thin, elderly man, rather threadbare and slovenly, somewhat indolent in manner, and with an easy, good-humoured look, not often met with in his craft. I have been interested in his favour by a few anecdotes which I have picked up concerning him.

He is a native of the village, and was a contemporary and playmate of Ready-Money Jack in the days of their boyhood. Indeed, they carried on a kind of league of mutual good offices. Slingsby was rather puny, and withal somewhat of a coward, but very apt at his learning; Jack, on the contrary, was a bully-boy out of doors, but a sad laggard at his books. Slingsby helped Jack, therefore, to all his lessons; Jack fought all Slingsby's battles; and they were inseparable friends. This mutual kindness continued even after they left the school, notwithstanding the dissimilarity of their characters. Jack took to ploughing and reaping, and prepared himself to till his paternal acres; while the other loitered negligently on in the path of learning, until he penetrated even into the confines of Latin and mathematics.

In an unlucky hour, however, he took to reading voyages and travels, and was smitten with a desire to see the world. This desire increased upon him as he grew up; so, early one bright, sunny morning, he put all his effects in a knapsack, slung it on his back, took staff in hand, and called in his way to take leave of his early schoolmate. Jack was just going out with the plough: the friends shook hands over the farm-house gate; Jack drove his team a-field, and Slingsby whistled, "Over the hills and far away," and sallied forth gayly to "seek his fortune."

Years and years passed by, and young Tom Slingsby was forgotten; when, one mellow Sunday afternoon in autumn, a thin man, somewhat advanced in life, with a coat out at elbows, a pair of old nankeen gaiters, and a few things tied in a handkerchief and slung on the end of a stick, was seen loitering through the village. He appeared to regard several houses attentively, to peer into the windows that were open, to eye the villagers wistfully as they returned from church, and then to pass some time in the church-yard reading the tombstones.

At length he found his way to the farm-house of Ready-Money Jack, but paused ere he attempted the wicket; contemplating the picture of substantial independence before him. In the porch of the house sat Ready-Money Jack, in his Sunday dress; with his hat upon his head, his pipe in his mouth, and his tankard before him, the monarch of all he surveyed. Beside him lay his fat house-dog. The varied sounds of poultry were heard from the well-stocked farm-yard; the bees hummed from their hives in the garden; the cattle lowed in the rich meadow; while the crammed barns and ample stacks bore proof of an abundant harvest.

The stranger opened the gate and advanced dubiously toward the house. The mastiff growled at the sight of the suspicious-looking intruder; but was immediately silenced by his master, who, taking his pipe from his mouth, awaited with inquiring aspect the address of this equivocal personage. The stranger eyed old Jack for a moment, so portly in his dimensions, and decked out in gorgeous apparel; then cast a glance upon his own thread-bare and starveling condition, and the scanty bundle which he held in his hand; then giving his shrunk waistcoat a twitch to make it meet its receding waistband, and casting another look, half sad, half humorous, at the sturdy yeoman, "I suppose," said he, "Mr. Tibbets, you have forgot old times and old playmates."

The latter gazed at him with scrutinizing look, but acknowledged that he had no recollection of him.

"Like enough, like enough," said the stranger, "every body seems to have forgotten poor Slingsby!"

"Why, no, sure! it can't be Tom Slingsby?"

"Yes, but it is, though!" replied the stranger, shaking his head.

Ready-Money Jack was on his feet in a twinkling, thrust out his hand, gave his ancient crony the gripe of a giant, and slapping the other hand on a bench, "Sit down there," cried he, "Tom Slingsby!"

A long conversation ensued about old times, while Slingsby was regaled with the best cheer that the farm-house afforded; for he was hungry as well as wayworn, and had the keen appetite of a poor pedestrian. The early playmates then talked over their subsequent lives and adventures. Jack had but little to relate, and was never good at a long story. A prosperous life, passed at home, has little incident for narrative; it is only poor devils, that are tossed about the world, that are the true heroes of story. Jack had stuck by the paternal farm, followed the same plough that his forefathers had driven, and had waxed richer and richer as he grew older. As to Tom Slingsby, he was an exemplification of the old proverb, "a rolling stone gathers no moss." He had sought his fortune about the world, without ever finding it, being a thing oftener found at home than abroad. He had been in all kinds of situations, and had learned a dozen different modes of making a living; but had found his way back to his native village rather poorer than when he left it, his knapsack having dwindled down to a scanty bundle.

As luck would have it, the Squire was passing by the farmhouse that very evening, and called there, as is often his custom. He found the two schoolmates still gossiping in the porch, and according to the good old Scottish song, "taking a cup of kindness yet, for auld lang syne." The Squire was struck by the contrast in appearance and fortunes of these early playmates. Ready-Money Jack, seated in lordly state, surrounded by the good things of this life, with golden guineas hanging to his very watch-chain, and the poor pilgrim Slingsby, thin as a weasel, with all his worldly effects, his bundle, hat, and walking-staff, lying on the ground beside him.

The good Squire's heart warmed towards the luckless cosmopolite, for he is a little prone to like such half-vagrant characters. He cast about in his mind how he should contrive once more to anchor Slingsby in his native village. Honest Jack had already offered him a present shelter under his roof, in spite of the hints, and winks, and half remonstrances of the shrewd Dame Tibbets; but how to provide for his permanent maintenance was the question. Luckily the Squire bethought himself that the village school was without a teacher. A little further conversation convinced him that Slingsby was as fit for that as for any thing else, and in a day or two he was seen swaying the rod of empire in the very school-house where he had often been horsed in the days of his boyhood.

Here he has remained for several years, and, being honoured by the countenance of the Squire, and the fast friendship of Mr. Tibbets, he has grown into much importance and consideration in the village. I am told, however, that he still shows, now and then, a degree of restlessness, and a disposition to rove abroad again, and see a little more of the world; an inclination which seems particularly to haunt him about springtime. There is nothing so difficult to conquer as the vagrant humour, when once it has been fully indulged.

Since I have heard these anecdotes of poor Slingsby, I have more than once mused upon the picture presented by him and his schoolmate, Ready-Money Jack, on their coming together again after so long a separation. It is difficult to determine between lots in life, where each one is attended with its peculiar discontents. He who never leaves his home repines at his monotonous existence, and envies the traveller, whose life is a constant tissue of wonder and adventure; while he who is tossed about the world, looks back with many a sigh to the safe and quiet shore which he has abandoned. I cannot help thinking, however, that the man that stays at home, and cultivates the comforts and pleasures daily springing up around him, stands the best chance for happiness. There is nothing so fascinating to a young mind as the idea of travelling; and there is very witchcraft in the old phrase found in every nursery tale, of "going to seek one's fortune." A continual change of place, and change of object, promises a continual succession of adventure and gratification of curiosity. But there is a limit to all our enjoyments, and every desire bears its death in its very gratification. Curiosity languishes under repeated stimulants, novelties cease to excite surprise, until at length we cannot wonder even at a miracle.

He who has sallied forth into the world, like poor Slingsby, full of sunny anticipations, finds too soon how different the distant scene becomes when visited. The smooth place roughens as he approaches; the wild place becomes tame and barren; the fairy tints that beguiled him on, still fly to the distant hill, or gather upon the land he has left behind; and every part of the landscape seems greener than the spot he stands on.

The School.

But to come down from great men and higher matters to my little children and poor school-house again; I will, God willing, go forward orderly, as I purposed, to instruct children and young men both for learning and manners.
—ROGER ASCHAM.

Having given the reader a slight sketch of the village schoolmaster, he may be curious to learn something concerning his school. As the Squire takes much interest in the education of the neighbouring children, he put into the hands of the teacher, on first installing him in office, a copy of Roger Ascham's Schoolmaster, and advised him, moreover, to con over that portion of old Peacham which treats of the duty of masters, and which condemns the favourite method of making boys wise by flagellation.

He exhorted Slingsby not to break down or depress the free spirit of the boys, by harshness and slavish fear, but to lead them freely and joyously on in the path of knowledge, making it pleasant and desirable in their eyes. He wished to see the youth trained up in the manners and habitudes of the peasantry of the good old times, and thus to lay a foundation for the accomplishment of his favorite object, the revival of old English customs and character. He recommended that all the ancient holidays should be observed, and that the sports of the boys, in their hours of play, should be regulated according to the standard authorities laid down in Strutt, a copy of whose invaluable work, decorated with plates, was deposited in the school-house. Above all, he exhorted the pedagogue to abstain from the use of birch, an instrument of instruction which the good Squire regards with abhorrence, as fit only for the coercion of brute natures that cannot be reasoned with.

Mr. Slingsby has followed the Squire's instructions, to the best of his disposition and abilities. He never flogs the boys, because he is too easy, good-humoured a creature to inflict pain on a worm. He is bountiful in holidays, because he loves holidays himself, and has a sympathy with the urchins' impatience of confinement, from having divers times experienced its irksomeness during the time that he was seeing the world. As to sports and pastimes, the boys are faithfully exercised in all that are on record, quoits, races, prison-bars, tipcat, trap-ball, bandy-ball, wrestling, leaping, and what not. The only misfortune is, that having banished the birch, honest Slingsby has not studied Roger Ascham sufficiently to find out a substitute; or rather, he has not the management in his nature to apply one; his school, therefore, though one of the happiest, is one of the most unruly in the country; and never was a pedagogue more liked, or less heeded by his disciples, than Slingsby.

He has lately taken a coadjutor worthy of himself, being another stray sheep that has returned to the village fold. This is no other than the son of the musical tailor, who had bestowed some cost upon his education, hoping to see him one day arrive at the dignity of an exciseman, or at least of a parish clerk. The lad grew up, however, as idle and musical as his father; and, being captivated by the drum and fife of a recruiting party, he followed them off to the army. He returned not long since, out of money, and out at the elbows, the prodigal son of the village. He remained for some time lounging about the place in half-tattered soldier's dress, with a foraging-cap on one side of his head, jerking stones across the brook, or loitering about the tavern-door, a burthen to his father, and regarded with great coldness by all warm householders.

Something, however, drew honest Slingsby towards the youth. It might be the kindness he bore to his father, who is one of the schoolmaster's great cronies; it might be that secret sympathy which draws men of vagrant propensities towards each other; for there is something truly magnetic in the vagabond feeling; or it might be, that he remembered the time when he himself had come back, like this youngster, a wreck, to his native place. At any rate, whatever the motive, Slingsby drew towards the youth. They had many conversations in the village tap-room about foreign parts and the various scenes and places they had witnessed during their wayfaring about the world. The more Slingsby talked with him, the more he found him to his taste; and finding him almost as learned as himself, he forthwith engaged him as an assistant, or usher, in the school. Under such admirable tuition, the school, as may be supposed, flourishes apace; and if the scholars do not become versed in all the holiday accomplishments of the good old times, to the Squire's heart's content, it will not be the fault of their teachers. The prodigal son has become almost as popular among the boys as the pedagogue himself. His instructions are not limited to school hours; and having inherited the musical taste and talents of his father, he has bitten the whole school with the mania. He is a great hand at beating a drum, which is often heard rumbling from the rear of the school-house. He is teaching half the boys of the village, also, to play the fife, and the pandean pipes; and they weary the whole neighbourhood with their vague pipings, as they sit perched on stiles, or loitering about the barn-doors in the evenings. Among the other exercises of the school, also, he has introduced the ancient art of archery, one of the Squire's favourite themes, with such success, that the whipsters roam in truant bands about the neighbourhood, practising with their bows and arrows upon the birds of the air, and the beasts of the field; and not unfrequently making a foray into the Squire's domains, to the great indignation of the gamekeepers. In a word, so completely are the ancient English customs and habits cultivated at this school, that I should not be surprised if the Squire should live to see one of his poetic visions realized, and a brood reared up, worthy successors to Robin Hood and his merry gang of outlaws.

A Village Politician.

I am a rogue if I do not think I was designed for the helm of state; I am so full of nimble stratagems, that I should have ordered affairs, and carried it against the stream of a faction, with as much ease as a skipper would laver against the wind.
—The Goblins.

In one of my visits to the village with Master Simon, he proposed that we should stop at the inn, which he wished to show me, as a specimen of a real country inn, the head-quarters of village gossips. I had remarked it before, in my perambulations about the place. It has a deep, old-fashioned porch, leading into a large hall, which serves for tap-room and travellers'-room; having a wide fire-place, with high-backed settles on each side, where the wise men of the village gossip over their ale, and hold their sessions during the long winter evenings. The landlord is an easy, indolent fellow, shaped a little like one of his own beer-barrels, and is apt to stand gossiping at his door, with his wig on one side, and his hands in his pockets, whilst his wife and daughter attend to customers. His wife, however, is fully competent to manage the establishment; and, indeed, from long habitude, rules over all the frequenters of the tap-room as completely as if they were her dependants instead of her patrons. Not a veteran ale-bibber but pays homage to her, having, no doubt, been often in her arrears. I have already hinted that she is on very good terms with Ready-Money Jack. He was a sweetheart of hers in early life, and has always countenanced the tavern on her account. Indeed, he is quite the "cock of the walk" at the tap-room.

As we approached the inn, we heard some one talking with great volubility, and distinguished the ominous words, "taxes," "poor's rates," and "agricultural distress." It proved to be a thin, loquacious fellow, who had penned the landlord up in one corner of the porch, with his hands in his pockets as usual, listening with an air of the most vacant acquiescence.

The sight seemed to have a curious effect on Master Simon, as he squeezed my arm, and, altering his course, sheered wide of the porch, as though he had not had any idea of entering. This evident evasion induced me to notice the orator more particularly. He was meagre, but active in his make, with a long, pale, bilious face; a black beard, so ill-shaven as to bloody his shirt-collar, a feverish eye, and a hat sharpened up at the sides, into a most pragmatical shape. He had a newspaper in his hand, and seemed to be commenting on its contents, to the thorough conviction of mine host.

At sight of Master Simon, the landlord was evidently a little flurried, and began to rub his hands, edge away from his corner, and make several profound publican bows; while the orator took no other notice of my companion than to talk rather louder than before, and with, as I thought, something of an air of defiance. Master Simon, however, as I have before said, sheered off from the porch, and passed on, pressing my arm within his, and whispering, as we got by, in a tone of awe and horror, "That's a radical! he reads Cobbett!"

I endeavoured to get a more particular account of him from my companion, but he seemed unwilling even to talk about him, answering only in general terms, that he was "a cursed busy fellow, that had a confounded trick of talking, and was apt to bother one about the national debt, and such nonsense;" from which I suspected that Master Simon had been rendered wary of him by some accidental encounter on the field of argument; for these radicals are continually roving about in quest of wordy warfare, and never so happy as when they can tilt a gentleman logician out of his saddle.

On subsequent inquiry, my suspicions have been confirmed. I find the radical has but recently found his way into the village, where he threatens to commit fearful devastations with his doctrines. He has already made two or three complete converts, or new lights; has shaken the faith of several others; and has grievously puzzled the brains of many of the oldest villagers, who had never thought about politics, or scarce any thing else, during their whole lives.

He is lean and meagre from the constant restlessness of mind and body; worrying about with newspapers and pamphlets in his pockets, which he is ready to pull out on all occasions. He has shocked several of the staunchest villagers, by talking lightly of the Squire and his family; and hinting that it would be better the park should be cut into small farms and kitchen-gardens, or feed good mutton instead of worthless deer.

He is a great thorn in the side of the Squire, who is sadly afraid that he will introduce politics into the village, and turn it into an unhappy, thinking community. He is a still greater grievance to Master Simon, who has hitherto been able to sway the political opinions of the place, without much cost of learning or logic; but has been much puzzled of late to weed out the doubts and heresies already sown by this champion of reform.

Indeed, the latter has taken complete command at the tap-room of the tavern, not so much because he has convinced, as because he has out-talked all the old-established oracles. The apothecary, with all his philosophy, was as nought before him. He has convinced and converted the landlord at least a dozen times; who, however, is liable to be convinced and converted the other way, by the next person with whom he talks. It is true the radical has a violent antagonist in the landlady, who is vehemently loyal, and thoroughly devoted to the king, Master Simon, and the Squire. She now and then comes out upon the reformer with all the fierceness of a cat-o'-mountain, and does not spare her own soft-headed husband, for listening to what she terms such "low-lived politics." What makes the good woman the more violent, is the perfect coolness with which the radical listens to her attacks, drawing his face up into a provoking supercilious smile; and when she has talked herself out of breath, quietly asking her for a taste of her home-brewed.

The only person that is in any way a match for this redoubtable politician, is Ready-Money Jack Tibbets, who maintains his stand in the tap-room, in defiance of the radical and all his works. Jack is one of the most loyal men in the country, without being able to reason about the matter. He has that admirable quality for a tough arguer, also, that he never knows when he is beat. He has half-a-dozen old maxims which he advances on all occasions, and though his antagonist may overturn them never so often, yet he always brings them anew to the field. He is like the robber in Ariosto, who, though his head might be cut off half-a-hundred times, yet whipped it on his shoulders again in a twinkling, and returned as sound a man as ever to the charge.

Whatever does not square with Jack's simple and obvious creed, he sets down for "French politics;" for, notwithstanding the peace, he cannot be persuaded that the French are not still laying plots to ruin the nation, and to get hold of the Bank of England. The radical attempted to overwhelm him, one day, by a long passage from a newspaper; but Jack neither reads nor believes in newspapers. In reply, he gave him one of the stanzas which he has by heart from his favourite, and indeed only author, old Tusser, and which he calls his Golden Rules:

Leave princes' affairs undescanted on,
And tend to such doings as stand thee upon;
Fear God, and offend not the king nor his laws,
And keep thyself out of the magistrate's claws.

When Tibbets had pronounced this with great emphasis, he pulled out a well-filled leathern purse, took out a handful of gold and silver,—paid his score at the bar with great punctuality, returned his money, piece by piece, into his purse, his purse into his pocket, which he buttoned up; and then, giving his cudgel a stout thump upon the floor, and bidding the radical "good-morning, sir!" with the tone of a man who conceives he has completely done for his antagonist, he walked with lion-like gravity out of the house. Two or three of Jack's admirers who were present, and had been afraid to take the field themselves, looked upon this as a perfect triumph, and winked at each other when the radical's back was turned. "Ay, ay!" said mine host, as soon as the radical was out of hearing, "let old Jack alone; I'll warrant he'll give him his own!"

The Rookery.

But cawing rooks, and kites that swim sublime
In still repeated circles, screaming loud;
The jay, the pie, and e'en the boding owl,
That hails the rising moon, have charms for me.
—COWPER.

In a grove of tall oaks and beeches, that crowns a terrace-walk just on the skirts of the garden, is an ancient rookery, which is one of the most important provinces in the Squire's rural domains. The old gentleman sets great store by his rooks, and will not suffer one of them to be killed: in consequence of which, they have increased amazingly; the tree-tops are loaded with their nests; they have encroached upon the great avenue, and have even established, in times long past, a colony among the elms and pines of the church-yard, which, like other distant colonies, has already thrown off allegiance to the mother country.

The rooks are looked up by the Squire as a very ancient and honourable line of gentry, highly aristocratical in their notions, fond of place, and attached to church and state; as their building so loftily, keeping about churches and cathedrals, and in the venerable groves of old castles and manor-houses, sufficiently manifests. The good opinion thus expressed by the Squire put me upon observing more narrowly these very respectable birds, for I confess, to my shame, I had been apt to confound them with their cousins-german the crows, to whom, at the first glance, they bear so great a family resemblance. Nothing, it seems, could be more unjust or injurious than such a mistake. The rooks and crows are, among the feathered tribes, what the Spaniards and Portuguese are among nations, the least loving, in consequence of their neighbourhood and similarity. The rooks are old established housekeepers, high-minded gentlefolk, that have had their hereditary abodes time out of mind; but as to the poor crows, they are a kind of vagabond, predatory, gipsy race, roving about the country without any settled home; "their hands are against every body, and every body's against them;" and they are gibbeted in every corn-field. Master Simon assures me that a female rook, that should so far forget herself as to consort with a crow, would inevitably be disinherited, and indeed would be totally discarded by all her genteel acquaintance.

The Squire is very watchful over the interests and concerns of his sable neighbours. As to Master Simon, he even pretends to know many of them by sight, and to have given names to them; he points out several, which he says are old heads of families, and compares them to worthy old citizens, beforehand in the world, that wear cocked hats, and silver buckles in their shoes. Notwithstanding the protecting benevolence of the Squire, and their being residents in his empire, they seem to acknowledge no allegiance, and to hold no intercourse or intimacy. Their airy tenements are built almost out of the reach of gun-shot; and, notwithstanding their vicinity to the Hall, they maintain a most reserved and distrustful shyness of mankind.

There is one season of the year, however, which brings all birds in a manner to a level, and tames the pride of the loftiest high-flyer—which is the season of building their nests. This takes place early in the spring, when the forest trees first begin to show their buds; the long, withy ends of the branches to turn green; when the wild strawberry, and other herbage of the sheltered woodlands, put forth their tender and tinted leaves; and the daisy and the primrose peep from under the hedges. At this time there is a general bustle among the feathered tribes; an incessant fluttering about, and a cheerful chirping; indicative, like the germination of the vegetable world, of the reviving life and fecundity of the year.

It is then that the rooks forget their usual stateliness and their shy and lofty habits. Instead of keeping up in the high regions of the air, swinging on the breezy tree-tops, and looking down with sovereign contempt upon the humble crawlers upon earth, they are fain to throw off for a time the dignity of the gentleman, to come down to the ground, and put on the pains-taking and industrious character of a labourer. They now lose their natural shyness, become fearless and familiar, and may be seen plying about in all directions, with an air of great assiduity, in search of building materials. Every now and then your path will be crossed by one of these busy old gentlemen, worrying about with awkward gait, as if troubled with the gout, or with corns on his toes, casting about many a prying look, turning down first one eye, then the other, in earnest consideration, upon every straw he meets with; until, espying some mighty twig, large enough to make a rafter for his air-castle, he will seize upon it with avidity, and hurry away with it to the tree-top; fearing, apparently, lest you should dispute with him the invaluable prize.

Like other castle-builders, these airy architects seem rather fanciful in the materials with which they build, and to like those most which come from a distance. Thus, though there are abundance of dry twigs on the surrounding trees, yet they never think of making use of them, but go foraging in distant lands, and come sailing home, one by one, from the ends of the earth, each bearing in his bill some precious piece of timber.

Nor must I avoid mentioning what, I grieve to say, rather derogates from the grave and honourable character of these ancient gentlefolk; that, during the architectural season, they are subject to great dissensions among themselves; that they make no scruple to defraud and plunder each other; and that sometimes the rookery is a scene of hideous brawl and commotion, in consequence of some delinquency of the kind. One of the partners generally remains on the nest, to guard it from depredation, and I have seen severe contests, when some sly neighbour has endeavoured to filch away a tempting rafter that has captivated his eye. As I am not willing to admit any suspicion hastily, that should throw a stigma on the general character of so worshipful a people, I am inclined to think that these larcenies are very much discountenanced by the higher classes, and even rigorously punished by those in authority; for I have now and then seen a whole gang of rooks fall upon the nest of some individual, pull it all to pieces, carry off the spoils, and even buffet the luckless proprietor. I have concluded this to be some signal punishment inflicted upon him, by the officers of the police, for some pilfering misdemeanour; or, perhaps, that it was a crew of bailiffs carrying an execution into his house.

I have been amused with another of their movements during the building season. The steward has suffered a considerable number of sheep to graze on a lawn near the house, somewhat to the annoyance of the Squire, who thinks this an innovation on the dignity of a park, which ought to be devoted to deer only. Be this as it may, there is a green knoll, not far from the drawing-room window, where the ewes and lambs are accustomed to assemble towards evening, for the benefit of the setting sun. No sooner were they gathered here, at the time when these politic birds were building, than a stately old rook, who Master Simon assured me was the chief magistrate of this community, would settle down upon the head of one of the ewes, who, seeming conscious of this condescension, would desist from grazing, and stand fixed in motionless reverence of her august burthen; the rest of the rookery would then come wheeling down, in imitation of their leader, until every ewe had two or three of them cawing, and fluttering, and battling upon her back. Whether they requited the submission of the sheep, by levying a contribution upon their fleece for the benefit of the rookery, I am not certain; though I presume they followed the usual custom of protecting powers.

The latter part of May is the time of great tribulation among the rookeries, when the young are just able to leave their nests, and balance themselves on the neighbouring branches. Now comes on the season of "rook shooting;" a terrible slaughter of the innocents. The Squire, of course, prohibits all invasion of the kind on his territories; but I am told that a lamentable havoc takes place in the colony about the old church. Upon this devoted commonwealth the village charges "with all its chivalry." Every idle wight that is lucky enough to possess an old gun or blunderbuss, together with all the archery of Slingsby's school, take the field on the occasion. In vain does the little parson interfere, or remonstrate, in angry tones from his study window that looks into the churchyard; there is a continual popping, from morning till night. Being no great marksmen, their shots are not often effective; but every now and then, a great shout from the besieging army of bumpkins makes known the downfall of some unlucky squab rook, which comes to the ground with the emphasis of a squashed apple-dumpling.

Nor is the rookery entirely free from other troubles and disasters. In so aristocratical and lofty-minded a community, which boasts so much ancient blood and hereditary pride, it is natural to suppose that questions of etiquette will sometimes arise and affairs of honour ensue. In fact, this is very often the case; bitter quarrels break out between individuals, which produce sad scufflings on tree-tops, and I have more than once seen a regular duel take place between two doughty heroes of the rookery. Their field of battle is generally the air; and their contest is managed in the most scientific and elegant manner; wheeling round and round each other, and towering higher and higher, to get the vantage-ground, until they sometimes disappear in the clouds before the combat is determined.

They have also fierce combats now and then with an invading hawk, and will drive him off from their territories by a *posse comitatus*. They are also extremely tenacious of their domains, and will suffer no other bird to inhabit the grove or its vicinity. There was a very ancient and respectable old bachelor owl, that had long had his lodgings in a corner of the grove, but has been fairly ejected by the rooks; and has retired, disgusted with the world, to a neighbouring wood, where he leads the life of a hermit, and makes nightly complaints of his ill-treatment.

The hootings of this unhappy gentleman may generally be heard in the still evenings, when the rooks are all at rest; and I have often listened to them of a moonlight night with a kind of mysterious gratification. This gray-bearded misanthrope, of course, is highly respected by the Squire; but the servants have superstitious notions about him, and it would be difficult to get the dairy-maid to venture after dark near to the wood which he inhabits.

Beside the private quarrels of the rooks, there are other misfortunes to which they are liable, and which often bring distress into the most respectable families of the rookery. Having the true baronial spirit of the good old feudal times, they are apt now and then to issue forth from their castles on a foray, and to lay the plebeian fields of the neighbouring country under contribution; in the course of which chivalrous expeditions, they now and then get a shot from the rusty artillery of some refractory farmer. Occasionally, too, while they are quietly taking the air beyond the park boundaries, they have the incaution to come within the reach of the truant bowman of Slingsby's school, and receive a flight shot from some unlucky urchin's arrow. In such case, the wounded adventurer will sometimes have just strength enough to bring himself home, and, giving up the ghost at the rookery, will hang dangling "all abroad" on a bough, like a thief on a gibbet—an awful warning to his friends, and an object of great commiseration to the Squire.

But, maugre all these untoward incidents, the rooks have, upon the whole, a happy holiday life of it. When their young are reared and fairly launched upon their native element, the air, the cares of the old folks seem over, and they resume all their aristocratical dignity and idleness. I have envied them the enjoyment which they appear to have in their ethereal heights, sporting with clamorous exultation about their lofty bowers; sometimes hovering over them, sometimes partially alighting upon the topmost branches, and there balancing with outstretched wings and swinging in the breeze. Sometimes they seem to take a fashionable drive to the church and amuse themselves by circling in airy rings about its spire; at other times a mere garrison is left at home to mount guard in their stronghold at the grove, while the rest roam abroad to enjoy the fine weather. About sunset the garrison gives notice of their return; their faint cawing will be heard from a great distance, and they will be seen far off like a sable cloud, and then nearer and nearer, until they all come soaring home. Then they perform several grand circuits in the air over the Hall and garden, wheeling closer and closer until they gradually settle down, when a prodigious cawing takes place, as though they were relating their day's adventures.

I like at such times to walk about these dusky groves, and hear the various sounds of these airy people roosted so high above me. As the gloom increases, their conversation subsides, and they seem to be gradually dropping asleep; but every now and then there is a querulous note, as if some one was quarrelling for a pillow, or a little more of the blanket. It is late in the evening before they completely sink to repose, and then their old anchorite neighbour, the owl, begins his lonely hooting from his bachelor's-hall in the wood.

May-Day.

It is the choice time of the year,
For the violets now appear;
Now the rose receives its birth,
And pretty primrose decks the earth.
Then to the May-pole come away,
For it is now a holiday.
—Acteon and Diana.

As I was lying in bed this morning, enjoying one of those half dreams, half reveries, which are so pleasant in the country, when the birds are singing about the window, and the sunbeams peeping through the curtains, I was roused by the sound of music. On going down-stairs I found a number of villagers, dressed in their holiday clothes, bearing a pole ornamented with garlands and ribands, and accompanied by the village band of music, under the direction of the tailor, the pale fellow who plays on the clarionet. They had all sprigs of hawthorn, or, as it is called, "the May," in their hats, and had brought green branches and flowers to decorate the Hall door and windows. They had come to give notice that the May-pole was reared on the green, and to invite the household to witness the sports. The Hall, according to custom, became a scene of hurry and delighted confusion. The servants were all agog with May and music; and there was no keeping either the tongues or the feet of the maids quiet, who were anticipating the sports of the green and the evening dance.

I repaired to the village at an early hour, to enjoy the merrymaking. The morning was pure and sunny, such as a May morning is always described. The fields were white with daisies, the hawthorn was covered with its fragrant blossoms, the bee hummed about every bank, and the swallow played high in the air about the village steeple. It was one of those genial days when we seem to draw in pleasure with the very air we breathe, and to feel happy we know not why. Whoever has felt the worth of worthy man, or has doted on lovely woman, will, on such a day, call them tenderly to mind, and feel his heart all alive with long-buried recollections. "For thenne," says the excellent romance of King Arthur, "lovers call ageyne to their mynde old gentilnes and old servyse, and many kind dedes that were forgotten by neglygence."

Before reaching the village, I saw the May-pole towering above the cottages with its gay garlands and streamers, and heard the sound of music. I found that there had been booths set up near it, for the reception of company; and a bower of green branches and flowers for the Queen of May, a fresh, rosy-cheeked girl of the village.

A band of morris-dancers were capering on the green in their fantastic dresses, jingling with hawks' bells, with a boy dressed up as Maid Marian, and the attendant fool rattling his box to collect contributions from the bystanders. The gipsy-women too were already plying their mystery in by-corners of the village, reading the hands of the simple country girls, and no doubt promising them all good husbands and tribes of children.

The Squire made his appearance in the course of the morning, attended by the parson, and was received with loud acclamations. He mingled among the country people throughout the day, giving and receiving pleasure wherever he went. The amusements of the day were under the management of Slingsby, the schoolmaster, who is not merely lord of misrule in his school, but master of the revels to the village. He was bustling about, with the perplexed and anxious air of a man who has the oppressive burthen of promoting other people's merriment upon his mind. He had involved himself in a dozen scrapes, in consequence of a politic intrigue, which, by-the-by, Master Simon and the Oxonian were at the bottom of, which had for object the election of the Queen of May. He had met with violent opposition from a faction of ale-drinkers, who were in favour of a bouncing bar-maid, the daughter of the innkeeper; but he had been too strongly backed not to carry his point, though it shows that these rural crowns, like all others, are objects of great ambition and heart-burning. I am told that Master Simon takes great interest, though in an Underhand way, in the election of these May-day Queens, and that the chaplet is generally secured for some rustic beauty that has found favour in his eyes.

In the course of the day, there were various games of strength and agility on the green, at which a knot of village veterans presided, as judges of the lists. Among these I perceived that Ready-Money Jack took the lead, looking with a learned and critical eye on the merits of the different candidates; and, though he was very laconic, and sometimes merely expressed himself by a nod, yet it was evident that his opinions far outweighed those of the most loquacious.

Young Jack Tibbets was the hero of the day, and carried off most of the prizes, though in some of the feats of agility he was rivalled by the "prodigal son," who appeared much in his element on this occasion; but his most formidable competitor was the notorious gipsy, the redoubtable "Starlight Tom." I was rejoiced at having an opportunity of seeing this "minion of the moon" in broad daylight. I found him a tall, swarthy, good-looking fellow, with a lofty air, something like what I have seen in an Indian chieftain; and with a certain lounging, easy, and almost graceful carriage, which I have often remarked in beings of the lazzaroni order, that lead an idle loitering life, and have a gentlemanlike contempt of labour.

Master Simon and the old general reconnoitred the ground together, and indulged a vast deal of harmless raking among the buxom country girls. Master Simon would give some of them a kiss on meeting with them, and would ask after their sisters, for he is acquainted with most of the farmers' families. Sometimes he would whisper, and affect to talk mischievously with them, and, if bantered on the subject, would turn it off with a laugh, though it was evident he liked to be suspected of being a gay Lothario amongst them.

He had much to say to the farmers about their farms; and seemed to know all their horses by name. There was an old fellow, with round ruddy face, and a night-cap under his hat, the village wit, who took several occasions to crack a joke with him in the hearing of his companions, to whom he would turn and wink hard when Master Simon had passed.

The harmony of the day, however, had nearly, at one time, been interrupted by the appearance of the radical on the ground, with two or three of his disciples. He soon got engaged in argument in the very thick of the throng, above which I could hear his voice, and now and then see his meagre hand, half a mile out of the sleeve, elevated in the air in violent gesticulation, and flourishing a pamphlet by way of truncheon. He was decrying these idle nonsensical amusements in time of public distress, when it was every one's business to think of other matters, and to be miserable. The honest village logicians could make no stand against him, especially as he was seconded by his proselytes; when, to their great joy, Master Simon and the general came drifting down into the field of action. I saw that Master Simon was for making off, as soon as he found himself in the neighbourhood of this fire-ship; but the general was too loyal to suffer such talk in his hearing, and thought, no doubt, that a look and a word from a gentleman would be sufficient to shut up so shabby an orator. The latter, however, was no respecter of persons, but rather seemed to exult in having such important antagonists. He talked with greater volubility than ever, and soon drowned them in declamation on the subject of taxes, poor's rates, and the national debt. Master Simon endeavoured to brush along in his usual excursive manner, which had always answered amazingly well with the villagers; but the radical was one of those pestilent fellows that pin a man down to facts; and, indeed, he had two or three pamphlets in his pocket, to support every thing he advanced by printed documents. The general, too, found himself betrayed into a more serious action than his dignity could brook; and looked like a mighty Dutch Indiaman, grievously peppered by a petty privateer. It was in vain that he swelled and looked big, and talked large, and endeavoured to make up by pomp of manner for poverty of matter; every home-thrust of the radical made him wheeze like a bellows, and seemed to let a volume of wind out of him.

In a word, the two worthies from the Hall were completely dumbfounded, and this too in the presence of several of Master Simon's staunch admirers, who had always looked up to him as infallible. I do not know how he and the general would have managed to draw their forces decently from the field, had there not been a match at grinning through a horse-collar announced, whereupon the radical retired with great expression of contempt, and, as soon as his back was turned, the argument was carried against him all hollow.

"Did you ever hear such a pack of stuff, general?" said Master Simon; "there's no talking with one of these chaps, when he once gets that confounded Cobbett in his head."

"S'blood, sir!" said the general, wiping his forehead, "such fellows ought all to be transported."

In the latter part of the day, the ladies from the Hall paid a visit to the green. The fair Julia made her appearance leaning on her lover's arm, and looking extremely pale and interesting. As she is a great favourite in the village, where she has been known from childhood; and as her late accident had been much talked about, the sight of her caused very manifest delight, and some of the old women of the village blessed her sweet face as she passed.

While they were walking about, I noticed the schoolmaster in earnest conversation with the young girl that represented the Queen of May, evidently endeavouring to spirit her up to some formidable undertaking. At length, as the party from the Hall approached her bower, she came forth, faltering at every step, until she reached the spot where the fair Julia stood between her lover and Lady Lillycraft. The little Queen then took the chaplet of flowers from her head, and attempted to put it on that of the bride elect; but the confusion of both was so great, that the wreath would have fallen to the ground, had not the officer caught it, and, laughing, placed it upon the blushing brows of his mistress. There was something charming in the very embarrassment of these two young creatures, both so beautiful, yet so different in their kinds of beauty. Master Simon told me, afterwards, that the Queen of May was to have spoken a few verses which the schoolmaster had written for her; but that she had neither wit to understand, nor memory to recollect them. "Besides," added he, "between you and I, she murders the king's English abominably; so she has acted the part of a wise woman, in holding her tongue, and trusting to her pretty face."

Among the other characters from the Hall was Mrs. Hannah, my Lady Lillycraft's gentlewoman; to my surprise, she was escorted by old Christy, the huntsman, and followed by his ghost of a grayhound; but I find they are very old acquaintances, being drawn together by some sympathy of disposition. Mrs. Hannah moved about with starched dignity among the rustics, who drew back from her with more awe than they did from her mistress. Her mouth seemed shut as with a clasp; excepting that I now and then heard the word "fellows!" escape from between her lips, as she got accidentally jostled in the crowd.

But there was one other heart present that did not enter into the merriment of the scene, which was that of the simple Phoebe Wilkins, the housekeeper's niece. The poor girl has continued to pine and whine for some time past, in consequence of the obstinate coldness of her lover; never was a little flirtation more severely punished. She appeared this day on the green, gallanted by a smart servant out of livery, and had evidently resolved to try the hazardous experiment of awakening the jealousy of her lover. She was dressed in her very best; affected an air of great gayety; talked loud and girlishly, and laughed when there was nothing to laugh at. There was, however, an aching, heavy heart in the poor baggage's bosom, in spite of all her levity. Her eye turned every now and then in quest of her reckless lover, and her cheek grew pale, and her fictitious gayety vanished, on seeing him paying his rustic homage to the little May-day Queen.

My attention was now diverted by a fresh stir and bustle. Music was heard from a distance; a banner was seen advancing up the road, preceded by a rustic band playing something like a march, and followed by a sturdy throng of country lads, the chivalry of a neighbouring and rival village.

No sooner had they reached the green, than they challenged the heroes of the day to new trials of strength and activity. Several gymnastic contests ensued, for the honour of the respective villages. In the course of these exercises, young Tibbets and the champion of the adverse party had an obstinate match at wrestling. They tugged, and strained, and panted, without either getting the mastery, until both came to the ground, and rolled upon the green. Just then, the disconsolate Phoebe came by. She saw her recreant lover in fierce contest, as she thought, and in danger. In a moment pride, pique, and coquetry, were forgotten; she rushed into the ring, seized upon the rival champion by the hair, and was on the point of wreaking on him her puny vengeance, when a buxom, strapping country lass, the sweetheart of the prostrate swain, pounced upon her like a hawk, and would have stripped her of her fine plumage in a twinkling, had she also not been seized in her turn.

A complete tumult ensued. The chivalry of the two villages became embroiled. Blows began to be dealt, and sticks to be flourished. Phoebe was carried off from the field in hysterics.

In vain did the sages of the village interfere. The sententious apothecary endeavoured to pour the soothing oil of his philosophy upon this tempestuous sea of passion, but was tumbled into the dust. Slingsby, the pedagogue, who is a great lover of peace, went into the midst of the throng, as marshal of the day, to put an end to the commotion; but was rent in twain, and came out with his garment hanging in two strips from his shoulders; upon which the prodigal son dashed in with fury, to revenge the insult which his patron had sustained. The tumult thickened; I caught glimpses of the jockey-cap of old Christy, like the helmet of a chieftain, bobbing about in the midst of the scuffle; whilst Mistress Hannah, separated from her doughty protector, was squalling and striking at right and left with a faded parasol; being tossed and tousled about by the crowd in such wise as never happened to maiden gentle woman before.

At length I beheld old Ready-Money Jack making his way into the very thickest of the throng; tearing it, as it were, apart, and enforcing peace, *vi et armis*. It was surprising to see the sudden quiet that ensued. The storm settled down at once into tranquillity. The parties, having no real grounds of hostility, were readily pacified, and in fact were a little at a loss to know why and how they had got by the ears. Slingsby was speedily stitched together again by his friend the tailor, and resumed his usual good-humour. Mrs. Hannah drew on one side, to plume her rumpled feathers; and old Christy, having repaired his damages, took her under his arm, and they swept back again to the Hall, ten times more bitter against mankind than ever.

The Tibbets family alone seemed slow in recovering from the agitation of the scene. Young Jack was evidently very much moved by the heroism of the unlucky Phoebe. His mother, who had been summoned to the field of action by news of the affray, was in a sad panic, and had need of all her management to keep him from following his mistress, and coming to a perfect reconciliation.

What heightened the alarm and perplexity of the good managing dame was, that the matter had aroused the slow apprehension of old Ready-Money himself; who was very much struck by the intrepid interference of so pretty and delicate a girl, and was sadly puzzled to understand the meaning of the violent agitation in his family.

When all this came to the ears of the Squire, he was grievously scandalized that his May-day fête should have been disgraced by such a brawl. He ordered Phoebe to appear before him; but the girl was so frightened and distressed, that she came sobbing and trembling, and, at the first question he asked, fell again into hysterics. Lady Lillycraft, who had understood that there was an affair of the heart at the bottom of this distress, immediately took the girl into great favour and protection, and made her peace with the Squire.

This was the only thing that disturbed the harmony of the day, if we except the discomfiture of Master Simon and the general by the radical. Upon the whole, therefore, the Squire had very fair reason to be satisfied that he had ridden his hobby throughout the day without any other molestation.

The reader, learned in these matters, will perceive that all this was but a faint shadow of the once gay and fanciful rites of May. The peasantry have lost the proper feeling for these rites, and have grown almost as strange to them as the boom of La Mancha were to the customs of chivalry, in the days of the valorous Don Quixote. Indeed, I considered it a proof of the discretion with which the Squire rides his hobby, that he had not pushed the thing any farther, nor attempted to revive many obsolete usages of the day, which, in the present matter-of-fact times, would appear affected and absurd. I must say, though I do it under the rose, the general brawl in which this festival had nearly terminated, has made me doubt whether these rural customs of the good old times were always so very loving and innocent as we are apt to fancy them; and whether the peasantry in those times were really so Arcadian, as they have been fondly represented. I begin to fear—

> —*"Those days were never; airy dream*
> *Sat for the picture, and the poet's hand,*
> *Imparting substance to an empty shade,*
> *Imposed a gay delirium for a truth.*
> *Grant it; I still must envy them an age*
> *That favour'd such a dream."*

The Manuscript.

Yesterday was a day of quiet and repose, after the bustle of May-day. During the morning, I joined the ladies in a small sitting-room, the windows of which came down to the floor, and opened upon a terrace of the garden, which was set out with delicate shrubs and flowers. The soft sunshine that fell into the room through the branches of trees that overhung the windows, the sweet smell of the flowers, and the singing of the birds, seemed to produce a pleasing yet calming effect on the whole party; for some time elapsed without any one speaking. Lady Lillycraft and Miss Templeton were sitting by an elegant work-table, near one of the windows, occupied with some pretty lady-like work. The captain was on a stool at his mistress' feet, looking over some music; and poor Phoebe Wilkins, who has always been a kind of pet among the ladies, but who has risen vastly in favour with Lady Lillycraft, in consequence of some tender confessions, sat in one corner of the room, with swoln eyes, working pensively at some of the fair Julia's wedding ornaments.

The silence was interrupted by her ladyship, who suddenly proposed a task to the captain. "I am in your debt," said she, "for that tale you read to us the other day; I will now furnish one in return, if you'll read it: and it is just suited to this sweet May morning, for it is all about love!"

The proposition seemed to delight every one present. The captain smiled assent. Her ladyship rung for her page, and despatched him to her room for the manuscript. "As the captain," said she, "gave us an account of the author of his story, it is but right I should give one of mine. It was written by the parson of the parish where I reside. He is a thin, elderly man, of a delicate constitution, but positively one of the most charming men that ever lived. He lost his wife a few years since; one of the sweetest women you ever saw. He has two sons, whom he educates himself; both of whom already write delightful poetry. His parsonage is a lovely place, close by the church, all overrun with ivy and honeysuckles; with the sweetest flower-garden about it; for, you know, our country clergymen are almost always fond of flowers, and make their parsonages perfect pictures.

"His living is a very good one, and he is very much beloved, and does a great deal of good in the neighbourhood, and among the poor. And then such sermons as he preaches! Oh, if you could only hear one taken from a text in Solomon's Song, all about love and matrimony, one of the sweetest things you ever heard! He preaches it at least once a year, in springtime, for he knows I am fond of it. He always dines with me on Sundays, and often brings me some of the sweetest pieces of poetry, all about the pleasures of melancholy, and such subjects, that make me cry so, you can't think. I wish he would publish. I think he has some things as sweet as any thing of Moore or Lord Byron.

"He fell into very ill health some time ago, and was advised to go to the continent; and I gave him no peace until he went, and promised to take care of his two boys until he returned.

"He was gone for above a year, and was quite restored. When he came back, he sent me the tale I'm going to show you.—Oh, here it is!" said she, as the page put in her hands a beautiful box of satinwood. She unlocked it, and from among several parcels of notes on embossed paper, cards of charades, and copies of verses, she drew out a crimson velvet case, that smelt very much of perfumes. From this she took a manuscript, daintily written on gilt-edged vellum paper, and stitched a light blue riband. This she handed to the captain, who read the following tale, which I have procured for the entertainment of the reader.

Annette Delarbre.

The soldier frae the war returns,
And the merchant from the main,
But I hae parted with my love,
And ne'er to meet again,
My dear,
And ne'er to meet again.
When day is gone, and night is come,
And a' are boun to sleep,
I think on them that's far awa
The lee-lang night, and weep,
My dear,
The lee-lang night, and weep.
—Old Scotch Ballad.

In the course of a tour that I once made in Lower Normandy, I remained for a day or two at the old town of Honfleur, which stands near the mouth of the Seine. It was the time of a fête, and all the world was thronging in the evening to dance at the fair, held before the chapel of Our Lady of Grace. As I like all kinds of innocent merry-making, I joined the throng.

The chapel is situated at the top of a high hill, or promontory, from whence its bell may be heard at a distance by the mariner at night. It is said to have given the name to the port of Havre-de-Grace, which lies directly opposite, on the other side of the Seine. The road up to the chapel went in a zigzag course, along the brow of the steep coast; it was shaded by trees, from between which I had beautiful peeps at the ancient towers of Honfleur below, the varied scenery of the opposite shore, the white buildings of Havre in the distance, and the wide sea beyond. The road was enlivened by groups of peasant girls, in their bright crimson dresses and tall caps; and I found all the flower of the neighbourhood assembled on the green that crowns the summit of the hill.

The chapel of Notre Dame de Grace is a favourite resort of the inhabitants of Honfleur and its vicinity, both for pleasure and devotion. At this little chapel prayers are put up by the mariners of the port previous to their voyages, and by their friends during their absence; and votive offerings are hung about its walls, in fulfilment of vows made during times of shipwreck and disaster. The chapel is surrounded by trees. Over the portal is an image of the Virgin and child, with an inscription which struck me as being quite poetical:

"Etoile de la mer, priez pour nous!"
(Star of the sea, pray for us.)

On a level spot near the chapel, under a grove of noble trees, the populace dance on fine summer evenings; and here are held frequent fairs and fêtes, which assemble all the rustic beauty of the loveliest parts of Lower Normandy. The present was an occasion of the kind. Booths and tents were erected among the trees; there were the usual displays of finery to tempt the rural coquette, and of wonderful shows to entice the curious; mountebanks were exerting their eloquence; jugglers and fortune-tellers astonishing the credulous; while whole rows of grotesque saints, in wood and wax-work, were offered for the purchase of the pious.

The fête had assembled in one view all the picturesque costumes of the Pays d'Auge, and the Coté de Caux. I beheld tall, stately caps, and trim bodices, according to fashions which have been handed down from mother to daughter for centuries, the exact counterparts of those worn in the time of the Conqueror; and which surprised me by their faithful resemblance to those which I had seen in the old pictures of Froissart's Chronicles, and in the paintings of illuminated manuscripts. Any one, also, that has been in Lower Normandy, must have remarked the beauty of the peasantry, and that air of native elegance that prevails among them. It is to this country, undoubtedly, that the English owe their good looks. It was from hence that the bright carnation, the fine blue eye, the light auburn hair, passed over to England in the train of the Conqueror, and filled the land with beauty.

The scene before me was perfectly enchanting: the assemblage of so many fresh and blooming faces; the gay groups in fanciful dresses; some dancing on the green, others strolling about, or seated on the grass; the fine clumps of trees in the foreground, bordering the brow of this airy height, and the broad green sea, sleeping in summer tranquillity in the distance.

Whilst I was regarding this animated picture, I was struck with the appearance of a beautiful girl, who passed through the crowd without seeming to take any interest in their amusements. She was slender and delicate in her form; she had not the bloom upon her cheek that is usual among the peasantry of Normandy, and her blue eyes had a singular and melancholy expression. She was accompanied by a venerable-looking man, whom I presumed to be her father. There was a whisper among the bystanders, and a wistful look after her as she passed; the young men touched their hats, and some of the children followed her at a little distance, watching her movements. She approached the edge of the hill, where there is a little platform, from whence the people of Honfleur look out for the approach of vessels. Here she stood for some time waving her handkerchief, though there was nothing to be seen but two or three fishing-boats, like mere specks on the bosom of the distant ocean.

These circumstances excited my curiosity, and I made some inquiries about her, which were answered with readiness and intelligence by a priest of the neighbouring chapel. Our conversation drew together several of the by-standers, each of whom had something to communicate, and from them all I gathered the following particulars.

Annette Delarbre was the only daughter of one of the higher order of farmers, or small proprietors, as they are called, who lived at Pont l'Eveque, a pleasant village not far from Honfleur, in that rich pastoral part of Lower Normandy called the Pays d'Auge. Annette was the pride and delight of her parents, and was brought up with the fondest indulgence. She was gay, tender, petulant, and susceptible. All her feelings were quick and ardent; and having never experienced contradiction or restraint, she was little practised in self-control: nothing but the native goodness of her heart kept her from running continually into error.

Even while a child, her susceptibility was evinced in an attachment which she formed to a playmate, Eugene La Forgue, the only son of a widow, who lived in the neighbourhood. Their childish love was an epitome of maturer passion; it had its caprices, and jealousies, and quarrels, and reconciliations. It was assuming something of a graver character, as Annette entered her fifteenth and Eugene his nineteenth year, when he was suddenly carried off to the army by the conscription.

It was a heavy blow to his widowed mother, for he was her only pride and comfort; but it was one of those sudden bereavements which mothers were perpetually doomed to feel in France, during the time that continual and bloody wars were incessantly draining her youth. It was a temporary affliction also to Annette, to lose her lover. With tender embraces, half childish, half womanish, she parted from him. The tears streamed from her blue eyes, as she bound a braid of her fair hair round his wrist; but the smiles still broke through; for she was yet too young to feel how serious a thing is separation, and how many chances there are, when parting in this wide world, against our ever meeting again.

Weeks, months, years flew by. Annette increased in beauty as she increased in years, and was the reigning belle of the neighbourhood. Her time passed innocently and happily. Her father was a man of some consequence in the rural community, and his house was the resort of the gayest of the village. Annette held a kind of rural court; she was always surrounded by companions of her own age, among whom she alone unrivalled. Much of their time was passed in making lace, the prevalent manufacture of the neighbourhood. As they sat at this delicate and feminine labour, the merry tale and sprightly song went round; none laughed with a lighter heart than Annette; and if she sang, her voice was perfect melody. Their evenings were enlivened by the dance, or by those pleasant social games so prevalent among the French; and when she appeared at the village ball on Sunday evenings, she was the theme of universal admiration.

As she was a rural heiress, she did not want for suitors. Many advantageous offers were made her, but she refused them all. She laughed at the pretended pangs of her admirers, and triumphed over them with the caprice of buoyant youth and conscious beauty. With all her apparent levity, however, could any one have read the story of her heart, they might have traced in it some fond remembrance of her early playmate, not so deeply graven as to be painful, but too deep to be easily obliterated; and they might have noticed, amidst all her gayety, the tenderness that marked her manner towards the mother of Eugene. She would often steal away from her youthful companions and their amusements, to pass whole days with the good widow; listening to her fond talk about her boy, and blushing with secret pleasure, when his letters were read, at finding herself a constant theme of recollection and inquiry.

At length the sudden return of peace, which sent many a warrior to his native cottage, brought back Eugene, a young sun-burnt soldier, to the village. I need not say how rapturously his return was greeted by his mother, who saw in him the pride and staff of her old age. He had risen in the service by his merits; but brought away little from the wars, excepting a soldier-like air, a gallant name, and a scar across the forehead. He brought back, however, a nature unspoiled by the camp. He was frank, open, generous, and ardent. His heart was quick and kind in its impulses, and was perhaps a little softer from having suffered: it was full of tenderness for Annette. He had received frequent accounts of her from his mother; and the mention of her kindness to his lonely parent, had rendered her doubly dear to him. He had been wounded; he had been a prisoner; he had been in various troubles, but had always preserved the braid of her hair, which she had bound round his arm. It had been a kind of talisman to him; he had many a time looked upon it as he lay on the hard ground, and the thought that he might one day see Annette again, and the fair fields about his native village, had cheered his heart, and enabled him to bear up against every hardship.

He had left Annette almost a child—he found her a blooming woman. If he had loved her before, he now adored her. Annette was equally struck with the improvement which time had made in her lover. She noticed, with secret admiration, his superiority to the other young men of the village; the frank, lofty, military air, that distinguished him from all the rest at their rural gatherings. The more she saw him, the more her light, playful fondness of former years deepened into ardent and powerful affection. But Annette was a rural belle.

She had tasted the sweets of dominion, and had been rendered wilful and capricious by constant indulgence at home, and admiration abroad. She was conscious of her power over Eugene, and delighted in exercising it. She sometimes treated him with petulant caprice, enjoying the pain which she inflicted by her frowns, from the idea how soon she would chase it away again by her smiles. She took a pleasure in alarming his fears, by affecting a temporary preference to some one or other of his rivals; and then would delight in allaying them, by an ample measure of returning kindness. Perhaps there was some degree of vanity gratified by all this; it might be a matter of triumph to show her absolute power over the young soldier, who was the universal object of female admiration. Eugene, however, was of too serious and ardent a nature to be trifled with. He loved too fervently not to be filled with doubt. He saw Annette surrounded by admirers, and full of animation; the gayest among the gay at all their rural festivities, and apparently most gay when he was most dejected. Every one saw through this caprice, but himself; everyone saw that in reality she doted on him; but Eugene alone suspected the sincerity of her affection. For some time he bore this coquetry with secret impatience and distrust; but his feelings grew sore and irritable, and overcame his self-command. A slight misunderstanding took place; a quarrel ensued. Annette, unaccustomed to be thwarted and contradicted, and full of the insolence of youthful beauty, assumed an air of disdain. She refused all explanations to her lover, and they parted in anger.

That very evening Eugene saw her, full of gayety, dancing with one of his rivals; and as her eye caught his, fixed on her with unfeigned distress, it sparkled with more than usual vivacity. It was a finishing blow to his hopes, already so much impaired by secret distrust. Pride and resentment both struggled in his breast, and seemed to rouse his spirit to all its wonted energy. He retired from her presence, with the hasty determination never to see her again.

A woman is more considerate in affairs of love than a man; because love is more the study and business of her life. Annette soon repented of her indiscretion; she felt that she had used her lover unkindly; she felt that she had trifled with his sincere and generous nature—and then he looked so handsome when he parted after their quarrel—his fine features lighted up by indignation. She had intended making up with him at the evening dance; but his sudden departure prevented her. She now promised herself that when next they met she would amply repay him by the sweets of a perfect reconciliation, and that, thenceforward, she would never—never tease him more! That promise was not to be fulfilled. Day after day passed—but Eugene did not make his appearance. Sunday evening came, the usual time when all the gayety of the village assembled—butEugene was not there. She inquired after him; he had left the village. She now became alarmed, and, forgetting all coyness and affected indifference, called on Eugene's mother for an explanation. She found her full of affliction, and learnt with surprise and consternation that Eugene had gone to sea.

While his feelings were yet smarting with her affected disdain, and his heart a prey to alternate indignation and despair, he had suddenly embraced an invitation which had repeatedly been made him by a relation, who was fitting out a ship from the port of Honfleur, and who wished him to be the companion of his voyage. Absence appeared to him the only cure for his unlucky passion; and in the temporary transports of his feelings, there was something gratifying in the idea of having half the world intervene between them. The hurry necessary for his departure left no time for cool reflection; it rendered him deaf to the remonstrances of his afflicted mother. He hastened to Honfleur just in time to make the needful preparations for the voyage; and the first news that Annette received of this sudden determination was a letter delivered by his mother, returning her pledges of affection, particularly the long-treasured braid of her hair, and bidding her a last farewell, in terms more full of sorrow and tenderness than upbraiding.

This was the first stroke of real anguish that Annette had ever received, and it overcame her. The vivacity of her spirits was apt to hurry her to extremes; she for a time gave way to ungovernable transports of affliction and remorse, and manifested, in the violence of her grief, the real ardour of her affection. The thought occurred to her that the ship might not yet have sailed; she seized on the hope with eagerness, and hastened with her father to Honfleur. The ship had sailed that very morning. From the heights above the town she saw it lessening to a speck on the broad bosom of the ocean, and before evening the white sail had faded from her sight. She turned full of anguish to the neighbouring chapel of Our Lady of Grace, and throwing herself on the pavement, poured out prayers and tears for the safe return of her lover.

When she returned home, the cheerfulness of her spirits was at an end. She looked back with remorse and self-upbraiding at her past caprices; she turned with distaste from the adulation of her admirers, and had no longer any relish for the amusements of the village. With humiliation and diffidence, she sought the widowed mother of Eugene; but was received by her with an overflowing heart; for she only beheld in Annette one who could sympathize in her doting fondness for her son. It seemed some alleviation of her remorse to sit by the mother all day, to study her wants, to beguile her heavy hours, to hang about her with the caressing endearments of a daughter, and to seek by every means, if possible, to supply the place of the son, whom she reproached herself with having driven away.

In the mean time, the ship made a prosperous voyage to her destined port. Eugene's mother received a letter from him, in which he lamented the precipitancy of his departure. The voyage had given him time for sober reflection. If Annette had been unkind to him, he ought not to have forgotten what was due to his mother, who was now advanced in years. He accused himself of selfishness, in only listening to the suggestions of his own inconsiderate passions. He promised to return with the ship, to make his mind up to his disappointment, and to think of nothing but making his mother happy—"And when he does return," said Annette, clasping her hands with transport, "it shall not be my fault if he ever leaves us again."

The time approached for the ship's return. She was daily expected, when the weather became dreadfully tempestuous. Day after day brought news of vessels foundered, or driven on shore, and the coast was strewed with wrecks. Intelligence was received of the looked-for ship having been seen dismasted in a violent storm, and the greatest fears were entertained for her safety.

Annette never left the side of Eugene's mother. She watched every change of her countenance with painful solicitude, and endeavoured to cheer her with hopes, while her own mind was racked by anxiety. She tasked her efforts to be gay; but it was a forced and unnatural gayety: a sigh from the mother would completely check it; and when she could no longer restrain the rising tears, she would hurry away and pour out her agony in secret. Every anxious look, every anxious inquiry of the mother, whenever a door opened, or a strange face appeared, was an arrow to her soul. She considered every disappointment as a pang of her own infliction, and her heart sickened under the careworn expression of the maternal eye. At length this suspense became insupportable. She left the village and hastened to Honfleur, hoping every hour, every moment, to receive some tidings of her lover. She paced the pier, and wearied the seamen of the port with her inquiries. She made a daily pilgrimage to the chapel of Our Lady of Grace; hung votive garlands on the wall, and passed hours either kneeling before the altar, or looking out from the brow of the hill upon the angry sea.

At length word was brought that the long-wished-for vessel was in sight. She was seen standing into the mouth of the Seine, shattered and crippled, bearing marks of having been sadly tempest-tost. There was a general joy diffused by her return; and there was not a brighter eye, nor a lighter heart, than Annette's, in the little port of Honfleur. The ship came to anchor in the river, and shortly after a boat put off for the shore. The populace crowded down to the pier-head, to welcome it. Annette stood blushing, and smiling, and trembling, and weeping; for a thousand painfully-pleasing emotions agitated her breast at the thoughts of the meeting and reconciliation about to take place.

Her heart throbbed to pour itself out, and atone to her gallant lover for all its errors. At one moment she would place herself in a conspicuous situation, where she might catch his view at once, and surprise him by her welcome; but the next moment a doubt would come across her mind, and she would shrink among the throng, trembling and faint, and gasping with her emotions. Her agitation increased as the boat drew near, until it became distressing; and it was almost a relief to her when she perceived that her lover was not there. She presumed that some accident had detained him on board of the ship; and she felt that the delay would enable her to gather more self-possession for the meeting. As the boat neared the shore, many inquiries were made, and laconic answers returned.

At length Annette heard some inquiries after her lover. Her heart palpitated—there was a moment's pause: the reply was brief, but awful. He had been washed from the deck, with two of the crew, in the midst of a stormy night, when it was impossible to render any assistance. A piercing shriek broke from among the crowd; and Annette had nearly fallen into the waves.

The sudden revulsion of feelings after such a transient gleam of happiness, was too much for her harassed frame. She was carried home senseless. Her life was for some time despaired of, and it was months before she recovered her health; but she never had perfectly recovered her mind: it still remained unsettled with respect to her lover's fate.

"The subject," continued my informant, "is never mentioned in her hearing; but she sometimes speaks of it herself, and it seems as though there were some vague train of impressions in her mind, in which hope and fear are strangely mingled—some imperfect idea of her lover's shipwreck, and yet some expectation of his return.

"Her parents have tried every means to cheer her, and to banish these gloomy images from her thoughts. They assemble round her the young companions in whose society she used to delight; and they will work, and chat, and sing, and laugh, as formerly; but she will sit silently among them, and will sometimes weep in the midst of their gayety; and, if spoken to, will make no reply, but look up with streaming eyes, and sing a dismal little song, which she has learned somewhere, about a shipwreck. It makes every one's heart ache to see her in this way, for she used to be the happiest creature in the village.

"She passes the greater part of the time with Eugene's mother; whose only consolation is her society, and who dotes on her with a mother's tenderness. She is the only one that has perfect influence over Annette in every mood. The poor girl seems, as formerly, to make an effort to be cheerful in her company; but will sometimes gaze upon her with the most piteous look, and then kiss her gray hairs, and fall on her neck and weep.

"She is not always melancholy, however; she has occasional intervals, when she will be bright and animated for days together; but there is a degree of wildness attending these fits of gayety, that prevents their yielding any satisfaction to her friends. At such times she will arrange her room, which is all covered with pictures of ships and legends of saints; and will wreathe a white chaplet, as if for a wedding, and prepare wedding ornaments. She will listen anxiously at the door, and look frequently out at the window, as if expecting some one's arrival. It is supposed that at such times she is looking for her lover's return; but, as no one touches upon the theme, nor mentions his name in her presence, the current of her thoughts is mere matter of conjecture. Now and then she will make a pilgrimage to the chapel of Notre Dame de Grace; where she will pray for hours at the altar, and decorate the images with wreaths that she had woven; or will wave her handkerchief from the terrace, as you have seen, if there is any vessel in the distance."

Upwards of a year, he informed me, had now elapsed without effacing from her mind this singular taint of insanity; still her friends hoped it might gradually wear away. They had at one time removed her to a distant part of the country, in hopes that absence from the scenes connected with her story might have a salutary effect; but, when her periodical melancholy returned, she became more restless and wretched than usual, and, secretly escaping from her friends, set out on foot, without knowing the road, on one of her pilgrimages to the chapel.

This little story entirely drew my attention from the gay scene of the fête, and fixed it upon the beautiful Annette. While she was yet standing on the terrace, the vesper-bell was rung from the neighbouring chapel. She listened for a moment, and then drawing a small rosary from her bosom, walked in that direction. Several of the peasantry followed her in silence; and I felt too much interested, not to do the same.

The chapel, as I said before, is in the midst of a grove, on the high promontory. The inside is hung round with little models of ships, and rude paintings of wrecks and perils at sea, and providential deliverances—the votive offerings of captains and crews that have been saved. On entering, Annette paused for a moment before a picture of the virgin, which, I observed, had recently been decorated with a wreath of artificial flowers. When she reached the middle of the chapel she knelt down, and those who followed her involuntarily did the same at a little distance. The evening sun shone softly through the checkered grove into one window of the chapel. A perfect stillness reigned within; and this stillness was the more impressive contrasted with the distant sound of music and merriment from the fair. I could not take my eyes off from the poor suppliant; her lips moved as she told her beads, but her prayers were breathed in silence. It might have been mere fancy excited by the scene, that, as she raised her eyes to heaven, I thought they had an expression truly seraphic. But I am easily affected by female beauty, and there was something in this mixture of love, devotion, and partial insanity, that was inexpressibly touching.

As the poor girl left the chapel, there was a sweet serenity in her looks; and I was told that she would return home, and in all probability be calm and cheerful for days, and even weeks; in which time it was supposed that hope predominated in her mental malady; and that, when the dark side of her mind, as her friends call it, was about to turn up, it would be known by her neglecting her distaff or her lace, singing plaintive songs, and weeping in silence.

She passed on from the chapel without noticing the fête, but smiling and speaking to many as she passed. I followed her with my eye as she descended the winding road towards Honfleur, leaning on her father's arm. "Heaven," thought I, "has ever its store of balms for the hurt mind and wounded spirit, and may in time rear up this broken flower to be once more the pride and joy of the valley. The very delusion in which the poor girl walks, may be one of those mists kindly diffused by Providence over the regions of thought, when they become too fruitful of misery. The veil may gradually be raised which obscures the horizon of her mind, as she is enabled steadily and calmly to contemplate the sorrows at present hidden in mercy from her view."

On my return from Paris, about a year afterwards, I turned off from the beaten route at Rouen, to revisit some of the most striking scenes of Lower Normandy. Having passed through the lovely country of the Pays d'Auge, I reached Honfleur on a fine afternoon, intending to cross to Havre the next morning, and embark for England. As I had no better way of passing the evening, I strolled up the hill to enjoy the fine prospect from the chapel of Notre Dame de Grace; and while there, I thought of inquiring after the fate of poor Annette Delarbre. The priest who had told me her story was officiating at vespers, after which I accosted him, and learnt from him the remaining circumstances. He told me that from the time I had seen her at the chapel, her disorder took a sudden turn for the worse, and her health rapidly declined. Her cheerful intervals became shorter and less frequent, and attended with more incoherency. She grew languid, silent, and moody in her melancholy; her form was wasted, her looks pale and disconsolate, and it was feared she would never recover. She became impatient of all sounds of gayety, and was never so contented as when Eugene's mother was near her. The good woman watched over her with patient, yearning solicitude; and in seeking to beguile her sorrows, would half forget her own. Sometimes, as she sat looking upon her pallid face, the tears would fill her eyes, which, when Annette perceived, she would anxiously wipe them away, and tell her not to grieve, for that Eugene would soon return; and then she would affect a forced gayety, as in former times, and sing a lively air; but a sudden recollection would come over her, and she would burst into tears, hang on the poor mother's neck, and entreat her not to curse her for having destroyed her son.

Just at this time, to the astonishment of every one, news was received of Eugene; who, it appeared, was still living. When almost drowned, he had fortunately seized upon a spar which had been washed from the ship's deck. Finding himself nearly exhausted, he had fastened himself to it, and floated for a day and night, until all sense had left him. On recovering, he had found himself on board a vessel bound to India, but so ill as not to move without assistance. His health had continued precarious throughout the voyage; on arriving in India, he had experienced many vicissitudes, and had been transferred from ship to ship, and hospital to hospital. His constitution had enabled him to struggle through every hardship; and he was now in a distant port, waiting only for the sailing of a ship to return home.

Great caution was necessary in imparting these tidings to the mother, and even then she was nearly overcome by the transports of her joy. But how to impart them to Annette, was a matter of still greater perplexity. Her state of mind had been so morbid; she had been subject to such violent changes, and the cause of her derangement had been of such an inconsolable and hopeless kind, that her friends had always forborne to tamper with her feelings. They had never even hinted at the subject of her griefs, nor encouraged the theme when she adverted to it, but had passed it over in silence, hoping that time would gradually wear the traces of it from her recollection, or, at least, would render them less painful. They now felt at a loss how to undeceive her even in her misery, lest the sudden recurrence of happiness might confirm the estrangement of her reason, or might overpower her enfeebled frame. They ventured, however, to probe those wounds which they formerly did not dare to touch, for they now had the balm to pour into them. They led the conversation to those topics which they had hitherto shunned, and endeavoured to ascertain the current of her thoughts in those varying moods that had formerly perplexed them. They found, however, that her mind was even more affected than they had imagined. All her ideas were confused and wandering. Her bright and cheerful moods, which now grew seldomer than ever, were all the effects of mental delusion. At such times she had no recollection of her lover's having been in danger, but was only anticipating his arrival. "When the winter has passed away," said she, "and the trees put on their blossoms, and the swallow comes back over the sea, he will return." When she was drooping and desponding, it was in vain to remind her of what she had said in her gayer moments, and to assure her that Eugene would indeed return shortly. She wept on in silence, and appeared insensible to their words. But at times her agitation became violent, when she would upbraid herself with having driven Eugene from his mother, and brought sorrow on her gray hairs. Her mind admitted but one leading idea at a time, which nothing could divert or efface; or if they ever succeeded in interrupting the current of her fancy, it only became the more incoherent, and increased the feverishness that preyed upon both mind and body. Her friends felt more alarm for her than ever, for they feared that her senses were irrecoverably gone, and her constitution completely undermined.

In the mean time, Eugene returned to the village. He was violently affected, when the story of Annette was told him. With bitterness of heart he upbraided his own rashness and infatuation that had hurried him away from her, and accused himself as the author of all her woes. His mother would describe to him all the anguish and remorse of poor Annette; the tenderness with which she clung to her, and endeavoured, even in the midst of her insanity, to console her for the loss of her son, and the touching expressions of affection that were mingled with her most incoherent wanderings of thought, until his feelings would be wound up to agony, and he would entreat her to desist from the recital. They did not dare as yet to bring him into Annette's sight; but he was permitted to see her when she was sleeping. The tears streamed down his sunburnt cheeks, as he contemplated the ravages which grief and malady had made; and his heart swelled almost to breaking, as he beheld round her neck the very braid of hair which she once gave him in token of girlish affection, and which he had returned to her in anger.

At length the physician that attended her determined to adventure upon an experiment, to take advantage of one of those cheerful moods when her mind was visited by hope, and to endeavour to engraft, as it were, the reality upon the delusions of her fancy. These moods had now become very rare, for nature was sinking under the continual pressure of her mental malady, and the principle of reaction was daily growing weaker. Every effort was tried to bring on a cheerful interval of the kind. Several of her most favourite companions were kept continually about her; they chatted gayly, they laughed, and sang, and danced; but Annette reclined with languid frame and hollow eye, and took no part in their gayety. At length the winter was gone; the trees put forth their leaves; the swallows began to build in the eaves of the house, and the robin and wren piped all day beneath the window. Annette's spirits gradually revived. She began to deck her person with unusual care; and bringing forth a basket of artificial flowers, she went to work to wreathe a bridal chaplet of white roses. Her companions asked her why she prepared the chaplet. "What!" said she with a smile, "have you not noticed the trees putting on their wedding dresses of blossoms? Has not the swallow flown back over the sea? Do you not know that the time is come for Eugene to return? that he will be home to-morrow, and that on Sunday we are to be married?"

Her words were repeated to the physician, and he seized on them at once. He directed that her idea should be encouraged and acted upon. Her words were echoed through the house. Every one talked of the return of Eugene, as a matter of course; they congratulated her upon her approaching happiness, and assisted her in her preparations. The next morning, the same theme was resumed. She was dressed out to receive her lover. Every bosom fluttered with anxiety. A cabriolet drove into the village. "Eugene is coming!" was the cry. She saw him alight at the door, and rushed with a shriek into his arms.

Her friends trembled for the result of this critical experiment; but she did not sink under it, for her fancy had prepared her for his return. She was as one in a dream, to whom a tide of unlooked-for prosperity, that would have overwhelmed his waking reason, seems but the natural current of circumstances. Her conversation, however, showed that her senses were wandering. There was an absolute forgetfulness of all past sorrow—a wild and feverish gayety, that at times was incoherent.

The next morning, she awoke languid and exhausted. All the occurrences of the preceding day had passed away from her mind, as though they had been the mere illusions of her fancy. She rose melancholy and abstracted, and, as she dressed herself, was heard to sing one of her plaintive ballads. When she entered the parlour, her eyes were swoln with weeping. She heard Eugene's voice without, and started. She passed her hand across her forehead, and stood musing, like one endeavouring to recall a dream. Eugene entered the room, and advanced towards her; she looked at him with an eager, searching look, murmured some indistinct words, and before he could reach her, sank upon the floor.

She relapsed into a wild and unsettled state of mind; but now that the first shock was over, the physician ordered that Eugene should keep continually in her sight. Sometimes she did not know him; at other times she would talk to him as if he were going to sea, and would implore him not to part from her in anger; and when he was not present, she would speak of him as if buried in the ocean, and would sit, with clasped hands, looking upon the ground, the picture of despair. As the agitation of her feelings subsided, and her frame recovered from the shock which it had received, she became more placid and coherent. Eugene kept almost continually near her. He formed the real object round which her scattered ideas once more gathered, and which linked them once more with the realities of life. But her changeful disorder now appeared to take a new turn. She became languid and inert, and would sit for hours silent, and almost in a state of lethargy. If roused from this stupor, it seemed as if her mind would make some attempts to follow up a train of thought, but would soon become confused. She would regard every one that approached her with an anxious and inquiring eye, that seemed continually to disappoint itself. Sometimes, as her lover sat holding her hand, she would look pensively in his face without saying a word, until his heart was overcome; and after these transient fits of intellectual exertion, she would sink again into lethargy.

By degrees, this stupor increased; her mind appeared to have subsided into a stagnant and almost death-like calm. For the greater part of the time, her eyes were closed; her face almost as fixed and passionless as that of a corpse. She no longer took any notice of surrounding objects. There was an awfulness in this tranquillity, that filled her friends with apprehensions. The physician ordered that she should be kept perfectly quiet; or that, if she evinced any agitation, she should be gently lulled, like a child, by some favourite tune.

She remained in this state for hours, hardly seeming to breathe, and apparently sinking into the sleep of death. Her chamber was profoundly still. The attendants moved about it with noiseless tread; every thing was communicated by signs and whispers. Her lover sat by her side, watching her with painful anxiety, and fearing that every breath which stole from her pale lips would be the last.

At length she heaved a deep sigh; and, from some convulsive motions, appeared to be troubled in her sleep. Her agitation increased, accompanied by an indistinct moaning. One of her companions, remembering the physician's instructions, endeavoured to lull her by singing, in a low voice, a tender little air, which was a particular favourite of Annette's. Probably it had some connexion in her mind with her own story; for every fond girl has some ditty of the kind, linked in her thoughts with sweet and sad remembrances.

As she sang, the agitation of Annette subsided. A streak of faint colour came into her cheeks; her eyelids became swoln with rising tears, which trembled there for a moment, and then, stealing forth, coursed down her pallid cheek. When the song was ended, she opened her eyes and looked about her, as one awakening in a strange place.

"Oh, Eugene! Eugene!" said she, "it seems as if I have had a long and dismal dream; what has happened, and what has been the matter with me?"

The questions were embarrassing; and before they could be answered, the physician, who was in the next room, entered. She took him by the hand, looked up in his face, and made the same inquiry. He endeavoured to put her off with some evasive answer;—"No, no!" cried she, "I know I have been ill, and I have been dreaming strangely. I thought Eugene had left us—and that he had gone to sea—and that—and that he was drowned!—But he *has* been to sea!" added she, earnestly, as recollection kept flashing upon her, "and he has been wrecked—and we were all so wretched—and he came home again one bright morning—and—Oh!" said she, pressing her hand against her forehead, with a sickly smile, "I see how it is; all has not been right here: I begin to recollect—but it is all past now—Eugene is here! and his mother is happy—and we shall never—never part again—shall we, Eugene?"

She sunk back in her chair, exhausted; the tears streamed down her cheeks. Her companions hovered round her, not knowing what to make of this sudden dawn of reason. Her lover sobbed aloud. She opened her eyes again, and looked upon them with an air of the sweetest acknowledgment. "You are all so good to me!" said she, faintly.

The physician drew the father aside. "Your daughter's mind is restored," said he; "she is sensible that she has been deranged; she is growing conscious of the past, and conscious of the present. All that now remains is to keep her calm and quiet until her health is re-established, and then let her be married in God's name!"

"The wedding took place," continued the good priest, "but a short time since; they were here at the last fête during their honeymoon, and a handsomer and happier couple was not to be seen as they danced under yonder trees. The young man, his wife, and mother, now live on a fine farm at Pont l'Eveque; and that model of a ship which you see yonder, with white flowers wreathed round it, is Annette's offering of thanks to Our Lady of Grace, for having listened to her prayers, and protected her lover in the hour of peril."

The captain having finished, there was a momentary silence. The tender-hearted Lady Lillycraft, who knew the story by heart, had led the way in weeping, and indeed had often begun to shed tears before they had come to the right place.

The fair Julia was a little flurried at the passage where wedding preparations were mentioned; but the auditor most affected was the simple Phoebe Wilkins. She had gradually dropt her work in her lap, and sat sobbing through the latter part of the story, until towards the end, when the happy reverse had nearly produced another scene of hysterics. "Go, take this case to my room again, child," said Lady Lillycraft, kindly, "and don't cry so much."

"I won't, an't please your ladyship, if I can help it;—but I'm glad they made all up again, and were married."

By the way, the case of this lovelorn damsel begins to make some talk in the household, especially among certain little ladies, not far in their teens, of whom she has made confidants. She is a great favourite with them all, but particularly so since she has confided to them her love secrets. They enter into her concerns with all the violent zeal and overwhelming sympathy with which little boarding-school ladies engage in the politics of a love affair.

I have noticed them frequently clustering about her in private conferences, or walking up and down the garden terrace under my window, listening to some long and dolorous story of her afflictions; of which I could now and then distinguish the ever-recurring phrases, "says he," and "says she."

I accidentally interrupted one of these little councils of war, when they were all huddled together under a tree, and seemed to be earnestly considering some interesting document. The flutter at my approach showed that there were some secrets under discussion; and I observed the disconsolate Phoebe crumpling into her bosom either a love-letter or an old valentine, and brushing away the tears from her cheeks.

The girl is a good girl, of a soft melting nature, and shows her concern at the cruelty of her lover only in tears and drooping looks; but with the little ladies who have espoused her cause, it sparkles up into fiery indignation: and I have noticed on Sunday many a glance darted at the pew of the Tibbets's, enough even to melt down the silver buttons on old Ready Money's jacket.

Travelling.

A citizen, for recreation sake,
To see the country would a journey take
Some dozen mile, or very little more;
Taking his leave with friends two months before,
With drinking healths, and shaking by the hand,
As he had travail'd to some new-found land.
—Doctor Merrie-Man, 1609.

The Squire has lately received another shock in the saddle, and been almost unseated by his marplot neighbour, the indefatigable Mr. Faddy, who rides his jog-trot hobby with equal zeal; and is so bent upon improving and reforming the neighbourhood, that the Squire thinks, in a little while, it will be scarce worth living in. The enormity that has thus discomposed my worthy host, is an attempt of the manufacturer to have a line of coaches established, that shall diverge from the old route, and pass through the neighbouring village.

I believe I have mentioned that the Hall is situated in a retired part of the country, at a distance from any great coachroad; insomuch that the arrival of a traveller is apt to make every one look out of the window, and to cause some talk among the ale-drinkers at the little inn. I was at a loss, therefore, to account for the Squire's indignation at a measure apparently fraught with convenience and advantage, until I found that the conveniences of travelling were among his greatest grievances.

In fact, he rails against stage-coaches, post-chaises, and turnpike-roads, as serious causes of the corruption of English rural manners. They have given facilities, he says, to every humdrum citizen to trundle his family about the kingdom, and have sent the follies and fashions of town, whirling, in coachloads, to the remotest parts of the island. The whole country, he says, is traversed by these flying cargoes; every by-road is explored by enterprising tourists from Cheapside and the Poultry, and every gentleman's park and lawns invaded by cockney sketchers of both sexes, with portable chairs and portfolios for drawing.

He laments over this, as destroying the charm of privacy, and interrupting the quiet of country life; but more especially as affecting the simplicity of the peasantry, and filling their heads with half-city notions. A great coach-inn, he says, is enough to ruin the manners of a whole village. It creates a horde of sots and idlers, makes gapers and gazers and newsmongers of the common people, and knowing jockeys of the country bumpkins.

The Squire has something of the old feudal feeling. He looks back with regret to the "good old times" when journeys were only made on horseback, and the extraordinary difficulties of travelling, owing to bad roads, bad accommodations, and highway robbers, seemed to separate each village and hamlet from the rest of the world. The lord of the manor was then a kind of monarch in the little realm around him. He held his court in his paternal hall, and was looked up to with almost as much loyalty and deference as the king himself. Every neighbourhood was a little world within itself, having its local manners and customs, its local history and local opinions. The inhabitants were fonder of their homes, and thought less of wandering. It was looked upon as an expedition to travel out of sight of the parish steeple; and a man that had been to London was a village oracle for the rest of his life.

What a difference between the mode of travelling in those days and at present! At that time, when a gentleman went on a distant visit, he sallied forth like a knight-errant on an enterprise, and every family excursion was a pageant. How splendid and fanciful must one of those domestic cavalcades have been, where the beautiful dames were mounted on palfreys magnificently caparisoned, with embroidered harness, all tinkling with silver bells, attended by cavaliers richly attired on prancing steeds, and followed by pages and serving-men, as we see them represented in old tapestry! The gentry, as they travelled about in those days, were like moving pictures. They delighted the eyes and awakened the admiration of the common people, and passed before them like superior beings; and, indeed, they were so; there was a hardy and healthful exercise connected with this equestrian style that made them generous and noble.

In his fondness for the old style of travelling, the Squire makes most of his journeys on horseback, though he laments the modern deficiency of incident on the road, from the want of fellow-wayfarers, and the rapidity with which every one else is whirled along in coaches and post-chaises. In the "good old times," on the contrary, a cavalier jogged on through bog and mire, from town to town and hamlet to hamlet, conversing with friars and franklins, and all other chance companions of the road; beguiling the way with travellers' tales, which then were truly wonderful, for every thing beyond one's neighbourhood was full of marvel and romance; stopping at night at some "hostel," where the bush over the door proclaimed good wine, or a pretty hostess made bad wine palatable; meeting at supper with travellers, or listening to the song or merry story of the host, who was generally a boon companion, and presided at his own board; for, according to old Tusser's "Innholder's Posie,"

> *"At meales my friend who vitleth here*
> *And sitteth with his host,*
> *Shall both be sure of better cheere,*
> *And 'scape with lesser cost."*

The Squire is fond, too, of stopping at those inns which may be met with here and there in ancient houses of wood and plaster, or calimanco houses, as they are called by antiquaries, with deep porches, diamond-paned bow-windows, pannelled rooms, and great fire-places. He will prefer them to more spacious and modern inns, and would cheerfully put up with bad cheer and bad accommodations in the gratification of his humour. They give him, he says, the feelings of old times, insomuch that he almost expects in the dusk of the evening to see some party of weary travellers ride up to the door with plumes and mantles, trunk-hose, wide boots, and long rapiers.

The good Squire's remarks brought to mind a visit that I once paid to the Tabbard Inn, famous for being the place of assemblage from whence Chaucer's pilgrims set forth for Canterbury. It is in the borough of Southwark, not far from London Bridge, and bears, at present, the name of "the Talbot." It has sadly declined in dignity since the days of Chaucer, being a mere rendezvous and packing-place of the great wagons that travel into Kent. The court-yard, which was anciently the mustering-place of the pilgrims previous to their departure, was now lumbered with huge wagons. Crates, boxes, hampers, and baskets, containing the good things of town and country, were piled about them; while, among the straw and litter, the motherly hens scratched and clucked, with their hungry broods at their heels. Instead of Chaucer's motley and splendid throng, I only saw a group of wagoners and stable-boys enjoying a circulating pot of ale; while a long-bodied dog sat by, with head on one side, ear cocked up, and wistful gaze, as if waiting for his turn at the tankard.

Notwithstanding this grievous declension, however, I was gratified at perceiving that the present occupants were not unconscious of the poetical renown of their mansion. An inscription over the gateway proclaimed it to be the inn where Chaucer's pilgrims slept on the night previous to their departure; and at the bottom of the yard was a magnificent sign representing them in the act of sallying forth. I was pleased, too, at noticing that though the present inn was comparatively modern, yet the form of the old inn was preserved. There were galleries round the yard, as in old times, on which opened the chambers of the guests. To these ancient inns have antiquaries ascribed the present forms of our theatres. Plays were originally acted in inn-yards. The guests lolled over the galleries, which answered to our modern dress-circle; the critical mob clustered in the yard, instead of the pit; and the groups gazing from the garret-windows were no bad representatives of the gods of the shilling gallery. When, therefore, the drama grew important enough to have a house of its own, the architects took a hint for its construction from the yard of the ancient "hostel."

I was so well pleased at finding these remembrances of Chaucer and his poem, that I ordered my dinner in the little parlour of the Talbot. Whilst it was preparing, I sat at the window musing and gazing into the court-yard, and conjuring up recollections of the scenes depicted in such lovely colours by the poet, until, by degrees, boxes, bales and hampers, boys, wagoners and dogs, faded from sight, and my fancy peopled the place with the motley throng of Canterbury pilgrims. The galleries once more swarmed with idle gazers, in the rich dresses of Chaucer's time, and the whole cavalcade seemed to pass before me. There was the stately knight on sober steed, who had ridden in Christendom and heathenesse, and had "foughten for our faith at Tramissene;"—and his son, the young squire, a lover, and a lusty bachelor, with curled locks and gay embroidery; a bold rider, a dancer, and a writer of verses, singing and fluting all day long, and "fresh as the month of May;"—and his "knot-headed" yeoman; a bold forester, in green, with horn, and baudrick, and dagger, a mighty bow in hand, and a sheaf of peacock arrows shining beneath his belt;—and the coy, smiling, simple nun, with her gray eyes, her small red mouth, and fair forehead, her dainty person clad in featly cloak and "'ypinched wimple," her choral beads about her arm, her golden brooch with a love motto, and her pretty oath by Saint Eloy;—and the merchant, solemn in speech and high on horse, with forked beard and "Flaundrish bever hat;"—and the lusty monk, "full fat and in good point," with berry brown palfrey, his hood fastened with gold pin. wrought with a love-knot, his bald head shining like glass, and his face glistening as though it had been anointed; and the lean, logical, sententious clerk of Oxenforde, upon his half-starved, scholar-like horse;—and the bowsing sompnour, with fiery cherub face, all knobbed with pimples, an eater of garlic and onions, and drinker of "strong wine, red as blood," that carried a cake for a buckler, and babbled Latin in his cups; of whose brimstone visage "children were sore aferd;"—and the buxom wife of Bath, the widow of five husbands, upon her ambling nag, with her hat broad as a buckler, her red stockings and sharp spurs;—and the slender, choleric reeve of Norfolk, bestriding his good gray stot; with close-shaven beard, his hair cropped round his ears, long, lean, calfless legs, and a rusty blade by his side;—and the jolly Limitour, with lisping tongue and twinkling eye, well-beloved franklins and housewives, a great promoter of marriages among young women, known at the taverns in every town, and by every "hosteler and gay tapstere." In short, before I was roused from my reverie by the less poetical but more substantial apparition of a smoking beef-steak, I had seen the whole cavalcade issue forth from the hostel-gate, with the brawny, double-jointed, red-haired miller, playing the bagpipes before them, and the ancient host of the Tabbard giving them his farewell God-send to Canterbury.

When I told the Squire of the existence of this legitimate descendant of the ancient Tabbard Inn, his eyes absolutely glistened with delight. He determined to hunt it up the very first time he visited London, and to eat a dinner there, and drink a cup of mine host's best wine in memory of old Chaucer. The general, who happened to be present, immediately begged to be of the party; for he liked to encourage these long-established houses, as they are apt to have choice old wines.

Popular Superstitions.

Farewell rewards and fairies,
Good housewives now may say;
For now fowle sluts in dairies
Do fare as well as they;
And though they sweepe their hearths no lease
Than maids were wont to doo,
Yet who of late for cleanlinesse
Finds sixpence in her shooe?
—BISHOP CORBET.

I have mentioned the Squire's fondness for the marvellous, and his predilection for legends and romances. His library contains a curious collection of old works of this kind, which bear evident marks of having been much read. In his great love for all that is antiquated, he cherishes popular superstitions, and listens, with very grave attention, to every tale, however strange; so that, through his countenance, the household, and, indeed, the whole neighbourhood, is well stocked with wonderful stories; and if ever a doubt is expressed of any one of them, the narrator will generally observe, that "the Squire thinks there's something in it."

The Hall of course comes in for its share, the common people having always a propensity to furnish a great superannuated building of the kind with supernatural inhabitants. The gloomy galleries of such old family mansions; the stately chambers, adorned with grotesque carvings and faded paintings; the sounds that vaguely echo about them; the moaning of the wind; the cries of rooks and ravens from the trees and chimney-tops; all produce a state of mind favourable to superstitious fancies.

In one chamber of the Hall, just opposite a door which opens upon a dusky passage, there is a full-length portrait of a warrior in armour; when, on suddenly turning into the passage, I have caught a sight of the portrait, thrown into strong relief by the dark pannelling against which it hangs, I have more than once been startled, as though it were a figure advancing towards me.

To superstitious minds, therefore, predisposed by the strange and melancholy stories that are connected with family paintings, it needs but little stretch of fancy, on a moonlight night, or by the flickering light of a candle, to set the old pictures on the walls in motion, sweeping in their robes and trains about the galleries.

To tell the truth, the Squire confesses that he used to take a pleasure in his younger days in setting marvellous stories afloat, and connecting them with the lonely and peculiar places of the neighbourhood. Whenever he read any legend of a striking nature, he endeavoured to transplant it, and give it a local habitation among the scenes of his boyhood. Many of these stories took root, and he says he is often amused with the odd shapes in which they will come back to him in some old woman's narrative, after they have been circulating for years among the peasantry, and undergoing rustic additions and amendments. Among these may doubtless be numbered that of the crusader's ghost, which I have mentioned in the account of my Christmas visit; and another about the hard-riding Squire of yore; the family Nimrod; who is sometimes heard in stormy winter nights, galloping, with hound and horn, over a wild moor a few miles distant from the Hall. This I apprehend to have had its origin in the famous story of the wild huntsman, the favourite goblin in German tales; though, by-the-by, as I was talking on the subject with Master Simon the other evening in the dark avenue, he hinted that he had himself once or twice heard odd sounds at night, very like a pack of hounds in cry; and that once, as he was returning rather late from a hunting dinner, he had seen a strange figure galloping along this same moor; but as he was riding rather fast at the time, and in a hurry to get home, he did not stop to ascertain what it was.

Popular superstitions are fast fading away in England, owing to the general diffusion of knowledge, and the bustling intercourse kept up throughout the country; still they have their strong-holds and lingering places, and a retired neighbourhood like this is apt to be one of them. The parson tells me that he meets with many traditional beliefs and notions among the common people, which he has been able to draw from them in the course of familiar conversation, though they are rather shy of avowing them to strangers, and particularly to "the gentry," who are apt to laugh at them. He says there are several of his old parishioners who remember when the village had its bar-guest, or bar-ghost—a spirit supposed to belong to a town or village, and to predict any impending misfortune by midnight shrieks and wailings. The last time it was heard was just before the death of Mr. Bracebridge's father, who was much beloved throughout the neighbourhood; though there are not wanting some obstinate unbelievers, who insisted that it was nothing but the howling of a watch-dog. I have been greatly delighted, however, at meeting with some traces of my old favourite, Robin Goodfellow, though under a different appellation from any of those by which I have heretofore heard him called. The parson assures me that many of the peasantry believe in household goblins, called Dubbies, which live about particular farms and houses, in the same way that Robin Goodfellow did of old. Sometimes they haunt the barns and outhouses, and now and then will assist the farmer wonderfully, by getting in all his hay or corn in a single night. In general, however, they prefer to live within doors, and are fond of keeping about the great hearths, and basking, at night, after the family have gone to bed, by the glowing embers. When put in particular good-humour by the warmth of their lodgings, and the tidiness of the house-maids, they will overcome their natural laziness, and do a vast deal of household work before morning; churning the cream, brewing the beer, or spinning all the good dame's flax. All this is precisely the conduct of Robin Goodfellow, described so charmingly by Milton:

> *"Tells how the drudging goblin sweat*
> *To earn his cream-bowl duly get,*
> *When in one night, ere glimpse of morn,*
> *His shadowy flail had thresh'd the corn*
> *That ten day-labourers could not end;*
> *Then lays him down the lubber-fiend,*
> *And, stretch'd out all the chimney's length,*
> *Basks at the fire his hairy strength,*
> *And crop-full, out of door he flings*
> *Ere the first cock his matin rings."*

But beside these household Dubbies, there are others of a more gloomy and unsocial nature, that keep about lonely barns at a distance from any dwelling-house, or about ruins and old bridges. These are full of mischievous and often malignant tricks, and are fond of playing pranks upon benighted travellers. There is a story, among the old people, of one that haunted a ruined mill, just by a bridge that crosses a small stream; how that, late one night, as a traveller was passing on horseback, the Dubbie jumped up behind him, and grasped him so close round the body that he had no power to help himself, but expected to be squeezed to death: luckily his heels were loose, with which he plied the sides of his steed, and was carried, with the wonderful instinct of a traveller's horse, straight to the village inn. Had the inn been at any greater distance, there is no doubt but he would have been strangled to death; as it was, the good people were a long time in bringing him to his senses, and it was remarked that the first sign he showed of returning consciousness was to call for a bottom of brandy.

These mischievous Dubbies bear much resemblance in their natures and habits to those sprites which Heywood, in his Heirarchie, calls pugs or hobgoblins:

> "———Their dwellings be
> In corners of old houses least frequented
> Or beneath stacks of wood, and these convented,
> Make fearfull noise in butteries and in dairies;
> Robin Goodfellow some, some call them fairies.
> In solitarie rooms these uprores keep,
> And beate at doores, to wake men from their slape,
> Seeming to force lockes, be they nere so strong,
> And keeping Christmasse gambols all night long.
> Pots, glasses, trenchers, dishes, pannes and kettles.
> They will make dance about the shelves and settles.
> As if about the kitchen tost and cast,
> Yet in the morning nothing found misplac't.
> Others such houses to their use have fitted,
> In which base murthers have been once committed.
> Some have their fearful habitations taken

In desolate houses, ruin'd and forsaken."

In the account of our unfortunate hawking expedition, I mentioned an instance of one of these sprites, supposed to haunt the ruined grange that stands in a lonely meadow, and has a remarkable echo. The parson informs me, also, that the belief was once very prevalent, that a household Dubbie kept about the old farm-house of the Tibbets. It has long been traditional, he says, that one of these good-natured goblins is attached to the Tibbets family, and came with, them when they moved into this part of the country; for it is one of the peculiarities of these household sprites, that they attach themselves to the fortunes of certain families, and follow them in all their removals.

There is a large old-fashioned fire-place in the farm-house, which affords fine quarters for a chimney-corner sprite that likes to lie warm; especially as Ready-Money Jack keeps up rousing fires in the winter-time. The old people of the village recollect many stories about this goblin, that were current in their young days. It was thought to have brought good luck to the house, and to be the reason why the Tibbets were always beforehand in the world, and why their farm was always in better order, their hay got in sooner, and their corn better stacked, than that of their neighbours. The present Mrs. Tibbets, at the time of her courtship, had a number of these stories told her by the country gossips; and when married, was a little fearful about living in a house where such a hobgoblin was said to haunt: Jack, however, who has always treated this story with great contempt, assured her that there was no spirit kept about his house that he could not at any time lay in the Red Sea with one flourish of his cudgel. Still his wife has never got completely over her notions on the subject, but has a horseshoe nailed on the threshold, and keeps a branch of rauntry, or mountain ash, with its red berries, suspended from one of the great beams in the parlour—a sure protection from all evil spirits.

These stories, however, as I before observed, are fast fading away, and in another generation or two will probably be completely forgotten. There is something, however, about these rural superstitions, that is extremely pleasing to the imagination; particularly those which relate to the good-humoured race of household demons, and indeed to the whole fairy mythology. The English have given an inexplicable charm to these superstitions, by the manner in which they have associated them with whatever is most homefelt and delightful in nature. I do not know a more fascinating race of beings than these little fabled people, that haunted the southern sides of hills and mountains, lurked in flowers and about fountain-heads, glided through key-holes into ancient halls, watched over farm-houses and dairies, danced on the green by summer moonlight, and on the kitchen-hearth in winter. They seem to accord with the nature of English housekeeping and English scenery. I always have them in mind, when I see a fine old English mansion, with its wide hall and spacious kitchen; or a venerable farm-house, in which there is so much fireside comfort and good housewifery. There was something of national character in their love of order and cleanliness; in the vigilance with which they watched over the economy of the kitchen, and the functions of the servants; munificently rewarding, with silver sixpence in shoe, the tidy housemaid, but venting their direful wrath, in midnight bobs and pinches, upon the sluttish dairymaid. I think I can trace the good effects of this ancient fairy sway over household concerns, in the care that prevails to the present day among English housemaids, to put their kitchens in order before they go to bed.

I have said, too, that these fairy superstitions seemed to me to accord with the nature of English scenery. They suit these small landscapes, which are divided by honeysuckled hedges into sheltered fields and meadows, where the grass is mingled with daisies, buttercups, and harebells. When I first found myself among English scenery, I was continually reminded of the sweet pastoral images which distinguish their fairy mythology; and when for the first time a circle in the grass was pointed out to me as one of the rings where they were formerly supposed to have held their moonlight revels, it seemed for a moment as if fairy-land were no longer a fable. Brown, in his Britannia's Pastorals, gives a picture of the kind of scenery to which I allude:

> "———A pleasant mead
> Where fairies often did their measures tread;
> Which in the meadows make such circles green,
> As if with garlands it had crowned been.
> Within one of these rounds was to be seen

A hillock rise, where oft the fairy queen
At twilight sat."

And there is another picture of the same, in a poem ascribed to Ben Jonson.

"Bywells and rills in meadows green,
We nightly dance our heyday guise,
And to our fairy king and queen
We chant our moonlight minstrelsies."

Indeed, it seems to me, that the older British poets, with that true feeling for nature which distinguishes them, have closely adhered to the simple and familiar imagery which they found in these popular superstitions; and have thus given to their fairy mythology those continual allusions to the farm-house and the dairy, the green meadow and the fountain-head, that fill our minds with the delightful associations of rural life. It is curious to observe how the most beautiful fictions have their origin among the rude and ignorant. There is an indescribable charm about the illusions with which chimerical ignorance once clothed every subject. These twilight views of nature are often more captivating than any which are revealed by the rays of enlightened philosophy. The most accomplished and poetical minds, therefore, have been fain to search back into these accidental conceptions of what are termed barbarous ages, and to draw from them their finest imagery and, machinery. If we look through our most admired poets, we shall find that their minds have been impregnated by these popular fancies, and that those have succeeded best who have adhered closest to the simplicity of their rustic originals. Such is the case with Shakspeare in his Midsummer-Night's Dream, which so minutely describes the employments and amusements of fairies, and embodies all the notions concerning them which were current among the vulgar. It is thus that poetry in England has echoed back every rustic note, softened into perfect melody; it is thus that it has spread its charms over every-day life, displacing nothing, taking things as it found them, but tinting them up with its own magical hues, until every green hill and fountain-head, every fresh meadow, nay, every humble flower, is full of song and story.

I am dwelling too long, perhaps, upon a threadbare subject; yet it brings up with it a thousand delicious recollections of those happy days of childhood, when the imperfect knowledge I have since obtained had not yet dawned upon my mind, and when a fairy tale was true history to me. I have often been so transported by the pleasure of these recollections, as almost to wish that I had been born in the days when the fictions of poetry were believed. Even now I cannot look upon those fanciful creations of ignorance and credulity, without a lurking regret that they have all passed away. The experience of my early days tells me, that they were sources of exquisite delight; and I sometimes question whether the naturalist who can dissect the flowers of the field, receives half the pleasure from contemplating them, that he did who considered them the abode of elves and fairies. I feel convinced that the true interests and solid happiness of man are promoted by the advancement of truth; yet I cannot but mourn over the pleasant errors which it has trampled down in its progress. The fauns and sylphs, the household sprite, the moonlight revel, Oberon, Queen Mab, and the delicious realms of fairy-land, all vanish before the light of true philosophy; but who does not sometimes turn with distaste from the cold realities of morning, and seek to recall the sweet visions of the night?

The Culprit.

From fire, from water, and all things amies,
Deliver the house of an honest justice.
—The Widow.

The serenity of the Hall has been suddenly interrupted by a very important occurrence. In the course of this morning a posse of villagers was seen trooping up the avenue, with boys shouting in advance. As it drew near, we perceived Ready-Money Jack Tibbets striding along, wielding his cudgel in one hand, and with the other grasping the collar of a tall fellow, whom, on still nearer approach, we recognized for the redoubtable gipsy hero, Starlight Tom. He was now, however, completely cowed and crestfallen, and his courage seemed to have quailed in the iron gripe of the lion-hearted Jack.

The whole gang of gipsy women and children came dragging in the rear; some in tears, others making a violent clamour about the ears of old Ready-Money, who, however, trudged on in silence with his prey, heeding their abuse as little as a hawk that has pounced upon a barn-door hero regards the outcries and cacklings of his whole feathered seraglio.

He had passed through the village on his way to the Hall, and of course had made a great sensation in that most excitable place, where every event is a matter of gaze and gossip. The report flew like wildfire, that Starlight Tom was in custody. The ale-drinkers forthwith abandoned the tap-room; Slingsby's school broke loose, and master and boys swelled the tide that came rolling at the heels of old Ready-Money and his captive.

The uproar increased, as they approached the Hall; it aroused the whole garrison of dogs, and the crew of hangers-on. The great mastiff barked from the dog-house; the stag-hound, and the grayhound, and the spaniel, issued barking from the hall-door, and my Lady Lillycraft's little dogs ramped and barked from the parlour window. I remarked, however, that the gipsy dogs made no reply to all these menaces and insults, but crept close to the gang, looking round with a guilty, poaching air, and now and then glancing up a dubious eye to their owners; which shows that the moral dignity, even of dogs, may be ruined by bad company!

When the throng reached the front of the house, they were brought to a halt by a kind of advanced guard, composed of old Christy, the gamekeeper, and two or three servants of the house, who had been brought out by the noise. The common herd of the village fell back with respect; the boys were driven back by Christy and his compeers; while Ready-Money Jack maintained his ground and his hold of the prisoner, and was surrounded by the tailor, the schoolmaster, and several other dignitaries of the village, and by the clamorous brood of gipsies, who were neither to be silenced nor intimidated.

By this time the whole household were brought to the doors and windows, and the Squire to the portal. An audience was demanded by Ready-Money Jack, who had detected the prisoner in the very act of sheep-stealing on his domains, and had borne him off to be examined before the Squire, who is in the commission of the peace.

A kind of tribunal was immediately held in the servants' hall, a large chamber, with a stone floor, and a long table in the centre, at one end of which, just under an enormous clock, was placed the Squire's chair of justice, while Master Simon took his place at the table as clerk of the court. An attempt had been made by old Christy to keep out the gipsy gang, but in vain, and they, with the village worthies, and the household, half filled the hall. The old housekeeper and the butler were in a panic at this dangerous irruption. They hurried away all the valuable things and portable articles that were at hand, and even kept a dragon watch on the gipsies, lest they should carry off the house clock, or the deal table.

Old Christy, and his faithful coadjutor the gamekeeper, acted as constables to guard the prisoner, triumphing in having at last got this terrible offender in their clutches. Indeed, I am inclined to think the old man bore some peevish recollection of having been handled rather roughly by the gipsy, in the chance-medley affair of May-day.

Silence was now commanded by Master Simon; but it was difficult to be enforced, in such a motley assemblage. There was a continual snarling and yelping of dogs, and, as fast as it was quelled in one corner, it broke out in another. The poor gipsy curs, who, like errant thieves, could not hold up their heads in an honest house, were worried and insulted by the gentlemen dogs of the establishment, without offering to make resistance; the very curs of my Lady Lillycraft bullied them with impunity.

The examination was conducted with great mildness and indulgence by the Squire, partly from the kindness of his nature, and partly, I suspect, because his heart yearned towards the culprit, who had found great favour in his eyes, as I have already observed, from the skill he had at various times displayed in archery, morris-dancing, and other obsolete accomplishments. Proofs, however, were too strong. Ready-Money Jack told his story in a straight-forward, independent way, nothing daunted by the presence in which he found himself. He had suffered from various depredations on his sheepfold and poultry-yard, and had at length kept watch, and caught the delinquent in the very act of making off with a sheep on his shoulders.

Tibbets was repeatedly interrupted, in the course of his testimony, by the culprit's mother, a furious old beldame, with an insufferable tongue, and who, in fact, was several times kept, with some difficulty, from flying at him tooth and nail. The wife, too, of the prisoner, whom I am told he does not beat above half-a-dozen times a week, completely interested Lady Lillycraft in her husband's behalf, by her tears and supplications; and several of the other gipsy women were awakening strong sympathy among the young girls and maid-servants in the back-ground. The pretty, black-eyed gipsy girl whom I have mentioned on a former occasion as the sibyl that read the fortunes of the general, endeavoured to wheedle that doughty warrior into their interests, and even made some approaches to her old acquaintance, Master Simon; but was repelled by the latter with all the dignity of office, having assumed a look of gravity and importance suitable to the occasion.

I was a little surprised, at first, to find honest Slingsby, the schoolmaster, rather opposed to his old crony Tibbets, and coming forward as a kind of advocate for the accused. It seems that he had taken compassion on the forlorn fortunes of Starlight Tom, and had been trying his eloquence in his favour the whole way from the village, but without effect. During the examination of Ready-Money Jack, Slingsby had stood like "dejected Pity at his side," seeking every now and then, by a soft word, to soothe any exacerbation of his ire, or to qualify any harsh expression. He now ventured to make a few observations to the Squire, in palliation of the delinquent's offence; but poor Slingsby spoke more from the heart than the head, and was evidently actuated merely by a general sympathy for every poor devil in trouble, and a liberal toleration for all kinds of vagabond existence.

The ladies, too, large and small, with the kind-heartedness of the sex, were zealous on the side of mercy, and interceded strenuously with the Squire; insomuch that the prisoner, finding himself unexpectedly surrounded by active friends, once more reared his crest, and seemed disposed, for a time, to put on the air of injured innocence. The Squire, however, with all his benevolence of heart, and his lurking weakness towards the prisoner, was too conscientious to swerve from the strict path of justice. There was abundant concurring testimony that made the proof of guilt incontrovertible, and Starlight Tom's mittimus was made out accordingly.

The sympathy of the ladies was now greater than ever; they even made some attempts to mollify the ire of Ready-Money Jack; but that sturdy potentate had been too much incensed by the repeated incursions that had been made into his territories by the predatory band of Starlight Tom, and he was resolved, he said, to drive the "varment reptiles" out of the neighbourhood. To avoid all further importunities, as soon as the mittimus was made out, he girded up his loins, and strode back to his seat of empire, accompanied by his interceding friend, Slingsby, and followed by a detachment of the gipsy gang, who hung on his rear, assailing him with mingled prayers and execrations.

The question now was, how to dispose of the prisoner—a matter of great moment in this peaceful establishment, where so formidable a character as Starlight Tom was like a hawk entrapped in a dove-cote. As the hubbub and examination had occupied a considerable time, it was too late in the day to send him to the county prison, and that of the village was sadly out of repair, from long want of occupation. Old Christy, who took great interest in the affair, proposed that the culprit should be committed for the night to an upper loft of a kind of tower in one of the outhouses, where he and the gamekeeper would mount guard. After much deliberation, this measure was adopted; the premises in question were examined and made secure, and Christy and his trusty ally, the one armed with a fowling-piece, the other with an ancient blunderbuss, turned out as sentries to keep watch over this donjon-keep.

Such is the momentous affair that has just taken place, and it is an event of too great moment in this quiet little world, not to turn it completely topsy-turvy. Labour is at a stand: the house has been a scene of confusion the whole evening. It has been beleagured by gipsy women, with their children on their backs, wailing and lamenting; while the old virago of a mother has cruised up and down the lawn in front, shaking her head, and muttering to herself, or now and then breaking into a paroxysm of rage, brandishing her fist at the Hall, and denouncing ill-luck upon Ready-Money Jack, and even upon the Squire himself.

Lady Lillycraft has given repeated audiences to the culprit's weeping wife, at the Hall door; and the servant maids have stolen out, to confer with the gipsy women under the trees. As to the little ladies of the family, they are all outrageous on Ready-Money Jack, whom they look upon in the light of a tyrannical giant of fairy tale. Phoebe Wilkins, contrary to her usual nature, is the only one that is pitiless in the affair. She thinks Mr. Tibbets quite in the right; and thinks the gipsies deserve to be punished severely, for meddling with the sheep of the Tibbets's.

In the mean time, the females of the family evinced all the provident kindness of the sex, ever ready to soothe and succour the distressed, right or wrong. Lady Lillycraft has had a mattress taken to the outhouse, and comforts and delicacies of all kinds have been taken to the prisoner; even the little girls have sent their cakes and sweetmeats; so that, I'll warrant, the vagabond has never fared so well in his life before. Old Christy, it is true, looks upon every thing with a wary eye; struts about with his blunderbuss with the air of a veteran campaigner, and will hardly allow himself to be spoken to.

The gipsy women dare not come within gun-shot, and every tatterdemalion of a boy has been frightened from the park. The old fellow is determined to lodge Starlight Tom in prison with his own hands; and hopes, he says, to see one of the poaching crew made an example of.

I doubt, after all, whether the worthy Squire is not the greatest sufferer in the whole affair. His honourable sense of duty obliges him to be rigid, but the overflowing kindness of his nature makes this a grievous trial to him.

He is not accustomed to have such demands upon his justice, in his truly patriarchal domain; and it wounds his benevolent spirit, that while prosperity and happiness are flowing in thus bounteously upon him, he should have to inflict misery upon a fellow-being.

He has been troubled and cast down the whole evening; took leave of the family, on going to bed, with a sigh, instead of his usual hearty and affectionate tone; and will, in all probability, have a far more sleepless night than his prisoner. Indeed, this unlucky affair has cast a damp upon the whole household, as there appears to be an universal opinion that the unlucky culprit will come to the gallows.

Morning.—The clouds of last evening are all blown over. A load has been taken from the Squire's heart, and every face is once more in smiles. The gamekeeper made his appearance at an early hour, completely shamefaced and crestfallen. Starlight Tom had made his escape in the night; how he had got out of the loft, no one could tell: the Devil, they think, must have assisted him. Old Christy was so mortified that he would not show his face, but had shut himself up in his stronghold at the dog-kennel, and would not be spoken with. What has particularly relieved the Squire, is, that there is very little likelihood of the culprit's being retaken, having gone off on one of the old gentleman's best hunters.

Family Misfortunes.

The night has been unruly; where we lay,
The chimneys were blown down.
—Macbeth.

We have for a day or two past had a flow of unruly weather, which has intruded itself into this fair and flowery month, and for a time has quite marred the beauty of the landscape. Last night, the storm attained its crisis; the rain beat in torrents against the casements, and the wind piped and blustered about the old Hall with quite a wintry vehemence. The morning, however, dawned clear and serene; the face of the heavens seemed as if newly washed, and the sun shone with a brightness that was undimmed by a single vapour. Nothing over-head gave traces of the recent storm; but on looking from my window, I beheld sad ravage among the shrubs and flowers; the garden-walks had formed the channels for little torrents; trees were lopped of their branches; and a small silver stream that wound through the park, and ran at the bottom of the lawn, had swelled into a turbid yellow sheet of water.

In an establishment like this, where the mansion is vast, ancient, and somewhat afflicted with the infirmities of age, and where there are numerous and extensive dependencies, a storm is an event of a very grave nature, and brings in its train a multiplicity of cares and disasters.

While the Squire was taking his breakfast in the great hall, he was continually interrupted by some bearer of ill-tidings from some part or other of his domains; he appeared to me like the commander of a besieged city, after some grand assault, receiving at his headquarters reports, of damages sustained in the various quarters of the place. At one time the housekeeper brought him intelligence of a chimney blown down, and a desperate leak sprung in the roof over the picture gallery, which threatened to obliterate a whole generation of his ancestors. Then the steward came in with a doleful story of the mischief done in the woodlands; while the gamekeeper bemoaned the loss of one of his finest bucks, whose bloated carcass was seen floating along the swoln current of the river.

When the Squire issued forth, he was accosted, before the door, by the old, paralytic gardener, with a face full of trouble, reporting, as I supposed, the devastation of his flower-beds, and the destruction of his wall-fruit. I remarked, however, that his intelligence caused a peculiar expression of concern, not only with the Squire and Master Simon, but with the fair Julia and Lady Lillycraft, who happened to be present. From a few words which reached my ear, I found there was some tale of domestic calamity in the case, and that some unfortunate family had been rendered houseless by the storm. Many ejaculations of pity broke from the ladies; I heard the expressions of "poor, helpless beings," and "unfortunate little creatures," several times repeated; to which the old gardener replied by very melancholy shakes of the head.

I felt so interested, that I could not help calling to the gardener, as he was retiring, and asking what unfortunate family it was that had suffered so severely? The old man touched his hat, and gazed at me for an instant, as if hardly comprehending my question. "Family!" replied he, "there be no family in the case, your honour; but here have been sad mischief done in the rookery!"

I had noticed, the day before, that the high and gusty winds which prevailed had occasioned great disquiet among these airy householders; their nests being all filled with young, who were in danger of being tilted out of their tree-rocked cradles. Indeed, the old birds themselves seemed to have hard work to maintain a foothold; some kept hovering and cawing in the air; or, if they ventured to alight, they had to hold fast, flap their wings, and spread their tails, and thus remain see-sawing on the topmost twigs.

In the course of the night, however, an awful calamity had taken place in this most sage and politic community. There was a great tree, the tallest in the grove, which seemed to have been a kind of court-end of the metropolis, and crowded with the residence of those whom Master Simon considers the nobility and gentry. A decayed limb of this tree had given way with the violence of this storm, and had come down with all its aircastles.

One should be well aware of the humours of the good Squire and his household, to understand the general concern expressed at this disaster. It was quite a public calamity in this rural empire, and all seemed to feel for the poor rooks as for fellow-citizens in distress.

The ground had been strewed with the callow young, which were now cherished in the aprons and bosoms of the maid-servants, and the little ladies of the family. I was pleased with this touch of nature; this feminine sympathy in the sufferings of the offspring, and the maternal anxiety of the parent birds.

It was interesting, too, to witness the general agitation and distress that seemed to prevail throughout the feathered community; the common cause that was made of it; and the incessant hovering, and fluttering, and lamenting, that took place in the whole rookery. There is a cord of sympathy, that runs through the whole feathered race, as to any misfortunes of the young; and the cries of a wounded bird in the breeding season will throw a whole grove in a flutter and an alarm. Indeed, why should I confine it to the feathered tribe? Nature seems to me to have implanted an exquisite sympathy on this subject, which extends through all her works. It is an invariable attribute of the female heart, to melt at the cry of early helplessness, and to take an instinctive interest in the distresses of the parent and its young. On the present occasion, the ladies of the family were full of pity and commiseration; and I shall never forget the look that Lady Lillycraft gave the general; on his observing that the young birds would make an excellent curry, or an especial good rook-pie.

Lovers' Troubles.

The poor soul sat singing by a sycamore tree,
Sing all a green willow;
Her hand on her bosom, her head on her knee
Sing willow, willow, willow;
Sing all a green willow must be my garland.
—Old Song.

The fair Julia having nearly recovered from the effects of her hawking disaster, it begins to be thought high time to appoint a day for the wedding. As every domestic event in a venerable and aristocratic family connexion like this is a matter of moment, the fixing upon this important day has of course given rise to much conference and debate.

Some slight difficulties and demurs have lately sprung up, originating in the peculiar humours that are prevalent at the Hall. Thus, I have overheard a very solemn consultation between Lady Lillycraft, the parson, and Master Simon, as to whether the marriage ought not to be postponed until the coming month.

With all the charms of the flowery month of May, there is, I find, an ancient prejudice against it as a marrying month. An old proverb says, "To wed in May is to wed poverty." Now, as Lady Lillycraft is very much given to believe in lucky and unlucky times and seasons, and indeed is very superstitious on all points relating to the tender passion, this old proverb seems to have taken great hold upon her mind. She recollects two or three instances, in her own knowledge, of matches that took place in this month, and proved very unfortunate. Indeed, an own cousin of hers, who married on a May-day, lost her husband by a fall from his horse, after they had lived happily together for twenty years.

The parson appeared to give great weight to her ladyship's objections, and acknowledged the existence of a prejudice of the kind, not merely confined to modern times, but prevalent likewise among the ancients. In confirmation of this, he quoted a passage from Ovid, which had a great effect on Lady Lillycraft, being given in a language which she did not understand. Even Master Simon was staggered by it; for he listened with a puzzled air; and then, shaking his head, sagaciously observed, that Ovid was certainly a very wise man.

From this sage conference I likewise gathered several other important pieces of information, relative to weddings; such as that, if two were celebrated in the same church, on the same day, the first would be happy, the second unfortunate. If, on going to church, the bridal party should meet the funeral of a female, it was an omen that the bride would die first; if of a male, the bridegroom. If the newly-married couple were to dance together on their wedding-day, the wife would thenceforth rule the roast; with many other curious and unquestionable facts of the same nature, all which made me ponder more than ever upon the perils which surround this happy state, and the thoughtless ignorance of mortals as to the awful risks they run in venturing upon it. I abstain, however, from enlarging upon this topic, having no inclination to promote the increase of bachelors.

Notwithstanding the due weight which the Squire gives to traditional saws and ancient opinions, yet I am happy to find that he makes a firm stand for the credit of this loving month, and brings to his aid a whole legion of poetical authorities; all which, I presume, have been conclusive with the young couple, as I understand they are perfectly willing to marry in May, and abide the consequences. In a few days, therefore, the wedding is to take place, and the Hall is in a buzz of anticipation. The housekeeper is bustling about from morning till night, with a look full of business and importance, having a thousand arrangements to make, the Squire intending to keep open house on the occasion; and as to the house-maids, you cannot look one of them in the face, but the rogue begins to colour up and simper.

While, however, this leading love affair is going on with a tranquillity quite inconsistent with the rules of romance, I cannot say that the under-plots are equally propitious. The "opening bud of love" between the general and Lady Lillycraft seems to have experienced some blight in the course of this genial season. I do not think the general has ever been able to retrieve the ground he lost, when he fell asleep during the captain's story. Indeed, Master Simon thinks his case is completely desperate, her ladyship having determined that he is quite destitute of sentiment.

The season has been equally unpropitious to the lovelorn Phoebe Wilkins. I fear the reader will be impatient at having this humble amour so often alluded to; but I confess I am apt to take a great interest in the love troubles of simple girls of this class. Few people have an idea of the world of care and perplexity that these poor damsels have, in managing the affairs of the heart.

We talk and write about the tender passion; we give it all the colourings of sentiment and romance, and lay the scene of its influence in high life; but, after all, I doubt whether its sway is not more absolute among females of an humbler sphere. How often, could we but look into the heart, should we find the sentiment throbbing in all its violence in the bosom of the poor lady's-maid, rather than in that of the brilliant beauty she is decking out for conquest; whose brain is probably bewildered with beaux, ball-rooms, and wax-light chandeliers.

With these humble beings, love is an honest, engrossing concern. They have no ideas of settlements, establishments, equipages, and pin-money. The heart—the heart, is all-in-all with them, poor things! There is seldom one of them but has her love cares, and love secrets; her doubts, and hopes, and fears, equal to those of any heroine of romance, and ten times as sincere. And then, too, there is her secret hoard of love documents;—the broken sixpence, the gilded brooch, the lock of hair, the unintelligible love scrawl, all treasured up in her box of Sunday finery, for private contemplation.

How many crosses and trials is she exposed to from some lynx-eyed dame, or staid old vestal of a mistress, who keeps a dragon watch over her virtue, and scouts the lover from the door! But then, how sweet are the little love scenes, snatched at distant intervals of holiday, and fondly dwelt on through many a long day of household labour and confinement! If in the country, it is the dance at the fair or wake, the interview in the church-yard after service, or the evening stroll in the green lane. If in town, it is perhaps merely a stolen moment of delicious talk between the bars of the area, fearful every instant of being seen; and then, how lightly will the simple creature carol all day afterwards at her labour!

Poor baggage! after all her crosses and difficulties, when she marries, what is it but to exchange a life of comparative ease and comfort, for one of toil and uncertainty? Perhaps, too, the lover for whom in the fondness of her nature she has committed herself to fortune's freaks, turns out a worthless churl, the dissolute, hard-hearted husband of low life; who, taking to the ale-house, leaves her to a cheerless home, to labour, penury, and child-bearing.

When I see poor Phoebe going about with drooping eye, and her head hanging "all o' one side," I cannot help calling to mind the pathetic little picture drawn by Desdemona:—

My mother had a maid, called Barbara;
She was in love; and he she loved proved mad,
And did forsake her; she had a song of willow,
An old thing 'twas; but it express'd her fortune,
And she died singing it.

I hope, however, that a better lot is in reserve for Phoebe Wilkins, and that she may yet "rule the roast," in the ancient empire of the Tibbets! She is not fit to battle with hard hearts or hard times. She was, I am told, the pet of her poor mother, who was proud of the beauty of her child, and brought her up more tenderly than a village girl ought to be; and ever since she has been left an orphan, the good ladies at the Hall have completed the softening and spoiling of her.

I have recently observed her holding long conferences in the church-yard, and up and down one of the lanes near the village, with Slingsby, the schoolmaster. I at first thought the pedagogue might be touched with the tender malady so prevalent in these parts of late; but I did him injustice. Honest Slingsby, it seems, was a friend and crony of her late father, the parish clerk; and is on intimate terms with the Tibbets family. Prompted, therefore, by his good-will towards all parties, and secretly instigated, perhaps, by the managing dame Tibbets, he has undertaken to talk with Phoebe upon the subject. He gives her, however, but little encouragement. Slingsby has a formidable opinion of the aristocratical feeling of old Ready-Money, and thinks, if Phoebe were even to make the matter up with the son, she would find the father totally hostile to the match. The poor damsel, therefore, is reduced almost to despair; and Slingsby, who is too good-natured not to sympathize in her distress, has advised her to give up all thoughts of young Jack, and has proposed as a substitute his learned coadjutor, the prodigal son. He has even, in the fullness of his heart, offered to give up the school-house to them; though it would leave him once more adrift in the wide world.

The Historian.

Hermione. Pray you sit by us,
And tell's a tale.

Mamilius. Merry or sad shall't be?

Hermione. As merry as you will.

Mamilius. A sad tale's best for winter.
I have one of sprites and goblins.

Hermione. Let's have that, sir.
—Winter's Tale.

As this is a story-telling age, I have been tempted occasionally to give the reader one of the many tales that are served up with supper at the Hall. I might, indeed, have furnished a series almost equal in number to the Arabian Nights; but some were rather hackneyed and tedious; others I did not feel warranted in betraying into print; and many more were of the old general's relating, and turned principally upon tiger-hunting, elephant-riding, and Seringapatam; enlivened by the wonderful deeds of Tippoo Saib, and the excellent jokes of Major Pendergast.

I had all along maintained a quiet post at a corner of the table, where I had been able to indulge my humour undisturbed: listening attentively when the story was very good, and dozing a little when it was rather dull, which I consider the perfection of auditorship.

I was roused the other evening from a slight trance into which I had fallen during one of the general's histories, by a sudden call from the Squire to furnish some entertainment of the kind in my turn. Having been so profound a listener to others, I could not in conscience refuse; but neither my memory nor invention being ready to answer so unexpected a demand, I begged leave to read a manuscript tale from the pen of my fellow-countryman, the late Mr. Diedrich Knickerbocker, the historian of New-York. As this ancient chronicler may not be better known to my readers than he was to the company at the Hall, a word or two concerning him may not be amiss, before proceeding to his manuscript.

Diedrich Knickerbocker was a native of New-York, a descendant from one of the ancient Dutch families which originally settled that province, and remained there after it was taken possession of by the English in 1664. The descendants of these Dutch families still remain in villages and neighbourhoods in various parts of the country, retaining with singular obstinacy, the dresses, manners, and even language of their ancestors, and forming a very distinct and curious feature in the motley population of the State. In a hamlet whose spire may be seen from New-York, rising from above the brow of a hill on the opposite side of the Hudson, many of the old folks, even at the present day, speak English with an accent, and the Dominie preaches in Dutch; and so completely is the hereditary love of quiet and silence maintained, that in one of these drowsy villages, in the middle of a warm summer's day, the buzzing of a stout bluebottle fly will resound from one end of the place to the other.

With the laudable hereditary feeling thus kept up among these worthy people, did Mr. Knickerbocker undertake to write a history of his native city, comprising the reign of its three Dutch governors during the time that it was yet under the domination of the Hogenmogens of Holland. In the execution of this design, the little Dutchman has displayed great historical research, and a wonderful consciousness of the dignity of his subject. His work, however, has been so little understood, as to be pronounced a mere work of humour, satirizing the follies of the times, both in politics and morals, and giving whimsical views of human nature.

Be this as it may:—among the papers left behind him were several tales of a lighter nature, apparently thrown together from materials which he had gathered during his profound researches for his history, and which he seems to have cast by with neglect, as unworthy of publication. Some of these have fallen into my hands, by an accident which it is needless at present to mention; and one of these very stories, with its prelude in the words of Mr. Knickerbocker, I undertook to read, by way of acquitting myself of the debt which I owed to the other story-tellers at the Hall. I subjoin it, for such of my readers as are fond of stories.[12]

[12] I find that the tale of Rip Van Winkle, given in the Sketch-Book, has been discovered by divers writers in magazines to have been founded on a little German tradition, and the matter has been revealed to the world as if it were a foul instance of plagiarism marvellously brought to light. In a note which follows that tale, I had alluded to the superstition on which it was founded, and I thought a mere allusion was sufficient, as the tradition was so notorious as to be inserted in almost every collection of German legends. I had seen it myself in three. I could hardly have hoped, therefore, in the present age, when every source of ghost and goblin story is ransacked, that the origin of the tale would escape discovery. In fact, I had considered popular traditions of the kind as fair foundations for authors of fiction to build upon, and made use of the one in question accordingly, I am not disposed to contest the matter, however, and indeed consider myself so completely overpaid by the public for my trivial performances, that I am content to submit to any deduction, which, in their after-thoughts, they may think proper to make.

The Haunted House.
FROM THE MSS. OF THE LATE DIEDRICH KNICKERBOCKER.

Formerly, almost every place had a house of this kind. If a house was seated on some melancholy place, or built in some old romantic manner, or if any particular accident had happened in it, such as murder, sudden death, or the like, to be sure that house had a mark set upon it, and was afterwards esteemed the habitation of a ghost.
—BOURNE'S Antiquities.

In the neighbourhood of the ancient city of the Manhattoes, there stood, not very many years since, an old mansion, which, when I was a boy, went by the name of the Haunted House. It was one of the very few remains of the architecture of the early Dutch settlers, and must have been a house of some consequence at the time when it was built. It consisted of a centre and two wings, the gable-ends of which were shaped like stairs. It was built partly of wood, and partly of small Dutch bricks, such as the worthy colonists brought with them from Holland, before they discovered that bricks could be manufactured elsewhere. The house stood remote from the road, in the centre of a large field, with an avenue of old locust[13] trees leading up to it, several of which had been shivered by lightning, and two or three blown down. A few apple-trees grow straggling about the field; there were traces also of what had been a kitchen-garden; but the fences were broken down, the vegetables had disappeared, or had grown wild, and turned to little better than weeds, with here and there a ragged rosebush, or a tall sunflower shooting up from among brambles, and hanging its head sorrowfully, as if contemplating the surrounding desolation. Part of the roof of the old house had fallen in, the windows were shattered, the panels of the doors broken, and mended with rough boards; and there were two rusty weathercocks at the ends of the house, which made a great jingling and whistling as they whirled about, but

---

[13] Acacias.

always pointed wrong. The appearance of the whole place was forlorn and desolate, at the best of times; but, in unruly weather, the howling of the wind about the crazy old mansion, the screeching of the weathercocks, the slamming and banging of a few loose window-shutters, had altogether so wild and dreary an effect, that the neighbourhood stood perfectly in awe of the place, and pronounced it the rendezvous of hobgoblins. I recollect the old building well; for I remember how many times, when an idle, unlucky urchin, I have prowled round its precincts, with some of my graceless companions, on holiday afternoons, when out on a freebooting cruise among the orchards. There was a tree standing near the house, that bore the most beautiful and tempting fruit; but then it was on enchanted ground, for the place was so charmed by frightful stories that we dreaded to approach it. Sometimes we would venture in a body, and get near the Hesperian tree, keeping an eye upon the old mansion, and darting fearful glances into its shattered window; when, just as we were about to seize upon our prize, an exclamation from some one of the gang, or an accidental noise, would throw us all into a panic, and we would scamper headlong from the place, nor stop until we had got quite into the road. Then there were sure to be a host of fearful anecdotes told of strange cries and groans, or of some hideous face suddenly seen staring out of one of the windows. By degrees we ceased to venture into these lonely grounds, but would stand at a distance and throw stones at the building; and there was something fearfully pleasing in the sound, as they rattled along the roof, or sometimes struck some jingling fragments of glass out of the windows.

The origin of this house was lost in the obscurity that covers the early period of the province, while under the government of their high mightinesses the states-general. Some reported it to have been a country residence of Wilhelmus Kieft, commonly called the Testy, one of the Dutch governors of New-Amsterdam; others said that it had been built by a naval commander who served under Van Tromp, and who, on being disappointed of preferment, retired from the service in disgust, became a philosopher through sheer spite, and brought over all his wealth to the province, that he might live according to his humour, and despise the world. The reason of its having fallen to decay, was likewise a matter of dispute; some said that it was in chancery, and had already cost more than its worth in legal expenses; but the most current, and, of course, the most probable account, was that it was haunted, and that nobody could live quietly in it. There can, in fact, be very little doubt that this last was the case, there were so many corroborating stories to prove it,—not an old woman in the neighbourhood but could furnish at least a score. There was a gray-headed curmudgeon of a negro that lived hard by, who had a whole budget of them to tell, many of which had happened to himself. I recollect many a time stopping with my schoolmates, and getting him to relate some. The old crone lived in a hovel, in the midst of a small patch of potatoes and Indian corn, which his master had given him on setting him free. He would come to us, with his hoe in his hand, and as we sat perched, like a row of swallows, on the rail of the fence, in the mellow twilight of a summer evening, he would tell us such fearful stories, accompanied by such awful rollings of his white eyes, that we were almost afraid of our own footsteps as we returned home afterwards in the dark.

Poor old Pompey! many years are past since he died, and went to keep company with the ghosts he was so fond of talking about. He was buried in a comer of his own little potato-patch; the plough soon passed over his grave, and levelled it with the rest of the field, and nobody thought any more of the gray-headed negro. By a singular chance, I was strolling in that neighbourhood several years afterwards, when I had grown up to be a young man, and I found a knot of gossips speculating on a skull which had just been turned up by a ploughshare. They of course determined it to be the remains of some one that had been murdered, and they had raked up with it some of the traditionary tales of the haunted house. I knew it at once to be the relic of poor Pompey, but I held my tongue; for I am too considerate of other people's enjoyment, ever to mar a story of a ghost or a murder. I took care, however, to see the bones of my old friend once more buried in a place where they were not likely to be disturbed. As I sat on the turf and watched the interment, I fell into a long conversation with an old gentleman of the neighbourhood, John Josse Vandermoere, a pleasant gossiping man, whose whole life was spent in hearing and telling the news of the province. He recollected old Pompey, and his stories about the Haunted House; but he assured me he could give me one still more strange than any that Pompey had related: and on my expressing a great curiosity to hear it, he sat down beside me on the turf, and told the following tale. I have endeavoured to give it as nearly as possible in his words; but it is now many years since, and I am grown old, and my memory is not over-good, I cannot therefore vouch for the language, but I am always scrupulous as to facts.

Dolph Heyliger.

"I take the town of Concord, where I dwell,
All Kilborn be my witness, if I were not
Begot in bashfulness, brought up in shamefacedness.
Let 'un bring a dog but to my vace that can
Zay I have beat 'un, and without a vault;
Or but a cat will swear upon a book,
I have as much as zet a vire her tail,
And I'll give him or her a crown for 'mends."
—Tale of a Tub.

In the early time of the province of New-York, while it groaned under the tyranny of the English governor, Lord Cornbury, who carried his cruelties towards the Dutch inhabitants so far as to allow no Dominie, or schoolmaster, to officiate in their language, without his special license; about this time, there lived in the jolly little old city of the Manhattoes, a kind motherly dame, known by the name of Dame Heyliger. She was the widow of a Dutch sea-captain, who died suddenly of a fever, in consequence of working too hard, and eating too heartily, at the time when all the inhabitants turned out in a panic, to fortify the place against the invasion of a small French privateer.[14] He left her with very little money, and one infant son, the only survivor of several children. The good woman had need of much management, to make both ends meet, and keep up a decent appearance. However, as her husband had fallen a victim to his zeal for the public safety, it was universally agreed that "something ought to be done for the widow;" and on the hopes of this "something" she lived tolerably for some years; in the meantime, every body pitied and spoke well of her; and that helped along.

She lived in a small house, in a small street, called Garden-street, very probably from a garden which may have flourished there some time or other. As her necessities every year grew greater, and the talk of the public

[14] 1705.

about doing "something for her" grew less, she had to cast about for some mode of doing something for herself, by way of helping out her slender means, and maintaining her independence, of which she was somewhat tenacious.

Living in a mercantile town, she had caught something of the spirit, and determined to venture a little in the great lottery of commerce. On a sudden, therefore, to the great surprise of the street, there appeared at her window a grand array of gingerbread kings and queens, with their arms stuck a-kimbo, after the invariable royal manner. There were also several broken tumblers, some filled with sugar-plums, some with marbles; there were, moreover, cakes of various kinds, and barley sugar, and Holland dolls, and wooden horses, with here and there gilt-covered picture-books, and now and then a skein of thread, or a dangling pound of candles. At the door of the house sat the good old dame's cat, a decent demure-looking personage, that seemed to scan every body that passed, to criticise their dress, and now and then to stretch her neck, and look out with sudden curiosity, to see what was going on at the other end of the street; but if by chance any idle vagabond dog came by, and offered to be uncivil—hoity-toity!—how she would bristle up, and growl, and spit, and strike out her paws! she was as indignant as ever was an ancient and ugly spinster, on the approach of some graceless profligate.

But though the good woman had to come down to these humble means of subsistence, yet she still kept up a feeling of family pride, having descended from the Vanderspiegels, of Amsterdam; and she had the family arms painted and framed, and hung over her mantel-piece. She was, in truth, much respected by all the poorer people of the place; her house was quite a resort of the old wives of the neighbourhood; they would drop in there of a winter's afternoon, as she sat knitting on one side of her fire-place, her cat purring on the other, and the tea-kettle singing before it; and they would gossip with her until late in the evening. There was always an arm-chair for Peter de Groodt, sometimes called Long Peter, and sometimes Peter Longlegs, the clerk and sexton of the little Lutheran church, who was her great crony, and indeed the oracle of her fire-side. Nay, the Dominie himself did not disdain, now and then, to step in, converse about the state of her mind, and take a glass of her special good cherry-brandy. Indeed, he never failed to call on new-year's day, and wish her a happy new year; and the good dame, who was a little vain on some points, always piqued herself on giving him as large a cake as any one in town.

I have said that she had one son. He was the child of her old age; but could hardly be called the comfort—for, of all unlucky urchins, Dolph Heyliger was the most mischievous. Not that the whipster was really vicious; he was only full of fun and frolic, and had that daring, gamesome spirit, which is extolled in a rich man's child, but execrated in a poor man's. He was continually getting into scrapes: his mother was incessantly harassed with complaints of some waggish pranks which he had played off; bills were sent in for windows that he had broken; in a word, he had not reached his fourteenth year before he was pronounced, by all the neighbourhood, to be a "wicked dog, the wickedest dog in the street!" Nay, one old gentleman, in a claret-coloured coat, with a thin red face, and ferret eyes, went so far as to assure Dame Heyliger, that her son would, one day or other, come to the gallows!

Yet, notwithstanding all this, the poor old soul loved her boy. It seemed as though she loved him the better, the worse he behaved; and that he grew more in her favour, the more he grew out of favour with the world. Mothers are foolish, fond-hearted beings; there's no reasoning them out of their dotage; and, indeed, this poor woman's child was all that was left to love her in this world;—so we must not think it hard that she turned a deaf ear to her good friends, who sought to prove to her that Dolph would come to a halter.

To do the varlet justice, too, he was strongly attached to his parent. He would not willingly have given her pain on any account; and when he had been doing wrong, it was but for him to catch his poor mother's eye fixed wistfully and sorrowfully upon him, to fill his heart with bitterness and contrition. But he was a heedless youngster, and could not, for the life of him, resist any new temptation to fun and mischief. Though quick at his learning, whenever he could be brought to apply himself, yet he was always prone to be led away by idle company, and would play truant to hunt after birds'-nests, to rob orchards, or to swim in the Hudson.

In this way he grew up, a tall, lubberly boy; and his mother began to be greatly perplexed what to do with him, or how to put him in a way to do for himself; for he had acquired such an unlucky reputation, that no one seemed willing to employ him.

Many were the consultations that she held with Peter de Groodt, the clerk and sexton, who was her prime counsellor. Peter was as much perplexed as herself, for he had no great opinion of the boy, and thought he would never come to good. He at one time advised her to send him to sea—a piece of advice only given in the most desperate cases; but Dame Heyliger would not listen to such an idea; she could not think of letting Dolph go out of her sight. She was sitting one day knitting by her fireside, in great perplexity, when the sexton entered with an air of unusual vivacity and briskness. He had just come from a funeral. It had been that of a boy of Dolph's years, who had been apprentice to a famous German doctor, and had died of a consumption. It is true, there had been a whisper that the deceased had been brought to his end by being made the subject of the doctor's experiments, on which he was apt to try the effects of a new compound, or a quieting draught. This, however, it is likely, was a mere scandal; at any rate, Peter de Groodt did not think it worth mentioning; though, had we time to philosophize, it would be a curious matter for speculation, why a doctor's family is apt to be so lean and cadaverous, and a butcher's so jolly and rubicund.

Peter de Groodt, as I said before, entered the house of Dame Heyliger, with unusual alacrity. He was full of a bright idea that had popped into his head at the funeral, and over which he had chuckled as he shovelled the earth into the grave of the doctor's disciple. It had occurred to him, that, as the situation of the deceased was vacant at the doctor's, it would be the very place for Dolph. The boy had parts, and could pound a pestle and run an errand with any boy in the town-and what more was wanted in a student?

The suggestion of the sage Peter was a vision of glory to the mother. She already saw Dolph, in her mind's eye, with a cane at his nose, a knocker at his door, and an M.D. at the end of his name—one of the established dignitaries of the town.

The matter, once undertaken, was soon effected; the sexton had some influence with the doctor, they having had much dealing together in the way of their separate professions; and the very next morning he called and conducted the urchin, clad in his Sunday clothes, to undergo the inspection of Dr. Karl Lodovick Knipperhausen.

They found the doctor seated in an elbow-chair, in one corner of his study, or laboratory, with a large volume, in German print, before him. He was a short, fat man, with a dark, square face, rendered more dark by a black velvet cap. He had a little, knobbed nose, not unlike the ace of spades, with a pair of spectacles gleaming on each side of his dusky countenance, like a couple of bow-windows.

Dolph felt struck with awe, on entering into the presence of this learned man; and gazed about him with boyish wonder at the furniture of this chamber of knowledge, which appeared to him almost as the den of a magician. In the centre stood a claw-footed table, with pestle and mortar, phials and gallipots, and a pair of small, burnished scales. At one end was a heavy clothes-press, turned into a receptacle for drugs and compounds; against which hung the doctor's hat and cloak, and gold-headed cane, and on the top grinned a human skull. Along the mantelpiece were glass vessels, in which were snakes and lizards, and a human foetus preserved in spirits. A closet, the doors of which were taken off, contained three whole shelves of books, and some, too, of mighty folio dimensions—a collection, the like of which Dolph had never before beheld. As, however, the library did not take up the whole of the closet, the doctor's thrifty housekeeper had occupied the rest with pots of pickles and preserves; and had hung about the room, among awful implements of the healing art, strings of red pepper and corpulent cucumbers, carefully preserved for seed.

Peter de Groodt, and his protégé, were received with great gravity and stateliness by the doctor, who was a very wise, dignified little man, and never smiled. He surveyed Dolph from head to foot, above, and under, and through his spectacles; and the poor lad's heart quailed as these great glasses glared on him like two full moons. The doctor heard all that Peter de Groodt had to say in favour of the youthful candidate; and then, wetting his thumb with the end of his tongue, he began deliberately to turn over page after page of the great black volume before him. At length, after many hums and haws, and strokings of the chin, and all that hesitation and deliberation with which a wise man proceeds to do what he intended to do from the very first, the doctor agreed to take the lad as a disciple; to give him bed, board, and clothing, and to instruct him in the healing art; in return for which, he was to have his services until his twenty-first year.

Behold, then, our hero, all at once transformed from an unlucky urchin, running wild about the streets, to a student of medicine, diligently pounding a pestle, under the auspices of the learned Doctor Karl Lodovick Knipperhausen. It was a happy transition for his fond old mother. She was delighted with the idea of her boy's being brought up worthy of his ancestors; and anticipated the day when he would be able to hold up his head with the lawyer, that lived in the large house opposite; or, peradventure, with the Dominie himself.

Doctor Knipperhausen was a native of the Palatinate of Germany; from whence, in company with many of his countrymen, he had taken refuge in England, on account of religious persecution. He was one of nearly three thousand Palatines, who came over from England in 1710, under the protection of Governor Hunter. Where the doctor had studied, how he had acquired his medical knowledge, and where he had received his diploma, it is hard at present to say, for nobody knew at the time; yet it is certain that his profound skill and abstruse knowledge were the talk and wonder of the common people, far and near.

His practice was totally different from that of any other physician; consisting in mysterious compounds, known only to himself, in the preparing and administering of which, it was said, he always consulted the stars. So high an opinion was entertained of his skill, particularly by the German and Dutch inhabitants, that they always resorted to him in desperate cases. He was one of those infallible doctors, that are always effecting sudden and surprising cures, when the patient has been given up by all the regular physicians; unless, as is shrewdly observed, the case has been left too long before it was put into their hands. The doctor's library was the talk and marvel of the neighbourhood, I might almost say of the entire burgh. The good people looked with reverence at a man that had read three whole shelves full of books, and some of them, too, as large as a family Bible. There were many disputes among the members of the little Lutheran church, as to which was the wiser man, the doctor or the Dominie. Some of his admirers even went so far as to say, that he knew more than the governor himself-in a word, it was thought that there was no end to his knowledge!

No sooner was Dolph received into the doctor's family, than he was put in possession of the lodging of his predecessor. It was a garret-room of a steep-roofed Dutch house, where the rain patted on the shingles, and the lightning gleamed, and the wind piped through the crannies in stormy weather; and where whole troops of hungry rats, like Don Cossacks, galloped about in defiance of traps and ratsbane.

He was soon up to his ears in medical studies, being employed, morning, noon, and night, in rolling pills, filtering tinctures, or pounding the pestle and mortar, in one corner of the laboratory; while the doctor would take his seat in another corner, when he had nothing else to do, or expected visitors, and, arrayed in his morning-gown and velvet cap, would pore over the contents of some folio volume. It is true, that the regular thumping of Dolph's pestle, or, perhaps, the drowsy buzzing of the summer flies, would now and then lull the little man into a slumber; but then his spectacles were always wide awake, and studiously regarding the book.

There was another personage in the house, however, to whom Dolph was obliged to pay allegiance. Though a bachelor, and a man of such great dignity and importance, yet the doctor was, like many other wise men, subject to petticoat government. He was completely under the sway of his housekeeper; a spare, busy, fretting housewife, in a little, round, quilted, German cap, with a huge bunch of keys jingling at the girdle of an exceedingly long waist. Frau Ilsé (or Frow Ilsy, as it was pronounced) had accompanied him in his various migrations from Germany to England, and from England to the province; managing his establishment and himself too: ruling him, it is true, with a gentle hand, but carrying a high hand with all the world beside. How she had acquired such ascendency, I do not pretend to say. People, it is true, did talk—but have not people been prone to talk ever since the world began? Who can tell how women generally contrive to get the upper hand? A husband, it is true, may now and then be master in his own house; but who ever knew a bachelor that was not managed by his housekeeper?

Indeed, Frau Ilsy's power was not confined to the doctor's household. She was one of those prying gossips that know every one's business better than they do themselves; and whose all-seeing eyes, and all-telling tongues, are terrors throughout a neighbourhood.

Nothing of any moment transpired in the world of scandal of this little burgh, but it was known to Frau Ilsy. She had her crew of cronies, that were perpetually hurrying to her little parlour, with some precious bit of news; nay, she would sometimes discuss a whole volume of secret history, as she held the street-door ajar, and gossiped with one of these garrulous cronies in the very teeth of a December blast.

Between the doctor and the housekeeper, it may easily be supposed that Dolph had a busy life of it. As Frau Ilsy kept the keys, and literally ruled the roast, it was starvation to offend her, though he found the study of her temper more perplexing even than that of medicine. When not busy in the laboratory, she kept him running hither and thither on her errands; and on Sundays he was obliged to accompany her to and from church, and carry her Bible. Many a time has the poor varlet stood shivering and blowing his fingers, or holding his frost-bitten nose, in the church-yard, while Ilsy and her cronies were huddled together, wagging their heads, and tearing some unlucky character to pieces.

With all his advantages, however, Dolph made very slow progress in his art. This was no fault of the doctor's, certainly, for he took unwearied pains with the lad, keeping him close to the pestle and mortar, or on the trot about town with phials and pill-boxes; and if he ever flagged in his industry, which he was rather apt to do, the doctor would fly into a passion, and ask him if he ever expected to learn his profession, unless he applied himself closer to the study. The fact is, he still retained the fondness for sport and mischief that had marked his childhood; the habit, indeed, had strengthened with his years, and gained force from being thwarted and constrained. He daily grew more and more untractable, and lost favour in the eyes both of the doctor and the housekeeper.

In the meantime the doctor went on, waxing wealthy and renowned. He was famous for his skill in managing cases not laid down in the books. He had cured several old women and young girls of witchcraft; a terrible complaint, nearly as prevalent in the province in those days as hydrophobia is at present. He had even restored one strapping country girl to perfect health, who had gone so far as to vomit crooked pins and needles; which is considered a desperate stage of the malady. It was whispered, also, that he was possessed of the art of preparing love-powders; and many applications had he in consequence from love-sick patients of both sexes. But all these cases formed the mysterious part of his practice, in which, according to the cant phrase, "secrecy and honour might be depended on." Dolph, therefore, was obliged to turn out of the study whenever such consultations occurred, though it is said he learnt more of the secrets of the art at the key-hole, than by all the rest of his studies put together.

As the doctor increased in wealth, he began to extend his possessions, and to look forward, like other great men, to the time when he should retire to the repose of a country-seat. For this purpose he had purchased a farm, or, as the Dutch settlers called it, a *bowerie*, a few miles from town. It had been the residence of a wealthy family, that had returned some time since to Holland. A large mansion-house stood in the centre of it, very much out of repair, and which, in consequence of certain reports, had received the appellation of the Haunted House. Either from these reports, or from its actual dreariness, the doctor had found it impossible to get a tenant; and, that the place might not fall to ruin before he could reside in it himself, he had placed a country boor, with his family, in one wing, with the privilege of cultivating the farm on shares.

The doctor now felt all the dignity of a landholder rising within him. He had a little of the German pride of territory in his composition, and almost looked upon himself as owner of a principality. He began to complain of the fatigue of business; and was fond of riding out "to look at his estate." His little expeditions to his lands were attended with a bustle and parade that created a sensation throughout the neighbourhood. His wall-eyed horse stood, stamping and whisking off the flies, for a full hour before the house. Then the doctor's saddle-bags would be brought out and adjusted; then, after a little while, his cloak would be rolled up and strapped to the saddle; then his umbrella would be buckled to the cloak; while, in the meantime, a group of ragged boys, that observant class of beings, would gather before the door. At length, the doctor would issue forth, in a pair of jack-boots that reached above his knees, and a cocked hat flapped down in front. As he was a short, fat man, he took some time to mount into the saddle; and when there, he took some time to have the saddle and stirrups properly adjusted, enjoying the wonder and admiration of the urchin crowd. Even after he had set off, he would pause in the middle of the street, or trot back two or three times to give some parting orders; which were answered by the housekeeper from the door, or Dolph from the study, or the black cook from the cellar, or the chambermaid from the garret-window; and there were generally some last words bawled after him, just as he was turning the corner.

The whole neighbourhood would be aroused by this pomp and circumstance. The cobbler would leave his last; the barber would thrust out his frizzed head, with a comb sticking in it; a knot would collect at the grocer's door; and the word would be buzzed from one end of the street to the other, "The doctor's riding out to his country-seat."

These were golden moments for Dolph. No sooner was the doctor out of sight, than pestle and mortar were abandoned; the laboratory was left to take care of itself, and the student was off on some madcap frolic.

Indeed, it must be confessed, the youngster, as he grew up, seemed in a fair way to fulfil the prediction of the old claret-coloured gentleman. He was the ringleader of all holiday sports, and midnight gambols; ready for all kinds of mischievous pranks, and harebrained adventures.

There is nothing so troublesome as a hero on a small scale, or, rather, a hero in a small town. Dolph soon became the abhorrence of all drowsy, housekeeping old citizens, who hated noise, and had no relish for waggery. The good dames, too, considered him as little better than a reprobate, gathered their daughters under their wings whenever he approached, and pointed him out as a warning to their sons. No one seemed to hold him in much regard, excepting the wild striplings of the place, who were captivated by his open-hearted, daring manners, and the negroes, who always look upon every idle, do-nothing youngster as a kind of gentleman. Even the good Peter de Groodt, who had considered himself a kind of patron of the lad, began to despair of him; and would shake his head dubiously, as he listened to a long complaint from the housekeeper, and sipped a glass of her raspberry brandy.

Still his mother was not to be wearied out of her affection, by all the waywardness of her boy; nor disheartened by the stories of his misdeeds, with which her good friends were continually regaling her. She had, it is true, very little of the pleasure which rich people enjoy, in always hearing their children praised; but she considered all this ill-will as a kind of persecution which he suffered, and she liked him the better on that account. She saw him growing up, a fine, tall, good-looking youngster, and she looked at him with the secret pride of a mother's heart. It was her great desire that Dolph should appear like a gentleman, and all the money she could save went towards helping out his pocket and his wardrobe. She would look out of the window after him, as he sallied forth in his best array, and her heart would yearn with delight; and once, when Peter de Groodt, struck with the youngster's gallant appearance on a bright Sunday morning, observed, "Well, after all, Dolph does grow a comely fellow!" the tear of pride started into the mother's eye: "Ah, neighbour! neighbour!" exclaimed she, "they may say what they please; poor Dolph will yet hold up his head with the best of them."

Dolph Heyliger had now nearly attained his one-and-twentieth year, and the term of his medical studies was just expiring; yet it must be confessed that he knew little more of the profession than when he first entered the doctor's doors. This, however, could not be from want of quickness of parts, for he showed amazing aptness in mastering other branches of knowledge, which he could only have studied at intervals. He was, for instance, a sure marksman, and won all the geese and turkeys at Christmas holidays. He was a bold rider; he was famous for leaping and wrestling; he played tolerably on the fiddle; could swim like a fish; and was the best hand in the whole place at fives or nine-pins.

All these accomplishments, however, procured him no favour in the eyes of the doctor, who grew more and more crabbed and intolerant, the nearer the term of apprenticeship approached. Frau Ilsy, too, was for ever finding some occasion to raise a windy tempest about his ears; and seldom encountered him about the house, without a clatter of the tongue; so that at length the jingling of her keys, as she approached, was to Dolph like the ringing of the prompter's bell, that gives notice of a theatrical thunderstorm. Nothing but the infinite good-humour of the heedless youngster, enabled him to bear all this domestic tyranny without open rebellion. It was evident that the doctor and his housekeeper were preparing to beat the poor youth out of the nest, the moment his term should have expired; a shorthand mode which the doctor had of providing for useless disciples.

Indeed, the little man had been rendered more than usually irritable lately, in consequence of various cares and vexations which his country estate had brought upon him. The doctor had been repeatedly annoyed by the rumours and tales which prevailed concerning the old mansion; and found it difficult to prevail even upon the countryman and his family to remain there rent-free. Every time he rode out to the farm, he was teased by some fresh complaint of strange noises and fearful sights, with which the tenants were disturbed at night; and the doctor would come home fretting and fuming, and vent his spleen upon the whole household. It was indeed a sore grievance, that affected him both in pride and purse. He was threatened with an absolute loss of the profits of his property; and then, what a blow to his territorial consequence, to be the landlord of a haunted house!

It was observed, however, that with all his vexation, the doctor never proposed to sleep in the house himself; nay, he could never be prevailed upon to remain in the premises after dark, but made the best of his way for town, as soon as the bats began to flit about in the twilight. The fact was, the doctor had a secret belief in ghosts, having passed the early part of his life in a country where they particularly abound; and indeed the story went, that, when a boy, he had once seen the devil upon the Hartz mountains in Germany.

At length, the doctor's vexations on this head were brought to a crisis. One morning, as he sat dozing over a volume in his study, he was suddenly started from his slumbers by the bustling in of the housekeeper.

"Here's a fine to do!" cried she, as she entered the room. "Here's Claus Hopper come in, bag and baggage, from the farm, and swears he'll have nothing more to do with it. The whole family have been frightened out of their wits; for there's such racketing and rummaging about the old house, that they can't sleep quiet in their beds!"

"Donner und blitzen!" cried the doctor, impatiently; "will they never have done chattering about that house? What a pack of fools, to let a few rats and mice frighten them out of good quarters!"

"Nay, nay," said the housekeeper, wagging her head knowingly, and piqued at having a good ghost story doubted, "there's more in it than rats and mice. All the neighbourhood talks about the house; and then such sights have been seen in it! Peter de Groodt tells me, that the family that sold you the house and went to Holland, dropped several strange hints about it, and said, 'they wished you joy of your bargain;' and you know yourself there's no getting any family to live in it."

"Peter de Groodt's a ninny—an old woman," said the doctor, peevishly; "I'll warrant he's been filling these people's heads full of stories. It's just like his nonsense about the ghost that haunted the church belfry, as an excuse for not ringing the bell that cold night when Hermanus Brinkerhoff's house was on fire. Send Claus to me."

Claus Hopper now made his appearance: a simple country lout, full of awe at finding himself in the very study of Dr. Knipperhausen, and too much embarrassed to enter into much detail of the matters that had caused his alarm. He stood twirling his hat in one hand, resting sometimes on one leg, sometimes on the other, looking occasionally at the doctor, and now and then stealing a fearful glance at the death's-head that seemed ogling him from the top of the clothes-press;

The doctor tried every means to persuade him to return to the farm, but all in vain; he maintained a dogged determination on the subject; and at the close of every argument or solicitation, would make the same brief, inflexible reply, "Ich kan nicht, mynheer." The doctor was a "little pot, and soon hot;" his patience was exhausted by these continual vexations about his estate. The stubborn refusal of Claus Hopper seemed to him like flat rebellion; his temper suddenly boiled over, and Claus was glad to make a rapid retreat to escape scalding.

When the bumpkin got to the housekeeper's room, he found Peter de Groodt, and several other true believers, ready to receive him. Here he indemnified himself for the restraint he had suffered in the study, and opened a budget of stories about the haunted house that astonished all his hearers. The housekeeper believed them all, if it was only to spite the doctor for having received her intelligence so uncourteously. Peter de Groodt matched them with many a wonderful legend of the times of the Dutch dynasty, and of the Devil's Stepping-stones; and of the pirate that was hanged at Gibbet Island, and continued to swing there at night long after the gallows was taken down; and of the ghost of the unfortunate Governor Leisler, who was hanged for treason, which haunted the old fort and the government house. The gossiping knot dispersed, each charged with direful intelligence. The sexton disburdened himself at a vestry meeting that was held that very day, and the black cook forsook her kitchen, and spent half the day at the street pump, that gossiping place of servants, dealing forth the news to all that came for water. In a little time, the whole town was in a buzz with tales about the haunted house. Some said that Claus Hopper had seen the devil, while others hinted that the house was haunted by the ghosts of some of the patients whom the doctor had physicked out of the world, and that was the reason why he did not venture to live in it himself.

All this put the little doctor in a terrible fume. He threatened vengeance on any one who should affect the value of his property by exciting popular prejudices. He complained loudly of thus being in a manner dispossessed of his territories by mere bugbears; but he secretly determined to have the house exorcised by the Dominie. Great was his relief, therefore, when, in the midst of his perplexities, Dolph stepped forward and undertook to garrison the haunted house. The youngster had been listening to all the stories of Claus Hopper and Peter de Groodt: he was fond of adventure, he loved the marvellous, and his imagination had become quite excited by these tales of wonder. Besides, he had led such an uncomfortable life at the doctor's, being subjected to the intolerable thraldom of early hours, that he was delighted at the prospect of having a house to himself, even though it should be a haunted one. His offer was eagerly accepted, and it was determined that he should mount guard that very night. His only stipulation was, that the enterprise should be kept secret from his mother; for he knew the poor soul would not sleep a wink, if she knew that her son was waging war with the powers of darkness.

When night came on, he set out on this perilous expedition. The old black cook, his only friend in the household, had provided him with a little mess for supper, and a rushlight; and she tied round his neck an amulet, given her by an African conjurer, as a charm against evil spirits. Dolph was escorted on his way by the doctor and Peter de Groodt, who had agreed to accompany him to the house, and to see him safe lodged. The night was overcast, and it was very dark when they arrived at the grounds which surrounded the mansion. The sexton led the way with a lantern. As they walked along the avenue of acacias, the fitful light, catching from bush to bush, and tree to tree, often startled the doughty Peter, and made him, fall back upon his followers; and the doctor grabbed still closer hold of Dolph's arm, observing that the ground was very slippery and uneven. At one time they were nearly put to a total rout by a bat, which came flitting about the lantern; and the notes of the insects from the trees, and the frogs from a neighbouring pond, formed a most drowsy and doleful concert.

The front door of the mansion opened with a grating sound, that made the doctor turn pale. They entered a tolerably large hall, such as is common in American country-houses, and which serves for a sitting-room in warm weather. From hence they went up a wide staircase, that groaned and creaked as they trod, every step making its particular note, like the key of a harpsichord. This led to another hall on the second story, from whence they entered the room where Dolph was to sleep. It was large, and scantily furnished; the shutters were closed; but as they were much broken, there was no want of a circulation of air. It appeared to have been that sacred chamber, known among Dutch housewives by the name of "the best bed-room;" which is the best furnished room in the house, but in which scarce any body is ever permitted to sleep. Its splendour, however, was all at an end. There were a few broken articles of furniture about the room, and in the centre stood a heavy deal table and a large arm-chair, both of which had the look of being coeval with the mansion. The fire-place was wide, and had been faced with Dutch tiles, representing scripture stories; but some of them had fallen out of their places, and lay shattered about the hearth. The sexton had lit the rushlight; and the doctor, looking fearfully about the room, was just exhorting Dolph to be of good cheer, and to pluck up a stout heart, when a noise in the chimney, like voices and struggling, struck a sudden panic into the sexton. He took to his heels with the lantern; the doctor followed hard after him; the stairs groaned and creaked as they hurried down, increasing their agitation and speed by its noises. The front door slammed after them; and Dolph heard them scrabbling down the avenue, till the sound of their feet was lost in the distance. That he did not join in this precipitate retreat, might have been owing to his possessing a little more courage than his companions, or perhaps that he had caught a glimpse of the cause of their dismay, in a nest of chimney swallows, that came tumbling down into the fire-place.

Being now left to himself, he secured the front door by a strong bolt and bar; and having seen that the other entrances were fastened, he returned to his desolate chamber. Having made his supper from the basket which the good old cook had provided, he locked the chamber door, and retired to rest on a mattress in one corner. The night was calm and still;

and nothing broke upon the profound quiet but the lonely chirping of a cricket from the chimney of a distant chamber. The rushlight, which stood in the centre of the deal table, shed a feeble yellow ray, dimly illumining the chamber, and making uncouth shapes and shadows on the walls, from the clothes which Dolph had thrown over a chair.

With all his boldness of heart, there was something subduing in this desolate scene; and he felt his spirits flag within him, as he lay on his hard bed and gazed about the room. He was turning over in his mind his idle habits, his doubtful prospects, and now and then heaving a heavy sigh, as he thought on his poor old mother; for there is nothing like the silence and loneliness of night to bring dark shadows over the brightest mind. By-and-by, he thought he heard a sound as if some one was walking below stairs. He listened, and distinctly heard a step on the great staircase. It approached solemnly and slowly, tramp—tramp—tramp! It was evidently the tread of some heavy personage; and yet how could he have got into the house without making a noise? He had examined all the fastenings, and was certain that every entrance was secure. Still the steps advanced, tramp—tramp—tramp! It was evident that the person approaching could not be a robber—the step was too loud and deliberate; a robber would either be stealthy or precipitate. And now the footsteps had ascended the staircase; they were slowly advancing along the passage, resounding through the silent and empty apartments. The very cricket had ceased its melancholy note, and nothing interrupted their awful distinctness. The door, which had been locked on the inside, slowly swung open, as if self-moved. The footsteps entered the room; but no one was to be seen. They passed slowly and audibly across it, tramp—tramp—tramp! but whatever made the sound was invisible. Dolph rubbed his eyes, and stared about him; he could see to every part of the dimly-lighted chamber; all was vacant; yet still he heard those mysterious footsteps, solemnly walking about the chamber. They ceased, and all was dead silence. There was something more appalling in this invisible visitation, than there would have been in anything that addressed itself to the eyesight. It was awfully vague and indefinite. He felt his heart beat against his ribs; a cold sweat broke out upon his forehead; he lay for some time in a state of violent agitation; nothing, however, occurred to increase his alarm. His light gradually burnt down into the socket, and he fell asleep. When he awoke it was broad daylight;

the sun was peering through the cracks of the window-shutters, and the birds were merrily singing about the house. The bright, cheery day soon put to flight all the terrors of the preceding night. Dolph laughed, or rather tried to laugh, at all that had passed, and endeavoured to persuade himself that it was a mere freak of the imagination, conjured up by the stories he had heard; but he was a little puzzled to find the door of his room locked on the inside, notwithstanding that he had positively seen it swing open as the footsteps had entered. He returned to town in a state of considerable perplexity; but he determined to say nothing on the subject, until his doubts were either confirmed or removed by another night's watching. His silence was a grievous disappointment to the gossips who had gathered at the doctor's mansion. They had prepared their minds to hear direful tales; and they were almost in a rage at being assured that he had nothing to relate.

The next night, then, Dolph repeated his vigil. He now entered the house with some trepidation. He was particular in examining the fastenings of all the doors, and securing them well. He locked the door of his chamber, and placed a chair against it; then, having despatched his supper, he threw himself on his mattress and endeavoured to sleep. It was all in vain—a thousand crowding fancies kept him waking. The time slowly dragged on, as if minutes were spinning out themselves into hours. As the night advanced, he grew more and more nervous; and he almost started from his couch, when he heard the mysterious footstep again on the staircase. Up it came, as before, solemnly and slowly, tramp—tramp—tramp! It approached along the passage; the door again swung open, as if there had been neither lock nor impediment, and a strange-looking figure stalked into the room. It was an elderly man, large and robust, clothed in the old Flemish fashion. He had on a kind of short cloak, with a garment under it, belted round the waist; trunk hose, with great bunches or bows at the knees; and a pair of russet boots, very large at top, and standing widely from his legs. His hat was broad and slouched, with a feather trailing over one side. His iron-gray hair hung in thick masses on his neck; and he had a short grizzled beard. He walked slowly round the room, as if examining that all was safe; then, hanging his hat on a peg beside the door, he sat down in the elbow-chair, and, leaning his elbow on the table, he fixed his eyes on Dolph with an unmoving and deadening stare.

Dolph was not naturally a coward; but he had been brought up in an implicit belief in ghosts and goblins. A thousand stories came swarming to his mind, that he had heard about this building; and as he looked at this strange personage, with his uncouth garb, his pale visage, his grizzly beard, and his fixed, staring, fish-like eye, his teeth began to chatter, his hair to rise on his head, and a cold sweat to break out all over his body. How long he remained in this situation he could not tell, for he was like one fascinated. He could not take his gaze off from the spectre; but lay staring at him with his whole intellect absorbed in the contemplation. The old man remained seated behind the table, without stirring or turning an eye, always keeping a dead steady glare upon Dolph. At length the household cock from a neighbouring farm clapped his wings, and gave a loud cheerful crow that rung over the fields. At the sound, the old man slowly rose and took down his hat from the peg; the door opened and closed after him; he was heard to go slowly down the staircase—tramp—tramp—tramp! —and when he had got to the bottom, all was again silent. Dolph lay and listened earnestly; counted every footfall; listened and listened if the steps should return—until, exhausted by watching and agitation, he fell into a troubled sleep.

Daylight again brought fresh courage and assurance. He would fain have considered all that had passed as a mere dream; yet there stood the chair in which the unknown had seated himself; there was the table on which he had leaned; there was the peg on which he had hung his hat; and there was the door, locked precisely as he himself had locked it, with the chair placed against it. He hastened down-stairs and examined the doors and windows; all were exactly in the same state in which he had left them, and there was no apparent way by which any being could have entered and left the house without leaving some trace behind. "Pooh!" said Dolph to himself, "it was all a dream;"—but it would not do; the more he endeavoured to shake the scene off from his mind, the more it haunted him.

Though he persisted in a strict silence as to all that he had seen or heard, yet his looks betrayed the uncomfortable night that he had passed. It was evident that there was something wonderful hidden under this mysterious reserve. The doctor took him into the study,—locked the door, and sought to have a full and confidential communication; but he could get nothing out of him. Frau Ilsy took him aside into the pantry, but to as little purpose; and Peter de Groodt held him by the button for a full hour in the church-yard, the very place to get at the bottom of a ghost story, but came off not a whit wiser than the rest. It is always the case, however, that one truth concealed makes a dozen current lies. It is like a guinea locked up in a bank, that has a dozen paper representatives. Before the day was over, the neighbourhood was full of reports. Some said that Dolph Heyliger watched in the haunted house with pistols loaded with silver bullets; others, that he had a long talk with the spectre without a head; others, that Doctor Knipperhausen and the sexton had been hunted down the Bowery lane, and quite into town, by a legion of ghosts of their customers. Some shook their heads, and thought it a shame that the doctor should put Dolph to pass the night alone in that dismal house, where he might be spirited away, no one knew whither; while others observed, with a shrug, that if the devil did carry off the youngster, it would be but taking his own.

These rumours at length reached the ears of the good Dame Heyliger, and, as may be supposed, threw her into a terrible alarm. For her son to have opposed himself to danger from living foes, would have been nothing so dreadful in her eyes as to dare alone the terrors of the haunted house. She hastened to the doctor's, and passed a great part of the day in attempting to dissuade Dolph from repeating his vigil; she told him a score of tales, which her gossiping friends had just related to her, of persons who had been carried off when watching alone in old ruinous houses. It was all to no effect. Dolph's pride, as well as curiosity, was piqued. He endeavoured to calm the apprehensions of his mother, and to assure her that there was no truth in all the rumours she had heard; she looked at him dubiously, and shook her head; but finding his determination was not to be shaken, she brought him a little thick Dutch Bible, with brass clasps, to take with him, as a sword wherewith to fight the powers of darkness; and, lest that might not be sufficient, the housekeeper gave him the Heidelburgh catechism by way of dagger.

The next night, therefore, Dolph took up his quarters for the third time in the old mansion. Whether dream or not, the same thing was repeated. Towards midnight, when every thing was still, the same sound echoed through the empty halls—tramp—tramp—tramp! The stairs were again ascended; the door again swung open; the old man entered, walked round the room, hung up his hat, and seated himself by the table. The same fear and trembling came over poor Dolph, though not in so violent a degree. He lay in the same way, motionless and fascinated, staring at the figure, which regarded him, as before, with a dead, fixed, chilling gaze. In this way they remained for a long time, till, by degrees, Dolph's courage began gradually to revive. Whether alive or dead, this being had certainly some object in his visitation; and he recollected to have heard it said, that spirits have no power to speak until they are spoken to. Summoning up resolution, therefore, and making two or three attempts before he could get his parched tongue in motion, he addressed the unknown in the most solemn form of adjuration that he could recollect, and demanded to know what was the motive of his visit.

No sooner had he finished, than the old man rose, took down his hat, the door opened, and he went out, looking back upon Dolph just as he crossed the threshold, as if expecting him to follow. The youngster did not hesitate an instant. He took the candle in his hand, and the Bible under his arm, and obeyed the tacit invitation. The candle emitted a feeble, uncertain ray; but still he could see the figure before him, slowly descend the stairs. He followed, trembling. When it had reached the bottom of the stairs, it turned through the hall towards the back door of the mansion. Dolph held the light over the balustrades; but, in his eagerness to catch a sight of the unknown, he flared his feeble taper so suddenly, that it went out. Still there was sufficient light from the pale moonbeams, that fell through a narrow window, to give him an indistinct view of the figure, near the door. He followed, therefore, down-stairs, and turned towards the place; but when he had got there, the unknown had disappeared. The door remained fast barred and bolted; there was no other mode of exit; yet the being, whatever he might be, was gone. He unfastened the door, and looked out into the fields. It was a hazy, moonlight night, so that the eye could distinguish objects at some distance. He thought he saw the unknown in a footpath that led from the door. He was not mistaken; but how had he got out of the house? He did not pause to think, but followed on. The old man proceeded at a measured pace, without looking about him, his footsteps sounding on the hard ground. He passed through the orchard of apple-trees that stood near the house, always keeping the footpath. It led to a well, situated in a little hollow, which had supplied the farm with water. Just at this well,

Dolph lost sight of him. He rubbed his eyes, and looked again; but nothing was to be seen of the unknown. He reached the well, but nobody was there. All the surrounding ground was open and clear; there was no bush nor hiding-place. He looked down the well, and saw, at a great depth, the reflection of the sky in the still water. After remaining here for some time, without seeing or hearing any thing more of his mysterious conductor, he returned to the house, full of awe and wonder. He bolted the door, groped his way back to bed, and it was long before he could compose himself to sleep.

His dreams were strange and troubled. He thought he was following the old man along the side of a great river, until they came to a vessel that was on the point of sailing; and that his conductor led him on board and vanished. He remembered the commander of the Tessel, a short swarthy man,—with crisped black hair, blind of one eye, and lame of one leg; but the rest of his dream was very confused. Sometimes he was sailing; sometimes on shore; now amidst storms and tempests, and now wandering quietly in unknown streets. The figure of the old man was strangely mingled up with the incidents of the dream; and the whole distinctly wound up by his finding himself on board of the vessel again, returning home, with a great bag of money!

When he woke, the gray, cool light of dawn was streaking the horizon, and the cocks passing the reveil from farm to farm throughout the country. He rose more harassed and perplexed than ever. He was singularly confounded by all that he had seen and dreamt, and began to doubt whether his mind was not affected, and whether all that was passing in his thoughts might not be mere feverish fantasy. In his present state of mind, he did not feel disposed to return immediately to the doctor's, and undergo the cross-questioning of the household. He made a scanty breakfast, therefore, on the remains of the last night's provisions, and then wandered out into the fields to meditate on all that had befallen him. Lost in thought, he rambled about, gradually approaching the town, until the morning was far advanced, when he was roused by a hurry and bustle around him. He found himself near the water's edge, in a throng of people, hurrying to a pier, where there was a vessel ready to make sail. He was unconsciously carried along by the impulse of the crowd, and found that it was a sloop, on the point of sailing up the Hudson to Albany. There was much leave-taking and kissing of old women and children, and great activity in carrying on board baskets of bread and cakes, and provisions of all kinds, notwithstanding, the mighty joints of meat that dangled over the stern; for a voyage to Albany was an expedition of great moment in those days. The commander of the sloop was hurrying about, and giving a world of orders, which were not very strictly attended to; one man being busy in lighting his pipe, and another in sharpening his snicker-snee.

The appearance of the commander suddenly caught Dolph's attention. He was short and swarthy, with crisped black hair; blind of one eye, and lame of one leg—the very commander that he had seen in his dream! Surprised and aroused, he considered the scene more attentively, and recalled still further traces of his dream: the appearance of the vessel, of the river, and of a variety of other objects, accorded with the imperfect images vaguely rising to recollection.

As he stood musing on these circumstances, the captain suddenly called out to him in Dutch, "Step on board, young man, or you'll be left behind!" He was startled by the sum mons; he saw that the sloop was cast loose, and was actually moving from the pier; it seemed as if he was actuated by some irresistible impulse; he sprang upon the deck, and the next moment the sloop was hurried off by the wind and tide. Dolph's thoughts and feelings were all in tumult and confusion. He had been strongly worked upon by the events that had recently befallen him, and could not but think that there was some connexion between his present situation and his last night's dream. He felt as if he was under supernatural influence; and he tried to assure himself with an old and favourite maxim of his, that "one way or other, all would turn out for the best." For a moment, the indignation of the doctor at his departure without leave, passed across his mind—but that was matter of little moment. Then he thought of the distress of his mother at his strange disappearance, and the idea gave him a sudden pang; he would have entreated to be put on shore; but he knew with such wind and tide the entreaty would have been in vain. Then, the inspiring love of novelty and adventure came rushing in full tide through his bosom; he felt himself launched strangely and suddenly on the world, and under full way to explore the regions of wonder that lay up this mighty river, and beyond those blue mountains that had bounded his horizon since childhood. While he was lost in this whirl of thought, the sails strained to the breeze; the shores seemed to hurry away behind him; and, before he perfectly recovered his self-possession, the sloop was ploughing her way past Spiking-devil and Yonkers, and the tallest chimney of the Manhattoes had faded from his sight.

I have said, that a voyage up the Hudson in those days was an undertaking of some moment; indeed, it was as much thought of as a voyage to Europe is at present. The sloops were often many days on the way; the cautious navigators taking in sail when it blew fresh, and coming to anchor at night; and stopping to send the boat ashore for milk for tea, without which it was impossible for the worthy old lady passengers to subsist. And there were the much-talked-of perils of the Tappaan Zee, and the highlands. In short, a prudent Dutch burgher would talk of such a voyage for months, and even years, beforehand; and never undertook it without putting his affairs in order, making his will, and having prayers said for him in the Low Dutch churches.

In the course of such a voyage, therefore, Dolph was satisfied he would have time enough to reflect, and to make up his mind as to what he should do when he arrived at Albany. The captain, with his blind eye and lame leg, would, it is true, bring his strange dream to mind, and perplex him sadly for a few moments; but, of late, his life had been made up so much of dreams and realities, his nights and days had been so jumbled together, that he seemed to be moving continually in a delusion. There is always, however, a kind of vagabond consolation in a man's having nothing in this world to lose; with this Dolph comforted his heart, and determined to make the most of the present enjoyment.

In the second day of the voyage they came to the highlands. It was the latter part of a calm, sultry day, that they floated gently with the tide between these stern mountains. There was that perfect quiet which prevails over nature in the languor of summer heat; the turning of a plank, or the accidental falling of an oar on deck, was echoed from the mountain side and reverberated along the shores; and if by chance the captain gave a shout of command, there were airy tongues that mocked it from every cliff.

Dolph gazed about him in mute delight and wonder, at these scenes of nature's magnificence. To the left the Dunderberg reared its woody precipices, height over height, forest over forest, away into the deep summer sky. To the right strutted forth the bold promontory of Anthony's

Nose, with a solitary eagle wheeling about it; while beyond, mountain succeeded to mountain, until they seemed to lock their arms together, and confine this mighty river in their embraces. There was a feeling of quiet luxury in gazing at the broad, green bosoms here and there scooped out among the precipices; or at woodlands high in air, nodding over the edge of some beetling bluff, and their foliage all transparent in the yellow sunshine.

In the midst of his admiration, Dolph remarked a pile of bright, snowy clouds peering above the western heights. It was succeeded by another, and another, each seemingly pushing onwards its predecessor, and towering, with dazzling brilliancy, in the deep-blue atmosphere: and now muttering peals of thunder were faintly heard rolling behind the mountains. The river, hitherto still and glassy, reflecting pictures of the sky and land, now showed a dark ripple at a distance, as the breeze came creeping up it. The fish-hawks wheeled and screamed, and sought their nests on the high dry trees; the crows flew clamorously to the crevices of the rocks, and all nature seemed conscious of the approaching thunder-gust.

The clouds now rolled in volumes over the mountain tops; their summits still bright and snowy, but the lower parts of an inky blackness. The rain began to patter down in broad and scattered drops; the wind freshened, and curled up the waves; at length it seemed as if the bellying clouds were torn open by the mountain tops, and complete torrents of rain came rattling down. The lightning leaped from cloud to cloud, and streamed quivering against the rocks, splitting and rending the stoutest forest trees. The thunder burst in tremendous explosions; the peals were echoed from mountain to mountain; they crashed upon Dunderberg, and rolled up the long defile of the highlands, each headland making a new echo, until old Bull hill seemed to bellow back the storm.

For a time the scudding rack and mist, and the sheeted rain, almost hid the landscape from the sight. There was a fearful gloom, illumined still more fearfully by the streams of lightning which glittered among the rain-drops. Never had Dolph beheld such an absolute warring of the elements: it seemed as if the storm was tearing and rending its way through this mountain defile, and had brought all the artillery of heaven into action.

The vessel was hurried on by the increasing wind, until she came to where the river makes a sudden bend, the only one in the whole course of its majestic career.[15] Just as they turned the point, a violent flaw of wind came sweeping down a mountain gully, bending the forest before it, and, in a moment, lashing up the river into white froth and foam. The captain saw the danger, and cried out to lower the sail. Before the order could be obeyed, the flaw struck the sloop, and threw her on her beam-ends. Everything was now fright and confusion: the flapping of the sails, the whistling and rushing of the wind, the bawling of the captain and crew, the shrieking of the passengers, all mingled with the rolling and bellowing of the thunder. In the midst of the uproar, the sloop righted; at the same time the mainsail shifted, the boom came sweeping the quarter-deck, and Dolph, who was gazing unguardedly at the clouds, found himself, in a moment, floundering in the river.

For once in his life, one of his idle accomplishments was of use to him. The many truant hours which he had devoted to sporting in the Hudson, had made him an expert swimmer, yet, with all his strength and skill, he found great difficulty in reaching the shore. His disappearance from the deck had not been noticed by the crew, who were all occupied by their own danger. The sloop was driven along with inconceivable rapidity. She had hard work to weather a long promontory on the eastern shore, round which the river turned, and which completely shut her from Dolph's view.

It was on a point of the western shore that he landed, and, scrambling up the rocks, he threw himself, faint and exhausted, at the foot of a tree. By degrees, the thunder-gust passed over. The clouds rolled away to the east, where they lay piled in feathery masses, tinted with the last rosy rays of the sun. The distant play of the lightning might be seen about the dark bases, and now and then might be heard the faint muttering of the thunder. Dolph rose, and sought about to see if any path led from the shore; but all was savage and trackless. The rocks were piled upon each other; great trunks of trees lay shattered about, as they had been blown down by the strong winds which draw through these mountains, or had fallen through age. The rocks, too, were overhung with wild vines and briers, which completely matted themselves together, and opposed a barrier to all ingress; every movement that he made, shook down a shower from the dripping foliage. He attempted to scale one of these almost perpendicular heights; but, though strong and agile, he found it an Herculean undertaking. Often he

---

[15] This must have been the bend at West-Point.

was supported merely by crumbling projections of the rock, and sometimes he clung to roots and branches of trees, and hung almost suspended in the air. The wood-pigeon came cleaving his whistling flight by him, and the eagle screamed from the brow of the impending cliff. As he was thus clambering, he was on the point of seizing hold of a shrub to aid his ascent, when something rustled among the leaves, and he saw a snake quivering along like lightning, almost from under his hand. It coiled itself up immediately, in an attitude of defiance, with flattened head, distended jaws, and quickly-vibrating tongue, that played like a little flame about its mouth. Dolph's heart turned faint within him, and he had well-nigh let go his hold, and tumbled down the precipice. The serpent stood on the defensive but for an instant; it was an instinctive movement of defence; and finding there was no attack, it glided away into a cleft of the rock. Dolph's eye followed with fearful intensity; and he saw at a glance that he was in the vicinity of a nest of adders, that lay knotted, and writhing, and hissing in the chasm. He hastened with all speed to escape from so frightful a neighbourhood. His imagination was full of this new horror; he saw an adder in every curling vine, and heard the tail of a rattlesnake in every dry leaf that rustled.

At length he succeeded in scrambling to the summit of a precipice; but it was covered by a dense forest. Wherever he could gain a look-out between the trees, he saw that the coast rose in heights and cliffs, one rising beyond another, until huge mountains overtopped the whole. There were no signs of cultivation, nor any smoke curling amongst the trees, to indicate a human residence. Every thing was wild and solitary. As he was standing on the edge of a precipice that overlooked a deep ravine fringed with trees, his feet detached a great fragment of rock; it fell, crashing its way through the tree tops, down into the chasm. A loud whoop, or rather yell, issued from the bottom of the glen; the moment after, there was the report of a gun; and a ball came whistling over his head, cutting the twigs and leaves, and burying itself deep in the bark of a chestnut-tree.

Dolph did not wait for a second shot, but made a precipitate retreat; fearing every moment to hear the enemy in pursuit. He succeeded, however, in returning unmolested to the shore, and determined to penetrate no farther into a country so beset with savage perils.

He sat himself down, dripping, disconsolately, on a wet stone. What was to be done? Where was he to shelter himself? The hour of repose was approaching; the birds were seeking their nests, the bat began to flit about in the twilight, and the night-hawk soaring high in heaven, seemed to be calling out the stars. Night gradually closed in, and wrapped every thing in gloom; and though it was the latter part of summer, yet the breeze, stealing along the river, and among these dripping forests, was chilly and penetrating, especially to a half-drowned man.

As he sat drooping and despondent in this comfortless condition, he perceived a light gleaming through the trees near the shore, where the winding of the river made a deep bay. It cheered him with the hopes that here might be some human habitation, where he might get something to appease the clamorous cravings of his stomach, and, what was equally necessary in his shipwrecked condition, a comfortable shelter for the night. It was with extreme difficulty that he made his way towards the light, along ledges of rocks down which he was in danger of sliding into the river, and over great trunks of fallen trees; some of which had been blown down in the late storm, and lay so thickly together, that he had to struggle through their branches. At length he came to the brow of a rock that overhung a small dell, from whence the light proceeded. It was from a fire at the foot of a great tree, that stood in the midst of a grassy interval, or plat, among the rocks. The fire cast up a red glare among the gray crags and impending trees; leaving chasms of deep gloom, that resembled entrances to caverns. A small brook rippled close by, betrayed by the quivering reflection of the flame. There were two figures moving about the fire, and others squatted before it. As they were between him and the light, they were in complete shadow; but one of them happening to move round to the opposite side, Dolph was startled at perceiving, by the full glare falling on painted features, and glittering on silver ornaments, that he was an Indian. He now looked more narrowly, and saw guns leaning against a tree, and a dead body lying on the ground.

Dolph began to doubt whether he was not in a worse condition than before; here was the very foe that had fired at him from the glen. He endeavoured to retreat quietly, not caring to entrust himself to these half-human beings in so savage and lonely a place. It was too late: the Indian, with that eagle quickness of eye so remarkable in his race, perceived something stirring among the bushes on the rock: he seized one of the guns that leaned against the tree; one moment more, and Dolph might have had his passion for adventure cured by a bullet. He hallooed loudly, with the Indian salutation of friendship: the whole party sprang upon their feet; the salutation was returned, and the straggler was invited to join them at the fire.

On approaching, he found, to his consolation, that the party was composed of white men as well as Indians. One, who was evidently the principal personage, or commander, was seated on the trunk of a tree before the fire. He was a large, stout man, somewhat advanced in life, but hale and hearty. His face was bronzed almost to the colour of an Indian's; he had strong but rather jovial features, an aquiline nose, and a mouth shaped like a mastiff's. His face was half thrown in shade by a broad hat, with a buck's-tail in it. His gray hair hung short in his neck. He wore a hunting-frock, with Indian leggings, and moccasons, and a tomahawk in the broad wampum belt round his waist. As Dolph caught a distinct view of his person and features, he was struck with something that reminded him of the old man of the haunted house. The man before him, however, was different in his dress and age; he was more cheery, too, in his aspect, and it was hard to define where the vague resemblance lay—but a resemblance there certainly was. Dolph felt some degree of awe in approaching him; but was assured by the frank, hearty welcome with which he was received. As he case his eyes about, too, he was still further encouraged, by perceiving that the dead body, which had caused him some alarm, was that of a deer; and his satisfaction was complete, in discerning, by the savoury steams which issued from a kettle suspended by a hooked stick over the fire, that there was a part cooking for the evening's repast.

He now found that he had fallen in with a rambling hunting party, such as often took place in those days among the settlers along the river. The hunter is always hospitable; and nothing makes men more social and unceremonious, than meeting in the wilderness. The commander of the party poured him out a dram of cheering liquor, which he gave him with a merry leer, to warm his heart; arid ordered one of his followers to fetch some garments from a pinnace, which was moored in a cove close by, while those in which our hero was dripping might be dried before the fire.

Dolph found, as he had suspected, that the shot from the glen, which had come so near giving him his quietus when on the precipice, was from the party before him. He had nearly crushed one of them by the fragment of rock which he had detached; and the jovial old hunter, in the broad hat and buck-tail, had fired at the place where he saw the bushes move, supposing it to be some wild animal. He laughed heartily at the blunder; it being what is considered an exceeding good joke among hunters; "but faith, my lad," said he, "if I had but caught a glimpse of you to take sight at, you would have followed the rock. Antony Vander Heyden is seldom known to miss his aim." These last words were at once a clue to Dolph's curiosity; and a few questions let him completely into the character of the man before him, and of his band of woodland rangers. The commander in the broad hat and hunting-frock, was no less a personage than the Heer Antony Vander Heyden, of Albany, of whom Dolph had many a time heard. He was, in fact, the hero of many a story; being a man of singular humours and whimsical habits, that were matters of wonder to his quiet Dutch neighbours. As he was a man of property, having had a father before him, from whom he inherited large tracts of wild land, and whole barrels full of wampum, he could indulge his humours without control. Instead of staying quietly at home, eating and drinking at regular meal times; amusing himself by smoking his pipe on the bench before the door, and then turning into a comfortable bed at night; he delighted in all kinds of rough, wild expeditions. He was never so happy as when on a hunting party in the wilderness, sleeping under trees or bark sheds, or cruising down the river, or on some woodland lake, fishing and hunting, and living the Lord knows how.

He was a great friend to Indians, and to an Indian mode of life; which he considered true natural liberty and manly enjoyment. When at home, he had always several Indian hangers-on, who loitered about his house, sleeping like hounds in the sunshine, or preparing hunting and fishing-tackle for some new expedition, or shooting at marks with bows and arrows.

Over these vagrant beings, Heer Antony had as perfect command as a huntsman over his pack; though they were great nuisances to the regular people of his neighbourhood. As he was a rich man, no one ventured to thwart his humours; indeed, he had a hearty, joyous manner about him, that made him universally popular. He would troll a Dutch song, as he tramped along the street; hail every one a mile off; and when he entered a house, he would slap the good man familiarly on the back, shake him by the hand till he roared, and kiss his wife and daughters before his face—in short, there was no pride nor ill-humour about Heer Antony.

Besides his Indian hangers-on, he had three or four humble friends among the white men, who looked up to him as a patron, and had the run of his kitchen, and the favour of being taken with him occasionally on his expeditions. It was with a medley of such retainers that he was at present on a cruise along the shores of the Hudson, in a pinnace which he kept for his own recreation. There were two white men with him, dressed partly in the Indian style, with moccasons and hunting-shirts; the rest of his crew consisted of four favourite Indians. They had been prowling about the river, without any definite object until thay found themselves in the highlands; where they had passed two or three days, hunting the deer which still lingered among these mountains.

"It is a lucky circumstance, young man," said Antony Vander Heyden, "that you happened to be knocked overboard to-day, as to-morrow morning we start early on our return homewards, and you might then have looked in vain for a meal among the mountains—but come, lads, stir about! stir about! Let's see what prog we have for supper; the kettle has boiled long enough; my stomach cries cupboard; and I'll warrant our guest is in no mood to dally with his trencher."

There was a bustle now in the little encampment. One took off the kettle, and turned a part of the contents into a huge wooden bowl; another prepared a flat rock for a table; while a third brought various utensils from the pinnace, which was moored close by; and Heer Antony himself brought a flask or two of precious liquor from his own private locker— knowing his boon companions too well to trust any of them with the key.

A rude but hearty repast was soon spread; consisting of venison smoking from the kettle, with cold bacon, boiled Indian corn, and mighty loaves of good brown household bread. Never had Dolph made a more delicious repast; and when he had washed it down with two or three draughts from the Heer Antony's flask, and felt the jolly liquor sending its warmth through his veins, and glowing round his very heart, he would not have changed his situation, no, not with the governor of the province.

The Heer Antony, too, grew chirping and joyous; told half-a-dozen fat stories, at which his white followers laughed immoderately, though the Indians, as usual, maintained an invincible gravity.

"This is your true life, my boy!" said he, slapping Dolph on the shoulder; "a man is never a man till he can defy wind and weather, range woods and wilds, sleep under a tree, and live on bass-wood leaves!"

And then would he sing a stave or two of a Dutch drinking song, swaying a short squab Dutch bottle in his hand, while his myrmidons would join in chorus, until the woods echoed again;—as the good old song has it:

> *"They all with a shout made the elements ring,*
> *So soon as the office was o'er;*
> *To feasting they went with true merriment.*
> *And tippled strong liquor gillore."*

In the midst of his jovialty, however, Heer Antony did not lose sight of discretion. Though he pushed the bottle without reserve to Dolph, yet he always took care to help his followers himself, knowing the beings he had to deal with; and he was particular in granting but a moderate allowance to the Indians. The repast being ended, the Indians having drunk their liquor and smoked their pipes, now wrapped themselves in their blankets, stretched themselves on the ground with their feet to the fire, and soon fell asleep, like so many tired hounds. The rest of the party remained chatting before the fire, which the gloom of the forest, and the dampness of the air from the late storm, rendered extremely grateful and comforting. The conversation gradually moderated from the hilarity of supper-time, and turned upon hunting adventures, and exploits and perils in the wilderness; many of which were so strange and improbable, that I will not venture to repeat them, lest the veracity of Antony Vander Heyden and his comrades should be brought into question. There were many legendary tales told, also, about the river, and the settlements on its borders; in which valuable kind of lore, the Heer Antony seemed deeply versed. As the sturdy bush-beater sat in the twisted root of a tree, that served him for a kind of arm-chair, dealing forth these wild stories, with the fire gleaming on his strongly-marked visage, Dolph was again repeatedly perplexed by something that reminded him of the phantom of the haunted house; some vague resemblance, that could not be fixed upon any precise feature or lineament, but which pervaded the general air of his countenance and figure.

The circumstance of Dolph's falling overboard being again discussed, led to the relation of divers disasters and singular mishaps that had befallen voyagers on this great river, particularly in the earlier periods of colonial history; most of which the Heer deliberately attributed to supernatural causes. Dolph stared at this suggestion; but the old gentleman assured him that it was very currently believed by the settlers along the river, that these highlands were under the dominion of supernatural and mischievous beings, which seemed to have taken some pique against the Dutch colonists in the early time of the settlement. In consequence of this, they have ever since taken particular delight in venting their spleen, and indulging their humours, upon the Dutch skippers; bothering them with flaws, head winds, counter currents, and all kinds of impediments; insomuch, that a Dutch navigator was always obliged to be exceedingly wary and deliberate in his proceedings; to come to anchor at dusk; to drop his peak, or take in sail, whenever he saw a swag-bellied cloud rolling over the mountains; in short, to take so many precautions, that he was often apt to be an incredible time in toiling up the river.

Some, he said, believed these mischievous powers of the air to be evil spirits conjured up by the Indian wizards, in the early times of the province, to revenge themselves on the strangers who had dispossessed them of their country. They even attributed to their incantations the misadventure which befell the renowned Hendrick Hudson, when he sailed so gallantly up this river in quest of a north-west passage, and, as he thought, run his ship aground; which they affirm was nothing more nor less than a spell of these same wizards, to prevent his getting to China in this direction.

The greater part, however, Heer Antony observed, accounted for all the extraordinary circumstances attending this river, and the perplexities of the skippers which navigated it, by the old legend of the Storm-ship, which haunted Point-no-point. On finding Dolph to be utterly ignorant of this tradition, the Heer stared at him for a moment with surprise, and wondered where he had passed his life, to be uninformed on so important a point of history. To pass away the remainder of the evening, therefore, he undertook the tale, as far as his memory would serve, in the very words in which it had been written out by Mynheer Selyne, an early poet of the New-Nederlandts. Giving, then, a stir to the fire, that sent up its sparks among the trees like a little volcano, he adjusted himself comfortably in his root of a tree; and throwing back his head, and closing his eyes for a few moments, to summon up his recollection, he related the following legend.

The Storm-Ship.

In the golden age of the province of the New-Netherlands, when it was under the sway of Wouter Van Twiller, otherwise called the Doubter, the people of the Manhattoes were alarmed, one sultry afternoon, just about the time of the summer solstice, by a tremendous storm of thunder and lightning. The rain descended in such torrents, as absolutely to spatter up and smoke along the ground. It seemed as if the thunder rattled and rolled over the very roofs of the houses; the lightning was seen to play about the church of St. Nicholas, and to strive three times, in vain, to strike its weather-cock. Garret Van Horne's new chimney was split almost from top to bottom; and Doffue Mildeberger was struck speechless from his bald-faced mare, just as he was riding into town. In a word, it was one of those unparalleled storms, that only happen once within the memory of that venerable personage, known in all towns by the appellation of "the oldest inhabitant."

Great was the terror of the good old women of the Manhattoes. They gathered their children together, and took refuge in the cellars; after having hung a shoe on the iron point of every bed-post, lest it should attract the lightning. At length the storm abated: the thunder sunk into a growl; and the setting sun, breaking from under the fringed borders of the clouds, made the broad bosom of the bay to gleam like a sea of molten, gold.

The word was given from the fort, that a ship was standing up the bay. It passed from mouth to mouth, and street to street, and soon put the little capital in a bustle. The arrival of a ship, in those early times of the settlement, was an event of vast importance to the inhabitants. It brought them news from the old world, from the land of their birth, from which they were so completely severed: to the yearly ship, too, they looked for their supply of luxuries, of finery, of comforts, and almost of necessaries. The good vrouw could not have her new cap, nor new gown, until the arrival of the ship; the artist waited for it for his tools, the burgomaster for his pipe and his supply of Hollands, the school-boy for his top and marbles, and the lordly landholder for the bricks with which he was to build his new mansion. Thus every one, rich and poor, great and small, looked out for the arrival of the ship. It was the great yearly event of the town of New-Amsterdam; and from one end of the year to the other, the ship—the ship—the ship—was the continual topic of conversation.

The news from the fort, therefore, brought all the populace down to the battery, to behold the wished-for sight. It was not exactly the time when she had been expected to arrive, and the circumstance was a matter of some speculation. Many were the groups collected about the battery. Here and there might be seen a burgomaster, of slow and pompous gravity, giving his opinion with great confidence to a crowd of old women and idle boys. At another place was a knot of old weatherbeaten fellows, who had been seamen or fishermen in their times, and were great authorities on such occasions; these gave different opinions, and caused great disputes among their several adherents: but the man most looked up to, and followed and watched by the crowd, was Hans Van Pelt, an old Dutch sea-captain retired from service, the nautical oracle of the place. He reconnoitred the ship through an ancient telescope, covered with tarry canvas, hummed a Dutch tune to himself, and said nothing. A hum, however, from Hans Van Pelt had always more weight with the public than a speech from another man.

In the meantime, the ship became more distinct to the naked eye: she was a stout, round Dutch-built vessel, with high bow and poop, and bearing Dutch colours. The evening sun gilded her bellying canvas, as she came riding over the long waving billows. The sentinel who had given notice of her approach, declared, that he first got sight of her when she was in the centre of the bay; and that she broke suddenly on his sight, just as if she had come out of the bosom of the black thunder-cloud. The bystanders looked at Hans Van Pelt, to see what he would say to this report: Hans Van Pelt screwed his mouth closer together, and said nothing; upon which some shook their heads, and others shrugged their shoulders.

The ship was now repeatedly hailed, but made no reply, and, passing by the fort, stood on up the Hudson. A gun was brought to bear on her, and, with some difficulty, loaded and fired by Hans Van Pelt, the garrison not being expert in artillery. The shot seemed absolutely to pass through the ship, and to skip along the water on the other side, but no notice was taken of it! What was strange, she had all her sails set, and sailed right against wind and tide, which were both down the river. Upon this Hans Van Pelt, who was likewise harbour-master, ordered his boat, and set off to board her; but after rowing two or three hours, he returned without success. Sometimes he would get within one or two hundred yards of her, and then, in a twinkling, she would be half a mile off. Some said it was because his oarsmen, who were rather pursy and short-winded, stopped every now and then to take breath, and spit on their hands; but this, it is probable, was a mere scandal. He got near enough, however, to see the crew; who were all dressed in the Dutch style, the officers in doublets and high hats and feathers: not a word was spoken by any one on board; they stood as motionless as so many statues, and the ship seemed as if left to her own government. Thus she kept on away up the river, lessening and lessening in the evening sunshine, until she faded from sight, like a little white cloud melting away in the summer sky.

The appearance of this ship threw the governor into one of the deepest doubts that ever beset him in the whole course of his administration. Fears were entertained for the security of the infant settlements on the river, lest this might be an enemy's ship in disguise, sent to take possession. The governor called together his council repeatedly to assist him with their conjectures. He sat in his chair of state, built of timber from the sacred forest of the Hague, and smoking his long jasmine pipe, and listened to all that his counsellors had to say on a subject about which they knew nothing; but, in spite of all the conjecturing of the sagest and oldest heads, the governor still continued to doubt.

Messengers were despatched to different places on the river; but they returned without any tidings—the ship had made no port. Day after day, and week after week, elapsed; but she never returned down the Hudson. As, however, the council seemed solicitous for intelligence, they had it in abundance. The captains of the sloops seldom arrived without bringing some report of having seen the strange ship at different parts of the river; sometimes near the Palisadoes; sometimes off Croton Point, and sometimes in the highlands; but she never was reported as having been seen above the highlands. The crews of the sloops, it is true, generally differed among themselves in their accounts of these apparitions; but they may have arisen from the uncertain situations in which they saw her. Sometimes it was by the flashes of the thunder-storm lighting up a pitchy night, and giving glimpses of her careering across Tappaan Zee, or the wide waste of Haverstraw Bay. At one moment she would appear close upon them, as if likely to run them down, and would throw them into great bustle and alarm; but the next flash would show her far off, always sailing against the wind. Sometimes, in quiet moonlight nights, she would be seen under some high bluff of the highlands, all in deep shadow, excepting her top-sails glittering in the moonbeams; by the time, however, that the voyagers would reach the place, there would be no ship to be seen; and when they had passed on for some distance, and looked back, behold! there she was again with her top-sails in tha moonshine! Her appearance was always just after, or just before, or just in the midst of, unruly weather; and she was known by all the skippers and voyagers of the Hudson, by the name of "the storm-ship."

These reports perplexed, the governor and his council more than ever; and it would be endless to repeat the conjectures and opinions that were uttered on the subject. Some quoted cases in point, of ships seen off the coast of New-England, navigated by witches and goblins. Old Hans Van Pelt, who had been more than once to the Dutch colony at the Cape of Good Hope, insisted that this must be the Flying Dutchman which had so long haunted Table Bay, but, being unable to make port, had now sought another harbour. Others suggested, that, if it really was a supernatural apparition, as there was every natural reason to believe, it might be Hendrick Hudson, and his crew of the Half-Moon; who, it was well-known, had once run aground in the upper part of the river, in seeking a north-west passage to China. This opinion had very little weight with the governor, but it passed current out of doors; for indeed it had already been reported, that Hendrick Hudson and his crew haunted the Kaatskill Mountain; and it appeared very reasonable to suppose, that his ship might infest the river, where the enterprise was baffled, or that it might bear the shadowy crew to their periodical revels in the mountain.

Other events occurred to occupy the thoughts and doubts of the sage Wouter and his council, and the storm-ship ceased to be a subject of deliberation at the board. It continued, however, to be a matter of popular belief and marvellous anecdote through the whole time of the Dutch government, and particularly just before the capture of New-Amsterdam, and the subjugation of the province by the English squadron. About that time the storm-ship was repeatedly seen in the Tappaan Zee, and about Weehawk, and even down as far as Hoboken; and her appearance was supposed to be ominous of the approaching squall in public affairs, and the downfall of Dutch domination.

Since that time, we have no authentic accounts of her; though it is said she still haunts the highlands and cruises about Point-no-point. People who live along the river, insist that they sometimes see her in summer moonlight; and that in a deep still midnight, they have heard the chant of her crew, as if heaving the lead; but sights and sounds are so deceptive along the mountainous shores, and about the wide bays and long reaches of this great river, that I confess I have very strong doubts upon the subject.

It is certain, nevertheless, that strange things have been seen in these highlands in storms, which are considered as connected with the old story of the ship. The captains of the river craft talk of a little bulbous-bottomed Dutch goblin, in trunk hose and sugar-loafed hat, with a speaking trumpet in his hand, which they say keeps about the Dunderberg.[16] They declare they have heard him, in stormy weather, in the midst of the turmoil, giving orders in Low Dutch for the piping up of a fresh gust of wind, or the rattling off of another thunder-clap. That sometimes he has been seen surrounded by a crew of little imps in broad breeches and short doublets; tumbling head-over-heels in the rack and mist, and playing a thousand gambols in the air; or buzzing like a swarm of flies about Antony's Nose; and that, at such times, the hurry-scurry of the storm was always greatest. One time, a sloop, in passing by the Dunderberg, was overtaken by a thunder-gust, that came scouring round the mountain, and seemed to burst just over the vessel. Though tight and well ballasted, yet she laboured dreadfully, until the water came over the gunwale. All the crew were amazed, when it was discovered that there was a little white sugar-loaf hat on the mast-head, which was known at once to be that of the Heer of the Dunderberg. Nobody, however, dared to climb to the mast-head, and get rid of this terrible hat. The sloop continued labouring and rocking, as if she would have rolled her mast overboard. She seemed in continual danger either of upsetting or of running on shore. In this way she drove quite through the highlands, until she had passed Pollopol's Island, where, it is said, the jurisdiction of the Dunderberg potentate ceases. No sooner had

---

[16] i.e., the "Thunder-Mountain," so called from its echoes.

she passed this bourne, than the little hat, all at once, spun up into the air like a top, whirled up all the clouds into a vortex, and hurried them back to the summit of the Dunderberg, while the sloop righted herself, and sailed on as quietly as if in a mill-pond. Nothing saved her from utter wreck, but the fortunate circumstance of having a horse-shoe nailed against the mast—a wise precaution against evil spirits, which has since been adopted by all the Dutch captains that navigate this haunted river.

There is another story told of this foul-weather urchin, by Skipper Daniel Ouslesticker, of Fish-Hill, who was never known to tell a lie. He declared, that, in a severe squall, he saw him seated astride of his bowsprit, riding the sloop ashore, full butt against Antony's Nose; and that he was exorcised by Dominie Van Gieson, of Esopus, who happened to be on board, and who sung the hymn of St. Nicholas; whereupon the goblin threw himself up in the air like a ball, and went off in a whirlwind, carrying away with him the nightcap of the Dominie's wife; which was discovered the next Sunday morning hanging on the weather-cock of Esopus church steeple, at least forty miles off! After several events of this kind had taken place, the regular skippers of the river, for a long time, did not venture to pass the Dunderberg, without lowering their peaks, out of homage to the Heer of the mountain; and it was observed that all such as paid this tribute of respect were suffered to pass unmolested.[17]

---

[17] Among the superstitions which prevailed in the colonies during the early times of the settlements, there seems to have been a singular one about phantom ships. The superstitious fancies of men are always apt to turn upon those objects which concern their daily occupations. The solitary ship, which, from year to year, came like a raven in the wilderness, bringing to the inhabitants of a settlement the comforts of life from the world from which they were cut off, was apt to be present to their dreams, whether sleeping or waking. The accidental sight from shore, of a sail gliding along the horizon, in those, as yet, lonely seas, was apt to be a matter of much talk and speculation. There is mention made in one of the early New-England writers, of a ship navigated by witches, with a great horse that stood by the mainmast. I have met with another story, somewhere, of a ship that drove on shore, in fair, sunny, tranquil weather, with sails all set, and a table spread in the cabin, as if to regale a number of guests, yet not a living being on board. These phantom ships always sailed

"Such," said Antony Vander Heyden, "are a few of the stories written down by Selyne the poet concerning this storm-ship; which he affirms to have brought this colony of mischievous imps into the province, from some old ghost-ridden country of Europe. I could give you a host more, if necessary; for all the accidents that so often befall the river craft in the highlands, are said to be tricks played off by these imps of the Dunderberg; but I see that you are nodding, so let us turn in for the night."

The moon had just raised her silver horns above the round back of old Bull-Hill, and lit up the gray rocks and shagged forests, and glittered on the waving bosom of the river. The night-dew was falling, and the late gloomy mountains began to soften, and put on a gray aerial tint in the dewy light. The hunters stirred the fire, and threw on fresh fuel to qualify the damp of the night air. They then prepared a bed of branches and dry leaves under a ledge of rocks, for Dolph; while Antony Vander Heyden, wrapping himself up in a huge coat made of skins, stretched himself before the fire. It was some time, however, before Dolph could close his eyes. He lay contemplating the strange scene before him: the wild woods and rocks around—the fire, throwing fitful gleams on the faces of the sleeping savages—and the Heer Antony, too, who so singularly, yet vaguely reminded him of the nightly visitant to the haunted house. Now and then he heard the cry of some animal from the forest; or the hooting of the owl; or the notes of the whip-poor-will, which seemed to abound among these solitudes; or the splash of a sturgeon, leaping out of the river, and falling back full length on its placid surface. He contrasted all this with his accustomed nest in the garret-room of the doctor's mansion; where the only sounds he heard at night were the church-clock telling the hour; the drowsy voice of the watchman, drawling out all was well; the deep snoring of the doctor's clubbed nose from below stairs; or the cautious labours of

---

in the eye of the wind; or ploughed their way with great velocity, making the smooth sea foam before their bows, when not a breath of air was stirring.

Moore has finely wrought up one of these legends of the sea into a little tale which, within a small compass, contains the very essence of this species of supernatural fiction. I allude to his Spectre-Ship bound to Dead-man's Isle.

some carpenter rat gnawing in the wainscot. His thoughts then wandered to his poor old mother: what would she think of his mysterious disappearance?—what anxiety and distress would she not suffer? This was the thought that would continually intrude itself, to mar his present enjoyment. It brought with it a feeling of pain and compunction, and he fell asleep with the tears yet standing in his eyes.

Were this a mere tale of fancy, here would be a fine opportunity for weaving in strange adventures among these wild mountains and roving hunters; and, after involving my hero in a variety of perils and difficulties, rescuing him from them all by some miraculous contrivance: but as this is absolutely a true story, I must content myself with simple facts, and keep to probabilities.

At an early hour the next day, therefore, after a hearty morning's meal, the encampment broke up, and our adventurers embarked in the pinnace of Antony Vander Heyden. There being no wind for the sails, the Indians rowed her gently along, keeping time to a kind of chant of one of the white men: The day was serene and beautiful; the river without a wave; and as the vessel cleft the glassy water, it left a long, undulating track behind. The crows, who had scented the hunters' banquèt, were already gathering and hovering in the air, just where a column of thin, blue smoke, rising from among the trees, showed the place of their last night's quarters. As they coasted along the bases of the mountains, the Heer Antony pointed out to Dolph a bald eagle, the sovereign of these regions, who sat perched on a dry tree that projected over the river; and, with eye turned upwards, seemed to be drinking in the splendour of the morning sun. Their approach disturbed the monarch's meditations. He first spread one wing, and then the other; balanced himself for a moment; and then, quitting his perch with dignified composure, wheeled slowly over their heads. Dolph snatched up a gun, and sent a whistling ball after him, that cut some of the feathers from his wing; the report of the gun leaped sharply from rock to rock, and awakened a thousand echoes; but the monarch of the air sailed calmly on, ascending higher and higher, and wheeling widely as he ascended, soaring up the green bosom of the woody mountain, until he disappeared over the brow of a beetling precipice. Dolph felt in a manner rebuked by this proud tranquillity, and almost reproached himself for having so wantonly insulted this majestic bird. Heer Antony told him, laughing, to remember that he was not yet out of the territories of the lord of the Dunderberg; and an old Indian shook his head, and observed that there was bad luck in killing an eagle—the hunter, on the contrary, should always leave him a portion of his spoils.

Nothing, however, occurred to molest them on their voyage. They passed pleasantly through magnificent and lonely scenes, until they came to where Pollopol's Island lay, like a floating bower, at the extremity of the highlands. Here they landed, until the heat of the day should abate, or a breeze spring up, that might supersede the labour of the oar. Some prepared the mid-day meal, while others reposed under the shade of the trees in luxurious summer indolence, looking drowsily forth upon the beauty of the scene. On the one side were the highlands, vast and cragged, feathered to the top with forests, and throwing their shadows on the glassy water that dimpled at their feet. On the other side was a wide expanse of the river, like a broad lake, with long sunny reaches, and green headlands; and the distant line of Shawungunk mountains waving along a clear horizon, or checkered by a fleecy cloud.

But I forbear to dwell on the particulars of their cruise along the river; this vagrant, amphibious life, careering across silver sheets of water; coasting wild woodland shores; banqueting on shady promontories, with the spreading tree overhead, the river curling its light foam to one's feet, and distant mountain, and rock, and tree, and snowy cloud, and deep-blue sky, all mingling in summer beauty before one; all this, though never cloying in the enjoyment, would be but tedious in narration.

When encamped by the water-side, some of the party would go into the woods and hunt; others would fish: sometimes they would amuse themselves by shooting at a mark, by leaping, by running, by wrestling; and Dolph gained great favour in the eyes of Antony Vander Heyden, by his skill and adroitness in all these exercises; which the Heer considered as the highest of manly accomplishments.

Thus did they coast jollily on, choosing only the pleasant hours for voyaging; sometimes in the cool morning dawn, sometimes in the sober evening twilight, and sometimes when the moonshine spangled the crisp curling waves that whispered along the sides of their little bark. Never had Dolph felt so completely in his element; never had he met with any thing so completely to his taste as this wild, hap-hazard life. He was the very man to second Antony Vander Heyden in his rambling humours, and gained continually on his affections. The heart of the old bushwhacker yearned toward the young man, who seemed thus growing up in his own likeness; and as they approached to the end of their voyage, he could not help inquiring a little into his history. Dolph frankly told him his course of life, his severe medical studies, his little proficiency, and his very dubious prospects. The Heer was shocked to find that such amazing talents and accomplishments were to be cramped and buried under a doctor's wig. He had a sovereign contempt for the healing art, having never had any other physician than the butcher. He bore a mortal grudge to all kinds of study also, ever since he had been flogged about an unintelligible book when he was a boy. But to think that a young fellow like Dolph, of such wonderful abilities, who could shoot, fish, run, jump, ride, and wrestle, should be obliged, to roll pills and administer juleps for a living—'twas monstrous! He told Dolph never to despair, but to "throw physic to the dogs;" for a young fellow of his prodigious talents could never fail to make his way. "As you seem to have no acquaintance in Albany," said Heer Antony, "you shall go home with me, and remain under my roof until you can look about you; and in the meantime we can take an occasional bout at shooting and fishing, for it is a pity such talents should lie idle."

Dolph, who was at the mercy of chance, was not hard to be persuaded. Indeed, on turning over matters in his mind, which he did very sagely and deliberately, he could not but think that Antony Vander Heyden was, "some how or other," connected with the story of the Haunted House; that the misadventure in the highlands, which had thrown them so strangely together, was, "some how or other," to work out something good: in short, there is nothing so convenient as this "some how or other" way of accommodating one's self to circumstances; it is the main-stay of a heedless actor, and tardy reasoner, like Dolph Heyliger; and he who can, in this loose, easy way, link foregone evil to anticipated good, possesses a secret of happiness almost equal to the philosopher's stone.

On their arrival at Albany, the sight of Dolph's companion seemed to cause universal satisfaction. Many were the greetings at the river side, and the salutations in the streets: the dogs bounded before him; the boys whooped as he passed; every body seemed to know Antony Vander Heyden. Dolph followed on in silence, admiring the neatness of this worthy burgh; for in those days Albany was in all its glory, and inhabited almost exclusively by the descendants of the original Dutch settlers, for it had not as yet been discovered and colonized by the restless people of New-England. Every thing was quiet and orderly; every thing was conducted calmly and leisurely; no hurry, no bustle, no struggling and scrambling for existence. The grass grew about the unpaved streets, and relieved the eye by its refreshing verdure. The tall sycamores or pendent willows shaded the houses, with caterpillars swinging, in long silken strings, from their branches, or moths, fluttering about like coxcombs, in joy at their gay transformation. The houses were built in the old Dutch style, with the gable-ends towards the street. The thrifty housewife was seated on a bench before her door, in close crimped cap, bright flowered gown, and white apron, busily employed in knitting. The husband smoked his pipe on the opposite bench, and the little pet negro girl, seated on the step at her mistress' feet, was industriously plying her needle. The swallows sported about the eaves, or skimmed along the streets, and brought back some rich booty for their clamorous young; and the little housekeeping wren flew in and out of a Lilliputian house, or an old hat nailed against the wall. The cows were coming home, lowing through the streets, to be milked at their owner's door; and if, perchance, there were any loiterers, some negro urchin, with a long goad, was gently urging them homewards.

As Dolph's companion passed on, he received a tranquil nod from the burghers, and a friendly word from their wives; all calling him familiarly by the name of Antony; for it was the custom in this strong-hold of the patriarchs, where they had all grown up together from childhood, to call every one by the Christian name. The Heer did not pause to have his usual jokes with them, for he was impatient to reach his home. At length they arrived at his mansion. It was of some magnitude, in the Dutch style, with large iron figures on the gables, that gave the date of its erection, and showed that it had been built in the earliest times of the settlement.

The news of Heer Antony's arrival had preceded him; and the whole household was on the look-out. A crew of negroes, large and small, had collected in front of the house to receive him. The old, white-headed ones, who had grown gray in his service, grinned for joy and made many awkward bows and grimaces, and the little ones capered about his knees.

But the most happy being in the household was a little, plump, blooming lass, his only child, and the darling of his heart. She came bounding out of the house; but the sight of a strange young man with her father called up, for a moment, all the bashfulness of a homebred damsel. Dolph gazed at her with wonder and delight; never had he seen, as he thought, any thing so comely in the shape of woman. She was dressed in the good old Dutch taste, with long stays, and full, short petticoats, so admirably adapted to show and set off the female form. Her hair, turned up under a small round cap, displayed the fairness of her forehead; she had fine, blue, laughing eyes, a trim, slender waist, and soft swell—but, in a word, she was a little Dutch divinity; and Dolph, who never stopt half-way in a new impulse, fell desperately in love with her.

Dolph was now ushered into the house with a hearty welcome. In the interior was a mingled display of Heer Antony's taste and habits, and of the opulence of his predecessors. The chambers were furnished with good old mahogany; the beau-fets and cupboards glittered with embossed silver, and painted china. Over the parlour fire-place was, as usual, the family coat-of-arms, painted and framed; above which was a long duck fowling-piece, flanked by an Indian pouch, and a powder horn. The room was decorated with many Indian articles, such as pipes of peace, tomahawks, scalping-knives, hunting pouches, and belts of wampum; and there were various kinds of fishing tackle, and two or three fowling-pieces in the corners. The household affairs seemed to be conducted, in some measure, after the master's humours; corrected, perhaps, by a little quiet management of the daughter's. There was a degree of patriarchal simplicity, and good-humoured indulgence. The negroes came into the room without being called, merely to look at their master, and hear of his adventures; they would stand listening at the door until he had finished a story, and then go off on a broad grin, to repeat it in the kitchen. A couple of pet negro children were playing about the floor with the dogs, and sharing with them their bread and butter. All the domestics looked hearty and happy; and when the table was set for the evening repast, the variety and abundance of good household luxuries bore testimony to the openhanded liberality of the Heer, and the notable housewifery of his daughter.

In the evening there dropped in several of the worthies of the place, the Van Rennsellaers, and the Gansevoorts, and the Rosebooms, and others of Antony Vander Heyden's intimates, to hear an account of his expedition; for he was the Sindbad of Albany, and his exploits and adventures were favourite topics of conversation among the inhabitants. While these sat gossiping together about the door of the hall, and telling long twilight stories, Dolph was cozily seated, entertaining the daughter on a window-bench. He had already got on intimate terms; for those were not times of false reserve and idle ceremony; and, besides, there is something wonderfully propitious to a lover's suit, in the delightful dusk of a long summer evening; it gives courage to the most timid tongue, and hides the blushes of the bashful. The stars alone twinkled brightly; and now and then a fire-fly streamed his transient light before the window, or, wandering into the room, flew gleaming about the ceiling.

What Dolph whispered in her ear, that long summer evening, it is impossible to say: his words were so low and indistinct, that they never reached the ear of the historian. It is probable, however, that they were to the purpose; for he had a natural talent at pleasing the sex, and was never long in company with a petticoat without paying proper court to it. In the meantime, the visitors, one by one, departed; Antony Vander Heyden, who had fairly talked himself silent, sat nodding alone in his chair by the door, when he was suddenly aroused by a hearty salute with which Dolph Heyliger had unguardedly rounded off one of his periods, and which echoed through the still chamber like the report of a pistol. The Heer started up, rubbed his eyes, called for lights, and observed, that it was high time to go to bed; though, on parting for the night, he squeezed Dolph heartily by the hand, looked kindly in his face, and shook his head knowingly; for the Heer well remembered what he himself had been at the youngster's age.

The chamber in which our hero was lodged was spacious, and panelled with oak. It was furnished with clothes-presses, and mighty chests of drawers, well waxed, and glittering with brass ornaments. These contained ample stock of family linen; for the Dutch housewives had always a laudable pride in showing off their household treasures to strangers.

Dolph's mind, however, was too full to take particular note of the objects around him; yet he could not help continually comparing the free, open-hearted cheeriness of this establishment with the starveling, sordid, joyless housekeeping at Doctor Knipperhausen's. Still there was something that marred the enjoyment—the idea that he must take leave of his hearty host and pretty hostess and cast himself once more adrift upon the world. To linger here would be folly; he should only get deeper in love; and for a poor varlet like himself to aspire to the daughter of the great Heer Vander Heyden—it was madness to think of such a thing! The very kindness that the girl had shown towards him prompted him, on reflection, to hasten his departure; it would be a poor return for the frank hospitality of his host to entangle his daughter's heart in an injudicious attachment. In a word, Dolph was like many other young reasoners, of exceeding good hearts and giddy heads, who think after they act, and act differently from what they think; who make excellent determinations overnight and forget to keep them the next morning.

"This is a fine conclusion, truly, of my voyage," said he, as he almost buried himself in a sumptuous feather-bed, and drew the fresh white sheets up to his chin. "Here am I, instead of finding a bag of money to carry home, launched in a strange place, with scarcely a stiver in my pocket; and, what is worse, have jumped ashore up to my very ears in love into the bargain. However," added he, after some pause, stretching himself and turning himself in bed, "I'm in good quarters for the present, at least; so I'll e'en enjoy the present moment, and let the next take care of itself; I dare say all will work out, 'some hew or other,' for the best."

As he said these words, he reached out his hand to extinguish the candle, when he was suddenly struck with astonishment and dismay, for he thought he beheld the phantom of the haunted house staring on him from a dusky part of the chamber. A second look reassured him, as he perceived that what he had taken for the spectre was, in fact, nothing but a Flemish portrait, that hung in a shadowy corner just behind a clothes-press. It was, however, the precise representation of his nightly visitor:—the same cloak and belted jerkin, the same grizzled beard and fixed eye, the same broad slouched hat, with a feather hanging over one side. Dolph now called to mind the resemblance he had frequently remarked between his host and the old man of the haunted house; and was fully convinced that they were in some way connected, and that some especial destiny had governed his voyage. He lay gazing on the portrait with almost as much awe as he had gazed on the ghostly original, until the shrill house-clock warned him of the lateness of the hour. He put out the light; but remained for a long time turning over these curious circumstances and coincidences in his mind, until he fell asleep. His dreams partook of the nature of his waking thoughts. He fancied that he still lay gazing on the picture, until, by degrees, it became animated; that the figure descended from the wall and walked out of the room; that he followed it and found himself by the well, to which the old man pointed, smiled on him, and disappeared.

In the morning when Dolph waked, he found his host standing by his bed-side, who gave him a hearty morning's salutation, and asked him how he had slept. Dolph answered cheerily; but took occasion to inquire about the portrait that hung against the wall. "Ah," said Heer Antony, "that's a portrait of old Killian Vander Spiegel, once a burgomaster of Amsterdam, who, on some popular troubles, abandoned Holland and came over to the province during the government of Peter Stuyvesant. He was my ancestor by the mother's side, and an old miserly curmudgeon he was. When the English took possession of New-Amsterdam in 1664, he retired into the country. He fell into a melancholy, apprehending that his wealth would be taken from him and that he would come to beggary. He turned all his property into cash, and used to hide it away. He was for a year or two concealed in various places, fancying himself sought after by the English, to strip him of his wealth; and finally was found dead in his bed one morning, without any one being able to discover where he had concealed the greater part of his money."

When his host had left the room, Dolph remained for some time lost in thought. His whole mind was occupied by what he had heard. Vander Spiegel was his mother's family name; and he recollected to have heard her speak of this very Killian Vander Spiegel as one of her ancestors. He had heard her say, too, that her father was Kollian's rightful heir, only that the old man died without leaving any thing to be inherited. It now appeared that Heer Antony was likewise a descendant, and perhaps an heir also, of this poor rich man; and that thus the Heyligers and the Vander Heydens were remotely connected. "What," thought he, "if, after all, this is the interpretation of my dream, that this is the way I am to make my fortune by this voyage to Albany, and that I am to find the old man's hidden wealth in the bottom of that well? But what an odd, round-about mode of communicating the matter! Why the plague could not the old goblin have told me about the well at once, without sending me all the way to Albany to hear a story that was to send me all the way back again?"

These thoughts passed through his mind while he was dressing. He descended the stairs, full of perplexity, when the bright face of Marie Vander Heyden suddenly beamed in smiles upon him, and seemed to give him a clue to the whole mystery. "After all," thought he, "the old goblin is in the right. If I am to get his wealth, he means that I shall marry his pretty descendant; thus both branches of the family will be again united, and the property go on in the proper channel."

No sooner did this idea enter his head, than it carried conviction with it. He was now all impatience to hurry back and secure the treasure, which, he did not doubt, lay at the bottom of the well, and which he feared every moment might be discovered by some other person. "Who knows," thought he, "but this night-walking old fellow of the haunted house may be in the habit of haunting every visitor, and may give a hint to some shrewder fellow than myself, who will take a shorter cut to the well than by the way of Albany?" He wished a thousand times that the babbling old ghost was laid in the Red Sea, and his rambling portrait with him. He was in a perfect fever to depart. Two or three days elapsed before any opportunity presented for returning down the river. They were ages to Dolph, notwithstanding that he was basking in the smiles of the pretty Marie, and daily getting more and more enamoured.

At length the very sloop from which he had been knocked overboard, prepared to make sail. Dolph made an awkward apology to his host for his sudden departure. Antony Vander Heyden was sorely astonished. He had concerted half-a-dozen excursions into the wilderness; and his Indians were actually preparing for a grand expedition to one of the lakes. He took Dolph aside, and exerted his eloquence to get him to abandon all thoughts of business, and to remain with him—but in vain; and he at length gave up the attempt, observing, "that it was a thousand pities so fine a young man should throw himself away." Heer Antony, however, gave him a hearty shake by the hand at parting, with a favourite fowling-piece, and an invitation to come to his house whenever he revisited Albany. The pretty little Marie said nothing; but as he gave her a farewell kiss, her dimpled cheek turned pale, and a tear stood in her eye.

Dolph sprang lightly on board of the vessel. They hoisted sail; the wind was fair; they soon lost sight of Albany, and its green hills, and embowered islands. They were wafted gayly past the Kaatskill mountains, whose fairy heights were bright and cloudless. They passed prosperously through the highlands, without any molestation from the Dunderberg goblin and his crew; they swept on across Haverstraw Bay, and by Croton Point, and through the Tappaan Zee, and under the Palisadoes, until, in the afternoon of the third day, they saw the promontory of Hoboken, hanging like a cloud in the air; and, shortly after, the roofs of the Manhattoes rising out of the water.

Dolph's first care was to repair to his mother's house; for he was continually goaded by the idea of the uneasiness she must experience on his account. He was puzzling his brains, as he went along, to think how he should account for his absence, without betraying the secrets of the haunted house. In the midst of these cogitations, he entered the street in which his mother's house was situated, when he was thunderstruck at beholding it a heap of ruins.

There had evidently been a great fire, which had destroyed several large houses, and the humble dwelling of poor Dame Heyliger had been involved in the conflagration. The walls were not so completely destroyed but that Dolph could distinguish some traces of the scene of his childhood. The fire-place, about which he had often played, still remained, ornamented with Dutch tiles, illustrating passages in Bible history, on which he had many a time gazed with admiration. Among the rubbish lay the wreck of the good dame's elbow-chair, from which she had given him so many a wholesome precept; and hard by it was the family Bible, with brass clasps; now, alas! reduced almost to a cinder.

For a moment Dolph was overcome by this dismal sight, for he was seized with the fear that his mother had perished in the flames. He was relieved, however, from this horrible apprehension, by one of the neighbours who happened to come by, and who informed him that his mother was yet alive.

The good woman had, indeed, lost every thing by this unlooked-for calamity; for the populace had been so intent upon saving the fine furniture of her rich neighbours, that the little tenement, and the little all of poor Dame Heyliger, had been suffered to consume without interruption; nay, had it not been for the gallant assistance of her old crony, Peter de Groodt, the worthy dame and her cat might have shared the fate of their habitation.

As it was, she had been overcome with fright and affliction, and lay ill in body, and sick at heart. The public, however, had showed her its wonted kindness. The furniture of her rich neighbours being, as far as possible, rescued from the flames; themselves duly and ceremoniously visited and condoled with on the injury of their property, and their ladies commiserated on the agitation of their nerves; the public, at length, began to recollect something about poor Dame Heyliger. She forthwith became again a subject of universal sympathy; every body pitied more than ever; and if pity could but have been coined into cash—good Lord! how rich she would have been!

It was now determined, in good earnest, that something ought to be done for her without delay. The Dominie, therefore, put up prayers for her on Sunday, in which all the congregation joined most heartily. Even Cobus Groesbeck, the alderman, and Mynheer Milledollar, the great Dutch merchant, stood up in their pews, and did not spare their voices on the occasion; and it was thought the prayers of such great men could not but have their due weight. Doctor Knipperhausen, too, visited her professionally, and gave her abundance of advice gratis, and was universally lauded for his charity. As to her old friend, Peter de Groodt, he was a poor man, whose pity, and prayers, and advice could be of but little avail, so he gave her all that was in his power—he gave her shelter.

To the humble dwelling of Peter de Groodt, then, did Dolph turn his steps. On his way thither, he recalled all the tenderness and kindness of his simple-hearted parent, her indulgence of his errors, her blindness to his faults; and then he bethought himself of his own idle, harum-scarum life. "I've been a sad scape-grace," said Dolph, shaking his head sorrowfully. "I've been a complete sink-pocket, that's the truth of it!—But," added he, briskly, and clasping his hands, "only let her live—only let her live—and I'll show myself indeed a son!"

As Dolph approached the house, he met Peter de Groodt coming out of it. The old man started back aghast, doubting whether it was not a ghost that stood before him. It being bright daylight, however, Peter soon plucked up heart, satisfied that no ghost dare show his face in such clear sunshine. Dolph now learned from the worthy sexton the consternation and rumour to which his mysterious disappearance had given rise. It had been universally believed that he had been spirited away by those hobgoblin gentry that infested the haunted house; and old Abraham Vandozer, who lived by the great button-wood trees, at the three-mile stone, affirmed, that he had heard a terrible noise in the air, as he was going home late at night, which seemed just as if a flight of wild geese were overhead, passing off towards the northward. The haunted house was, in consequence, looked upon with ten times more awe than ever; nobody would venture to pass a night in it for the world, and even the doctor had ceased to make his expeditions to it in the day-time.

It required some preparation before Dolph's return could be made known to his mother, the poor soul having bewailed him as lost; and her spirits having been sorely broken down by a number of comforters, who daily cheered her with stories of ghosts, and of people carried away by the devil. He found her confined to her bed, with the other member of the Heyliger family, the good dame's cat, purring beside her, but sadly singed, and utterly despoiled of those whiskers which were the glory of her physiognomy. The poor woman threw her arms about Dolph's neck: "My boy! my boy! art thou still alive?" For a time she seemed to have forgotten all her losses and troubles, in her joy at his return. Even the sage grimalkin showed indubitable signs of joy, at the return of the youngster. She saw, perhaps, that they were a forlorn and undone family, and felt a touch of that kindliness which fellow-sufferers only know. But, in truth, cats are a slandered people; they have more affection in them than the world commonly gives them credit for.

The good dame's eyes glistened as she saw one being, at least, beside herself, rejoiced at her son's return. "Tib knows thee! poor dumb beast!" said she, smoothing down the mottled coat of her favourite; then recollecting herself, with a melancholy shake of the head, "Ah, my poor Dolph!" exclaimed she, "thy mother can help thee no longer! She can no longer help herself! What will become of thee, my poor boy!"

"Mother," said Dolph, "don't talk in that strain; I've been too long a charge upon you; it's now my part to take care of you in your old days. Come! be of good heart! you, and I, and Tib, will all see better days. I'm here, you see, young, and sound, and hearty; then don't let us despair; I dare say things will all, some how or other, turn out for the best."

While this scene was going on with the Heyliger family, the news was carried to Doctor Knipperhausen, of the safe return of his disciple. The little doctor scarcely knew whether to rejoice or be sorry at the tidings. He was happy at having the foul reports which had prevailed concerning his country mansion thus disproved; but he grieved at having his disciple, of whom he had supposed himself fairly disencumbered, thus drifting back, a heavy charge upon his hands. While he was balancing between these two feelings, he was determined by the counsels of Frau Ilsy, who advised him to take advantage of the truant absence of the youngster, and shut the door upon him for ever.

At the hour of bed-time, therefore, when it was supposed the recreant disciple would seek his old quarters, every thing was prepared for his reception. Dolph, having talked his mother into a state of tranquillity, sought the mansion of his quondam master, and raised the knocker with a faltering hand. Scarcely, however, had it given a dubious rap, when the doctor's head, in a red night-cap, popped out of one window, and the housekeeper's, in a white night-cap, out of another. He was now greeted with a tremendous volley of hard names and hard language, mingled with invaluable pieces of advice, such as are seldom ventured to be given excepting to a friend in distress, or a culprit at the bar. In a few moments, not a window in the street but had its particular night-cap, listening to the shrill treble of Frau Ilsy, and the guttural croaking of Dr. Knipperhausen; and the word went from window to window, "Ah! here's Dolph Heyliger come back, and at his old pranks again." In short, poor Dolph found he was likely to get nothing from the doctor but good advice—a commodity so abundant as even to be thrown out of the window; so he was fain to beat a retreat, and take up his quarters for the night under the lowly roof of honest Peter de Groodt.

The next morning, bright and early, Dolph was at the haunted house. Every thing looked just as he had left it. The fields were grass-grown and matted, and it appeared as if nobody had traversed them since his departure. With palpitating heart, he hastened to the well. He looked down into it, and saw that it was of great depth, with water at the bottom. He had provided himself with a strong line, such as the fishermen use on the banks of Newfoundland. At the end was a heavy plummet and a large fish-hook. With this he began to sound the bottom of the well, and to angle about in the water. He found that the water was of some depth; there appeared also to be much rubbish, stones from the top having fallen in. Several times his hook got entangled, and he came near breaking his line. Now and then, too, he hauled up mere trash, such as the skull of a horse, an iron hoop, and a shattered iron-bound bucket. He had now been several hours employed without finding any thing to repay his trouble, or to encourage him to proceed. He began to think himself a great fool, to be thus decoyed into a wild-goose-chase by mere dreams, and was on the point of throwing line and all into the well, and giving up all further angling.

"One more cast of the line," said he, "and that shall be the last." As he sounded, he felt the plummet slip, as it were, through the interstices of loose stones; and as he drew back the line, he felt that the hook had taken hold of something heavy. He had to manage his line with great caution, lest it should be broken by the strain upon it. By degrees, the rubbish that lay upon the article which he had hooked gave way; he drew it to the surface of the water, and what was his rapture at seeing something like silver glittering at the end of his line! Almost breathless with anxiety, he drew it up to the mouth of the well, surprised at its great weight, and fearing every instant that his hook would slip from its hold, and his prize tumble again to the bottom. At length he landed it safe beside the well. It was a great silver porringer, of an ancient form, richly embossed, and with armorial bearings, similar to those over his mother's mantel-piece, engraved on its side.

The lid was fastened down by several twists of wire; Dolph loosened them with a trembling hand, and on lifting the lid, behold! the vessel was filled with broad golden pieces, of a coinage which he had never seen before! It was evident he had lit on the place where Killian Vander Spiegel had concealed his treasure.

Fearful of being seen by some straggler, he cautiously retired, and buried his pot of money in a secret place. He now spread terrible stories about the haunted house, and deterred every one from approaching it, while he made frequent visits to it on stormy days, when no one was stirring in the neighbouring fields; though, to tell the truth, he did not care to venture there in the dark. For once in his life he was diligent and industrious, and followed up his new trade of angling with such perseverance and success, that in a little while he had hooked up wealth enough to make him, in those moderate days, a rich burgher for life.

It would be tedious to detail minutely the rest of this story:—to tell how he gradually managed to bring his property into use without exciting surprise and inquiry—how he satisfied all scruples with regard to retaining the property, and at the same time gratified his own feelings, by marrying the pretty Marie Vander Heyden—and how he and Heer Antony had many a merry and roving expedition together.

I must not omit to say, however, that Dolph took his mother home to live with, him, and cherished her in her old days. The good dame, too, had the satisfaction of no longer hearing her son made the theme of censure; on the contrary, he grew daily in public esteem; every body spoke well of him and his wines, and the lordliest burgomaster was never known to decline his invitation to dinner. Dolph often related, at his own table, the wicked pranks which had once been the abhorrence of the town; but they were now considered excellent jokes, and the gravest dignitary was fain to hold his sides when listening to them. No one was more struck with Dolph's increasing merit, than his old master the doctor; and so forgiving was Dolph, that he actually employed the doctor as his family physician, only taking care that his prescriptions should be always thrown out of the window. His mother had often her junto of old cronies, to take a snug cup of tea with her in her comfortable little parlour; and Peter de Groodt, as he sat by the fire-side, with one of her grandchildren on his knee, would many a time congratulate her upon her son turning out so great a man; upon which the good old soul would wag her head with exultation, and exclaim, "Ah, neighbour, neighbour! did I not say that Dolph would one day or other hold up his head with the best of them?"

Thus did Dolph Heyliger go on, cheerily and prosperously, growing merrier as he grew older and wiser, and completely falsifying the old proverb about money got over the devil's back; for he made good use of his wealth, and became a distinguished citizen, and a valuable member of the community. He was a great promoter of public institutions, such as beef-steak societies and catch-clubs. He presided at all public dinners, and was the first that introduced turtle from the West Indies. He improved the breed of race-horses and game-cocks, and was so great a patron of modest merit, that any one who could sing a good song, or tell a good story, was sure to find a place at his table.

He was a member, too, of the corporation, made several laws for the protection of game and oysters, and bequeathed to the board a large silver punch-bowl, made out of the identical porringer before mentioned, and which is in the possession of the corporation to this very day.

Finally, he died, in a florid old age, of an apoplexy, at a corporation feast, and was buried with great honours in the yard of the little Dutch church in Garden-street, where his tombstone may still be seen, with a modest epitaph in Dutch, by his friend Mynheer Justus Benson, an ancient and excellent poet of the province.

The foregoing tale rests on better authority than most tales of the kind, as I have it at second-hand from the lips of Dolph Heyliger himself. He never related it till towards the latter part of his life, and then in great confidence, (for he was very discreet,) to a few of his particular cronies at his own table over a supernumerary bowl of punch; and, strange as the hobgoblin parts of the story may seem, there never was a single doubt expressed on the subject by any of his guests. It may not be amiss, before concluding, to observe that, in addition to his other accomplishments, Dolph Heyliger was noted for being the ablest drawer of the long-bow in the whole province.

The Wedding.

No more, no more, much honour aye betide
The lofty bridegroom and the lovely bride;
That all of their succeeding days may say,
Each day appears like to a wedding-day.
—BRAITHWAITE.

Notwithstanding the doubts and demurs of Lady Lillycraft, and all the grave objections that were conjured up against the month of May, yet the wedding has at length happily taken place. It was celebrated at the village church, in presence of a numerous company of relatives and friends, and many of the tenantry. The Squire must needs have something of the old ceremonies observed on the occasion; so, at the gate of the church-yard, several little girls of the village, dressed in white, were in readiness with baskets of flowers, which they strewed before the bride; and the butler bore before her the bride-cup, a great silver embossed bowl, one of the family relics from the days of the hard drinkers. This was filled with rich wine, and decorated with a branch of rosemary, tied with gay ribands, according to ancient custom.

"Happy is the bride that the sun shines on," says the old proverb; and it was as sunny and auspicious a morning as heart could wish. The bride looked uncommonly beautiful; but, in fact, what woman does not look interesting on her wedding-day? I know no sight more charming and touching than that of a young and timid bride, in her robes of virgin white, led up trembling to the altar. When I thus behold a lovely girl, in the tenderness of her years, forsaking the house of her fathers and the home of her childhood; and, with the implicit confiding, and the sweet self-abandonment, which belong to woman, giving up all the world for the man of her choice: when I hear her, in the good old language of the ritual, yielding herself to him "for better for worse, for richer for poorer, in sickness and in health, to love, honour and obey, till death us do part," it brings to my mind the beautiful and affecting self-devotion of Ruth:

"Whither thou goest I will go, and where thou lodgest I will lodge; thy people shall be my people, and thy God my God."

The fair Julia was supported on the trying occasion by Lady Lillycraft, whose heart was overflowing with its wonted sympathy in all matters of love and matrimony. As the bride approached the altar, her face would be one moment covered with blushes, and the next deadly pale; and she seemed almost ready to shrink from sight among her female companions.

I do not know what it is that makes every one serious, and, as it were, awe-struck, at a marriage ceremony—which is generally considered as an occasion of festivity and rejoicing. As the ceremony was performing, I observed many a rosy face among the country girls turn pale, and I did not see a smile throughout the church. The young ladies from the Hall were almost as much frightened as if it had been their own case, and stole many a look of sympathy at their trembling companion. A tear stood in the eye of the sensitive Lady Lillycraft; and as to Phoebe Wilkins, who was present, she absolutely wept and sobbed aloud; but it is hard to tell, half the time, what these fond foolish creatures are crying about.

The captain, too, though naturally gay and unconcerned, was much agitated on the occasion; and, in attempting to put the ring upon the bride's finger, dropped it on the floor; which Lady Lillycraft has since assured me is a very lucky omen. Even Master Simon had lost his usual vivacity, and had assumed a most whimsically solemn face, which he is apt to do on all occasions of ceremony. He had much whispering with the parson and parish-clerk, for he is always a busy personage in the scene, and he echoed the clerk's amen with a solemnity and devotion that edified the whole assemblage.

The moment, however, that the ceremony was over, the transition was magical. The bride-cup was passed round, according to ancient usage, for the company to drink to a happy union; every one's feelings seemed to break forth from restraint. Master Simon had a world of bachelor pleasantries to utter; and as to the gallant general, he bowed and cooed about the dulcet Lady Lillycraft, like a mighty cock-pigeon about his dame.

The villagers gathered in the church-yard, to cheer the happy couple as they left the church; and the musical tailor had marshalled his band, and set up a hideous discord, as the blushing and smiling bride passed through a lane of honest peasantry to her carriage. The children shouted, and threw up their hats; the bells rung a merry peal, that set all the crows and rooks flying and cawing about the air, and threatened to bring down the battlements of the old tower; and there was a continual popping off of rusty fire-locks from every part of the neighbourhood.

The prodigal son distinguished himself on the occasion, having hoisted a flag on the top of the school-house, and kept the village in a hubbub from sunrise, with the sound of drum and fife and pandean pipe; in which species of music several of his scholars are making wonderful proficiency. In his great zeal, however, he had nearly done mischief; for on returning from church, the horses of the bride's carriage took fright from the discharge of a row of old gun-barrels, which he had mounted as a park of artillery in front of the school-house, to give the captain a military salute as he passed.

The day passed off with great rustic rejoicing. Tables were spread under the trees in the park, where all the peasantry of the neighbourhood were regaled with roast-beef and plum-pudding and oceans of ale. Ready-Money Jack presided at one of the tables, and became so full of good cheer, as to unbend from his usual gravity, to sing a song out of all tune, and give two or three shouts of laughter, that almost electrified his neighbours, like so many peals of thunder. The schoolmaster and the apothecary vied with each other in making speeches over their liquor; and there were occasional glees and musical performances by the village band, that must have frightened every faun and dryad from the park. Even old Christy, who had got on a new dress from top to toe, and shone in all the splendour of bright leather breeches and an enormous wedding favour in his cap, forgot his usual crustiness, became inspired by wine and wassel, and absolutely danced a hornpipe on one of the tables, with all the grace and agility of a manikin hung upon wires.

Equal gayety reigned within doors, where a large party of friends were entertained. Every one laughed at his own pleasantry, without attending to that of his neighbours. Loads of bride-cake were distributed. The young ladies were all busy in passing morsels of it through the wedding-ring to dream on, and I myself assisted a few little boarding-school girls in putting up a quantity for their companions, which I have no doubt will set all the little heads in the school gadding, for a week at least.

After dinner, all the company, great and small, gentle and simple, abandoned themselves to the dance: not the modern quadrille, with its graceful gravity, but the merry, social, old country-dance; the true dance, as the Squire says, for a wedding occasion, as it sets all the world jigging in couples, hand in hand, and makes every eye and every heart dance merrily to the music. According to frank old usage, the gentlefolks of the Hall mingled for a tune in the dance of the peasantry, who had a great tent erected for a ball-room; and I think I never saw Master Simon more in his element, than when figuring about among his rustic admirers, as master of the ceremonies; and, with a mingled air of protection and gallantry, leading out the quondam Queen of May, all blushing at the signal honour conferred upon her.

In the evening the whole village was illuminated, excepting the house of the radical, who has not shown his face during the rejoicings. There was a display of fire-works at the school-house, got up by the prodigal son, which had well-nigh set fire to the building. The Squire is so much pleased with the extraordinary services of this last mentioned worthy, that he talks of enrolling him in his list of valuable retainers, and promoting him to some important post on the estate; per-adventure to be falconer, if the hawks can ever be brought into proper training.

There is a well-known old proverb, that says "one wedding makes many,"—or something to the same purpose; and I should not be surprised if it holds good in the present instance. I have seen several flirtations among the young people, that have been brought together on this occasion; and a great deal of strolling about in pairs, among the retired walks and blossoming shrubberies of the old garden: and if groves were really given to whispering, as poets would fain make us believe, Heaven knows what love tales the grave-looking old trees about this venerable country-seat might blab to the world.

The general, too, has waxed very zealous in his devotions within the last few days, as the time of her ladyship's departure approaches. I observed him casting many a tender look at her during the wedding dinner, while the courses were changing; though he was always liable to be interrupted in his adoration by the appearance of any new delicacy. The general, in fact, has arrived at that time of life when the heart and the stomach maintain a kind of balance of power, and when a man is apt to be perplexed in his affections between a fine woman and a truffled turkey. Her ladyship was certainly rivalled, through the whole of the first course, by a dish of stewed carp; and there was one glance, which was evidently intended to be a point-blank shot at her heart, and could scarcely have failed to effect a practicable breach, had it not unluckily been directed away to a tempting breast of lamb, in which it immediately produced a formidable incision. Thus did this faithless general go on, coquetting during the whole dinner, and committing an infidelity with every new dish; until, in the end, he was so overpowered by the attentions he had paid to fish, flesh, and fowl; to pastry, jelly, cream, and blanc-mange, that he seemed to sink within himself: his eyes swam beneath their lids, and their fire was so much slackened, that he could no longer discharge a single glance that would reach across the table. Upon the whole, I fear the general ate himself into as much disgrace, at this memorable dinner, as I have seen him sleep himself into on a former occasion.

I am told, moreover, that young Jack Tibbets was so touched by the wedding ceremony, at which he was present, and so captivated by the sensibility of poor Phoebe Wilkins, who certainly looked all the better for her tears, that he had a reconciliation with her that very day, after dinner, in one of the groves of the park, and danced with her in the evening; to the complete confusion of all Dame Tibbets' domestic politics. I met them walking together in the park, shortly after the reconciliation must have taken place. Young Jack carried himself gayly and manfully; but Phoebe hung her head, blushing, as I approached. However, just as she passed me, and dropped a curtsy, I caught a shy gleam of her eye from, under her bonnet; but it was immediately cast down again. I saw enough in that single gleam, and in the involuntary smile that dimpled about her rosy lips, to feel satisfied that the little gipsy's heart was happy again.

What is more, Lady Lillycraft, with her usual benevolence and zeal in all matters of this tender nature, on hearing of the reconciliation of the lovers, undertook the critical task of breaking the matter to Ready-Money Jack. She thought there was no time like the present, and attacked the sturdy old yeoman that very evening in the park, while his heart was yet lifted up with the Squire's good cheer. Jack was a little surprised at being drawn aside by her ladyship, but was not to be flurried by such an honour: he was still more surprised by the nature of her communication, and by this first intelligence of an affair which had been passing under his eye. He listened, however, with his usual gravity, as her ladyship represented the advantages of the match, the good qualities of the girl, and the distress which she had lately suffered: at length his eye began to kindle, and his hand to play with the head of his cudgel. Lady Lillycraft saw that something in the narrative had gone wrong, and hastened to mollify his rising ire by reiterating the soft-hearted Phoebe's merit and fidelity, and her great unhappiness; when old Ready-Money suddenly interrupted her by exclaiming, that if Jack did not marry the wench, he'd break every bone in his body! The match, therefore, is considered a settled thing: Dame Tibbets and the housekeeper have made friends, and drank tea together; and Phoebe has again recovered her good looks and good spirits, and is carolling from morning till night like a lark.

But the most whimsical caprice of Cupid is one that I should be almost afraid to mention, did I not know that I was writing for readers well experienced in the waywardness of this most mischievous deity. The morning after the wedding, therefore, while Lady Lillycraft was making preparations for her departure, an audience was requested by her immaculate hand-maid, Mrs. Hannah, who, with much primming of the mouth, and many maidenly hesitations, requested leave to stay behind, and that Lady Lillycraft would supply her place with some other servant. Her ladyship was astonished: "What! Hannah going to quit her, that had lived with her so long!"

"Why, one could not help it; one must settle in life some time or other."

The good lady was still lost in amazement; at length, the secret was gasped from the dry lips of the maiden gentlewoman: "She had been some time thinking of changing her condition, and at length had given her word, last evening, to Mr. Christy, the huntsman."

How, or when, or where this singular courtship had been carried on, I have not been able to learn; nor how she has been able, with the vinegar of her disposition, to soften the stony heart of old Nimrod: so, however, it is, and it has astonished every one. With all her ladyship's love of match-making, this last fume of Hymen's torch has been too much for her. She has endeavoured to reason with Mrs. Hannah, but all in vain; her mind was made up, and she grew tart on the least contradiction. Lady Lillycraft applied to the Squire for his interference. "She did not know what she should do without Mrs. Hannah, she had been used to have her about her so long a time."

The Squire, on the contrary, rejoiced in the match, as relieving the good lady from a kind of toilet-tyrant, under whose sway she had suffered for years. Instead of thwarting the affair, therefore, he has given it his full countenance; and declares that he will set up the young couple in one of the best cottages on his estate. The approbation of the Squire has been followed by that of the whole household; they all declare, that if ever matches are really made in heaven, this must have been; for that old Christy and Mrs. Hannah were as evidently formed to be linked together, as ever were pepper-box and vinegar-cruet.

As soon as this matter was arranged, Lady Lillycraft took her leave of the family at the Hall; taking with her the captain and his blushing bride, who are to pass the honeymoon with her. Master Simon accompanied them on horseback, and indeed means to ride on ahead to make preparations. The general, who was fishing in vain for an invitation to her seat, handed her ladyship into the carriage with a heavy sigh; upon which his bosom friend, Master Simon, who was just mounting his horse, gave me a knowing wink, made an abominably wry face, and, leaning from his saddle, whispered loudly in my ear, "It won't do!" Then, putting spurs to his horse, away he cantered off. The general stood for some time waving his hat after the carriage as it rolled down the avenue, until he was seized with a fit of sneezing, from exposing his head to the cool breeze. I observed that he returned rather thoughtfully to the house; whistling softly to himself, with his hands behind his back, and an exceedingly dubious air.

The company have now almost all taken their departure; I have determined to do the same to-morrow morning; and I hope my reader may not think that I have already lingered too long at the Hall. I have been tempted to do so, however, because I thought I had lit upon one of the retired places where there are yet some traces to be met with of old English character. A little while hence, and all these will probably have passed away. Ready-Money Jack will sleep with his fathers: the good Squire, and all his peculiarities, will be buried in the neighbouring church. The old Hall will be modernized into a fashionable country-seat, or, peradventure, a manufactory. The park will be cut up into petty farms and kitchen-gardens. A daily coach will run through the village; it will become, like all other commonplace villages, thronged with coachmen, post-boys, tipplers, and politicians: and Christmas, May-day, and all the other hearty merry-makings of the "good old times," will be forgotten.

The Author's Farewell.

And so without more circumstance at all,
I hold it fit that we shake hands and part.
—Hamlet.

Having taken leave of the Hall and its inmates, and brought the history of my visit to something like a close, there seems to remain nothing further than to make my bow, and exit. It is my foible, however, to get on such companionable terms with my reader in the course of a work, that it really costs me some pain to part with him; and I am apt to keep him by the hand, and have a few farewell wards at the end of my last volume.

When I cast an eye back upon the work I am just concluding, I cannot but be sensible how full it must be of errors and imperfections: indeed, how should it be otherwise, writing as I do about subjects and scenes with which, as a stranger, I am but partially acquainted? Many will doubtless find cause to smile at very obvious blunders which I may have made; and many may, perhaps, be offended at what they may conceive prejudiced representations. Some will think I might have said much more on such subjects as may suit their peculiar tastes; whilst others will think I had done wiser to have left those subjects entirely alone.

It will probably be said, too, by some, that I view England with a partial eye. Perhaps I do; for I can never forget that it is my "father land." And yet, the circumstances under which I have viewed it have by no means been such as were calculated to produce favourable impressions. For the greater part of the time that I have resided in it, I have lived almost unknowing and unknown; seeking no favours, and receiving none: "a stranger and a sojourner in the land," and subject to all the chills and neglects that are the common lot of the stranger.

When I consider these circumstances, and recollect how often I have taken up my pen, with a mind ill at ease, and spirits much dejected and cast down, I cannot but think I was not likely to err on the favourable side of the picture. The opinions I have given of English character have been the result of much quiet, dispassionate, and varied observation. It is a character not to be hastily studied, for it always puts on a repulsive and ungracious aspect to a stranger. Let those, then, who condemn my representations as too favourable, observe this people as closely and deliberately as I have done, and they will, probably, change their opinion. Of one thing, at any rate, I am certain, that I have spoken honestly and sincerely, from the convictions of my mind, and the dictates of my heart. When I first published my former writings, it was with no hope of gaining favour in English eyes, for I little thought they were to become current out of my own country: and had I merely sought popularity among my own countrymen, I should have taken a more direct and obvious way, by gratifying rather than rebuking the angry feelings that were then prevalent against England.

And here let me acknowledge my warm, my thankful feelings, at the effect produced by one of my trivial lucubrations. I allude to the essay in the Sketch-Book, on the subject of the literary feuds between England and America. I cannot express the heartfelt delight I have experienced, at the unexpected sympathy and approbation with which those remarks have been received on both sides of the Atlantic. I speak this not from any paltry feelings of gratified vanity; for I attribute the effect to no merit of my pen. The paper in question was brief and casual, and the ideas it conveyed were simple and obvious. "It was the cause: it was the cause" alone. There Vras a predisposition on the part of my readers to be favourably affected. My countrymen responded in heart to the filial feelings I had avowed in their name towards the parent country: and there was a generous sympathy in every English bosom towards a solitary individual, lifting up his voice in a strange land, to vindicate the injured character of his nation. There are some causes sosacred as to carry with them an irresistible appeal to every virtuous bosom; and he needs but little power of eloquence, who defends the honour of his wife, his mother, or his country.

I hail, therefore, the success of that brief paper, as showing how much good may be done by a kind word, however feeble, when spoken in season—as showing how much dormant good-feeling actually exists in each country, towards the other, which only wants the slightest spark to kindle it into a genial flame—as showing, in fact, what I have all along believed and asserted, that the two nations would grow together in esteem and amity, if meddling and malignant spirits would but throw by their mischievous pens, and leave kindred hearts to the kindly impulses of nature.

I once more assert, and I assert it with increased conviction of its truth, that there exists, among the great majority of my countrymen, a favourable feeling toward England. I repeat this assertion, because I think it a truth that cannot too often be reiterated, and because it has met with some contradiction. Among all the liberal and enlightened minds of my countrymen, among all those which eventually give a tone to national opinion, there exists a cordial desire to be on terms of courtesy and friendship. But at the same time, there exists in those very minds a distrust of reciprocal good-will on the part of England. They have been rendered morbidly sensitive by the attacks made upon their country by the English press; and their occasional irritability on this subject has been misinterpreted into a settled and unnatural hostility.

For my part, I consider this jealous sensibility as belonging to generous natures. I should look upon my countrymen as fallen indeed from that independence of spirit which is their birth-gift; as fallen indeed from that pride of character which they inherit from the proud nation from which they sprung, could they tamely sit down under the infliction of contumely and insult. Indeed, the very impatience which they show as to the misrepresentations of the press, proves their respect for English opinion, and their desire for English amity; for there is never jealousy where there is not strong regard.

It is easy to say, that these attacks are all the effusions of worthless scribblers, and treated with silent contempt by the nation; but, alas! the slanders of the scribbler travel abroad, and the silent contempt of the nation is only known at home. With England, then, it remains, as I have formerly asserted, to promote a mutual spirit of conciliation; she has but to hold the language of friendship and respect, and she is secure of the good-will of every American bosom.

In expressing these sentiments, I would utter nothing that should commit the proper spirit of my countrymen. We seek no boon at England's hands: we ask nothing as a favour. Her friendship is not necessary, nor would her hostility be dangerous to our well-being. We ask nothing from abroad that we cannot reciprocate. But with respect to England, we have a warm feeling of the heart, the glow of consanguinity that still lingers in our blood. Interest apart—past differences forgotten—we extend the hand of old relationship. We merely ask, do not estrange us from you; do not destroy the ancient tie of blood; do not let scoffers and slanderers drive a kindred nation from your side; we would fain be friends; do not compel us to be enemies.

There needs no better rallying-ground for international amity, than that furnished by an eminent English writer: "There is," say she, "a sacred bond between us of blood and of language, which no circumstances can break. Our literature must always be theirs; and though their laws are no longer the same as ours, we have the same Bible, and we address our common Father in the same prayer. Nations are too ready to admit that they have natural enemies; why should they be less willing to believe that they have natural friends?"[18]

To the magnanimous spirits of both countries must we trust to carry such a natural alliance of affection into full effect. To pens more powerful than mine, I leave the noble task of promoting the cause of national amity. To the intelligent and enlightened of my own country, I address my parting voice, entreating them to show themselves superior to the petty attacks of the ignorant and the worthless, and still to look with dispassionate and philosophic eye to the moral character of England, as the intellectual source of our rising greatness; while I appeal to every generous-minded Englishman from the slanders which disgrace the press, insult the understanding, and belie the magnanimity of his country: and I invite him to look to America, as to a kindred nation, worthy of its origin; giving, in the healthy vigour of its growth, the best of comments on its parent stock; and reflecting, in the dawning brightness of its fame, the moral effulgence of British glory.

I am sure that such an appeal will not be made in vain. Indeed, I have noticed, for some time past, an essential change in English sentiment with regard to Amerioar. In parliament, that fountain-head of public opinion, there seems to be an emulation, on both sides of the house, in holding the language of courtesy and friendship. The same spirit is daily becoming

---

[18] From an article (said to be by Robert Southey, Esq.) published in the Quarterly Review. It is to be lamented that that publication should so often forget the generous text here given!

more and more prevalent in good society. There is a growing curiosity concerning my country; a craving desire for correct information, that cannot fail to lead to a favourable understanding. The scoffer, I trust, has had his day; the time of the slanderer is gone by; the ribald jokes, the stale commonplaces, which have so long passed current when America was the theme, are now banished to the ignorant and the vulgar, or only perpetuated by the hireling scribblers and traditional jesters of the press. The intelligent and high-minded now pride themselves upon making America a study.

But however my feelings may be understood or reciprocated on either side of the Atlantic, I utter them without reserve, for I have ever found that to speak frankly is to speak safely. I am not so sanguine as to believe that the two nations are ever to be bound together by any romantic ties of feeling; but I believe that much may be done towards keeping alive cordial sentiments, were every well-disposed mind occasionally to throw in a simple word of kindness. If I have, indeed, produced any such effect by my writings, it will be a soothing reflection to me, that for once, in the course of a rather negligent life, I have been useful; that for once, by the casual exercise of a pen which has been in general but too unprofitably employed, I have awakened a cord of sympathy between the land of my fathers and the dear land that gave me birth.

In the spirit of these sentiments, I now take my farewell of the paternal soil. With anxious eye do I behold the clouds of doubt and difficulty that are lowering over it, and earnestly do I hope that they may all clear up into serene and settled sunshine. In bidding this last adieu, my heart is filled with fond, yet melancholy emotions; and still I linger, and still, like a child leaving the venerable abodes of his forefathers, I turn to breathe forth a filial benediction: Peace be within thy walls, O England! and plenteousness within thy palaces; for my brethren and my companions' sake I will now say, Peace be within thee!